THE GRAV MATTER

AG
Claymore

Also by A.G. Claymore:

THE GRAY MATTER

By A.G. Claymore
Edited by B.H. MacFadyen
Copyright © 2016 A.G. Claymore

ISBN: 9781730916809

free stories

When you sign up for my new-release mail list!

Follow this link to get started:
http://eepurl.com/ZCP-z

TABLE OF CONTENTS

NEW OPPORTUNITIES

Thanks for the hospitality…

Detention Specialist, Second-Grade Edmund Riley tuned out the echoing bedlam of Tango Block. Ignoring things was a valuable part of getting along in the Imperium. He approached the small knot of laughing guards, his features sour.

He usually managed to ignore the fact that his own quarters, as a Block Superintendent, were nearly as small as a one-man cell. In reality, the only place a guard could stretch his legs on a supermax asteroid like Mictlan was out on the gen-pop decks, surrounded by the scum of a thousand worlds.

He reached his small group of subordinates. "Why's 'Captain Indigestion', here, wearing an EVA suit?" He waved through the heavy plate of glaz-armor to where a size 1.3 prisoner was crammed into a size 1 suit.

The men chuckled. Alvarez, the next most senior in Tango after Riley, spoke for the group. "Ain't no biggie, Riles – he just kept insisting 'they' were talking to him and he needed a suit." Alvarez shrugged. "He's quiet now and, considering how many antacid tabs he goes through, I'd rather keep his carbon-dioxide-filled ass inside that suit." A grin. "Let him hotbox himself to death – save us having to space him if a sentence ever comes down."

"I'd like to know how he's gonna eat that meatloaf with his helmet on," Melchit, the youngest and newest member of Tango's guard force, spoke up.

Riley turned to look. Prisoner ap Rhys was scooping his dinner from the acrylic serving platter. He turned to the steel toilet at the foot of his bed and shook the gray chunk of meatloaf from his gloved hand, dropping it into the bowl with a splash.

"Can't really say I blame him," Melchit said. "That last shipment of beef must have come from an infected vat. I've no objections to feeding it to prisoners, but they should at least send *us* something that won't leave us too sick to hold down the riots."

"No," Alvarez warned darkly, "don't do it..."

Prisoner ap Rhys put a hand to the side of his helmet as though trying to hear the guard through the thick wall of glaz-armor. His left foot was resting gently on the flush knob of the toilet.

"Ain't nobody gonna clean that up for you," Alvarez shouted uselessly.

"You're at least gonna have to clean up whatever comes out into the corridor, Javi," Riley insisted, "'cause I don't want him in that suit."

"Aw, come on, Riles," Alvarez protested. "What's the harm in letting him wear the suit?"

"He's an engineer, Javi. The same engineer that turned an old piece of *gŏushĭ* into an effective strike-carrier. The same engineer who invented the source-directed wormhole generator."

"*Cái bù shì!*" Alvarez looked back at the prisoner, who now had five centimeters of meatloaf-fouled water on the floor of his cell. "That oaf?"

"That's right." Riley sighed. "And you idiots gave him a suit that's packed with all sorts of electronics and emergency

8

equipment. Get him out of it before he works some kind of mischief."

Before anyone could move to follow Riley's order, prisoner ap Rhys grabbed his mattress and pulled the end zipper open. He grabbed it by the middle and started shaking the open end over the growing pond in his cell. A shower of antacid tabs fluttered down to the liquid.

"What... an... asshole," Riley muttered as the hundreds of tabs began to jump and hiss across the surface of the water. There'd be no getting the door open with the extra pressure those carbon dioxide tabs were releasing.

Riley's eyes grew wide. "Oh *jiàn tā de guǐ.*" He gripped Alvarez' shoulder. "The pressure!"

"Relax, Riles." Javi waved a dismissive hand. "That glaz-armor's rated to forty-eight atmos. It's impossible to blow it."

"Yeah, but the back side of this cell's an outer wall. It's hull-plating, Imperial Standard, designed to hold in the atmo and keep the crew from falling out when you make a sharp turn."

"So," Javi frowned. "How much..."

"One point four atmos," Riley answered, his face a mask of fury.

Prisoner ap Rhys had turned around to point his backside at the guards and he was smacking his left cheek when the outer hull blew. He went cartwheeling out the ragged hole, smacking his right arm on the edge of the torn seam.

"That'll leave a nasty bruise, at least," Alvarez muttered.

"Get over to Maintenance," Riley told him. "Have them take you out on a sled and pick him up before he freezes to death out there. He may not even have enough oxygen to..."

He trailed off as a large, dark gray mass came into view, just beyond their drifting prisoner.

"That's the same piece of *gŏucàode* debris that came drifting out of the asteroid field yesterday," Alvarez exclaimed. "Wasn't Maintenance going to check it for survivors?"

Riley's shoulders slumped. "Somehow, I don't think they got around to it, Javi. Who'd have thought that thing could actually *fly*?"

As they watched helplessly, a lightly armed shuttle bearing three stars and a '1GD' on the hull came to a stop next to the prisoner and he was thrown a boarding net.

"Fixing that breach is gonna eat up our bonus for the next five cycles," Riley groused. "And they're gonna want somebody's head for this. He wasn't an ordinary *zek*. That guy was a political detainee."

"*Tāmāde!*" Alvarez suddenly found it hard to meet Riley's eye. Even though he'd been the one to give the prisoner a suit, it would be the Block Superintendent who'd quietly disappear.

And Alvarez would get his job – promoted by his own incompetence. His ears were turning red with the shame of it.

"It's a shame Maintenance's avaricious attitude made this all possible." Melchit scratched at his patchy chin-stubble. "They probably dragged their feet, hoping any survivors aboard the derelict would die from exposure, thereby giving them a nice fat salvage fee." He belched delicately into his fist. "S'cuse me. And so their greed ends up facilitating a prisoner's escape."

Riley looked at Alvarez, who'd lost his reluctance to meet his gaze. They grinned.

Happiness in the Imperium didn't take much. Three squares a day, a place to lay your head...

And a plausible scapegoat.

Reassignment

Julia sat on the low stone wall of the third-level ventilation gallery. A hundred meters down the canyon, she could see a large, scaled pterobat drifting in and out of the deep shadows. Its high-pitched shriek echoed up to her as the sightless creature mapped the surroundings and searched for prey.

A smaller, fur-bearing avian darted across its path, bouncing a chittering call of its own off the cliff face before turning to circle its forty-kilo adversary. It began emitting a piercing shriek as it flew circles around its prey, confusing the pterobat and calling in reinforcements.

Julia shivered, despite the warm sunlight of the gallery. She'd lost four people to the quarter-kilo *not fur nothings,* as the smaller creatures were known. Now, nobody went down the canyon unless they'd been trained by young Caleb on how to avoid drawing the wrong sort of attention.

A blur of the smaller creatures came pouring out of the cracks in the rock, circling the large creature, darting in to take small bites. They worked with a communal precision, disabling the large avian's flight muscles, so its only remaining choices were to glide on or dive to its death.

They continued to feed on the doomed animal until it finally chose a quicker death and relaxed the extensor muscles that the smaller attackers had left intact. It plummeted out of the ravenous cloud to the rocks below, the sound of its impact lost in the roar of the fast-flowing river at the base of the canyon.

She turned from the scene as the sound of approaching footsteps heralded her next meeting. A man in a hood was flanked by Rodrigues, the Marine they'd turned from

Kinsey's service, and an imposingly built man with a clean-shaven head. Mullins.

Oddly enough, Mullins' distinctive look didn't get in the way of his almost supernatural ability to blend into a crowd. If nothing else, that one fact told her that he'd truly mastered his trade.

He was a retired Maegi and he now led her intelligence network, consisting largely of commandeered Maegi. The secretive society, dedicated to the task of ensuring the Imperium continued to forget about the colonies, was a logical choice. Their members were excellent information gatherers and skilled influencers.

The insectoid monks who'd agreed to serve in that role had been shuffled aside when the Grays had been tricked into a civil war.

Brother N'Zim and any other members of the Brotherhood who'd served on any of Julia's ships were on this world for the duration of the conflict and so they'd been re-assigned to the Gray Brainwashing problem.

The minute any one of them left, *every* member of the Brotherhood would know who'd plunged the Grays into a civil war. Julia wasn't keen on taking that kind of risk and N'Zim's team understood the reasons. They weren't very happy about it, though.

That left her forces with an intelligence shortfall but she'd found an excellent spymaster in Mullins.

Julia turned, dropping her left foot to the rock floor, sitting with her back to the canyon, and nodded to Rodrigues.

He yanked the hood from the man's head and Julia felt a wince of conscience at his pale face and ragged beard. Still, considering the circumstances surrounding his capture, she hadn't been inclined to make him a priority.

Mullins came to stand in the sunlight to her left as she addressed the prisoner. "You gave your name as Edgar Prestonby," she told him, "which, I gather, was intended to draw the attention of people like Mullins, here." She nodded beyond him to where Rodrigues stood.

Prestonby glanced at the Marine over his shoulder and turned back to her with a grin. "Nah." He shook his head. "That ain't Mullins." He nodded at the actual article. "That's Mullins."

Mullins nodded slightly. "A Roanokan, a Spirian and a bandicoon all meet in a clearing in the forest, facing each other to form a perfect triangle. Which shadow is the shortest?"

Prestonby cocked his head in thought for a moment. "Tricky," he muttered appreciatively. "Did the bandicoon bring his own vehicle?"

Julia frowned but kept silent. As far as she knew, the bandicoon was a small, nocturnal forest animal.

"Of course," Mullins replied as though such a thing should have been self evident.

Prestonby's features lightened. "Well then, that means they all cast an equal shadow which, I'm sure, aggravates the poor little bandicoon to no end!"

Mullins nodded. "He's one of ours, Commodore."

Rodrigues stepped forward to cut the bindings on Prestonby's wrists.

"Grade and assignment," Mullins demanded.

Prestonby sighed as he rubbed his wrists. "Field agent, 1st grade. I was enroute to take up a new posting to TC-452e when our ship got waylaid by the same fellows who raided this place."

Mullins' eyebrow lifted a full centimeter. "Not many Maegi of your rank stay in the field. Promotion to 1st always comes with a choice of jobs. You could have a nice office in one of the chapter-houses, managing an entire sector of agents. Why were you taking another assignment in the Imperium?"

"I like the work." Prestonby's gaze slid over to Julia. "And I don't care for the *confining* spaces of office work."

Mullins kept his eyes on Prestonby, a thoughtful look on his face. He nodded to himself at whatever it was he saw there.

Julia felt the heat in her ears at the veiled rebuke. "It's true that we took far too long in getting around to you but, considering the company you were keeping when we found you..."

The crew that had plucked him from the debris of his original ship had gone on to raid the mine where Prestonby was now being questioned. They'd killed every man, woman and child, except for Caleb, who'd hidden in the crypt. Prestonby had been found with one of the last surviving enemy crewmen. The rest had either been killed in a cutting-out expedition against the *Walter Currie* or they'd killed *themselves*, victims of Gray brainwashing.

He nodded. "I'm just glad you were looking for prisoners to interrogate. Otherwise, I wouldn't have had the luxury of complaining about my incarceration, for which I'm absurdly grateful."

"Well, I'm glad we sorted this out," she told him. "And I'm also glad to hear you like field work because we're giving you to Resident Mullins."

Prestonby's gaze darted to Mullins, his eyes slightly widened but he quickly brought his reaction under control and gave the man a respectful nod. "A Resident." He allowed a tone of mild surprise. "It seems I'm not the only Maegi who prefers field work."

Mullins returned the nod. "A retired resident, obviously, or I'd still be running a station on a Rim world right now. Nonetheless, even a retired Resident can invoke the right of override on any agent's mission. I'm in charge of the field agents for this force and I'll be sending you out to join them."

Prestonby frowned. "Resident, has this been approved by the Maegi Council?"

"It hasn't," Mullins admitted, "and you're perfectly correct to ask me that." Mullins sat on the low wall, gesturing for Prestonby to sit between him and Julia.

"Let's put your new mission in context," he offered as Prestonby sat. "Your mission, indeed, all Maegi missions, share the common goal of keeping the Imperium out of the colonies. Mostly, you make sure the folks that come our way aren't looking to open trade routes or sneak back to the Imperium with news bulletins that the public can't conveniently ignore."

He grinned. "The Imperium helps the process by not *wanting* to know about us. They still assume we'd be more trouble to assimilate than we're actually worth."

Mullins waved to indicate the mine they lived in. "The forces based here are engaged in nurturing and maintaining a civil war between the Gray Quorum and a splinter faction, the Purists, who want no contact or involvement with Humans whatsoever. If they should learn of our role in their conflict..." He took a deep breath.

"Then they'd declare open war on us," Prestonby finished the thought for Mullins.

A nod from Julia. "And that would almost certainly draw the Imperium into the conflict. They may pretend the colonies were lost, but enough Imperial agents have been captured out here, over the centuries, for us to know that a steady flow of information makes its way back to CentCom."

"So you see," Mullins continued, "we need to manage the balance of this conflict and keep a lid on our own role in it. For better or worse, it's where our choices have led us and we need to stay the course if we're to have any chance of saving the colonies. The only other choice we saw before us was to sit back and watch our worlds be turned into subject farms for Gray experiments."

"Alright," Prestonby said heavily. "I'm under your orders, then. Where do you need me?"

Mullins stood, waiting for Prestonby to follow suit. "The *Mot Juste* is leaving for a 'trading run' through the Spiral Archipelago. They'll depart the moment you step aboard. Do what we always do," he advised. "Keep your eyes open and your ears tuned."

Just Passing Through

Daffyd stopped at the entry to the forward riser. "Is it possible she's even lovelier than she was on the day we took her from the Grays?" His right hand came to rest gently on the grav-control panel, just to the right of the riser door.

"Well, that sulphurous Gray smell is gone, if that's what you mean." Edrich offered morosely. "So that's an improvement..."

Daffyd quirked an eyebrow over his shoulder at his fourth engineer. You could give Edrich his own planet and he'd still find a reason to be glum about it. "You're sure you entered the right coordinates while I was making an ass of myself in Engineering?"

Edrich grunted. "You've never doubted my solutions before..."

"Yeah, well, there's a lot riding on it this time."

"And there wasn't when we inserted the 488 directly into Narsa and brought out all those civvies?"

"Fair enough," Daffyd conceded. "It just shocked me to see how the Imperials have pulled the reactors half apart. I'm surprised she's still able to pinch space at all."

Now Edrich's blood was up, or at least by his standards it was. "Are *you* ready to play your part when we get up there?"

A chuckle. "You mean the part of a half-drunk *hooy morzhovy* who's pretending to be the inventor of the source-directed wormhole generator?" Daffyd jabbed a thumb at his own chest. "The Imperial Exchequer's been paying me to rehearse the role for more than a year now. I'd better be ready for this!"

"Not exactly a *yes*," Edrich groused.

"Maybe not, but I'm feeling a sudden operational need to fill that vacant wiper position in the auxiliary reactor room." Daffyd nodded at the riser. "Get your ass in gear and try to act like filming me's a big deal."

When Daffyd stepped out into the main companionway leading to the bridge, he found two confused-looking technicians standing watch outside the doors.

"Look natural now," Edrich called to them. "Act like you see him every day..."

Daffyd breezed past as if they didn't even exist. If there'd been Marines guarding the bridge, he'd have had a much harder time of it, but these two were simply stationed here as some sort of secondary duty.

The two ratings clearly had no idea what they were doing, so they were unlikely to interfere with someone who *did*.

"It's alright, everybody," Daffyd proclaimed loudly as he swept onto the bridge.

All eyes turned to him as he grimaced, tapping his chest with his fist. "I'm here to help." He managed to spit the words out just ahead of an impressive belch.

The young man at the engineering panel regarded Daffyd without an abundance of hope on his face. "Maybe you should have kept notes when you invented this thing. *Tiānxiǎode!* I must have been a senator in a past life to get shafted with this *gǒucàode* posting..."

"Don't you worry, lad," Daffyd assured him, throwing in a slight sway for dramatic effect, "we'll get it sorted out and, when we do, the ladies'll be all over you!" He was laying it on thick, but the bridge crew were all engineers and, as a rule, very sceptical.

The young man rolled his eyes. "Oh, sure. Surviving a top-secret, unheard-of project really helps your chances with the opposite sex."

"Mr. ap Rhys!"

Daffyd turned at the loud address to find the officer of the deck staring at him. The officer jerked his head toward the ready room. "A word, if you please."

He stood by the door as Daffyd entered, then put a hand on Edrich's chest to stop him. "Why don't you just wait out here?" he said, clearly not meaning it as a suggestion.

Commander Pulver waved the door shut and rounded on the gin-scented intruder. "I won't have you giving my men false hope, Mr. ap Rhys." It was one thing to cut the team off from the outside universe while on a project, but to subject them to visits from imbeciles without notice was really too much.

Daffyd tilted his head slightly. "*False* is a bit strong, don't you think?"

Pulver treated himself to a sardonic smile as he strode around to the far side of the control table that dominated the room. "So, what you're asking me to believe is that *you* managed to invent a source-directed wormhole generator?" He raised a hand. "And this is the really clever part – you somehow managed to trick a Gray shipyard into building an attack carrier with ready-made housings for all three rings as well as setting aside space for the generator array?"

He didn't really expect an answer to that, and ap Rhys clearly had no intention of providing one.

Pulver turned to look out the large window on the outer wall. "We're down to a matter of weeks, at best." He took a deep breath and blew it out between pursed lips. "Senator Nathaniel got me appointed to this project because he knew we'd never figure out how that generator works. All he has to do is wait until the right moment. One of his cronies will make waves about how dangerous it is to have an alien ship that Humans can't understand, and the entire program will be eliminated, along with the engineers who know just enough to tarnish Imperial prestige."

"Like the old saying, eh?" ap Rhys offered. "Two men may keep a secret, providing one of them has just killed the other?"

Pulver spun to face the man, noticing he was sniffing at his coffee mug.

Daffyd gave him an apologetic little shrug and set it on the control table. "Seems to me, your daddy bought you the wrong commission. You should have asked for something a little safer than the Imperial Corps of Engineers. Maybe a nice cozy combat posting out on the Rim..."

Pulver felt a sudden urge to hit the man but the control table stood between them. An angry lunge across the surface might make him feel better, but he'd randomly trigger any number of the surface or holographic command macros that were currently open.

"Maybe you're right," he retorted, "but I can take comfort in the knowledge that, even if we do manage to unlock the secrets of this ship, *you* will still end up dead from some 'unfortunate accident'. The longer you're in front of cameras, the more people will come to realize what an idiot you really are. You won't live much longer than us."

21

He jerked his head toward the door. "Now, get off my bridge!"

He watched the two men shuffle out of the bridge before picking up his coffee and carrying it over to a heating pad. The fool wasn't entirely wrong. Pulver had already caught himself wishing he'd ignored the lure of secret work and shipped aboard a cruiser or an LHV. Engineering officers on combat postings had a much higher life expectancy than those involved in black projects.

A curl of steam rose from the mug and he reached out to retrieve it. He sipped as he walked to the window to look out at the small constellation of ships surrounding Nidaveller Station. Some were involved in other projects but a large number of them were warships, posted there for security. One of these days, a cruiser might have an 'accidental discharge' and Pulver's troubles would come to an abrupt end.

His eyes narrowed as he saw an escape pod drift past. A Gray-built escape pod. "Maxwell!" he roared.

Maxwell, the second lieutenant stationed at the sensor suite, appeared in the doorway. "Sir?"

Pulver turned to Maxwell as he pointed out the window at the pod. "Do you have an explanation for that?"

Maxwell looked past him. "Huh!" he grunted. "I'd imagine it has to do with that shuttle." He pointed out the same window.

Pulver wheeled back to look. "*Ō, zhè zhēn shì gè kuàilè de guòchéng!*"

A shuttle, bearing three stars and the letters 1GD was bearing down on the pod. As the two engineers watched, it scooped the pod into its front loading bay and turned toward the next surprise.

"It's that old derelict they towed in here two days ago!" Maxwell exclaimed. "I thought one of the other projects was going to use her for parts. How is that thing even moving under its own power?"

Pulver thought it fitting that ap Rhys would die in the old relic. "Comms, signal the security force. Advise them that we…"

Just as the shuttle flew in through an improvised landing bay door in the stern of the old ship, a wormhole plunged into existence directly in front of them. As Pulver watched in silent rage, the ship slipped out of sight, taking most of his remaining life expectancy with it.

He turned back to the control table. Sure enough, a green authorization icon was quietly pulsing, just under the spot where ap Rhys had set his coffee. The damned oaf had authorized a wormhole right under Pulver's nose. His ears grew hot.

If ap Rhys was a buffoon, what did that make Pulver?

Cherchez le Oaf

"**D**affyd ap Rhys?" General Sir Edmund Windemere blinked in surprise. "Why in twelve purgatories would that imbecile come here?" He leaned forward in his chair, raising one eyebrow. It was a gesture to tighten the sphincter of any Engineering project leader. "And how did he get access to the wormhole generator on the *Sucker Punch*?"

Commander Pulver had pretty much resigned himself to death after ap Rhys had played him for a fool, so he wasn't terribly worried about Windemere's displeasure. Being chewed out by his superior meant he was still alive, for the moment.

"I'd imagine he did it the same way he got past the security pickets around Nidaveller Station in the first place," he said mildly, enjoying the barb against his general who, to be fair, was responsible for the interlopers being at the research station in the first place. "He acted like he was supposed to be here."

"We know better." Windemere pounded a fist on his desk.

"You and I do, certainly," Pulver conceded, "but we can't tell the staff, now, can we?" It was clearly not meant as a question. "I have enough people aboard the *Sucker Punch* to take her into combat and you have enough troops guarding Nidaveller to fight a small war." He waved a dismissive hand. "Tell them and you can forget about secrecy. Some of them are bound to make it home one day, and you don't want them contradicting the official Imperial line on this project."

"Sod the Imperial line." Windemere looked down at his desk. "I'm in this up to my eyeballs."

"Sir?" Pulver knew that the project teams were often liquidated in the name of political expediency, but Windemere was in charge of the entire station. He'd been here since the discovery of pointy rocks. Was his head on the block as well?

A sigh. "No sense hiding it." He looked up to meet Pulver's gaze. "They're coming for us both." He got up and went to the sideboard where he kept an impressive array of intoxicants. "The Windemeres are part of the Santa Clara Block."

Pulver nodded to himself as he accepted a tumbler of whiskey. The Windemere family must be heavy shareholders in the circuit production at Santa Clara. Their wealth would take a beating from Senator Nathaniel's plan to break the Santa Claran monopoly and disperse circuit production throughout the Imperium.

He frowned at the general who motioned for him to sit. "I don't see how that makes you a target, unless..."

"Unless I've been running a project on the sly to implement compatibility codes on computing components." He took a swig of the amber liquid and sighed appreciatively. "Once they implement the new standards, you'll need the handshake-circuits in every component. Cortical processors, quantum busses, memory crystals, even I/O devices will fail to work if they don't have the circuit."

"So..." Pulver took a drink. "... If Ganges sets up a factory to build cortical processors, they won't work without this new coding circuit?"

"Which will be proprietary, of course," the general added. "So it would increase the difficulty of Nathaniel's little plan by several orders of magnitude. The Gangians can't just set up shop to produce circuits; they'd need to build an entire computer industry from the ground up."

"But that leaves a major bottleneck in the computing industry," Pulver said, "and it's sitting on the edge of Gray space. They've already tried to destroy the main factory ship once. It would be madness to think they won't try again!"

Windemere chuckled. "Madness and money usually go hand in hand. Show me a single person of wealth who'd put the Imperium ahead of personal fortune!" He shook his head. "The Imperium is nothing more than a framework for families like ours to squeeze money out of the poor." He waved his tumbler at Pulver. "Or are you going to tell me your father got the money for your commission from hard work and good intentions, and not from raiding the planetary coffers on Kansas?"

"Are you saying that my project and now my probable death is just part of a plot by Senator Nathaniel to root you out of here before you can implement this compatibility program of yours?" Pulver's death might save the Imperium, when viewed from that angle, but he was in no mood to feel noble.

He'd much rather keep on breathing.

"Hmm..." Windemere looked straight through Pulver as though he wasn't even there. A grin began to soften his ordinarily angry features.

"I wonder," he began quietly, "did that drunken oaf had a direct role in this or is this simply a coincidence and Nathaniel hasn't even heard of it yet. Even if that's so, he'll waste no time when he *does* hear of it." He focused on Pulver, eyes shining with mischief.

"I've always liked you, lad..."

"Umm…" Now it was time for Pulver's eyebrows to raise. "No, you haven't. Just last week you invited me to visit you on Loki… so you could feed me to your dogs…"

Windemere sat up a little straighter, squinting at the young engineer. "That was you?" He shook his head. "A little advice, young man – never remind your boss that he doesn't like you. Honestly, how did you make it all the way to commander?" He waved off the question.

"Never mind that," he breezed. "I like you well enough now. You've shaken the tree, as they say, and the solution has dropped in our laps. You have a full crew, even if they're mostly engineers, and I've got a few ships and troops at my disposal, as you so inelegantly pointed out earlier. We're going after that gin-soaked *hundan* and, when we've got him, we'll make him say Senator Nathaniel put him up to the whole thing."

"In front of a holocam and a recognizable notary?" Pulver asked helpfully.

A nod. "And then we'll tuck him away somewhere safe. That should keep Nathaniel out of my hair for the time being."

"*Our* hair, if you don't mind, sir."

"What? Oh… yes. Of course, that's implied, young man. Do try to keep up."

Pulver nodded to be polite, but he didn't want to leave his life entirely in Windemere's hands. Part of a general's job was to spend lives in accomplishing his goal and he had no doubt that Windemere would shove him into the intake, as the saying goes, if the general's goal of self-preservation called for it. He wanted to keep his boss close.

"I assume you'll be moving your flag to the *Sucker Punch* then, sir?" It was a safe bet. The Gray ship was the only one capable of generating a wormhole to return to Imperial space. If the small fleet ended up separated, Windemere would want to stay close to his ticket home.

The general was selecting ship icons in the defense force holo, appending a command for the captains to report to his office immediately. "Of course I will, so you'd better clear out of that cabin behind the bridge." He looked up at the engineer. "You still have the coordinates that Mr. ap Rhys used?"

A nod. "Yes, sir."

"Good! As soon as I brief the captains, I'll head over to join you. We'll jump as soon as everybody's back on their bridges."

Live Bait

"**M**ayday, mayday, mayday! This is the *Bastile* out of Beaumont. Coordinates are Unity Primary, 125689774 Nu, 43.8843, 22.9933. Have taken heavy damage from raiders. Weapons are down, main reactor offline, twenty-three dead, six wounded. Urgently require medical assistance and a set of flash capacitors to initiate the support generator. Mayday..."

"Keep it running," Fall ordered, "but mute the replay. We could be here for a few centidays before we get a nibble and that'll get old pretty damn quick."

The signal was being sent from a Human-built antenna jury-rigged onto the hull of his captured Gray cruiser.

He turned to Julia. "With respect, Commodore," he said quietly, "this is too similar to the last ambush for my comfort. The Grays may not be great tactical innovators, but they can recognize a pattern better than any Human."

Julia nodded. "And it's that very trait that constrains us, Captain." She leaned in a little closer and lowered her voice. "If we get too creative in our tactics, how long before they realize the majority of attacks against Quorum ships were carried out by us and not a splinter faction of their own people?"

"Oh, I understand well enough," Fall assured her, "but I still don't like the idea of dumbing down our tactics. It's giving us the results we want but it also gives away one of our best advantages."

Julia had already seen examples of Captain Fall's 'edge' in tactical and strategic thinking. He more or less favored direct assaults on Gray worlds, throwing in words like 'surprise' and 'unexpected' here and there to make it sound like he'd come up with something clever.

It was little more than putting lipstick on a pig, as far as she was concerned. He was a privateer, after all. His combat experience had been focused mainly on raiding commercial shipping and he clearly had no idea what he'd be getting into, assaulting a properly defended enemy planet.

Especially when the enemy wasn't aware they were *considered* the enemy. It would only take the destruction of one Human-manned cruiser in orbit to bring the combined might of the Gray Quorum down on the Human colonies. Finding Human corpses floating with the debris of a ship that should have carried Gray Purists would prove to the Quorum that Humans were behind the Gray civil war.

"Squadron reports ready for action," Tactical announced. "All four cruisers are in position."

Patterns. Predictability.

It may have been risky to emulate Gray tactics, but you could lay out an effective ambush secure in the knowledge that the enemy would follow the same old routine.

Usually.

When capturing Human vessels to seize experimental subjects, the Grays typically employed their version of shock and awe. Two cruisers would drop out of distortion, one ahead of the victim's bow and the other astern. They'd come in perpendicular to the prey's vessel, releasing a blast of drop-wash plasma in front and behind the Humans before turning to bring their mains to bear on the target from less than a half kilometer.

They liked to get nice and close to frighten their victims as well as to minimize transit time between the ships.

Ferrying captives to their holds would take too long if they stayed too far out.

The ships in the Human's ambush squadron were arranged in a diamond formation. A cruiser waited to port, starboard, ventral and dorsal, each one five hundred meters out. Two were aligned aft and two forward, all aiming at the point where the Gray ships would appear. Fall's ship, as the bait, sat at the middle of the diamond.

She'd felt the occasional twinge of conscience, over the years, at a few of her more questionable *ruse de guerres,* but this one had a certain poetic justice to it that appealed to her.

"Ambush is ready, ma'am," Fall informed her.

"Very good, Captain Fall. Your crew knows what to do." She cast a quick glance around the bridge, nodding confidently. "You don't need me looking over your shoulders. I'll grab some food and get back to our intel reports."

She noticed a few grins as she left. It rarely hurt to show confidence in subordinates and it usually did wonders for morale. She had no intention of being off the bridge when the fight started, but it would take at least a deciday before the distress call could filter through the Gray repeater network and result in the dispatch of a capture team.

She frowned slightly as she entered the main companionway. Did they seem a little too surprised at her mild display of approval or were her impressions clouded by her concerns over Fall's quality as a leader? Like it or not, he was her flag captain for this operation and she'd have to work with what she had.

She dropped down to twelve deck, where the main mess hall was located. She could have eaten from the auxiliary mess set up directly aft of the bridge but she wanted to get a better feel for the crew. As always, with just over a thousand crew operating three shifts, there were close to a hundred crewmen in the mess, either eating a full meal or simply having a coffee and swapping stories.

The buzz of voices trailed off quickly as she walked in. Visible traces of her combat implants, running along her jawline and up to circle her ear, made her easily recognizable. Keeping her head closely shaved for a better calibration in her heavy Marine armor also marked her as a professional warrior.

The buzz quickly picked up again. It's one thing to know that Marines have augments. It's quite another to remember, specifically, that they have augmented hearing, especially when a Marine general walks into a common mess for lunch.

...turned those Sector Defense units into an elite regiment in just six months. They even kicked some Marine ass...

...captured a Gray cruiser within hours of escaping their custody...

...have a proper fighting officer with us, we'll make it home ok, regardless of what old 'Pride before a Fall' might blunder into...

...in that underarmor suit, I'd follow her anywhere!

She frowned. Crews always griped about their officers – It was a law of nature – but when they started giving them disparaging nicknames, it indicated a distinct lack of respect. She grabbed a tray of food and headed for a table with an open seat.

The chatter at her table died out as she approached, but quickly resumed as they switched their discussion from her to the pending fight.

She suppressed a smile. The young crewman who'd restarted the conversation with the new topic was sharp. He'd bear watching.

She returned their politely nervous nods. "Forgot to bring hot sauce," she told them. "Anybody here have a canister I can use?"

The food on their ships was nourishing but hopelessly monotonous, and she laughed as five canisters appeared in the hands of her table-mates. She took one from the young woman across the table and gave her food a liberal spray of Xel Ha's finest export.

"That's pretty hot stuff, ma'am," the young woman warned as Julia handed back the canister. "You might want to start with a small, oh…" she trailed off as her commodore shoveled in a large mouthful.

"Shorry to be such a pig," Julia apologized around her food. "Old habit from training at Twenty-nine Moons. They give you fifteen minutes to eat lunch and the course senior always wants you lined up ten minutes early, so you end up stuffing your face in the chow line and running right back out to the boarding ledge." Her voice was becoming more intelligible as she chewed and talked.

"Walking into a mess hall seems to put me back in the old OCS mindset." She grinned at the young woman. "Antonov, isn't it? That's good spice but I went a little light on it. Would you mind?"

Eyes wide, the young woman handed over the canister and watched as Julia gave the food a second, heavier dose of the spicy spray.

"Different from what I'm used to," she said as she handed it back. "Sharper… less pungent. Gives mess-deck food a real kick in the pants." She'd proven she could handle the stuff; no harm in showing a little respect for it.

"How long till our ambush brings in a catch?" Antonov asked, more at ease now that she was sharing with her commodore.

Julia looked over the young woman's shoulder as she thought it through. "We've been here a half-centi," she mused. "Another one and a half centis should see us killing something."

"How did the Grays ever build such an advanced civilization when they're so stuck in their ways?" the young man at the end asked.

Julia shrugged. "Maybe they were different when they were a younger race. Perhaps this final generation, the one that lives through an endless succession of clone bodies, has simply lost the ability to think creatively." She grinned. "You have to admit, knowing you're gonna die in a few short decades has a way of lighting a fire under your ass."

The Gray reluctance to employ innovative tactics was actually turning out to be a problem for Julia and not simply because of the restrictions it placed on those who sought to impersonate them. The real Purists were a motivated group dedicated to their own goals but, at the end of the day, they were still Grays. Their dedication didn't lead to any great leaps of tactical or strategic innovation. They fought with the same scientifically precise battle drills as the forces loyal to the Gray Quorum.

Without any tactical advantages, it simply boiled down to a numbers game and the Quorum had vastly more force than the Purists. They were dwindling quickly.

Julia's forces were posing as Purists, like a fleece-wolf hiding among a grazing herd of claw-toed sheep. It was rare that one was detected before it made its final lunge at an unsuspecting deer. It was an effective tactic.

But the herd was shrinking fast.

Julia finished her food and stood with the tray. "Thanks for the hot sauce." She nodded at Antonov.

She headed for the tray conveyor but stopped next to the crewman who'd mentioned her underarmor suit. His comrades cast him nervous glances as she looked down at him. "If *you* were wearing this suit," she told him, deliberately misinterpreting his earlier remark, "you wouldn't be following anyone anywhere." She leaned down to give his protruding belly a light smack with the back of her hand. "You'd have no circulation left in your legs!"

A chorus of guffaws broke out at the man's expense but he took it well, grinning up at her. "I doubt they make 'em my size anyway – I'd hate to see the armor that'd fit *me*!"

She laughed, giving him a thump on the shoulder as she resumed her course for the conveyor.

Julia returned to the bridge and took a tablet from a locker at the back. She settled into one of the command chairs with a polite nod to Fall before immersing herself in the latest disposition reports.

The tablet let her avoid conversation. Fall was content to ignore his subordinates but he just couldn't keep quiet when his superiors were around. If she didn't have the tablet, she'd be subjected to an endless stream of inane comments about the ship, the current plan, the state of the engines...

She wished she'd found another way to fend off chatter. The reports were becoming more alarming each day. The projected Purist force strength was shrinking faster than she'd thought and it wouldn't take the enemy long to figure out that some of the Purists were not like the others.

She needed to come up with a new plan. The Grays would be heavily damaged by the end of the short civil war she'd managed to engineer. The Purists represented nearly a fifth of Gray forces and they'd probably take close to that much with them as they were destroyed, but that still left an overwhelming amount of enemy ships.

There'd be more than enough force left over to wipe out the colonies once they learned they'd been fooled by the Humans. It wasn't a question of *if.* With the Gray's civil war winding down, there'd be little chance of keeping her crews bottled up at the mining world they'd been hiding on. Word would definitely get out.

She frowned at the tablet. Was there another race out here somewhere who could give the Grays a run for their credits? She looked up at Fall but decided not to ask him. Not only was she reluctant to get him talking, but she also didn't trust his judgement.

Captain Fall possessed clarity of vision but only where it involved immediate personal advantage.

She entered a scheduling note that would invite Brother N'Zim and Resident Mullins to join her the morning after she returned to Defiance, the small mining outpost they were currently calling home.

She stared down at the small hologram projected by the tablet without really seeing it. They needed to find a rival for the Grays to focus on before the colonies got wiped out. Maybe…

"Contact!" The tactical officer announced. "Two enemy cruisers conforming to standard Gray tactics. They're sliding straight into the kill-zones."

Julia closed the tablet and looked up to see Fall, eyes blazing with anticipation, turn to the weapons officer, his mouth opening to say something.

She wouldn't put it past him to open fire too early.

"They'll be in the sweet spot in a couple of ten-millis," she said with an affected wolfish tone as she came out of her chair. She was genuinely concerned he'd trigger the fight too soon and let the enemy escape and so she'd provided him with a plausibly deniable reminder of the plan.

She came to stand next to him in the central, tactical holo.

The last thing she wanted was for him to turn an easy ambush into a running firefight. Not only would he have denied his role in the failure, but he'd almost certainly blame *her* for it, citing her orders to use Gray tactics.

She didn't think he was bad enough to do such a thing consciously, but she'd seen more than her fair share of officers in the Imperial Marines who'd built a career out of blaming others for their own shortcomings. Some had known they were terrible combat officers, but others, like Fall, simply didn't *know* how much they didn't know.

"They're both in the zone," Weapons announced.

"Signal the squadron," Fall ordered. "Weapons free!"

As usual, the Gray captains were confused about the presence of a small Gray squadron where a distress call indicated the presence of a stricken Human ship. Just like every other ambush, they continued on toward their originally planned positions, no doubt assuming that they'd be better able to focus fire on the central ship if it came to a fight.

Fall's order came back as confirmed, activating a signal at the weapons station to tell the weapons officer he could now open fire without jumping the gun on his counterparts in the other four ships.

The enemy ship to their front was intimidatingly close. They wanted to minimize the time required to ferry their Human victims aboard and it meant the outgoing rounds from the ambush ships would impact their targets before the Gray captain could draw breath and mumble a single order.

A hail of enhanced conventional ammunition hammered at the enemy's forward shield. The smaller-caliber rounds focused on the area directly in front of their main armament. No shot could be fired without the shield generator creating a small aperture for the rounds to pass through and no aperture could be opened while an enemy was firing at that area or the launch rails would be damaged by incoming fire.

"We've got them sealed up at the bow," the weapons officer said.

"That salvo from the *Emma* nearly broke through their dorsal shielding," the tactical officer advised. "The next might even... Whoa!" he shouted. "Complete overmatch! A round from the *Oliver* went through from ventral before detonating against the inside of the dorsal shield."

He enlarged a holographic menu. "Given the path taken by that round, I'd estimate heavy damage to the command and control links. The departments are probably isolated until they can activate new pathways."

"Give 'em another salvo from our mains," Fall ordered, commendably eager to pound them while they were on their heels.

Before the rounds were fired, the enemy started backing off, but the front half of the Gray cruiser began to rotate slightly to port.

"Looks like the damage was even worse than we thought," the tactical officer said. "The stress of backing up has sheared off whatever held her together on the starboard side. The front half is hanging on by a few primary longitudinal frames."

The deck rumbled as the mains fired again, their soul-rending shriek vibrating the jury-rigged Human-sized bridge chairs. The projectiles slammed into the unshielded hulk ahead of them, tearing through both the fore and aft sections and trailing a haze of debris behind them.

"She's dead," the tactical officer pronounced, then raised his voice to a near-shout. "Collision alert! Contact astern of us is accelerating and opening an aperture for her mains!"

"All ahead, full!" Fall shouted. "Twenty degrees up angle. Take us over that wreckage..."

Before he could finish, the deck shook and the pressure on the bridge jumped a few Pascals.

"Grazing hit to port," the tactical officer reported. "The shields held but we had some energy bleed-through. He highlighted the affected sections in the ship-status holo. A long stretch of hull plating on the port side was crumpled and torn.

"Catastrophic venting in eighteen compartments," he continued. "Estimated thirty two dead. Damage control teams are working to seal the affected areas and get two point defense weapons back online."

"Helm, keep us moving," Fall ordered. He turned to Tactical. "Let's shift some of the forward shielding aft to shore up our stern."

The tactical officer looked up at him, one eyebrow raised. "We can certainly do that, sir, but we're danger-close. We have four friendlies trying to get a solution and if one of my counterparts leads the target too much..."

"Do it," Fall ordered. "We might take friendly fire, but we know for a fact that those *húndàn* behind us are trying to hit us, so I'll take my chances."

"Aft contact is showing heavy damage to the outer hull," the tactical officer offered. "They're following us into the envelope for the *Emma* and the *Oliver*. There's no way they can take much more."

Emma and *Oliver* were turning to bear on the remaining contact and they opened up almost in punctuation to the officer's statement. The combined, concentrated fire of the four ships was too much for the enemy's shield emitters and the blue haze began to fail in multiple locations.

That spelled the end for her. One moment, she was a fighting ship – a heavy cruiser – and, the next, she was a failing habitat for her crew as enhanced conventional rounds tore bulkheads, stanchions and deck plates to lethal shreds. Fragments flew away from the hull, propelled by escaping atmosphere, and the bodies – and body parts – soon followed.

Julia nodded to herself as she watched the tactical holo. The remnants of both enemy ships were ejecting their escape pods. Some of the small, unshielded capsules were colliding with wreckage and rupturing.

"Captain Fall, signal phase two, if you'd be so kind," she requested. "The goods have a very short shelf-life in this environment."

Fall passed on the order to the squadron while she assessed the beacons on the escape pods, touching each high-priority signal to mark them for pickup.

Shuttles from the five ships launched and began picking up the pods, slowly scooping them into their open boarding ramps.

This was becoming the main purpose of the ambush program. With the end of the civil war in sight, the Humans were scrambling to capture as many prisoner specialists as they could get their hands on. Gray ships engaged in the capture of Human experimental subjects were equipped and staffed to begin the conditioning process from the moment the victims were brought aboard.

Experts in Human conditioning were a rare commodity among the Grays and they got top priority in a rescue scenario, higher even than the ship's command staff.

Progress was being made on reversing the effects of the conditioning, but Brother N'Zim wanted more trained Grays to accelerate his work. A large portion of Humans in the colonies had been conditioned and then set free. They were committed to the constant, draining conflict between the colonies and they rarely failed, if captured, to destroy the evidence.

Seeing as that evidence resided in their brains...

They were grabbing as many specialists as they could, while the Gray civil war lasted.

"That's all of 'em, ma'am," Fall announced.

"Very well, Captain," Julia replied. "Leave a message drone and let's go home."

The communications officer released the drone and a slight rumble began to build as the ship turned for the jump to the primary RV point.

"I do hope the distortion drive hasn't been knocked out of alignment," Fall said mildly but with a slightly accusatory glance at Julia. "Wouldn't do to drop out in the middle of one of Defiance's stars..."

Julia affected not to hear him, despite her military augments, and the ship slid into distorted space. If he was worrying over nothing, she could afford to be gracious about it. If he was right and they reappeared inside a planet or star, then nobody would be left to raise a fuss about it anyway.

They left behind nothing but a Gray drone, repeating the Purist manifesto over and over.

Beating the Bushes

Daffyd paid for his coffee and walked over to a small table on the edge of the half-deserted market square. He dragged a finger across the seat and made a small grunt of approval at the cleanliness. Masra was built on a desert world and he'd expected a great deal more heat and dust, given the way the city was laid out.

Unlike the Imperial way of dropping a massive arcology into the desert and sealing it up, Masra was a *collection* of buildings, none more than five stories high, set close to provide shaded alleys for pedestrian traffic. Wind towers caught the breeze, electrostatically filtered out the dust and released the wind to cool the pedestrian level. Without even tapping into the city's fusion plants, the average temperature was nearly twenty degrees lower than the surrounding desert.

He sat and took a closer look at the strange, velvety ornaments someone had hung in the tree. He squinted. The yellow/orange, slightly irregular orbs seemed to somehow be grafted right onto the tree. He shrugged, taking another look around the square before trying the coffee. His eyebrows shot up in delight.

He'd been leery of the beverage, knowing the shopkeeper had *made* it right in front of his eyes, but it actually tasted... better... than proper coffee from a heat-serve bag. Those little brown beans he'd been crushing really seemed to add complexity to the coffee. He took another sip and leaned back in his chair with a sigh.

It was a pleasant relief to drop the drunken oaf act.

A low rumble from the far side of the square caught his attention. He looked over to see the awning of a produce shop lifting up from the shipping level. He'd gotten the basics on how Masra's markets worked while the shopkeeper was making the coffee.

The Market was dotted with forty square holes, each surrounded by a protective railing. At night, when the shops closed, they lowered down to the more secure level. In the morning, when the sale goods were brought in by ground trucks, the shops were already at the level set aside for mechanized transport.

As each shop was stocked, it would return to the market level and, as Daffyd watched, the market quickly came to life. As he'd hoped, a large part of the early clientele made the coffee shop their first waypoint.

The seats around him filled quickly and he'd deliberately put himself within hearing range of several circular conversation pits. The conversations ran the usual gambit, work, family and war. There was a lot of discussion about the long-running conflict between the colonies, though Daffyd had come down to the surface thinking they'd found the only Human world in this region.

Hearing there were more worlds – enough to keep a low-level war going for decades – came as a bit of a surprise. Less surprising was the number of times the names Urbica and Grimm popped up. He nodded to himself. The general knew her business. If there was a war out here, she wouldn't be sitting on the sidelines.

He grinned. Evidently, she was rumored to have seized a Gray cruiser within hours of being freed from their clutches. He figured that might not even be an exaggeration. He'd been with her when they seized the *Sucker Punch*. They'd actually seized a cruiser first but, when the Gray crew activated the self-destruct, they abandoned the ship in favor of the brand new attack carrier that the cruiser was supposed to be protecting.

A man to his right, so close he was practically in Daffyd's back pocket, was loudly denying the admittedly tall tale and Daffyd saw a chance to join in the discussion and, perhaps, steer it in a more productive direction.

"At Irricana," he said, turning to face the men seated in the round pit, "she and her dragoons took a Gray cruiser by boarding but then abandoned it for a chance to seize a carrier instead." He tilted his head at the man who didn't believe in her more recent exploits, as if to say 'you can't argue with the facts'. "Total time between leaving the *Rope a Dope* and securing the *Sucker Punch* was less than two centidays."

"You're basing that on Imperial records, friend," a man on the other side of the pit pointed out reasonably. "I wouldn't put too much faith in Mankind's longest running serial fiction, if I were you."

Daffyd joined in the laughter good naturedly, taking it as a chance to pick up his drink and join them. "You don't need to rely on Imperial records, friend," he told the man. "Just ask the eyewitnesses. It happened in Irricanan orbit, in full view of the station, hundreds of ships and a full shift on duty at Orbital Control."

He leaned forward. "Or you could just ask someone who was there with her."

The skeptic on his right snorted in derision. "And I suppose we're supposed to believe that means *you*?"

"What's so unbelievable about that?" Daffyd shrugged. "Our general went missing and we decided to come looking for her."

The man across the pit grinned. "I'd heard a slightly more... nuanced... story than that."

Daffyd nodded. He and his fellow dragoons were trying to find General Urbica and it looked like she wasn't currently in a mood to be found. Their best bet was to make a public spectacle of themselves. The General would hear of them and come looking.

So there was no sense in holding anything back.

"By 'nuanced' I assume you're referring to my incarceration and the fact that the 1st Gliessan Dragoons were ordered by CentCom to lay down arms and return to civilian pursuits?"

The man nodded.

"All the more reason, don't you think," Daffyd asked, "for us to come find our stranded commander?" He stuck out his arm. "No need to stand on faith. Just scan my implant."

The skeptic beat the others to the punch, pulling out his data-unit and waving it over Daffyd's arm. The holographic readout appeared over the scanner and the man grunted in surprise. "Imperial chip," he muttered. "Says he's Daffyd ap Rhys."

"*You* invented the source-directed wormhole generator?" the other man asked.

"*Wǒ de mā*," Daffyd exclaimed. "And you were just talking about serial fiction! That was a cover story to keep CentCom from having it scrapped. The Grays invented that drive and, hopefully, died when we used it to raid the world they were working on. If we didn't..."

A hand fell on his shoulder, the grip firm.

The men at the table were looking past him, their eyes growing wide.

Luck is a Harsh Mistress

"**We**'re at the rendezvous coordinates," Robin announced from the helm. "Captain Fall's combat group is already here." Despite the good news, she frowned at her display as though it had just insulted her sister.

Julia nodded, relieved that Fall had returned to the Odin's Eye nebula from another ambush without straying from the program and getting anyone killed. "Very well," she replied. We'll..."

"Contact!" the tactical officer broke in. "We have distortion alerts consistent with multiple enemy inbounds."

"Beat to quarters," Hale ordered in a calm but loud voice. "Weapons free."

Julia knew there was no need to pass that order to the rest of Hale's small combat group. They were well drilled and they'd be maneuvering to get the best shots on the inbound vessels without any prompting from her.

"Reading fifteen cruisers, twenty frigates and one carrier," the tactical officer announced.

Julia walked into the midst of the tactical holo projected in the center of the bridge. Did that carrier have the same kind of wormhole generator they'd found on the *Sucker Punch?* Regardless, it was a juicy target.

Since the Battle of Greenland Roads, carriers had been viewed as the successor to the super-dreadnought. No longer were naval engagements a matter of putting out as much ordnance as possible and hoping for hits as forces closed on one another. Naval doctrine among most of the advanced species now called for carrier-launched ship destroyers that could get in close and deal damage more effectively.

An enemy carrier was automatically a primary target in any engagement but Julia had only nine ships at her disposal.

She caught Hale's questioning look. "Standing orders, Captain Hale. If anyone happens to get off a shot at that carrier in passing, I won't complain, but we're to break contact and escape with all due haste."

Robin turned to look back at Julia. "Why aren't the Grays firing? They've definitely got the drop on us."

"Why indeed," Julia muttered. "Were they hoping to capture prisoners?" It would mark a drastic departure from Gray doctrine, if they were. They weren't in the business of capturing their own kind.

"*Chto za Huy?*" Hale exclaimed. "Fall's taking his squadron straight at the carrier." He seemed to catch himself on the verge of uttering a scathing criticism in front of his own bridge crew. "Ballsy, but not a course of action afflicted with an abundance of good sense."

"Something isn't right," the tactical officer warned. "Some of those Gray cruisers are sitting where gravimetric ribbons should be. Why in Hades aren't they falling in?"

"*Jiàn tā de guǐ!*" Julia grabbed Hale by the shoulder. "They set off some nukes in here and re-aligned the ribbons. Our current cartography will get us killed!"

"Must have been recent," Hale replied. "The gases still haven't re-aligned, which is why we didn't notice."

"No wonder they aren't firing." Julia looked at the holographic enemy. "They don't want the trajectory of their rounds to curve in the wrong place and alert our tactical computer to the discrepancy."

"And we can use that," Hale enthused, "now that we know about it." He looked to Robin. "The distortion drive is spooled up?"

"Aye, sir."

He turned to the left. "Tactical, get every gun firing and task the computer to map the new ribbon locations. Helm will jump the ship as soon as we resolve a clear path out."

There was no need to risk sending an explanation in Human language. The targeting computers on the other ships would pick up on the discrepancy in the outbound trajectories and alert the crews. Any confusion would be cleared up in short order.

As Julia watched, a haze of lines began tracing their way out from the *Ava Klum's* projected image. Some ran true enough, to the naked eye, but tiny calculations began showing next to each trajectory. Some of the rounds even disappeared entirely, confirming the system's predictions.

"*Tāmāde!*" Hale muttered. "Fall's got a cruiser and a frigate stuck." Sure enough, the two ships were caught in the gravity well of an unmapped ribbon. "Get out of there," he urged quietly. "Don't reinforce failure."

The three remaining ships of Fall's combat group continued to press the attack, seemingly oblivious to their comrades' plight.

"They're losing ground," Julia almost whispered. The two ships, carrying more than two thousand of her crewmen, were sliding back into the ribbon. External equipment and hull plating began tearing loose, tumbling into oblivion as the bigger cruiser drifted back against her engine's best efforts.

As she watched in horror, the engines themselves broke loose and fell into the abyss. The ship herself, with nothing to slow her fate, was snatched out of existence in the blink of an eye.

The frigate captain must have decided to throw the dice because he engaged his distortion drive and, for a brief instant, it looked as though they might escape. The vessel took on an elongated look, as her engines began to create the compression differential that would move the universe past her, but then she broke in two. With her engines snatched into the void, the front half dropped back out of distortion at a standstill, only to be pulled into the quick, brutal embrace of the ribbon.

"Captain Hale," she began, barely keeping her voice under control, "send the withdrawal signal again, if you please." Grief and rage fought for control, but she forced them both aside. She still had eight ships and their crews to save. She could deal with the rest later.

If there *was* a later.

"We have a path," the navigation officer announced urgently. "Our other call-signs are lining up for the jump."

Under standing orders for situations just like this one, each ship would jump at the earliest opportunity. There was no need to send signals that might blow their cover, revealing who the Grays were really up against. Julia looked at the tactical holo.

Fall's remaining three ships seemed to have stopped their forward motion and were angling away from the enemy carrier.

The holo flickered, stabilized and then dissolved into a green haze of static.

"We're out," Robin reported. "ETA to secondary rendezvous is eight centi-days."

Julia looked over at Hale. "We can only hope he manages to jump his ships out of there," she said, keeping her voice low because she knew she couldn't trust it right now at a higher volume.

Hale raised an eyebrow. "Or that they fly into a ribbon." He shrugged. "If the Grays find any Human corpses floating around in the wreckage, we're in for a bit of trouble."

She looked around at the subdued bridge crew. She resisted the urge to shake her head. The longer you ride a lucky streak, the more certain it becomes that you'll run into trouble.

And one way or another, trouble would be following them home.

You're not on Kansas Anymore

Pulver gave Daffyd's shoulder what he hoped to be a particularly painful squeeze. "Get up!"

Daffyd finished his drink, nodded to the men he'd been talking to and came to his feet with a slight waver. He turned slowly, giving Pulver a mildly surprised look. "Commander Pulver," he chided, "it's unseemly for a man of your station to follow me around like this. If you wanted my autograph, all you had to do is..."

"As an officer holding his Imperial Majesty's commission," Pulver cut in impatiently, "I hereby place you under arrest."

"Ah..." ap Rhys nodded sympathetically "... this would be about that business at Nidaveller Station." He smiled. "Who could blame you and this fine gentleman here..." he pointed over Pulver's left shoulder, "for thinking I had something to do with it?"

Frowning, Pulver glanced over his shoulder and cursed his own stupidity as he heard ap Rhys' mug shatter on the flagstones amid the scuffle of rapidly accelerating feet. He swung his head back around to see the prisoner racing across the seating area, knocking over tables and patrons in his haste.

Rolling his eyes, Pulver pulled out the stun launcher he'd taken from the armory on the *Sucker Punch* before coming down to Masra. He aimed it at the fleeing back and pulled the trigger, sending a cloud of tiny spheres after the quarry.

Several struck innocent bystanders, but they were usually non-lethal. No officer in the Imperium would worry about shocking a few civilians as long as they got their target.

The spheres hit with more than enough force to compress the intervening layers of clothing and plant their tiny barbs into skin. Once embedded, their micro-capacitors released their electrical charges, overloading the victim's nervous system.

With a strange squawk, ap Rhys went down twitching. Several others were on the ground as well, but Pulver kept his eyes on the target. "Grab him!" he shouted.

Several of his men jumped to their feet, throwing off the local robes they'd been wearing to blend in. They raced over to the twitching prisoner and rolled him onto his belly to place polymer joint locks at his wrists and ankles.

Pulver became aware of a growing current of anger in the crowd. Surprise at seeing Imperial uniforms was quickly giving way to anger. He suddenly realized that, though he'd behaved in a perfectly ordinary way for a commissioned officer in the Imperium, Masra was definitely not part of the Imperium.

He'd already noticed that few of the locals went without weapons. He'd noticed, but it hadn't really meant much to him until now, when he'd cavalierly stunned six or seven of their people in order to get his prisoner.

"You have no business here," shouted one of the men who'd been talking to ap Rhys, "and no rights, either."

"And nobody to claim your blood-price," another man in the small seating pit added as he stood, his right hand straying to the butt of a pistol.

Pulver was no combat officer, but it didn't take a tactical genius to see there was little to be gained from trying to win an argument with hundreds of angry, armed individuals. He gave them a bow, bending at the waist but keeping his eyes on the locals. "My apologies," he offered. "I have overstepped in my zeal. We will leave you in peace."

Maxwell was quick enough to realize that was the cue to get the prisoner moving. He detailed three men to the task, one to each arm, and one to the feet.

Pulver gave the men in the pit a polite nod before following his men. Shouts followed them, mostly referring to his ancestry or to the lack of enthusiasm for the Imperium in general. "Hands off your weapons," he hissed. "If one of us pulls a gun, we're all dead."

He'd spent most of his engineering career with the constant threat of liquidation hanging over his head but he'd never felt the adrenaline-fueled rush of imminent danger before. He fought to keep his thoughts in order. He knew any wrong move would get them killed. Even making all the right moves might end in the same result.

Paradoxically, time seemed to dilate for him, much like the distortion bubble of a ship's drive. Though their progress through the endless alleyways of Masra seemed painfully slow, he still seemed to perceive everything at an accelerated pace.

Was this what it was like for combat personnel? He saw one local fling a rock at Maxwell and Pulver reached out to put a steadying hand on his energy specialist cum sensor officer as the missile struck.

"We're leaving," he soothed the local. "No need for trouble." He reckoned it wouldn't hurt to remind the man that the men in Pulver's party were armed and capable of making trouble. He also knew it was a bluff.

Shouts echoed off the alley walls as they made their way to the shuttle pad. Running feet echoed from every side alley and he hoped they were running away, but he had a sinking feeling that they weren't. They passed through a larger intersection, walking under a wind tower, the relatively cool jet of air reminding him how sweaty he was.

He could smell the stink of fear on his own sweat as their way forward became more and more congested. The Masrans were starting to push at Pulver's men, loudly declaring that they would never allow their world to be annexed and expressing anger at his use of the stun gun.

In the Imperium, this kind of reaction was simply unthinkable. Clearly, the citizens of this world were accustomed to a great deal more in the way of personal liberties and Pulver was starting to think his transgression would spell his death.

Then he saw the shuttle.

A Marine lance corporal must have noticed the approach of Pulver's party. He led six fellow Marines down the boarding ramp in full HMA. Two of the armored Marines stayed at the ramp to guard the craft while the other four followed the lance corporal, parting the tide of Humanity.

The locals were still angry, but they fell back in awe at the sight of heavy Marine armor.

Pulver felt a rush of euphoria as well as a healthy dose of affection for the Corps. The armored escorts fell in on either side of the engineers, walking between them and the locals, who were now falling back to leave a wide path open for the Imperials.

They rushed up the ramp and the shuttle lifted off while it was just beginning to close. The pilot swung the craft around, giving the crowd a good look at the rail-gun in the nose as well as the half dozen rotary cannon built into the fuselage.

Not a single rock was thrown as the craft lifted above the roofs of the city.

He looked across to where the lance corporal was locked into an HMA restraint. The helmet was retracted and he gave the man a nod of thanks. He moved aft to where ap Rhys lay on the deck. The dragoon engineer had regained his senses.

"Your ship jumped away the instant we arrived in orbit," Pulver told him. "They must have had the drives spooled up and ready to go on an instant's notice. We figured that meant somebody would have been left behind and it looks like we figured right."

"*Tcho sa ga'lima!*" the prisoner commented pungently. "After all I've done for them? So much for the honor of the 1st Gliessan Dragoons."

With the ramp up, the shuttle's progress toward orbit accelerated drastically and Pulver had to slump down into a side bench. He gave the prisoner a speculative look. "Why not help us find them?" he suggested. "Clearly they don't care what happens to you. I'd want to give them a piece of my mind, if I were in your shoes..."

"Oh, I can do a damn sight better than help you *look* for them," ap Rhys growled. "I know where they'll head next. Standard operating procedure. If they have to leave without everybody back aboard, they'll be heading for a rendezvous where they're supposed to wait a couple of days; give the missing crew a chance to catch up." He looked away. "Not that I expect the rat bastards to wait more than a couple of centi-days before moving on..."

Pulver grinned. He was starting to develop a liking for this cloak and dagger stuff. "You'll take us to the rendezvous?"

Daffyd raised an eyebrow. "Will it improve your opinion of me enough for you to let me go free afterwards?" He held out his bound wrists.

Pulver pulled out his knife and sliced through the bonds. "You have my guarantee," he said. He wondered if the prisoner had noticed that no specific guarantee had been proffered. He'd said nothing about freedom himself.

As phrased, it was a pretty empty promise. One might argue about context, but Pulver was an engineer, he preferred to stick to absolutes.

Confidence

Julia sat on the ledge of the main gallery, looking down into the canyon where the overburden ramp was steadily disappearing beneath a relentless carpet of green. The rain kicked up a slightly dusty scent as it pounded the waste rock.

She took another deep, calming breath as shouts echoed up the passageway from the main chamber. Almost two thousand crewmen were dead after the ambush at Odin's Eye. Two thousand men and women who'd looked to her for victory.

She clenched a fist, staring down into the narrow canyon where a swarm of *not fur nothings* were ascending from a corpse they'd just picked clean. Their chittering calls raised the hair on the back of her neck. Those dead crewmen had also looked to Captain Fall for victory and he'd led them to their deaths.

He'd still managed to come home safely, though, and now he was in the main chamber painting her as the cause of all their woes.

A deeper call echoed from further along the canyon, forcing the small predators into a tighter, defensive formation. As they grouped together in fear, a large, four-meter wingspan creature dove on them, scooping most of the *not fur nothings* into its gaping jaw in one pass.

She watched it fly off, trying not to think as the large creature faded into the rain. Caleb, the sole survivor of the miners and therefore the owner of this world, insisted the large predator was a stage in the life-cycle of the *not fur nothings*.

It was hard to believe the smaller, hand-sized predators could transform into the much larger beast, but he'd pointed out a small clutch of metamorphosis-sacs one morning as they were scouting a nearby canyon and, after managing to control her revulsion at the sight, she'd admitted the truth of it.

She turned her head at the polite moment as Ava approached. With Julia's Marine enhancements, she'd heard Ava and her guards far sooner than most would have. Still, she refrained from reminding everybody that she was different.

"Am I intruding?" Ava waved a hand to indicate the ledge where Julia sat.

Julia shook her head and Ava sat next to her. Her guards attached her tether to a ring in the floor before backing off to a discrete distance. They were charged with protecting Roanoke's greatest warrior from the Gray suicide imperative programmed into her mind.

They'd be in a great deal of trouble if their charge had thrown herself over the gallery ledge.

Julia looked back out into the rain. "How's the research program coming along?"

"Hmm," Ava began noncommittally, "Brother N'Zim is far more optimistic than I am but, then, my conditioning probably discourages me from circumventing what the Grays have done to me." She let out a half chuckle as she gave her tether a tug.

"The less I fight it, the less I feel the urge to kill myself."

Julia nodded. "He tells me the latest batch of specialists we captured are starting to make a difference."

Ava turned to put a foot up on the ledge. Julia could hear the startled shifting of the guard's feet, but their leader was simply trying to get a better view of the canyon.

"Brother N'Zim and his kind have a way with the Grays," Ava replied. "One from the last batch has a deeper theoretical knowledge than the others. It seems the conditioning is built in layers, lots of them, and they lock from the inside, if that makes any sense to you."

Julia frowned. "Does that mean there might be an innermost layer that we can unlock and the whole thing will unravel?"

A nod. "N'Zim is calling it the keystone. If we can find it, I might be able to sleep without having somebody stand over my bed all night."

Julia shuddered. "Sounds like an old ex of mine. Just couldn't let go." She looked at Ava. "At least until I broke his fingers..."

Ava laughed. "If only our problems were so easily solved." She tilted her head. "But that's not why I came to see you."

Controlled exhale as Julia looked back out into the rain. "I know," she replied.

"This is war," Ava reminded her. "Ships will be lost, crew killed. You're a Marine, a professional. You know this. Losing people isn't always a sign of failure."

"My failure is more specific," Julia insisted. "I knew Fall was dangerous but I didn't remove him from command. It was negligence on my part, pure and simple."

"What could you have done? He was voted in. It takes a vote or an outright mutiny to remove him. This isn't the Imperial military, where you can do as you wish with your subordinates."

Julia waved a hand. "I know that, but I could have called for a vote of no-confidence."

"Just out of the black?" Ava's tone indicated her opinion clearly enough. "Certainly anyone can call a vote, but there was no real proof of incompetence. His tactical sense is limited, I grant you, but he's a skillful networker. Usually our system weeds out the politicians but, every now and then, one of them slips through."

Ava leaned in toward Julia. "It's an open vote. It has to be in order to protect serving officers from constant politically motivated interference. You have to stand up in front of all your crewmates and state your decision, so you really need to believe in what you're doing to remove an officer. There's no taking cheap shots from anonymity."

She pointed down the corridor to indicate the source of the shouting in the main chamber. As if on cue, a roar of anger reverberated up the rocky passage. "Fall is down there right now telling everybody that it's your fault we lost those ships. Once he thinks he has enough votes, he'll make his *own* call for a vote of no confidence."

She looked over to her guards and nodded. One of them turned and trotted around the corner. Julia knew someone was scuffling around in the semi-darkness but she'd assumed they were simply eavesdropping. She revised that estimate when the guard returned with Antonov following.

Ava nodded her head at Julia. "Tell Commodore Urbica what you told me."

Antonov's eyes blazed. "Ma'am, we're pissed. Fall told everybody on his bridge crew to keep their mouths shut, but there's too many of 'em to keep any kind of secret. As soon as they started rotating off their duty watches we started hearing how he ignored standing orders, not to mention direct orders, in order to go after that carrier.

Her right hand was resting on the grip of her sidearm, though she didn't seem to be aware of it. "Bastard didn't care about his crews. He just wanted the glory of taking out an enemy carrier." Her fingers tightened on the grip. "Even had the nerve to say we were lucky... *lucky* that our dead were pulled into the gravimetric ribbons, as if that somehow redeemed his stupidity."

"He assumes he's relatively secure because the officers who'd need to vote on him owe their own positions to his influence." Ava nodded at Antonov. "Kat tells me the tactical officer, navigator and XO were all eager to pursue the carrier and they even shouted down officers who urged a withdrawal as per your standing orders."

"The chief engineer was locked up," Antonov added, "because he wouldn't go along with them. He's still under guard." She pointed down the corridor to where the ruckus was building. "I'm going to walk in there and call for a vote of no-confidence for his three cronies. When we get them out of the way, we can call a vote for Fall himself."

"It would help if you went in there first," Ava suggested. "Contrast your own professionalism with his empty bluster. Remind the people in that chamber they've been listening to a fool before we ask them to vote on his cronies.

"Right now, they think you're sitting up here wallowing in guilt." Ava looked up to meet Julia's eyes. "They need to know they're wrong."

"They *are*," Julia replied evenly. "There's a big difference between the weight of responsibility and self-indulgent guilt." She stood. "You're right, though. It's time to get in there and put a stop to Fall's scheming. He'll tear us apart and the colonies along with us."

She waited for the guards to release Ava from the ring in the floor and then led the way down to the main chamber. The shouts began to resolve into individual voices as she moved down the echoing passage.

The noise began to die out as word spread through the crowd that she was among them, much like a misbehaving class when the teacher returns unexpectedly. Even Fall had stopped talking and he stood on the raised rock platform, watching her approach, his face unreadable.

She walked up to stand next to him, but gave no further indication that she was aware of his presence.

She swept her eyes across the crowd. The faces looking up at her ranged from friendly, to confused, to downright belligerent.

Not a bad start.

"I *will* admit," she began, "that Captain Fall and I don't agree on matters of strategic policy." She saw a few heads bobbing in agreement and many of the belligerents had a look of triumph stealing across their features.

"He feels that the best results will come from an aggressive posture, a willingness to press the attack under any circumstance." She paused again to let that one sink in. Clearly, his attack on the carrier had yielded anything but positive results.

In a heated discussion, facts are easily melted down and moulded into something else entirely. Even in an argument where the facts favor you, you can't simply state them. Angry people don't want to be confused with facts.

But if you can let their anger steer them back to the truth, you can talk about it without losing the crowd.

"No doubt that's why he ignored standing orders during the fight at Odin's Eye," she continued. "No doubt that's why he ignored direct orders to disengage, deciding instead to lead his three ships in an attack on that Gray carrier.

"Capturing or destroying a carrier is a notable achievement," she allowed, "but notoriety doesn't serve our cause. In case anyone has forgotten..." she paused for a heartbeat. "... we're in the business of imitating the Purists. They don't seize the ships of their enemies; they fight when they can and they run when they can't.

"This is a war. It may be a secret war, but it's a *war*. If we don't commit, if we stray from the program, we lose." She finally acknowledged Fall's presence by looking directly at him. "If the Grays ever figure out who we really are, it'll cost us more than a couple of ships; it will result in the destruction of every single Human colony."

She turned away from him, stepping to the edge of the platform and, before Fall could frame a response, Antonov took Julia's place.

"All secondary voting officers of the *Dumas,* I'm calling for a vote of no-confidence in... Morrison – Tactical Officer, Connolly – Navigation Officer and Burke – XO. In accordance with the forms and custom of our ship's company, step forward and assemble for the vote."

Fall's jaw hung open as he watched the officers push forward to vote on the three men.

"We have fourteen officers present from the secondary voting class," Antonov announced. "The voting may proceed. Gentlemen, in the case of Morrison – Tactical Officer, do you confirm his present position or shall he return to his duties in the gunroom?"

Thirteen of the officers crossed their arms. One hold-out kept his arms to the side.

"Crewman Morrison returns to the gunroom by a vote of thirteen to one," she confirmed. "In the case of Connolly – Navigation Officer, how do you vote?"

Again, thirteen pairs of crossed arms but, this time, the other crewmen jeered at the hold-out.

"Crewman Connolly returns to the cartographic section. In the case of Burke –Executive Officer, how do you vote?"

There was a commotion in the crowd as two late arriving officers of the secondary voting class hurried to the front to add their votes to the final cast. This time, sixteen pairs of arms were crossed. Apparently, the hold-out knew better than to reinforce failure. The crowd raised an ironic cheer in honor of his sudden *courage.*

"Crewman Burke returns to..." She frowned. "... to wherever the hell he came from." An XO would have spent years working his way up from his original posting.

"Oh, hell no!" A deep voice boomed from the back of the chamber, near the entrance. "That trouble-making jackass isn't welcome in *my* engineering department!"

Heads turned and a wild cheer burst from the crew of the *Dumas.* Someone had seen which way the wind was blowing and gotten the chief engineer out of lockdown.

Julia knew that reflected a major shift. The chief engineer led the single largest division on almost any ship outside of the Imperial Marines, who were the exception due to their huge troop complements. His presence, ten minutes earlier, would have been enough to swing the vote against Fall, even without removing his three cronies. Now that he was here, Fall's removal became a more leisurely affair.

"I call for a vote of no-confidence in Captain Fall," the chief engineer shouted.

By now, the crowd was almost fully behind the idea and they raised a shout of approval as the newly arrived officer pushed his way to the front. "I nominate Kat to convene," he shouted. "I can't convene and vote at the same time and I wouldn't miss this for anything!"

"Primary voting tier officers are accounted for," Antonov declared amidst the noise. "Administration not yet elected." It was a strange quirk among the privateers that the XO also served as the administration officer, but he was out of the way so Julia wasn't about to complain.

"Chief Medical Officer," Antonov shouted into the sudden silence, grinning at being caught out by the quick drop in noise, "how do you vote?"

The doctor crossed his arms.

"Engineering?"

Another pair of crossed arms and a flurry of pleased shouts.

"Navigation Officer not yet elected."

Chuckles.

"Operations?"

Folded arms.

"Supply?"

Folded arms.

"Tactical..."

"Not yet elected," the crowd shouted, almost in perfect harmony.

"Crewman Fall," Antonov began...

"Is *also* not welcome back to my engine room," the chief engineer shouted.

Julia stepped forward. "As the former positions held by crewmen Fall and Burke are no longer available, we'll find work for them at this facility."

Fall, his face as near crimson as any Human's might possibly get, gave her a stiff nod. She held out a hand, inviting him to leave ahead of her.

As she followed him out, she wondered what she'd do with him. She certainly wouldn't let him have a position of any real influence but he was likely to cause more trouble if he felt his skills were being underutilized. She wondered if she could live with herself if she simply snapped his neck and threw him to the local wildlife.

Julia shuddered. She was reasonably confident of the argument in favor of killing Fall. He'd likely get more people killed if left to his own devices but she knew, once the genie was out of the bottle, it would be easier to justify subsequent killings.

She felt a sudden urge to spin him around and knock his teeth out. It wasn't enough he'd just killed two ship's companies; he had to destroy her soul as well?

It's Never Simple...

Pulver was putting on a confident face. He even condescended to notice Daffyd, standing near the damage control station on the *Sucker Punch's* bridge. "If your coordinates pay off," he told Daffyd, "I'll speak for you when we get back to the Imperium." He frowned slightly. "Assuming we capture your fellow dragoons, of course."

Daffyd didn't have a great deal of faith in Pulver's promises – not so much an issue of trust but, rather, from an understanding of what kind of trouble the research engineer had waiting for him on his return.

The young engineering lieutenant at the tactical station shook his head, ever so slightly, his lips drawn tight. Clearly the crew understood the politically sensitive nature of their assignment... their *actual* assignment.

Being tasked with the reverse engineering of an alien jump drive, at a time when the Imperial Engineering Corps was having trouble keeping their own jumpgate system running, was a nearly impossible task.

Admitting that aliens had built something that Humans couldn't figure out ran counter to the Human assumption of superiority over their neighbors. An entire team of engineers that possessed such damaging knowledge would be a serious threat to Imperial prestige.

"Believe me, Commander," Daffyd replied, "I know how to find the feckless bastards."

He noticed the officers from the next shift filing into the bridge. Each one leaned over the shoulder of his counterpart, getting a quick rundown on what had transpired on the previous shift before taking over the seat.

"You'd better," General Windemere growled. "If you don't, I might just leave you behind when we head home." His grin raised the hairs on the back of Daffyd's neck. "Whether we leave you somewhere with an atmosphere remains to be seen..."

Daffyd had no intention of being among these gray-bellies long enough to find out if Windemere was merely posturing, but he had a role to play and so he gave the threat a nervous, dismissive wave. He broke eye contact, affecting an interest in the departing bridge shift.

He realized, with mild amusement, that his interest wasn't entirely faked. He turned back to Windemere. "I'll just, ummm..." he nodded at the portside bridge hatch, raising his fist to his mouth. "S'cuse me! I'll just be..." He grimaced, tried to force a smile, failed and then simply turned and left.

He knew the crew were under tremendous pressure and they had little hope of surviving their return to the Imperium. He knew where *he'd* be heading in their shoes. When 1GD had seized the *Sucker Punch* from the Grays, one of his first orders of business had been setting up an all-ranks mess in one of the storage holds.

He doubted his brother engineers would have re-purposed the room. He followed them down the companionway and most of them seemed to be heading in the right direction. More than half of the bridge shift made a direct path to the mess and Daffyd walked in behind them, heading straight for the bar.

He walked behind the counter and shooed the NCO bartender back with a few flicks of his hands. As soon as the man had stepped back far enough, Daffyd crouched down to pull up one of the deck plates. Sure enough, six bottles of quality bourbon were still down there, undiscovered by the engineers.

He pulled one out and set it on the counter, noting the surprise on everyone's faces. He grinned. It was ok for him to appear competent where alcohol was involved. He turned to the bartender. "Grab those shot glasses, will you?" He nodded at an access panel next to the cargo scanning station. "Yep, that's the one," Daffyd assured the man. "Should be at least a couple dozen in there."

"Hells," the navigation officer muttered. "We've been sitting on that stuff all this time?"

"Well, actually..." Daffyd pointed at the bartender. "... He's been *standing* on it." He looked at the navigator. "*You've* been sitting on..." He frowned for a moment. "The Mumbai Pale Ale, if I recall correctly."

The navigator looked over his shoulder at the damage controller. Without a single word, both got off their stools and pushed them aside to get at the release for the deck plate that was under them.

"*Zhēnde shì tiāncái!*" the damage controller muttered, staring down at the stash.

"I don't know if I'd go so far as that," Daffyd demurred modestly.

She looked up at Daffyd. "Packing them around the secondary entropic bypass qualifies as *tiāncái* in my book! It's the perfect temperature. The only cooling unit we have on this gŏushĭ Gray ship is five decks down. Any beer we bring up gets warm pretty damned quick."

"Not to mention it's the standard ration issue," the navigator added.

"Oh!" Daffyd didn't have to put on a fake grimace. "Not that *Old Gray* that the Navy hands out?" He shuddered.

"I've had it cold. I can't imagine how much worse it would be warm." He motioned for the damage controller to pull a few out.

She laughed, standing up with four bottles. "Give me a half-centi and I'll turn this into a passable imitation of warm *Old Gray*."

Daffyd chuckled. "I'll take your word for it." He poured shots of bourbon and handed them around. "*Vsego khoroshego!*" He knocked back the shot.

The damage controller took a drink from her ale and pinned him with a stare. "You planning on leaving us, then?"

Daffyd shrugged to conceal his surprise. He knew he was being a little too clever for his own good. "Not at all. Just wishing us all the best." He figured a change in tack was in order. The atmosphere in the room had been vastly improved by the appearance of quality beverages and he judged he might be able to steer the conversation in the right direction now.

"Your boy Pulver seems to have all the angles figured out," he ventured, leaning on the bar from the tender's side.

The navigator held out his glass and the tender refilled it for him. "He's not a bad guy to work for," he began defensively, "he's just trying to put the best face on a bad situation."

Daffyd nodded. "I've seen leaders fall apart under far less stress. Considering what all of you have hanging over your heads..."

"You mean liquidation, if we fail," the engineer serving as navigator cut in, "and possibly liquidation, even if we manage to figure out this drive?"

"It is a pretty juicy secret for hundreds of engineers and techs to keep," Daffyd admitted. "You have to hope CentCom sees the strategic value in a source-directed wormhole generator. They might be willing to admit it's alien tech, if they can say we stole it out from under their noses, but we'd still have to say we can understand how it works."

"If expecting CentCom to see sense is our Plan A," the damage controller growled, "then the gene pool is probably better off without us!"

Daffyd knocked back a shot of bourbon. "I'm in the same boat, figuratively *and* literally. As the guy who supposedly invented the damn thing, they can't leave me running around, whether you figure it out or not."

The bartender nodded. "So you're going back to a certain death."

"*If* I go back," Daffyd allowed. "It sounds like there's a lot of places where a fella could settle down out here."

"Leave the Imperium?" The damage controller stared at him, her eyes wide. "Are you crazy?"

A shrug. "Maybe. Maybe not. Taxes are light out here, set by each colony world, and the folks I've talked to don't even believe me when I tell them my apartment on Irricana only had a five foot high ceiling."

"Really?" The navigator stared at him. "What kind of cost per cube do they pay out here for rent?"

Daffyd grinned at him. "The rents out here are in cost per *square*. Oh, sure, some places with high ceilings probably come with a premium, but most planetary building codes state a two meter minimum height." He shrugged. "Bought a fella on Trondheim a few drinks day before yesterday. Turned out he was a civil engineer."

"Monty's hairy arse!" the damage controller said in surprise. She looked at her crewmates. "We should just scuttle the damn ship and take our chances out here." She'd used a joking tone, but just barely.

Daffyd joined in the laughter, but he knew he'd struck the right nerve. "Stay clear of hot places like Masra," he offered, affecting a sarcastic tone as though he didn't take the conversation seriously. "Lots of Serp raids on worlds like that. Place like Trondheim, a fella could settle down without worrying about scaly visitors..."

The Serps, or Serpentia Sapiens, were active in this region of space. Called *snakes* in the Imperium, the reptilian aliens were ectotherms and quickly slowed down in cold climates.

The damage controller shook her head, but her reply was interrupted.

A klaxon sounded from speakers in the ceiling.

Daffyd, as a passenger or perhaps a prisoner, had no duty station to report to during a general-quarters alarm and so he followed the bridge officers. He arrived on the bridge just as the alarm cut out.

Pulver stared at the tactical holo, his lips drawn tight. General Windemere was beside him and he'd definitely lost some of the color in his face. Daffyd followed their gaze to where the holo showed a medium-sized moon in orbit around a gas giant.

Orbiting the moon was a Gray heavy cruiser.

Daffyd resisted the urge to comment. Windemere had brought sufficient force to deal with a single cruiser but he seemed unsure of what to do next.

"We'd better hail the bastards," Windemere finally announced. "Wouldn't do to start a war if we can avoid it."

A Human figure with a long welt on his forehead replaced the hologram of the moon and ship. Pulver's eyes narrowed and Windemere took an involuntary step back in surprise.

"This is Commander Pulver of His Imperial Majesty's vessel the... *Sucker Punch*," Pulver didn't seem to share General Urbica's sense of humor in ship names. "Identify yourself."

The hologram nodded politely. "Hi Commander. I'm Beam."

Daffyd supressed a grin as he watched the skin on the back of Pulver's neck grow red.

"Well, Beam," Pulver replied acidly, "perhaps you could tell me what you're doing on a Gray cruiser?"

Beam shrugged. "I was a loadmaster aboard the *Pony Express* but we were captured by the Grays. They brought us aboard this ship and shoved us all into pods, down in the cargo bays."

Beam's attention seemed to wander for a moment and then he snapped his eyes back to Pulver. "Some kind of brain-washing setup, we think. But my friend and I turned out to be un-washable. I managed to get the drop on a Marine and..."

"Grays don't have infantry," Pulver interrupted. "Try again..."

"They have *Human* infantry," Beam insisted. "Imperial Marines with gods-damned hand cannons." He gestured at the scar on his forehead. "Recoil caught me off guard when I shot the first one and nearly knocked me unconscious"

"Right." Pulver nodded, dragging out the word. "You single-handedly took out a ship full of Marines and..."

"Three Marines," Beam corrected, "and only two of 'em were armed. I managed to stitch two of them with the first volley, thank the gods for dumb luck, and the unarmed one became very cooperative after that. He helped us release the rest of our crew. They're down on the surface, looking for the *Pony*. The Grays have some kind of breaking yard down there."

Pulver made a cutting motion across his throat and turned to Windemere. "I bet the crew left them behind to maintain their salvage claim while they try to get their original ship back. I doubt this guy's even able to conn a ship that large..."

"Y'know," Beam cut in, "I can still hear you, and of course we were left here to maintain our claim on this ship. I'm just a loadmaster so, no, I can't conn a ship." The hologram sighed. "It seems that a loadmaster's chief duty on a ship like ours is to know as little as possible."

Pulver glared at the communications operator before looking to meet Windemere's gaze. The general clearly had no better idea what the young man was talking about.

Daffyd stepped forward. "If I might put my three credits in here, I've seen the *Pony Express* a few times. She's a regular at Irricana – shows up every couple of months."

"So what's he talking about?" Windemere demanded.

Daffyd inclined his head a bit to the right. "Can you think of no reason why it might be advantageous to have a loadmaster with no clue what's going on in his own ship?"

He got the distinct impression Windemere wasn't a fan of puzzles. "When they call in at an Imperial possession, they have to give the standard electro-encephalographic declaration..."

The cloud front cleared from the general's expression. "Smugglers!" He shot a predatory glance at the holographic Beam.

"Now hold on a second, your generalship." Daffyd stepped between Windemere and the projected Human. "You're not thinking of arresting them, are you? Where the hells would we stick them all, not to mention the obvious jurisdictional issues."

"The Emperor's Regulations and Orders are clear on the matter of smugglers," Windemere replied darkly.

It was entirely possible that this one mundane issue was drawing the general's attention simply because it was more within his comfort zone than his other problems.

"And what do the ER&O's have to say about pursuing a renegade dragoon unit while carting a few hundred prisoners along with us and trying to keep them supplied with water and food?" Daffyd wanted to make the general realise just how much trouble he'd be making for himself if he decided to start making arrests.

Having the *Sucker Punch* full of prisoners would complicate things, requiring a serious change in Daffyd's plans. Still, he could offer the general a small bit of ordinary trouble, just to make him happy.

"That cruiser's in a very shaky orbit," he added. "They probably know enough glyphs to figure out the broad strokes but you need a deeper understanding of their systems to set up a stable orbit. I can help them with that."

He waved at the spot where the moon had been projected. "Even if the *Pony Express* hasn't been broken up yet, they'd still need help getting their reactors back online." He raised an eyebrow. "First rule of spacefaring..."

"Don't quote the Rule-of-Assistance to an engineer, Mr. Ap Rhys," Windemere cut him off, his tone a warning in itself. "Of course we aren't just leaving Humans to the whim of fate." He looked over to Pulver. "Commander, take a damage control team and a full security detail over to that ship, give them what aid you can and then find the crew on the surface."

He waved at Daffyd. "Take our guest with you. He's familiar with their ship, so he may be of use."

Humint

Edgar Prestonby stared at the middle aged Masran man, his coffee held halfway to his mouth where he'd stopped it in feigned surprise.

Truth be told, Edgar *was* surprised but, being a highly trained Maegi, he'd suppressed his initial surprise before deciding the man across the conversation pit from him would be more inclined to talk freely if he felt his words were having an impact.

"And he said he was Daffyd ap Rhys?" Edgar demanded. "The same Daffyd ap Rhys who belongs to the 1st Gliessan Dragoons?"

The man raised one eyebrow. "Would there be *several* men called Daffyd ap Rhys looking for the commanding officer of 1GD?"

"It *is* unlikely," Edgar admitted, finally having a sip of the brown liquid. "And where did he go from here?"

The man grinned nastily. "They."

"They?"

A nod. "Captured by gray-bellies, right in front of my eyes."

Edgar supressed a shudder but such was his shock that he failed to substitute a fake one. Imperials here in the colonies ran counter to everything he stood for.

He tried to work out the implications. The Imperium recognized this region as the property of the Gray Quorum, so they'd be unlikely to send an expedition that might start a war. The Imperial military was a rotting dragon, more than able to destroy any enemy, but too conscious of its own decline to have any real confidence.

That meant a rogue element or a clandestine unit that could easily be disavowed and forgotten. He devoutly hoped it was the former. A clandestine unit meant a direct Imperial interest in this region.

He drained his coffee, nodded politely to the man and took his leave.

He arrived at the shuttle pad to find a small collection of new passengers waiting for a ride up to the *Mot Juste*. One young man sat a little to himself and Edgar dropped onto the bench next to him with a sigh.

"You play the pintarel?" Edgar asked, nodding down at the traditional stringed instrument in the young man's hands. "Interesting choice of instrument for a Human."

The young man frowned. The pintarel was a Human instrument and he said as much to Edgar.

"Oh, certainly," Edgar replied cheerfully, "but you have to admit that with so many aliens not playing it, one can get the wrong idea..."

The pintarel player opened his mouth to reply but then shut it again as there seemed to be no sensible answer to such a statement.

Edgar plowed on, peppering his patter with ever more contradictory statements and the young man continued to let them pass unremarked, becoming an unwitting participant in his own hypnotic induction.

By the time the shuttle landed in the forward hangar of the *Mot Juste*, the young musician was ready to find Julia Urbica and her merry band. He'd be getting off at the next stop to find a ship heading the other way. The trigger phrases planted in his mind would ensure that Mullins or one of his subordinates would discover him and the message he carried.

He walked into the refectory and filled a tray with what the crew jokingly referred to as food. He looked around the room for his next target. He'd need a second messenger to ensure the news got through. He spotted the man with ease, having already marked him for use.

The Roanokan was heading nowhere in particular. He was taking a recent breakup with his girlfriend badly and had simply left his world with no real plan in mind. Edgar supressed any visible evidence of the sadness that suddenly washed over him.

He understood the man's loss.

He walked over and sat next to him. "Food..." he said sarcastically, waving a hand at the man's plate. It was a pretty good example of contradiction, if he did say so himself.

Uruk

Daffyd resisted the urge to grin as the shuttle bucked its way through a rainstorm that covered half the moon. Uruk was very wet and incredibly turbulent and the crew of the *Sucker Punch*, engineers and techs from Nidaveller Station, were accustomed to working aboard stations and ships in the vacuum of space.

Doubtless, most of them were wishing they'd stayed aboard the Gray cruiser in orbit. The deck would need a good wash-down.

They should try landing on Irricana sometime. A bad particulate storm there could strip the vanes off an atmo engine in no time flat.

He treated himself to a ration bar as the men and women around him held onto the seat bars for dear life.

The wind lessened as they neared the surface. The intensity of the rain seemed to increase but it was simply the slowing of the shuttle relative to the falling water drops. The increased pounding on the upper surfaces of the shuttle leveled off just as the landing points touched down.

Daffyd walked over to the ramp as it opened and a man jumped in out of the rain as soon as it was halfway down. He looked around the passenger compartment seeing fifteen grey uniforms.

"Didn't quite believe it until just now," he said. "Imperial engineers, all the way out here on Uruk!" He extended a hand to Daffyd. "Name's Marco Stanic, captain of the *Pony Express*. We're damn glad to have you show up down here!"

Daffyd waved his hand over Marco's. "Daffyd ap Rhys," he replied, nodding over his shoulder. "That's Commander Pulver. He's the one in charge of our little mission of mercy."

Marco nodded at Pulver but stopped to do a double take on Daffyd. "Really?" he asked, his brows knitting together. "One of Urbica's famous dragoons?"

"That's me," Daffyd agreed. "And I've seen your ship around Irricana more than once. What brings you all the way out here?"

"Got nabbed by the Grays," Marco replied, looking back and forth between Daffyd and Pulver, who'd come to stand next to his right. "They shoved us into pods and the next thing I knew, one of my loadmasters is pulling me back out and we were in orbit around this moon."

"Yeah, we heard that from your boys in orbit," Daffyd cut in. "What I don't quite get is how they managed to stay conscious when they went into the pods."

A charming grin. "Well, as a hypothetical exercise..." He raised his eyebrows at Pulver.

Pulver sighed, waving a dismissive hand.

Marco nodded. "Well, let's say, for example, that a ship was carrying a small stash of FMG, purely for medical purposes you understand, and say that your loadmasters are both fond of the stuff..."

"So your loadmasters were stoned," Daffyd cut in, then grinned, "hypothetically, of course!"

"Exactly!" Marco nodded. "It might just be possible that a captive in that exact set of circumstances could find himself resistant to the effects of the Gray pods."

"Fabulous," Pulver drawled. He waved a hand at the stack of components that were strapped down on the deck. "Let's get your boat back in the black so we can all get on with what we were doing."

None of Pulver's people wanted to touch the stack, seeing as it was now decorated with somebody's lunch. All eyes turned to the freighter captain.

"Fair enough," Marco chuckled. "What's a little stomach acid among friends, eh?" He pulled the strap-release and scooped the stack of flash capacitors into his arms. "They'll be clean anyway, by the time we get inside the breaking yards." He strolled down the back ramp and led the way, through pounding rain, to a set of massive, open doors in the cliff-side that showed a freighter sitting inside.

Just before they reached shelter, the rain let up.

"Always seems to happen *after* you get soaked," Marco mused. He handed off the equipment to one of his crewmen who carried it inside the large structure.

A horde of avians were wheeling and diving in a swarm, just beyond the roof of the large building.

The smuggler nodded to Pulver. "My thanks, Commander. Those flash-caps should get our reactor back on its feet."

"Why didn't you have any in the first place?" Pulver asked.

"We did, but one of the containment emitters was dead. We didn't know until we'd dumped the charge into the ignition sequence."

"You didn't check?" One of engineering techs demanded.

"Not while we were sitting in a hostile Gray facility, sonny." Marco replied mildly. "We had no idea when another cruiser might happen along and find us standing next to a pile of their dead pals."

"Well we have a small fleet up there." Pulver nodded upwards. "We should be able to hold this place long enough to do a proper job this time. Let's have my team go over everything before you try to flash up."

They were halfway to the freighter when Pulver slowed, putting a hand to his ear with a frown. He looked to Daffyd. "With me," he ordered and peeled off to the left. A smattering of gunfire echoed from somewhere down the hall as they walked and Pulver, to his credit, quickened his pace toward the sound.

They passed through a glazed walkway into another building where three of Pulver's Marines were holding back a collection of strange looking aliens, one of whom had several layers of what appeared to be a chitinous husk shot away from the side of his head.

"We walked in here," a lance corporal began explaining, "and they converged on us. Tried to take our weapons and equipment. We managed to convince 'em that we don't feel like cooperating, but now they seem confused as hell."

Before Pulver could respond, they noticed the sound of running feet and turned to look at the other exit from the room. The lance corporal signaled to his two men and they took aim at the opening.

A Human face appeared around the doorframe and ducked back. Daffyd had formed a fleeting impression of a man who hadn't washed or eaten well for a very long time. His skin hung loosely from his skull and his eyes had flashed a look of confused disbelief before disappearing again.

"Don't shoot!" a voice shouted hoarsely. "I'm a Marine. I'm coming out unarmed." True to his word, a hand dropped a 10mm caseless pistol to the floor in the middle of the doorway.

"Advance one and be recognized," the lance corporal shouted back.

The man stepped out, his hands raised and his chest heaving from his run. "I was starting to think nobody would come to relieve me," he croaked. "Michaels bought the plot three months back when a scavenger dove on him. He tripped and fell through the *zapper*. Been alone ever since, unless you count these helmet-heads." He waved at the aliens.

"Why are you here?" Pulver demanded.

The filthy Marine blinked at him. "Those *hundan* didn't even tell you what the duty would be?" He shook his head. "Simple enough. The sooner I can show you the ropes, the sooner I can get off this poor excuse for a planet.

"The captives who die in the pods or just can't absorb the programming get sent down here because they know too much." He waved at the aliens. "These guys, who seem to be some kind of 'wild' version of the Grays, from before they started cloning themselves, process the prisoners."

He shuffled over to a panel on the wall and hit a large green button.

The Marines' weapons twitched a little closer to their shoulders as the entire floor of the room began lowering.

"They take away any tech or clothes and send it down for sorting." As they came to a halt on the next level down, five more of the aliens began approaching but stopped in confusion when they saw the armed Humans.

"These guys sort everything." He waved at the conveyors, built into the floor. Objects, no doubt from the previous batch of prisoners, lay on the various belts, halted until more material made it economical to start them up again.

Daffyd wandered over to one of the belts and bent over to pick up a small holo-toy. It was set to project a cuddly, furry creature that probably never existed, unless it was on the original home-world, lost in the mists of time.

He stood, looking up from the creature in his hand to the filthy Marine. "Where do the prisoners go from here?" His voice had a hard edge. He'd seen how little regard the Grays had for Human life, and he didn't think this facility had been placed here for the good of their captives.

The man pointed. "Through there," he said simply. He led the way out to an open walkway, five meters long. Canyon walls rose up around them. "We take 'em out one at a time or we'd have trouble on our hands," he explained with a wild-eyed grin.

At the end was a gate with what looked like a greenish energy shield. "Michaels had just put a prisoner through when an avian tried to take a slice out of his shoulder. He bobbed, when he should have weaved, and fell right through..."

He stood there, staring through the shimmering green portal.

Daffyd edged closer to the railing to the right of the opening. The last thing he wanted to do was take a look, but he knew he had to. He reached the rail and looked down.

"*Bozhemoi!*" He stepped back from the railing and brought a hand to his mouth, his stomach suddenly his own worst enemy.

"Yeah," the filthy Marine conceded, "I had the same reaction, when they brought me here, but you learn to tune it out." He shrugged. "They're enemies of the Imperium. Can't just turn 'em loose ..."

"Enemies?" Daffyd roared as Pulver took a look over the railing. Daffyd waved the holo-bear in the Marine's face. "The child you took this from was an enemy?"

Pulver scrambled away from the railing, stumbling to the deck plating where he gave up his lunch. The lance corporal stepped to the railing and shuddered in disgust. He turned to his two men, shaking his head. "You don't want to see this," he told them as a squadron of hungry avians dove past behind the gate. "There's thousands of 'em. Just thrown down there for the animals to eat."

"It's like the massacre at Gilgamesh," Pulver whispered.

"No!" the skeletal Marine insisted. "The killers at Gilgamesh were all evil monsters. The Navy chased them back to their world and destroyed it. This is unpleasant but we have orders..."

He fell back in surprise when the back of Daffyd's meaty hand slammed against the side of his mouth.

"*Zatkinice!*" Daffyd shook his hand to ease the sting. "I always thought the Navy line was a load of *dermo*. They let folks think that this kind of thing only happens when *evil* people get nasty ideas. They miss the point entirely.

"We *all* possess the capacity for evil. Any group of people, on any world, can slip into unspeakable atrocity if they aren't on guard against it." He pointed a finger at the man. "You're just as bad as the bastards who destroyed Gilgamesh or those renegades that burnt the atmosphere off New Damascus."

"Kinsey didn't send you," the man blurted in sudden awareness.

"*Chto za huy?*" Daffyd grabbed the man's tunic and pulled him back to his feet, bringing his face close to his own. "Rufus Kinsey? That *predátil*?"

"Traitor?" The man shook his head. "No, he's a..."

"Traitor!" Pulver grabbed the man by the collar and tore him out of Daffyd's grip. He swung him around and released him on a trajectory that would take him through the green shielding.

The Marine's arms flailed for balance as he passed through the portal. The light went out of his eyes the instant his head passed through and he fell, limply, to the corpses below.

Daffyd stared at Pulver, waiting for him to come back to his senses. "You know, Commander," he ventured quietly, "that man might have led us to one of the key players in a plot that nearly crushed the Imperium."

Pulver's eyes narrowed as he stared at the portal. He'd heard Daffyd, but still needed time to absorb the meaning. He nodded. "Yeah, we should have pumped him for information but I just couldn't stand the thought of a thing like that drawing breath when he'd killed all those poor people."

"Can't say I disagree with that," Daffyd admitted and, anyway, bringing Kinsey back to the Imperium probably wouldn't win any favour at Court. He'd be a reminder of how fragile Imperial society continued to be.

The erbium mines on Irricana and the circuit factories on Santa Clara still remained as single-failure points. Sitting close to the Rim, either world, if destroyed, could bring the Imperial Military and the economy to a halt in a matter of months. The circuits only lasted for a quarter of a year at most and if there were no new replacements available, ships, weapons and computers would start failing rapidly.

Too many aristocrats and Grand Senators were being enriched by the status quo and they were far more concerned about their bank balances than they were about the future of the Imperium. Bringing Kinsey back wouldn't extricate them from their current predicament.

But killing him would be a service to the universe.

Daffyd sighed. "How about we get that ship off the ground?"

Pulver nodded. "The sooner we're out of here, the better."

It was unclear whether he meant the planet or Gray space in general.

This Just In…

"three, two, one…" Robin checked her screen. "Distortion drive secured. We're in the pipe." She touched a hand to her ear. "Roger that, Orbital Control. Holding coordinates confirmed. Will confirm when we reach position."

She turned to Julia. "Five-day slot confirmed, ma'am. We'll be five clicks out from the station, in the outer holding pattern."

"Very well." Julia turned to Oliver, another of Mullins' semi-retired Maegi. "How long to find him and clear that signal out of the stations nav beacon?"

Oliver pursed his lips for a moment. "Maybe a couple of centis," he ventured, grinning at her look of surprise. "Finding him'll be easy enough and, as for the rest…" He shrugged. "…The Maegi recruited me on Norseman, where I was hacking for hire. Shouldn't be all that long at all." He sketched a salute and left the bridge.

Julia could feel the eyes on her. This station was one of the old designs, based on a large rotating ring and designed with a sense of scale and grandeur. Her ragtag force of fake Gray Purists were getting tired of their ships and even more tired of the mine where they'd made their base.

"Sorry, folks. Nobody else goes ashore. Not unless we want a full war with the Grays."

Less than a centi-day later, she was just stepping out of the shower when her door chime sounded. "Just a moment,"

she told the audio pickups. She moved through the dryer cubicle as quickly as possible before stepping into some clean clothes. Her underarmor suits lay unused in her bag. The last suit of Heavy Marine Armor had failed three months ago and she'd switched to dressing like a local.

"What?" she demanded when she noticed Paul's grin. He'd been sitting on the couch going over intelligence reports but he'd set them aside when she'd come out of the shower.

A shrug. "I just like how you look in regular civilian clothes," he said. "I was so used to seeing you in those skin-tight UA suits..."

"You saying I've got something that's better off hidden beneath loose clothing?" Her tone wasn't entirely playful, but it wasn't exactly dangerous either.

"No, I think you know I'm an avid enthusiast..." He got a chuckle from her with that. "It's just more fun when the process of discovery is factored in."

"I suppose a cop would take an angle like that." She gave him a playful smile but it was short-lived. "Come," she ordered and the door slid open.

Oliver ushered a young man inside. His eyes lit up when he saw Julia.

"Commodore Urbica?" he asked, holding up a small stringed instrument. "I've come to play for you."

Julia sat on the couch next to Paul and waved the man to sit across from her in one of the club chairs. She let him tune his instrument before delivering the trigger phrase.

"Gravity is a function of probability gradients."

The young man kept tuning his instrument but he began talking in a wooden tone. "Standard Date 235326, second era. Edgar Prestonby reporting from Orbit over Masra." A stubborn string failed to tune and he began removing the over-stretched line of gut. "On or about 235302, a male Human arrived in the central market and spoke with the locals, introducing himself as Daffyd ap Rhys. He was searching for Brigadier General Julia Urbica."

The musician set his instrument aside while he fished around in his pockets for a new string.

Julia looked at Paul. *Daffyd?* she mouthed, not wanting to speak out loud and accidentally knock the messenger out of his trance before he could deliver the full message.

"While he was still in the market..." The young musician's voice drew their gaze back to him. "... he was apprehended by Imperial forces and taken off world. They had support from Imperial Marines in full HMA. Estimate grab team to be either a clandestine unit or a rogue element of some sort. Some locals report that the grab team were all in engineering uniforms, which makes them more likely to be some kind of bizarre rogue element. Masran Orbital Control indicates the Imperials went deeper into Gray territory when they left."

The string was in place and tuned. "Report ends. All that blather about probability is bollox. Gravity is just gravity." The young man looked up, slightly confused to find himself in the room.

Julia clapped, Paul and Oliver quickly joining in. "Very nice," she told him. She stood and held out a hand to the door. "Oliver will see you back to the station and arrange for payment. Thank-you for sharing your wonderful talent with us."

In truth, she was very glad to escape listening to him play. He seemed very much one of those young men who learn a smattering of music to impress young women. If they'd been sitting in the Imperium, she'd have bet heavily that he'd grown up on a world like Greenland but that he'd never admit it. He'd probably try to give the vague impression that he was from Bohemia.

Whatever colonial world he might have adopted to add to his mystique, she didn't care. She simply wanted him off the ship before he tried talking to any of her crew.

The door slid shut behind him and she dropped back onto the couch. "Daffyd..."

"Out here, beyond the Rim," Paul added, "and we would have heard from the Maegi if he'd come on a Fools' Hope. That leaves the wormhole engine on the *Sucker Punch*." He reached out to the tablet on the low table and turned it off.

"The fact that he's been nabbed by engineers could mean he used the *Sucker Punch* without their cooperation." He stared down at the table, frowning.

"So the question we need to ask," Julia jumped in, "is where will Daffyd head, once he gives his captors the slip?"

Paul nodded his agreement. It wasn't a question of *if* but, rather, *when* Daffyd would escape from the engineers who currently held him.

If they still had him at all.

"He made a big splash at Masra," Paul mused. "Engineers wouldn't expect him to go back there but it's the most likely place for us to find him." He gave her a kiss. "I'll go to the station and find a ship for Masra."

"Do you think he brought the unit with him?"

Paul stopped at the door and looked back at her. "I think it's likely. He wouldn't come out here to the great unknown in a shuttle, not if he could help it, and the guys who grabbed him went deeper into Gray space once they had him, which tells me they're still looking for someone."

She nodded. "Find them first."

Left in a Lurch

"**Y**ou're about to redeem yourself," General Windemere told Daffyd, "assuming your dragoons are there when we arrive."

Pulver couldn't quite read the expression on ap Rhys' face. It figured the man would be a little conflicted about betraying his unit, but he'd been pretty pissed off at them for leaving him behind on Masra.

Either way, they were already at battle stations and they'd be dropping out in less than a centi. Once they'd secured the dragoons, Pulver could get on with the important business of wondering how he'd keep body and soul together when they got back to the Imperium. He had several thousand men and women depending on him and he had no concrete plan, as of yet.

And he was reasonably certain Windemere didn't have one either. If the man had had a plan, it probably involved a plea to his aristocratic allies and it would only be enough to save his own life.

"If nobody minds," Daffyd began quietly with a wave toward the exit portal, "I'll sit this one out."

"Of course, of course," Windemere responded bluffly, though a trifle sarcastically. "Why don't you go back down and carry on *organizing* the equipment on the hangar deck?"

Pulver was sure he'd caught a flicker of alarm on the prisoner's face, but then the man shrugged and ambled off.

He didn't have time to dwell on the man's odd behavior. They were about to confront a renegade unit, one with an aggressive reputation and a long track record of successful engagements. Pulver's hopes were pinned on talking them down.

He didn't have a great deal of confidence in the garrison forces from Nidaveller Station if it came to a stand-up fight against 1GD. He even doubted it would be a stand-up fight to begin with. Urbica's famous dragoons had taken to the concept of carrier warfare far more quickly than the Imperial Navy. He frowned down at the icon representing the LHV they'd brought along from Nidaveller.

A few new LHV-class carriers were coming online, but they were more in response to economic factors than any strategic leadership from CentCom. With a shrunken budget, no new super-dreadnaughts had been built for centuries. The smaller LHVs were cheaper and so they were starting to supplant the massive SDNs, but that didn't mean that the Imperium understood, in Pulver's opinion, what they really had in their LHVs.

Every engagement he could think of involving the LHVs was an up-close, pound-the-enemy-into-submission kind of fight. Perhaps it was his logical engineering background, but he firmly believed, and told anyone who would listen, that an LHVs primary batteries were not the 200mm guns built into her structure.

An LHV's primaries were her ship destroyer squadrons as well as, in the case of the Marine variant, her assault landing shuttles. There was no need to bring your fleet within range of an enemy formation, not when a ship destroyer squadron could cripple a SDN in a single pass (*some luck required – see targeting models for weak-points*).

He knew 'Windy Bag' was one of the old-school officers, old school in the Imperial Navy meaning anything from a gray-hair like the general to half the new grads from this year's academy crop. He'd want to get in nice and close so everybody's secondary batteries could be brought to bear on the target.

If they managed to take the *Rope a Dope* by surprise, it might work.

He knew 1GD had yet to be taken by surprise, so he very much doubted a gaggle of garrison forces led by an engineering administrator would fare any better than all the dead people who'd already tried. His shoulders drooped a fraction.

Maybe it would be for the best. A quick death out here, in a fair fight, was a much better way to go than a bullet in the back of the head from some CentCom goon.

He'd studied the schematics of the ship they pursued. The *Rope a Dope* was an old luxury passenger liner converted into a carrier by none other than prisoner ap Rhys, who was currently puttering around on the hangar deck to avoid watching the pending fight.

Half her passenger staterooms had been pulled out to create quick-launch slots. Pulver had to admit a certain admiration for Daffyd. He'd created a carrier that could launch two entire squadrons on a heartbeat's notice. Even if this force could catch them unaware, they'd *still* start launching their third squadron while their pursuers were getting started on their second.

His stomach suddenly protested violently and, before he could even wonder at the cause, he went lurching forward, through the tactical hologram, and slammed face first onto the decking. Alarm chimes sounded soothingly, reminding him, uselessly, that they were on a Gray ship.

He shook his head to clear the fuzzy thoughts. "Launch all squadrons!" he shouted as he climbed back to his feet. All around him, the bridge crew were pulling themselves back up to their duty stations and Windemere sat against the forward viewport, a trickle of blood running freely down over his right eye from his scalp.

"What wash it?" the general slurred. "Arti-Sing?"

Pulver's blood ran cold. If the dragoons had left an artificial singularity in their path, it meant *they* were the ones springing the surprise.

A host of soothing tones told him something was going terribly wrong. He staggered over to the ops station. "Why the hell are our squadrons still in the hangar?" he demanded.

"Sir, their engines can't reach critical," the near-panicked engineer serving as the ops officer replied. "Not a single one on our ship or over on the *Intrepid*."

"Same with our own engines," the helmsman added. "The pitch field has collapsed and we're reading no energy at all in the jump drives." He looked calm enough, when Pulver turned to glare at him, though he still showed a healthy amount of concern. "Sir, we're dead in the black."

"*Tchyo za ga `lima?*" the sensor officer exclaimed. He pre-empted the central holo image with a new projection. "It's a pulsar – a big one. Damn thing's supressing the fields in our engines. We're going to have to restart them but I don't know if we'll have enough time to get 'em running before the effect hits us again. We sure as hell don't have the time to get the jump drives up, so if we do get propulsion, it'll only take us a short distance before we're shut down again."

"Security," Pulver shouted, his face nearly crimson, "secure prisoner ap Rhys immediately." They'd been led into a trap like a pack of idiots, but he'd be damned if he let ap Rhys get away with it.

"What do we have that *isn't* affected by the pulsar?" he demanded.

"Sir, there's a rocket sledge," the damage control officer offered. "It was aboard when the dragoons seized this ship from the Grays and we never bothered to offload it at Nidaveller. She can carry ten men and runs on liquid fuel."

"Good!" Windemere staggered over to the center of the bridge. "We'll tow this ship out and head back to Nidaveller for help."

Pulver turned to Windemere in amazement. He felt certain the man would simply forget about the ships left behind if he managed to get back to the Imperium. He'd gotten himself in way over his head and he probably just wanted to concentrate on saving his own hide.

"Oh!" Windemere brightened considerably as he gazed out the forward viewport. "Good job, that man!"

Pulver looked out at the rocket sledge pulling ahead of the *Sucker Punch*. He was quick to analyse the sinking feeling in the pit of his stomach this time. He turned to the damage control officer. "That sledge," he asked, wishing he could avoid the answer, "was it in the main hangar or the transit bay?"

"Main hangar."

Pulver nodded, his lips drawn tight. He looked out the forward viewport at the sledge as it continued to grow smaller in the distance. "The main hangar, where the prisoner was organizing the loose equipment..."

He sighed. "Secure from general quarters."

A.G. Claymore

His hatred and respect for Daffyd ap Rhys were increasing in equal measure.

THE OLD GANG

It's a Trap!

t was an ambush; Paul had absolutely no doubt. Still, he followed the old Masran through the cool breeze in the alleyways of the fourth level down from the surface. The old gaffer had shown no interest in his search for a missing friend until he'd heard Daffyd's name.

Suddenly, the elderly gent had become the font of all knowledge, all grins, nods and assurances that he'd take Paul to meet Daffyd. Robbery was unlikely, as he'd changed his tune only *after* hearing who Paul was searching for. If he were simply rounding up rubes for his pals to rob, he'd have shown more interest from the start.

That told Paul the man knew something about Daffyd and so he was following him down into the bowels of Masra. The rumble of cargo vehicles, three levels above, sounded like distant thunder but he could see why some people preferred it down here. Despite the relative cool of the surface level, it was almost cold down here.

The man who'd been signaled by the old fella was somewhere ahead of them. Despite their circumspection, Paul's years as a cop and his numerous physical enhancements let him see what most others missed. The runner had exhibited signs of apprehension and Paul's trusty guide was also exhibiting elevated stress levels.

They were preparing a surprise for him and it wasn't a baklava platter.

Not that he had much of an appetite. This level clearly hadn't been designed with habitation in mind, or perhaps the system had simply broken down, because the homes and businesses here used a modular sewage system. Paul and his guide had to wait for a moment while a 'honey cart' backed its carrousel up to the module on the front of a bar, picking up the full canister and inserting an empty.

The faint odor of sewage was everywhere but definitely stronger behind this vehicle. Fortunately, the guide turned down an even smaller alley and they got away from the honey wagon's contribution to the local atmosphere.

Despite the smell, Paul was impressed by the cleanliness. The homes and establishments down here must be *owned* by the inhabitants because they took care of their neighborhoods in a way the denizens of an Imperial rezza never would have.

The old man ducked in the door of a coffee house, waving for Paul to follow. Several of the men inside gave the man a nod of recognition and a quick once-over for Paul. He caught several tics that indicated curiosity, but none of them appeared apprehensive.

Either the runner had had an accident or this wasn't where he'd gone with his warning. Then again, a hasty nod and twitch of the eyes can be a pretty vague way to signal an accomplice. It could mean 'Get over to O'Zorgnax's Pub and warn them I'm bringing in a troublemaker' or 'We've got trouble; run for it!'

Any way you sliced it, nobody was trying to add new holes to Paul's body, at the moment, and so he moved to the far left corner before the old fella could pick out a seat. Paul dropped into a chair that kept his back to the wall, letting him see the front entrance as well as the back door to his left.

The old man sat across from him, motioning to an attractive, dark-haired young woman who nodded and slipped behind the bar to do battle with the barista equipment. From the cordura strap showing through the slit in the side of her dress, she was carrying a small-caliber automatic on the inside of her thigh. The slight bulge in her left sleeve told him she also had a molecular stiletto.

"Now," the man began, "you're looking for this Daffyd but what kind of cut will you give us?"

Four men got up from their tables and sauntered over, hands resting on the butts of their pistols. They stood flanking their seated comrade, faces devoid of expression.

Paul kept his hands flat on the table. "Cut?"

"Of the bounty, of course. If you want him, you need to pay our cut before we let you take him."

"You think there's a bounty?"

"Oh, yes." He stroked his beard. "A very large one." He leaned forward, pointing at Paul. "But you know that, don't you?"

Paul noticed a slight pause preceding the answer. His augmented senses picked up a temperature drop in the man's ears, nose and lips and the pointing was an attempt to turn attention away from his statement. They didn't think there was a bounty, so why even mention one, unless they were trying to test him?

Did they think he might be willing to pay them or were they up to something else? Either way, Paul didn't want them knowing who he was. With the Purists almost completely beaten by the Gray Quorum, Julia needed a way to keep them out of the colonies and Daffyd's arrival had given him the nucleus of an idea. It wouldn't work, though, if the Grays found out how he'd found the engineer from 1GD.

Best to use the truth or, at least, selected elements of the truth.

"I know nothing about any bounty," he told the man as the young woman set three mugs of coffee on the table. He picked up a mug, enjoying the earthy scent before looking back to the man across from him. "Even if there *was* one, I wouldn't want to earn it by betraying an old friend."

"A friend, you say?"

Paul nodded. "I know him from the 1st Gliessan Dragoons."

"Then you'll already know they're all out here as well…"

"Look at his eyes, Garum," one of the men standing by the guide's chair exclaimed. "Shocked all to hells. He has no idea about 1GD!"

"He's just another one of those damned gray-bellies," another growled. "Snuck back here in civvies this time to look for him. I say we just dump his corpse out in the bled. Let the sand have him."

"Niffleheim!" a new voice sounded from behind the large and angry men. "At least let the man finish his drink first." Daffyd, in local garb, stepped from behind the small group and dropped into an empty chair at the table.

Before, when they'd been fighting to stop Seneca and his catspaw, Kinsey, from destroying the Imperium, Daffyd had just been one of Julia's many dragoons. They'd rarely spoken and, when they did, Paul was always 'Inspector Grimm'.

Here on Masra, Daffyd was a welcome face from home.

"Good to see you again, Paul!" Daffyd picked up the third mug and peered into it before leaning back to look behind the bar.

The young woman brought a sugar bowl. "Just one spoonful," she scolded.

Daffyd nodded meekly, to the chuckles of the other men. His one spoonful was piled as high as he could get it when it came out of the bowl. "They weren't kidding about dumping you out in the desert, by the way." He took a sip and let out a sigh.

"Didn't know there was such a thing as coffee beans," he admitted to Paul. "You know the locals insist this stuff is garbage, compared to the pricey stuff you get on some of the wetter worlds?"

Paul grinned. He'd already sampled the culinary wonders of the colonial worlds. "Damn good to see you, Daffyd, though I'd only expected to pick up your *trail* here." He tilted a head toward their companions. "Why are they so protective of you?"

"Old friends," Daffyd said simply before taking another drink. He grinned at Paul. "Well," he pointed to the two large men to the older man's left, "these two used to beat me up when we were kids back in Vermillion and Garum, here," he indicated the older man, "is their dad."

"You came out her on a Fool's Hope?" Paul asked.

"Years ago," Daffyd confirmed, reaching for the spoon, but the young woman had returned, shifting the sugar bowl to another table before sitting down in the fourth seat. "She's concerned about my diet," he explained.

"Garum's daughter?" Paul inquired.

"Elsa Garumsdottir," she confirmed. She smiled at Daffyd. "You can imagine my surprise at seeing this fool in the market square. When I heard you were looking for him, I asked my father to bring you in."

"Elsa's coffee house is a real business," Daffyd told him, "but it's more a means to an end. She *collects* information." He smiled at her. "A freelance intelligence service, if you will."

Elsa shrugged. "The Serps keep us on our toes," she explained, "but you can tell when a raid is coming, if you know what to look for." She leaned in. "So what's your interest in Daffyd? Does this have something to do with the imminent collapse of the Gray Purists?"

Paul took a drink to cover his surprise.

She raised a hand in a negligent wave. "I'm probably not the only one making the connection between the arrival of Commodore Urbica and the sudden outbreak of civil conflict among the Grays. Frankly, I doubt the Grays acknowledge what's really going on."

It was a strange choice of wording but Paul thought he understood her reasons. The Grays felt they were vastly superior to Humans, a feeling that was reciprocated, for the most part. They wouldn't want to believe Humans had been able to manipulate them into a full-blown civil war, even if the evidence was there, waiting to be found.

If the evidence was a little too insistent, they might just be persuaded to believe it and to take 'corrective' action. The colonies wouldn't last long if that ever happened.

And that was where Daffyd came into the picture.

He looked over at Daffyd. "The old gang came out here with you?"

"With the Imperial Corps of Engineers hot on our heels."

"Why'd you come out here, of all places?"

Daffyd grimaced. "Got orders to lay down arms and disband the unit. You ask me, the next step would have been a round of arrests."

Paul nodded. "Anybody who was connected to the *Sucker Punch*. They finally realized they weren't going to figure out the engines so they're moving into damage control mode."

"Including the supposed inventor," Daffyd said, the picture of injured dignity. "Had me cooped up on Mictlan for weeks before 1GD came."

"Putting *you* in prison is like putting a goat in a pen made of breadsticks." Paul won a look of approval from Elsa with that. He shuddered. "Still, a super-max like Mictlan... Purgatory!"

"More like purge-atory," Daffyd corrected. "One bite of the meatloaf and you're in for one hells of a ride."

"Those engineers..." Paul ventured. "What kind of assets did they bring with them?"

"LHV carrier, Navy variant, so no ground assault, just ship destroyer squadrons; Hasty Ferrets; Iron Hands, that kind of stuff." He frowned. "Three heavy gunboats and two frigates that may have seen action with Montgomery himself, for all I know, but those boys at Nidaveller must have given 'em a good overhaul 'cause they're better than new now."

Paul nodded, his idea crystalizing quickly now. "So, they'd look like a respectable Imperial force to the casual observer, then." His moderately foolhardy idea was turning into an almost-clever one.

"And who are we trying to impress?"

Elsa snorted. "The most casual observers in the universe, that's who."

Paul inclined his head in salute. "Would you consider working with us, Elsa? We have some re-purposed Maegi passing through, every now and then. It would help if they could check in with you and compare notes."

She paused for a moment. "I'm not saying no," she hedged. "I'll pass on what I hear about the Grays, but you need to let the dragoons help us if we hear the Serps are getting ready for a raid." Her lips drew tight. "We don't much fancy waking up with Serp eggs in our bellies."

"Done," Paul said, "but I'll need to borrow your old friend for a few weeks. Turns out he may be key to our exit strategy." He looked to Daffyd. "If we can pull this off, we might just be able to save the colonies from annihilation."

Daffyd finished his coffee. "Well, I did have a haircut booked but what the hells." He stood. "Always wanted a ponytail..."

Paul took a deep breath as they left the small café, remembering too late the sewer smell of the alleyways at this level.

"So what's your clever scheme," Daffyd asked, "or would that spoil the showmanship of the whole thing?"

Paul shook his head, as much in an attempt to clear the smell as to negate Daffyd's suggestion. "Oh, I'll tell you," he assured him, "and you can probably help refine the whole thing. It's just that there's still a complication we need to sort out if we want our chances of success to reach an acceptable level. I'd forgotten about it until I stepped out into this stink..."

Daffyd pointed to the left. "Quickest way topside," he advised, leading the way. "So what's the hitch?"

"A lot of folks have been nabbed over the years and their brains tinkered with. They're compelled to keep the civil war between the colonies going. If anyone tries to interfere with that, they're programmed to kill themselves."

Daffyd stopped and turned to face Paul, one eyebrow raised. "Nabbed by the Grays?"

Paul stepped back, having nearly run into him. He nodded.

Daffyd grinned. "I really don't know what you'd do without me," he declared. "Here you are, bigtime inspector for The Eye, and I find the cure the same day I learn of the disease itself!"

Paul knew his slack-jawed expression was doing little for the reputation of The Eye, but he couldn't help it. "A cure?" he finally managed.

"Sure as death and taxes," Daffyd boomed cheerfully. "Have 'em spark a tube, ride the lazy Susan, y'know... *For My Glaucoma...*"

Paul shook himself free of his mental block. "FMG? How do you know this?" he demanded.

"We found the planet where the Grays are processing their subjects," Daffyd told him, his voice suddenly growing dark. "A Fool's Hope ship, the *Pony Express*, was there with a couple of real stoners for loadmasters. They were so goofed on FMG, their brains couldn't wash."

"Yeah, well, that means you can prevent it if you're already stoned but..."

"We rounded up the crew and un-washed them with a few grams each," Daffyd cut him off. "They're fine now."

Paul slumped back against the front window of a machinist shop, oblivious to the scents wafting from a sewage module a few feet away. "We can cure my sister," he muttered.

"Sister?" Now it was Daffyd's turn to gape. "Paul, do you mean to say..."

Paul grabbed Daffyd by the arm. "Where did that ship go?" His face was only inches from Daffyd's.

"We cut 'em loose." Daffyd leaned back a bit, alarmed by his friend's intensity. "They'll be back on the route to Irricana by now, I'd imagine. They went through a hells of a shock but that doesn't mean they don't still have bills to pay."

"And I know how they pay them," Paul said darkly. "I was a cop on the Rim," he reminded the engineer. "I've seen how much FMG they bring in." He straightened, giving Daffyd some breathing space. "We need that ship. I want to talk to those loadmasters *and* I need that cargo."

He gestured for Daffyd to lead on. "Let's get topside before we do anything else." He fell in behind the dragoon engineer. "Where do we find the *Rope a Dope*? We're going to need their help."

"I can just call them and they'll have a shuttle here in less than a centi," Daffyd called over his shoulder.

Paul brought his eyebrows back in line. "They're here, in orbit? Isn't that a little risky?"

"Bah..." Daffyd waved off the concern. "Even if General Windbag manages to get a grip on his current predicament, he'll be thinking of where I and the dragoons will head *next*. He wouldn't dream of us coming back to the city where he actually captured me."

He cast a grin over his shoulder as he turned a corner. "It's elegantly stupid, if I do say so myself."

Paul inclined his head. "I'd say you have an extra word in that description, somewhere..."

They found one of Elsa's brothers at the shuttle pad standing watch over a knee-high storage cube marked 'coffee'. He picked it up and followed them up the ramp of a waiting shuttle, setting it on the floor before giving the engineer a guarded nod. "If you don't return," he warned, "you'd better be dead." He left without a further word.

Daffyd watched him disappear in the crowd as the shuttle ramp lifted. A fatalistic shrug. "He's a little protective of his sister."

"Maybe he's suspicious," Paul offered. "I mean, how does an average, ordinary guy rate an impressive woman like Elsa?"

Daffyd beamed, clearly taking it for a compliment, as intended, rather than the insult it could have been. "I do think she may be a little sweet on me..."

Stepping out of the shuttle was like a homecoming. Hangar crew, pilots and techs crowded them the moment they stepped off the ramp. Paul was buffeted about by slaps on the back as the cheerful dragoons welcomed him 'home'.

Paul had always been somewhat insular and it was a little overwhelming to have a large group treat him so warmly. He was even more surprised, though, by the realization that he actually cared a great deal about these lunatics. His voice almost faltered when he asked Eddie, one of the three squadron commanders, where Dmitry was.

"Up on the bridge," Liang answered before Eddie could. "We take it in three shifts. Old Hendricksen got left behind at Home World along with a handful of bridge officers."

"Had to make it look like we were all present and accounted for," Eddie explained. "Big standing-down ceremony at the Hamtramck shipyard. Supposed to hand in our weapons and sign amnesties." He glared at Paul. "Can you believe that? Amnesties... as if we'd done anything illegal!

"Hendricksen went over to the ceremony on the station, along with the boys who had strong attachments in the Imperium, but it was just to keep CENTCOM off their guard. The rest of us jumped through the Kowalski gate for Nidaveller."

"Paul," Liang cut in, "what about the General? Where is she?"

Silence replaced the babble. Every face was riveted on Paul as they waited for news of their leader.

These were people who'd need to know the full plan, but where to start?

"She's a commodore out here," he began. "Elected to lead a fleet of colonial privateers."

That took a bit of explaining, though nobody was terribly surprised to hear they'd seized a Gray cruiser within hours of waking up on one of their prison ships, especially seeing as they had help from a privateer ship. The business of electing officers was a little harder for them to swallow.

"How does that even work?" a red-vested ordnance specialist demanded. "Sounds like anarchy to me."

"Well, it's not like they stop in the middle of combat to elect a replacement for a dead officer." Paul chuckled. "The guy under him just steps in, the same way he would in the Navy or on this ship. If he does a good enough job, they confirm him with a quick vote and elect a replacement for him, but not until after the fight is done."

He glanced at Liang, Eddie and Daffyd. "Let's get to the bridge and have a chat with Dmitry. I've got a problem you boys can help solve."

Liang raised an eyebrow. "You've got some shenanigans in mind?"

A shrug. "The usual," Paul replied, "a little light-hearted piracy, maybe provoke a full-on war with the Grays..."

How to Ride an Landslide

"**F**acility Manager Fall has a point," Julia shouted to be heard over the drone of voices in the main chamber. Dozens of arguments had broken out and hundreds of angry voices echoed off the rock walls and ceiling of the huge chamber.

She'd decided to wait them out but then young Caleb, the legal owner of the mine, and, in fact, the entire planet, stepped up onto the platform to join her. She leaned in to hear him.

"...used to spend a lot of time down here, before the raiders came and killed everyone else," he shouted. "I think I can shut them up for you."

She waved a hand at the angry crowd, handing them over to him.

Caleb took a deep breath and then started to whistle. The tone was somewhere in the mid-range and he began modifying it, up and down until he found some point of harmonic resonance with the rock. Once he zeroed in on the right tone, he put more breath into it and the effect grew dramatically.

The shouting faded and faces began turning to the rock faces, apprehension evident on most of them at this unnerving sound.

When the crowd had become entirely silent, Caleb stopped whistling and the effect died out in a matter of heartbeats. "You are all guests in my home," he spoke into the sudden silence. "You will oblige me by not acting like animals." He nodded to Julia.

"You all let Mr. Fall have his say, now the commodore has the floor."

"Thank you, Caleb." She looked around the chamber. "As I was trying to say, Mr. Fall has a point. We're almost out of real Purists, so the Grays are bound to catch on if we keep imitating them."

She held up her hand to calm the shouts that erupted at this admission. "And racing off to the colony worlds to warn everybody and organize a defense sounds good, until you realize that a lot of the defenders might just blow their own heads off when you need them the most. We still have the small matter of a brainwashed population to deal with."

"And what progress have we made on that front?" Burke, Fall's former executive officer, demanded. "We're stuck here like rats but Fall, at least, has a plan."

"Captain... Mr. Fall," Julia retorted, deliberately reminding the assembly that the man had been so incompetent as to be relieved of his command by a majority vote, "is right that we have to do something."

That muddied the waters nicely. The Fall faction was primed for a frontal engagement, typical of the man himself.

Julia was going to come at them sideways.

"There might come a time to rally the colonies and fight a Gray invasion but they probably won't invade until they've figured out we've been playing them for fools." She gave them a few minutes to work that one through. "The moment we leave here to follow the Fall Plan, the clock starts ticking. Our people will talk and the Grays will hear what we've been doing."

You'll never diffuse an angry mob with reason. It was one of the first rules of crowd control taught at the twenty-nine moons. You needed to shock them enough to derail them. In the Imperium, that usually meant small arms fire. Shoot a few ringleaders and the rest can be counted on to find a new way to use their free time.

Julia didn't want to shoot this particular mob, seeing as they were her responsibility. But she had news that might be enough to postpone the problem.

"We have an Imperial unit in the neighborhood," she told them. "And they're looking for us." Calling Daffyd a unit might be stretching things, but she was reasonably certain he hadn't come alone.

It was like waving a red flag in front of a Roanokan taurus. The chamber erupted in fear and anger. Nobody here was keen on being annexed by the Imperium, regardless of what benefits a Navy presence might convey on the colonies.

She looked at Caleb and gave a slight shake of her head. Better to let them carry on for a while, imagine all the terrible things that would happen under the boot-heels of the Imperium. She knew she wouldn't need his help to quiet them again. They were afraid before, but there had been little cohesion.

Now she was the focus of their fears, the bearer of terrible tidings.

She waited until the ruckus was starting to die down before raising a hand. The crowd didn't settle entirely but they were mostly quiet.

"That unit," she said patiently, having tolerated their outburst, "is the 1st Gliessan Dragoons, not the Imperial Navy or Marines."

Well, that was a different matter entirely. There were even a few cheers. The colonies knew of 1GD from news brought in by the *Fools' Hope* ships carrying immigrants from the Imperium. 1GD was as much a threat to CentCom as they were to the Grays. They were formed by Julia herself, welding numerous Sector Defense Force units together in a series of battles along the Rim.

Their officers were promoted or dismissed based entirely on their own competence rather than their ancestry. They were an aggressive unit and fiercely loyal to their general, who happened to be fighting for the colonies.

Julia almost felt the moment needed some clever phrase to sum up this turn in the debate, but she decided to just leave. The crews were excitedly chattering about what they could accomplish with 1GD at their side. Reasonable expectations were trotted out and were promptly trampled by wild exaggerations.

They were still an irrational mob, but at least now they were a mob willing to wait it out for a few more days.

The Pressgang

Beam lurched through the starboard bridge hatch. "Is it the Grays again?" He grimaced as his stomach tried to leap out of his throat. Being knocked out of a distortion envelope once was more than enough for a lifetime. Having it happen twice on his first voyage as a loadmaster was making him remember his job at Soylent Orange in a much more favorable light.

He waved a medi-kit. "Twenty tubes packed with FMG," he gasped. "Spark up, fellas. This time, let's kill them all and steal their gods-damned ship..."

"Ain't no Grays in sight," Captain Marco Stanic cut him off. He waved at the nav holo. "Just an old derelict passenger liner." He shook his head. "Poor bastards are probably either brainwashed or dead by now."

Stanic turned to Beam, fishing out a light gray ceramic tube and waving it at him. "Thanks for making the effort, but we're all carrying the ones you gave out day before yesterday."

"Oh," Beam temporized, ears turning a little red. "Yeah, Cap'n." He rubbed the back of his neck. "I forgot is all; I mean, it's not like you'd be, ummm... partaking of the stuff or anything..."

Stanic chuckled. "Keep packing those 'ready doses'," he told him. "Might find a good market, once word gets around that..."

"Captain!" the sensor officer nearly shouted. "That ship!"

Stanic turned to see a horde of attack craft boiling out of the supposed derelict and his face went white. "*Wo de ma,*" he breathed. "Hichefs, Khlens... it *is* the *goucaode* Grays after all.

He fished in his pocket for a lighter, eyes riveted on the display. "You'd better pass those out to any passengers who don't already…"

"*Pony Express*, this is the *Rope a Dope*, 1st Gliessan Dragoons. Stand by to receive our boarding party."

The signal cut off without waiting for a confirmation.

"Oh, thank the Gods," Stanic whispered as the *thwunk* of an airlock capture sounded just aft of the bridge hatch.

Rob stepped through the port bridge hatch, chain-lighting a second tube of FMG and tossing the first to the deck. "Sons'f'bitches are gonna get a good size-nine-wide suppository this time," the secondary loadmaster declared. "Wash my brain, will they? Well, it's dirty as hell and I aim to keep it that way."

"Rob," Beam tried to cut in.

"Never would've come out here if I'd known how dangerous space is," Rob ploughed on. "Should've clued in when we were hired while standing next to the corpses of our predecessors. Y'know, my momma used to…"

"ROB!" Stanich barely kept his voice below a yell. "Shut your cakehole. These are Humans."

"And they said…" Beam looked aft as the airlock hatch-pins retracted with a reverberating clang. "… that they were the 1st Gliessan Dragoons." Beam had expected a bit of adventure, working as a loadmaster for a few runs, but he'd never expected to meet living legends.

This was as close as it got to walking into the pages of history. The girls back on Roanoke would go bananas over a story like this.

"One GD?" Rob laughed. "You fell for that? What are the chances…" He trailed off as troops poured into the bridge.

A.G. Claymore

They wore armored EVA suits and carried what looked like the standard Imperial assault rifles you see in adventure holo-stories. Each one had a crest with three small stars and the characters '1GD' beneath them on their shoulder armor. It would be easy enough to fake a crest, but that armor was like nothing you could find anywhere in the colonies.

Beam couldn't hold back the grin. These guys were the real deal.

Probably.

The dragoons pulled the bridge crew away from their consoles and moved everybody up against the lockers along the aft bulkhead. One of them retracted his helmet.

"I apologize for the inconvenience," the man said mildly, "but you boys represent a critical strategic advantage to the colonies." He suddenly seemed to remember his weapon and lowered it, gesturing at his comrades to do the same. "I'm inspector Paul Grimm," he began but then caught himself. "Make that Justice Grimm of Roanoke," he amended with a wry grin.

Beam's eyes grew wide. He was in a room with a man who'd executed an Imperial Grand Senator, strangled the life out of him with a silk scarf right on the podium. Beam had signed on with the *Pony Express* to make a new start, to become someone interesting.

This even beat the prize money he'd be getting for helping to seize the Gray cruiser that had captured them earlier.

As far as he was concerned, he could ship out on a thousand more runs and never be able to top a story like this.

"We're sorry to *Bergen* you like this but you boys are holding the key to the coming war with the Grays. A couple of your crewmen are about to become real-life, larger-than-Monty heroes. I'm talking commemorative statues and everything."

Beam felt another thrill run down his spine. He could just imagine pointing to some giant statue back home and telling his children that he'd shipped with that guy.

"We're going to need you to call Beam Wehr and Rob Midline up here." Grimm checked the chronometer on his wrist holo. "We need to shove off as soon as possible. We'll take your boys aboard the 'Dope and chat with them in transit."

Holy hells! His kids, if he'd ever have any, should be able to recognize the statue without any help from him! Still, how the hells could any of this be making sense?

Rob was quick to advise them as to his and Beam's whereabouts, along with a steady stream of chatter. If they wanted a chat, they'd sure as hells get one. The man had no inner dialogue at all. If he thought it, he said it.

Without really giving it much thought, Beam followed Grimm toward the rear bridge hatch. It wasn't like he could resist a squad of armed and armored combat veterans.

"We'll leave you a navigator and some crew to help you find the place," Grimm called over his shoulder.

"Find what place?" Stanic asked.

Grimm turned around and smiled. "Our boarders tell me you're carrying nearly twenty thousand talents of FMG." He watched as four of his men retracted their helmets and took up posts around the bridge. He looked back at Stanic. "Let's just say we've got a surprisingly large number of glaucoma cases that need medication…"

Beam found himself sitting opposite Grim on the shuttle flight to their ersatz carrier. He tuned out Rob's chatter but he couldn't ignore the growing sense of unease.

It was one thing to be on the sidelines, watching history be made. It was quite another to be directly involved. A lot of those guys ended up dead. He leaned back and closed his eyes as the shuttle banked to head for the *Rope a Dope*. He could just picture Stanic pointing up to a pair of statues. *They were on my crew,* Stanic would tell his kids. *Real shame, what happened to them...*

People dream about being famous, about saving the universe, but they rarely gave thought to the difficulties involved. This sounded like a dangerous gig. Grimm *did* say there was a war coming and that Beam had a role in that.

They slipped in through the aft hangar doors and settled on the deck. The hangar itself had the sort of clangor and bustle he'd have expected of a combat carrier but the ornate arches that spanned the large space, forty cubits above them, were an eloquent reminder of the ship's original role.

It was a story Beam had reveled in, daydreaming behind the counter at Soylent Orange, doing his best to ignore the idiot customers. The hardy colonial stock of Roanoke was fertile ground for the story of 1GD, citizen warriors who'd retrofitted an old luxury liner into a carrier. They'd defeated Gray forces and defied CentCom through a mix of daring, wit and sheer luck.

Their Gray-built attack craft were only export versions, inferior in every technical aspect to both the renegade Marines they'd fought and the Gray forces themselves. Still, they'd come off the better force every time.

Grimm led them through an oval section that had probably served as an overpriced shopping promenade but which now held orderly racks of spare parts. Forward of that, the passage ended in a large lounge-area where dozens of off-duty dragoons were taking their ease.

The inspector waved them to a couch, angling off to the bar by himself to get drinks. He returned with one of the dragoons from the boarding party and they set mugs of coffee in front of Beam and Rob.

Beam suddenly straightened his back, leaning forward a bit. "You're Daffyd! You were with those Imperials who rescued us at Uruk."

"I accept tips in any denomination," the engineer told him cheerfully. "I had to put my Imperial pals in storage for a few deccas so I could come rescue Paul, here."

"I might be a little dense," Rob said, "but I'm still not clear on any of this. Are the gray-bellies planning to start a war?"

"Not so they know," Grimm answered. "But before we get into that, we've got thousands of people brainwashed by the Grays to keep the civil war going between the colonies. We've had a huge team working on ways to get around it, but the best we've managed so far is to trigger their conditioning and watch them kill themselves.

Beam shuddered. "They were trying to do that to us, just a few days ago..."

"And they failed, didn't they?" Grimm set his mug down and rested his elbows on his knees, leaning in toward Beam. "It was the FMG?"

Beam scratched at the stubble on his cheeks. FMG might not be illegal in most colonies but the Imperium was dedicated to stamping it out and this man was an inspector from the *Eye*. "Umm, Inspector..."

Grimm held up a hand. "Please, just call me Paul," he urged. "I'm not an inspector out here, just a man who's trying to save his sister."

That took a second to assimilate. Of course it was common knowledge that Grimm... Paul... was the brother of Commodore Klum, but there was a limit to how much crazy shit a man could parallel-process in a situation like this.

Ava Klum had been brainwashed by the Grays!

And Beam had found the cure?

Paul cut into the mental wandering. "How much did it take to break the conditioning on your crewmates after you freed yourselves? We need to spread the cure as efficiently as possible."

"And then we take the fight to the Grays," Daffyd added with relish.

"We gave each one a half tube," Beam told him, fishing out the tube in his chest pocket and handing it over. "We were just guessing it would help, but an engineering supervisor had killed himself, so we had to try something."

"The biggest difference between us and the rest of the crew," Rob cut in, "was the fact that we had regular access to the hold where the FMG was stored and, brother, we were accessing the living shit out of that hold!"

Paul leaned back in the seat and looked at Rob for a moment, just long enough to be slightly uncomfortable. "I've worked as a cop on Rim worlds," Paul told him. "And I think you're missing the point of being loadmasters on a *Fool's Hope*. What were you going to do when you hit Irricanan orbit and you had to report to the station and give a manifest engram? Your value was in your ignorance..."

"Hey, don't look at me like that," Rob told Beam. "If we'd kept our value as loadmasters, we'd be a couple of brainwashed zombies right now."

Beam sighed. He'd been pissed at Rob for getting into the cargo they weren't supposed to know about. Their value to the crew had been nullified and it was looking like they'd be dropped off at the nearest planet with an atmosphere (if they were lucky).

Still, Rob's lack of forethought and insatiable appetite for mischief had accidentally allowed them to save the crew of the *Pony Express* and, if Paul was right, the colonies as well.

He wondered how many statues were put up because some self-indulgent jackass accidentally became a hero.

Probably most of them...

The Recruiting Office is Open

"**D**istortion at zero," the engineering rating announced. "Securing the drive."

"Stars match the plot," the navigation officer began. "We're...

"Contact!" a young officer called out from the tactical station. She turned to face Julia. "They're exactly what you said we'd find, ma'am."

"Very well." Julia shook her head at Hale, who was offering her the command chair. "Your bridge, Captain. I may command the squadron, but this is your ship."

She ran a hand over her freshly shaved head. She'd grown accustomed to hair but it wasn't compatible with Heavy Marine Armor. That her own HMA suit no longer worked was beside the point. There was an impression to be made and she wasn't one to half-ass the details.

"Should we hail them?" the comms officer asked.

"No," Julia stepped over to Hale's right side and leaned against a railing circling the rear of the bridge. "They'll call us soon enough."

She'd come here to take new ships into her fleet and that wouldn't be helped by hailing first. She had a pretty good idea of how she would play this out, but it had to start with patience.

"Ma'am?"

She turned to the space behind the railing. "Rodrigues, any luck?"

The Marine shrugged. "Two suits," he told her. "We pulled a few modules from the suits Grimm shot up on Roanoke so they're physically in top condition." His eyes lit up. "And Oliver, that Maegi that you asked to help us, is some kind of wizard with code! He killed off close to sixty percent of the bloat-ware in the HMA operating system. Those suits boot up in a milli and they look like they'd run a hells of a lot longer than a new model straight off the line!"

"Which of us will they fit?"

"Well, we only have four Marines aboard, counting you of course, but the suits are male. You could wear them but you'd be pretty damned uncomfortable."

HMA was gender specific and sized for the user. It could adjust for different-sized users and even for the wrong gender, but the adjustments had their limits. Using the wrong suit gender was invariably a bad experience.

"So suit up and bring 'Army' with you," she decided. "I'll wear a local EVA suit."

"We could bring Garfield in an EVA suit as well," Rodrigues volunteered. "Three Marine guards are better than two..."

"Not when one of them is missing his HMA," she countered. "Raises questions that we'd rather leave unasked till we settle things." She waved to the rear hatch. "Suit up and wait for me in Bay Five."

Rodrigues nodded and moved off.

She'd selected Armstead to come with Rodrigues because they'd been recruited to her service together. The two had been holding Ava's daughter hostage but they'd been acting on Colonel Kinsey's orders. If young Saoirse wasn't holding a grudge against them, then Julia could see it in her heart to forgive, especially seeing as the girl had the two men completely wrapped around her little finger.

She turned her gaze back to the holo showing the engineer fleet. How would they react to the sudden appearance of six Human ships of unidentified class and three Gray heavy cruisers? They'd be desperate for help, as they obviously still hadn't seen through their trap yet, but would they ask for help from what might be a Gray force?

She'd met Vance Windemere during the hand-off of the *Sucker Punch*. He might be a windbag, but he was no idiot. He'd realize pretty quickly that Grays wouldn't be cruising around with Human escort ships. That left only one possibility. The crews aboard the cruisers couldn't be Grays...

"Incoming hail from the *Sucker Punch*, ma'am."

"On this holo," she replied.

Windemere appeared in front of her, his eyebrows showing he'd recognized her.

"Afternoon, Vance," she offered casually. It had to be afternoon somewhere, after all. "I trust we find you in good health."

"Urbica," he nodded pompously. "I must say, it's a bit of a surprise, finding you out here." His gaze drifted off focus a little. "Though it might just explain a few things..." He looked to his right for a moment, then waved off whoever had caught his attention. "Yes, yes, of course."

"Look, Urbica," he began than paused. He darted an irritated glance to his right. "Look, we seem to have a bit of a problem over here. Any assistance would be appreciated..."

She nodded. "Not to worry. I'll bring a team over right away."

Windemere's eyes grew large, a hand came up in a warning gesture. "No..."

She cut the connection.

She looked at Hale. "Standby to notify the fleet when my flag transfers."

She headed directly for Bay Five. Armstead and Rodrigues were both waiting by the navshield that held the atmosphere in the large space. Black back-packs with vacuum nozzles held their personal gear and a third pack sat by Rodrigues' armored feet. Thirteen other crewmen were there, suited up and ready to go.

Julia stepped over to a row of lockers next to an EVA exit trunk and backed into one with a female symbol above it.

"I've never seen HMA work so well," Armstrong enthused. "If we could take Oliver back to the Imperium with us, we'd make a fortune fixing Marine gear!"

"No, you wouldn't," she warned him. The EVA suit snapped into place around her body and she stepped out, taking her pack from Rodrigues with a nod of thanks.

She shrugged her arms into the straps. "There's a massive industry built around the problems with HMA. Hundreds of thousands of jobs specializing in code patching and line splicing would disappear overnight if you boys showed up with Oliver and set up shop."

"Yeah," Armstead frowned at her. "General, that's kind of the point I'm making." Unlike the privateers, her Marines preferred to use the rank given her by the Senate.

"And you're a Marine, Army," she reminded him, unable to resist grinning at the slight tic of annoyance the nickname always brought out in the man, "so you can estimate the battle damage from that course of action."

"Well," he tilted his head a little, "we'd replace that whole industry with just a handful of folks and..." He suddenly looked back at Julia. "*Tamade!*" he growled. "All those *voting* employees laid off and more than a few Grand Senators seeing jobs lost in their constituencies..."

Julia sighed. "You'd be lucky to live through your first Sol in a business like that. In the Imperium, votes are more precious than Marine's lives. Doesn't matter how many of your brethren you'd save, you'd be refused the chance to bid on a contract and then you'd get a free bullet to the back of the neck one quiet night."

"*Zhentama yaoming!*" Rodrigues exploded. "I'm never going back! The whole damned Imperium is a massive tangle of interconnected stupidity."

"And on that note," Julia said, "let's get over to my carrier and convince her crew they'd rather stay here as well." She led the team onto a shuttle and the ramp slid shut.

They passed out through the shielding and lined up on the *Sucker Punch*. A quick burst from the pitch engines and they were on a trajectory for the stranded engineers. "The real trick in the next few weeks," she told the group, "will be to preserve the differences that make the colonies a place where an idea like yours would have made you rich men instead of corpses."

Thrusters in the nose fired to slow their approach.

"You've heard, by now, that 1GD is out here?"

Rodrigues nodded.

"Well, they wear a lighter armor that the local industries will probably be able to build and maintain." She raised an eyebrow. "A group with experience in armor and a plan to fix the operating system – LDA OS is almost as bugged as HMA OS – can place themselves at the leading edge of that tech and set themselves up for life."

The two Marines shared a glance. Julia had no doubt they'd be trying to get back onto the same ship as Oliver as soon as possible. She made a mental note to have him transferred to the *Sucker Punch*. She could use his skills fine tuning the ship's jury-rigged Human interface anyway.

A blue haze played through the portals as they passed into the aft hangar. Julia stood as the ramp began to drop and walked over to the bottom end, stepping off as it thumped on the decking.

Pulver was already there, waiting for her.

She'd half expected him to make her come up to the bridge.

"You don't really expect to pull us out on thrusters, do you?" Windemere demanded. "That'd take a month for just one..." He trailed off at the sight of fifteen people exiting the shuttle, including two Marines in HMA.

"Windemere," she nodded. "Not to worry, it's under control, but, first, there's the small matter of my ship."

"Your ship?" He glanced out the hangar bay door to where her fleet lay.

"The Imperial Exchequer thought to save money by taking the *Sucker Punch* under lease rather than paying for her outright," she reminded him. The price assessed by Nordegg and Fischer had been astronomical, given the incredible potential represented by the source-directed wormhole generator she carried. By leasing her for research use, the Corps of Engineers would have access at a fraction of the cost.

"That lease explicitly states Nidaveller Station as the location of use," she continued. Once they removed the broken pieces of the *Sucker Punch* from Nidaveller, the lease would end and Julia would be free to reclaim what remained of her ship.

Now, however, the ship was intact and most definitely *not* at Nidaveller. The lease was, technically, at an end.

"As the holder of a fifty percent share of this vessel, I hereby resume control and reserve the right to appoint her officers and crew," she stated formally, wishing a silent blessing on the stingy administrators at the Exchequer.

Windemere opened his mouth, closed it, then repeated the procedure a second time.

Third time's the charm...

"You can't just take ownership of this vessel," he spluttered. "You...

"Droits of Admiralty..." she cut him off with a voice usually reserved for issuing orders in combat, "... para nine-forty-two, second amendment. *Any vessels seized at the outbreak of hostilities in the defense of Imperial territories or properties shall be treated as legitimate prizes of war and are not subject to seizure by the state.*

"It's already been ruled on by the prize courts, Vance, hence the modest lease payments that I've been using to buy the occasional coffee."

"But..."

"But nothing." She looked around the hangar as if to signal that this conversation was coming to an end. "The moment you passed beyond the warning beacons at Nidaveller, this ship reverted to me." She allowed him a smile and a comradely thump on the back. "And you have my thanks for being so good as to bring her back to me.

"In fact," she said in a suddenly lowered voice, leaning in closer, "I'm going to make you an offer you'd be wise to accept – one that solves most of your troubles in a single fit of decisiveness."

Windemere darted another glance out the hangar door at the menace represented by Urbica's fleet. "What's your offer?"

"First things first," she said, holding up a hand. "Do you, or any of your people really want to return to the Imperium, at this point?"

"Well, we..."

"Face it, Vance. You're well and totally screwed. The project was going nowhere. The Corps of Engineers can barely figure out how to keep our own network of jump-gates running. What were the chances of sorting out an even more advanced alien version?"

Windemere's shoulders dropped a fraction.

She shook her head. "Your project was pretty much set up to be an embarrassment to Imperial prestige. You were never going to survive that project. All Daffyd did was accelerate affairs a little bit and offer you a way out."

"A way out? Surely you don't suggest we stay here!"

She smiled, but in a way that made the man shiver. "Let me put it this way: if I put it to a vote, your crews would choose to stay. They don't have massive funds and properties waiting for them back home. Out here, they can find apartments where they can stand up at a fraction of the price they're used to."

She caught Rodrigues' eye for a heartbeat before looking back to Windemere. "And you brought the makings of a top-notch engineering firm. I know just the right client for your first contract, too. A product that every security and military force in the colonies will be drooling to buy."

It had been a spur of the moment thought, but she knew it was the right thing to say. It promised riches to all concerned and gave them a vested interest in keeping Imperial influence at bay.

Or, rather, a second interest.

"It would certainly beat being liquidated to cover up knowledge of superior alien technology," she reminded him.

He let out a deep sigh. "It seems the gun to my head isn't the obvious one, after all." He straightened his back and turned away from her fleet to face her. "You suggest we stay here. I assume you wish us to crew *your* vessel for the time being?"

He'd sounded a little bitter about who owned the *Sucker Punch*, but he'd at least described it as hers, so she chose not to take issue. "You're authority is needed also," she told him. "I want the rest of your ships to work with us as well. You'll have to tell them to follow my orders."

"You want me to take orders from you?" No matter how screwed Windemere might be, he still had an ingrained attitude about women in the military. "What's the date of your commission?"

She allowed herself to laugh. If this was going to be the linchpin of the man's resistance then she'd already won. "Vance, what are the chances that a woman who's reached the rank of Brigadier General in the Marines would have done so more quickly than a *man* with your kind of connections?"

She waved a hand dismissively. "Don't trouble yourself over it. I've already checked. I've been in uniform forty percent longer than you."

Windemere paused for the barest of moments before accepting the situation. Even an ingrained attitude had to take a back seat when facing an officer with a superior record. Everyone knew who Urbica was, while his own name was connected to very few combat actions.

"I place myself under your command," he announced formally.

"Excellent. Let's get underway." Julia started toward the nearest riser.

Windemere thought to point out the small matter of the pulsar but decided against it. If she'd forgotten, he'd just be annoying her. If she already had the whole thing under control, as she'd indicated earlier, he'd simply look the fool.

"General on the bridge!" the sentry at the entry portal announced as they stepped through.

All eyes turned to look at them and Windemere felt a twinge of envy at the hopeful faces. They knew who Urbica was and they clearly felt she could help them. He couldn't blame them. He felt the same sense of hope himself. She'd been on the ship for less than a centi-day and he'd already replaced his dread of returning home with a hope for a future in what appeared to be a fairly large colonial territory.

"I should notify the fleet," he suggested.

She nodded.

"Open a channel to all our ships," he ordered.

Five holographic captains appeared in the middle of the bridge.

"As senior officer, General Urbica of the Imperial Marines is now assuming command of our forces." He turned to Julia. "General..."

"I relieve you, General Windemere."

"I stand relieved."

"Helm," Julia called out, "confirm receipt of coordinates from my implant and pass them to the rest of the fleet."

"Received and passing now, ma'am." He turned to look at her. "But, ma'am, we're still stranded by the pulsar."

Julia looked at the holographic captains. One of them had muted the audio while talking to someone on his right.

He turned back to find his new commanding officer staring at him and sheepishly unmuted.

"Apologies, ma'am. My chief engineer was trying to explain his escape plan and I didn't want to clutter the channel."

"Been a while since you've been in action, Captain?"

The hologram nodded. "Just guard duty, General."

"Well, Captain, we'll be seeing action soon enough so I'll tell you, just this once, that you never mute your boss, ever."

"Won't happen again, General."

"What was his idea?"

"Ma'am?" He frowned, then glanced to his side. "Oh, yes. Cables. Ship's cables with roller drums. Use the biggest ship to pull the second biggest forward, then the third and so-on until we slingshot the smallest gunboat out of the effect horizon. Then we slowly tow the whole fleet out."

"Wouldn't work," she told him, "because you would have only had your own ship to work with. The rest of us are leaving and you'd still be sitting here, if you'd kept the channel muted.

"If I never see meatloaf again," she said loudly, "I'll die a happy man."

Now everybody was looking at her again but, instead of hope, they showed mild confusion. A few consoles began to chime softly, announcing updated information.

"*Hooy na ny!*" the nav officer suddenly exclaimed, looking at his console. "The pulsar... it's gone!"

"It was never there," Julia corrected. "Daffyd had free run of this ship. He managed to program an emergency shutdown for all six ships and a sensor ghost to keep you from looking for his virus. It loaded onto the frigates and gunboats when you synched up for your last jump."

"So that business about meatloaf was his code to return control?" Commander Pulver asked.

"It was," she confirmed, "and, considering his sense of humor, I'm lucky it was just about meatloaf."

"Comms, tie in the rest of our ships on the frequency I'm sending to your console." She turned back to the holographic display, watching as nine more captains shimmered into view.

She activated a control set, placing icons above both Commander Pulver and herself. "I'm transferring my flag to the *Sucker Punch*," she announced. "Captain Pulver will serve as fleet captain."

She resisted the urge to laugh. Hale actually looked pleased to get rid of that particular headache.

"Confirm receipt of new coordinates and spool up. We jump out in ten millis."

Blazing New Trails

"**W**e're gonna have to put a tracker on you!" a breathless voice announced.

Beam didn't bother to take his gaze off the canyon below the landing platform. "I take it you're ready to try the first patient?"

Daffyd walked over and sat next to him, legs dangling over the dizzying drop. "We are, and we have more than a few folks with experience in FMG but you've got the most experience at curing the 'Gray Blues' with it."

"Me and Rob, you mean."

"Well, yes," Daffyd conceded, "but we'd like to hear ourselves think during the process so we've got Rob supervising the crew down in the workshop while they turn out the ceramic tubes and stuff 'em with doses."

The mine's workshop was the kind of setup that could produce just about anything the miners would have needed. Extruding and baking ceramic tubing was a cinch.

"Why don't any of these guys live back there," Beam asked irrelevantly, nodding toward the tunnel. It led to the habitats where the original miners had lived and it got a lot of sunlight, far more than the cold tunnels below

"Too many ghosts, they tell me." Daffyd tossed a pebble over the edge, watching it fade into the hazy distance below. "As an Irricanan, I prefer living underground anyway. C'mon." He gave Beam a nudge. "Ava Klum's your first customer, so let's not keep her waiting."

Beam slid back from the edge and jumped to his feet, fighting a growing bout of panic. For someone whose most valued skill was passing out FMG, he was sure getting tangled up with a lot of famous people.

He followed Daffyd back to the elevator that connected the habitat level with the mine proper and rode down, lost in his own thoughts. They walked to the room selected for dose storage and found that nobody was there yet.

He tried to imagine Ava, Roanoke's foremost privateer leader, buzzed on FMG and the picture failed to form. The stern beauty he knew from her recruiting posters simply refused to take on the slightly slack look of a regular user.

He did manage to imagine one thing, though. "Daffyd..." he came out of the storage room to find the dragoon engineer across the passageway, sitting on the ledge of the outer gallery, feet pressed up against the heavy wire cage that hung outside the opening. "Can you grab a plate of wraps or something from the canteen?"

The man raised an eyebrow at Beam for a moment, then he broke into a wide grin. "Good man!" he enthused, swinging his legs around to the inside of the railing and standing. "Dotting the 'I's and crossing the thorns. I like how you think, young fella." He ambled off just as footsteps began approaching from the up-slope passage.

Paul, Julia and Ava came into the relatively light area by the open gallery. Ava was flanked by two guards and her hands were restrained.

Beam took a deep breath. "Morning, ma'am." He held up a ceramic tube filled with FMG. "I'm ready when you are..."

"It's there to keep the, ummm..." Ava waved at the wire cage, frowning when the waving failed to call the name to mind. "You know," she insisted, frowning again when Beam simply shrugged. "Oh, *Wuh duh ma huh tah duh fong kwong duh wai shung...* not... not-fur-nothings."

Paul, the only other observer present, slowly clapped his hands. "Bravo, sis. Right on the first stumble."

She giggled helplessly, which had sent shivers of terror up Beam's spine the first time he'd heard her do it. This was Ava Klum, the warrior goddess of Roanoake. The shield that protected insignificant folk like himself from raiders, Grays and gods only knew what else.

He was slowly coming to grips with it. Everybody, even iconic leaders, needed a chance to step out of themselves and decompress from time to time. Still, he doubted she'd ever use the stuff again. She wasn't the type to give up her self-control willingly and certainly not without a compelling reason.

Like the removal of a conditioned suicide reflex.

"They'll strip your bones in a heartbeat," she declared. "Have you dead before you finish falling down and there's a few folks around here I'd like to shove out through that door over there." She started to look toward a door next to the gallery but got distracted by the sight of the empty plate.

"Say," she mused, "could've sworn that had sandwiches on it, not two millis ago." She gave Beam an accusing glance. "You eat those?"

"Um..." Beam looked over to Paul, caught the laughter in the cop's eyes.

"Stay with the patient," he suggested as he stood up and stretched. "I'll go refill the plate."

"Bring back some of those little dumplings," she called out as he walked away. She turned to Beam. "I could eat every damn dumpling in this whole damn base.

"So, what's her name?"

"Ma'am?"

"The girl you couldn't get the time of day from so you decided to run off and be a spacer." Ava giggled again. "I'd have thought that was obvious. You wouldn't be the first guy to run away and join a crew to forget about a woman... or to impress her."

She nodded. "Your ears are red. So you haven't given up on her, huh?"

Beam sighed. "I don't know. I think I care a lot less about all that now. The longer I'm away from Roanoke the less important it seems."

"Thank the gods for that," she said with a glance down the hall where her brother had gone in search of food. "Mooning after some girl isn't going to impress her, but a confident swagger might have an impact."

"And if it doesn't," Beam added, surprised at what he was admitting, "I really don't think I care all that much."

"What did I miss?"

Paul's sudden reappearance caught Beam by surprise. He'd been so focused on the conversation that he'd missed the approaching footsteps. He took an eggroll with a nod of thanks.

"We just found out that Beam is interesting," Ava said around a mouthful of eggroll. "Not to me, in particular, of course. Nothing personal," she mumbled hastily. "But then, I'm not really looking for romance."

She scarfed down three more eggrolls. As she swallowed the third, she seemed to remember where she'd left off and reached over to put a hand on Beam's shoulder. "If anyone tells you that hunting down the raiders who killed your husband and skinning them alive won't leave a scar on your psyche, don't you believe them!"

"Um..." Beam replied thoughtfully.

"Alright, huffie..." Paul pulled out a knife and cut her hands free, "... let's see if the cure worked."

Before anyone could even form the phrase 'so what do we do next?', Ava grabbed the Nuttall special from his holster, flipped off the safety and pointed the weapon at her temple.

"Whoa!" Paul urged, one hand held out toward Ava, palm facing her. "That wasn't what I had in mind."

Ava shrugged and handed the weapon back. "Well at least we know I'm cured, seeing as how my head is still in one piece."

"What the hells are you two playing at?" Beam demanded. He reached under his jacket and pulled out a vastly cheaper handgun and brandished it. "I was going to 'accidentally' drop this unloaded weapon as part of the test."

Paul reddened. "Yeah, that sounds like a much better plan."

"Well..." Beam had been ready to launch into an angry tirade but Paul's admission had taken the edge off, "no more coming down here with loaded weapons, and the two of you have to keep quiet about the test; otherwise, it's too easy to cheat.

"Matter of fact," he mused, "let's ship 'em all up to the *Sucker Punch* after each cure so word doesn't get out."

Paul nodded, approval evident on his face. "Good plan. C'mon, sis. You're in no shape to keep a secret right now."

Ava stood, turned to Beam and gave him a slightly exaggerated nod. "Thanks for this." she said. "If there's anything you need, you let me know."

By the Numbers

Julia slid down the grav-free column of space that connected the command deck to the hangar. The captains of the combined fleet were gathered in a rough circle on the forward inertial trap, safe enough as long as the *Sucker Punch* wasn't conducting flight operations. They'd pulled cargo containers over to provide makeshift seats and she noticed that not all of the Imperial captains were keeping to themselves.

She was reasonably certain she could see Pulver's influence there. In the short time she'd had to observe the engineer, she'd formed a provisionally favorable opinion of his leadership skills.

She extended a hand, feeling the sudden gravity the way you do when you lift your arm out of a pool. She grabbed the egress stanchion and pulled herself forward at the right moment, stepping lightly onto the deck.

She walked over to sit with her back to the bay opening, the mining world known as Caleb's Rock turning slowly behind her. Ava was already there, sitting opposite her.

She took a moment to scan the faces in front of her. Wary eagerness seemed the best description.

She smiled. "Thanks for coming, folks. I'm happy to report that we'll be able to get out of our young host's hair in the very near future!"

One of the privateer captains leaned forward. "How near?"

"So near," Ava replied, "that we've already launched Phase One."

"Which involves what, exactly?" another captain asked.

"No details," Julia said firmly. "You'll be out there fighting while the tail end of the first phase is still active, so we don't want that information falling into Gray hands." She gave them a moment to take that in. She'd shut him down, but she'd done so because they'd be in action soon.

"You've seen the cure," she went on. "Phase One is the propagation of that cure through the colonies."

"Fair enough," the first captain conceded. "We're Phase Two?"

Ava shook her head. "Tim, we're Phase Three. When the cure-estimate reaches ninety percent, we orchestrate a PR campaign, exposing the Grays as the cause of our own civil war. Then we take our existing privateer forces into Gray space. We'll be launching a series of lightning raids to disrupt their communication and logistics."

"Just the colonials?" Tim cut in, waving a hand toward the spot where three Imperial captains were clustered together. "What about our Imperial friends, here?"

"They're already going to be busy," Julia told him, "ensuring that Phase Two keeps the Grays too afraid to launch a full scale retaliation for your own attacks."

Pulver frowned. "General, I doubt the Grays will take our threats seriously. We're too small a force to be sent as a warning."

"Agreed, Captain," she said, granting him the courtesy of his position instead of his rank. "As a deterrent force, we're too small. The Grays would assume we're simply a renegade unit and wipe us out."

A round of chuckles ensued. The small Imperial flotilla was exactly that – a renegade force.

"So we leave off any thoughts of threats or dire warnings," she continued, "and politely greet any Grays we meet."

Pulver started to nod, a grin eating his face alive. "Of course! We're simply responding to a request for medical aid for the citizens of whatever planet, or technical assistance in an industrial accident."

"Exactly." Julia inclined her head slightly in recognition of his grasp. "Or we say we're responding to a distress call. Believe me, that will have them wondering what we know about their activities out here.

"By stating benign interests, we give them the definite impression that the Imperium has long-term designs on the colonies or, at the very least, an interest in what goes on out here. We'd never tell the truth about something like that!"

"They'd definitely think twice about wiping out the colonies," Tim allowed, "but they won't just sit still while we attack them."

"Which is why we'll end Phase Two with the 'discovery' of some egregious Gray atrocities against colonials and use the *Sucker Punch's* wormhole generator," she waved a hand to indicate the ship they sat in, "to start launching a flurry of raids.

"We'll hit targets that border Imperial space. They'll be certain a full-scale Imperial invasion is building up."

Windemere had been silent so far, but now he stepped in. "They'd try to hit Santa Clara again." He turned a shrewd eye on Julia. "That's exactly what you have in mind, isn't it?"

The Grays had already tried once before. If they could destroy the factory ships beneath the ice crust of Santa Clara, the Imperium would run out of organic circuits in a matter of months.

With no chips, ships would grind to a halt as the circuits started to fail. It was an accepted fact of the industry. The circuits were incredibly powerful, but they had a short lifespan. The only thing you could rely on was the fact that they'd fail on schedule.

The Navy and Marines would quickly lose their ability to deploy. Even their personal weapons needed the chips to operate.

If the Grays could wipe out Santa Clara, then they need only fight a delaying action for a few weeks before they could start taking the upper hand.

"Dangerously close to treason, don't you think?' he asked her.

"Closer to patriotism," she said. "The Grays *will* try again, but they'll wait a decade or so. If we push them into it now, they'll throw the dice while CentCom still has that huge emergency force stationed in orbit." She shrugged. "It *will* happen, Vance. If we set the schedule instead of them, we give the Imperium its best chance of survival."

"There's also Irricana," Pulver reminded them.

Julia nodded. "They'd almost certainly send an attack to Irricana as well. It has less value than hitting Santa Clara, but if they can choke off the flow of erbium from Irricana, the end effect will still be the same, once the factory ships run out."

"It would take longer for us to grind to a halt," Pulver added, "but we'd still be screwed."

"Which is why *we* will have to stop the attack on Irricana." She held up a hand to forestall a privateer captain. Before she could explain, Ava jumped in.

"No, Franco, we won't be sent off to fight for the Imperium. The colonial forces will be too busy fighting for our own territory." She nodded at Julia. "General Urbica will lead her dragoons and the Imperial forces from here on, and they'll look after Irricana."

"General?" Tim frowned.

"As of now," Julia stated formally, raising her voice to ensure all could hear, "I resign from the commission voted for me by the officers and crew of the colonial forces. With Commodore Klum fully recovered, you have no need of the split command structure we've struggled under for the last few months.

"Those who've served directly under me, I advise you to ratify the leadership of Commodore Ava Klum. I'm sure I needn't remind you of her record!"

Tim took a quick look around the crowd. "As a quick expedient," he called out, "all those in favor of ratification, remain seated; all those opposed to serving under Commodore Klum, stand now."

"And see how long you can stay on your feet," a captain at the back joked.

Amid the ensuing laughter, it became clear there were only a few challenges.

Captain Hale, who'd served as Julia's flag captain for most of her tenure and Captain Savage, who'd risen from chief engineer to captain one of the captured cruisers, were both standing. Savage nodded to Hale.

"Ma'am," Hale began, "Karen and I figured you might be playing some kind of Imperial distraction card and that you'd be glad of a couple of heavy cruisers to guard the *Sucker Punch* and secure your rendezvous sites."

"Otherwise, you'd be using some of your Imperial ships for security when they could be more profitably employed in giving the Grays something to worry about," Savage added.

She grinned. "And our guns will come in handy when the Grays attack Irricana. Might even confuse them further, seeing colonial forces fighting for an Imperial world."

They had a point, or perhaps several, and they were all good. When the 'Imperial' raids began, they'd be launched and recovered through wormholes created by the *Sucker Punch*. Having two cruisers to defend the exit strategy would be a definite plus.

And, knowing she'd be drawing the Imperium into the fight, having colonial forces defend Imperial holdings might just prove a valuable bargaining chip, later on.

She nodded. "Commodore Klum, are you willing to lose two ships?"

Ava shook her head. "We have lots of prize crews. We can just take a few replacement ships from the Grays while we're raiding." She grinned. "It's you Imperials that can't recover your force strengths without an approved shipyard..."

Julia grinned. "Have you forgotten who built my current flagship?" The assembled leaders laughed.

Julia turned back to Hale and Savage. "Glad to have you with us. You'll make life a hell of a lot easier for us"

"Alright folks," Ava stood. "Get your commands ready. We've got a war to start."

And neither official participant had any idea it was coming.

Spreading the Love

"**T**ry it now," Paul suggested.

"That's definitely the strongest point we've seen so far." Oliver's voice sounded in Paul's helmet. "Can you move a little closer to the centerline? I think we'll get a better link over there."

Paul looked across the station's cluttered hull. Ceres had been built to an older Imperial design, when grav-plating was so expensive that these larger, rotating models were preferred. The central block had grav-plates but, unlike the newer stations that relied entirely on artificially generated gravity, these older models routed their sub systems outside the hull to minimize the area served by the expensive plates. There was an endless jungle of pipes, protrusions and railings for him to hold onto.

"How far do you need me to go?" He grimaced as he heard the sound of a mug setting down on a table. Oliver's voice was half muted as he thanked the server.

"Last thing we need is a break in the connection while I'm still coding," Oliver reminded him, "so I'd like to at least double our signal index, if we can."

"You're buying me one of those espressos when I get back inside."

"Sure, sure. Just keep moving."

Paul was about to move around a large heat pump when a shadow stopped him. He suppressed an angry curse, knowing it would alarm Oliver, who was supposed to be acting like the standard coffee shop poser with his data slate.

A guy who was writing the 'next big holo movie' wasn't supposed to suddenly put a hand to his ear and demand to know what was wrong.

149

But Paul was angry with himself for ignoring simple precautions. He subvocalized a command and the electronic warfare suite in his new dragoon armor suit activated. Sure enough, a Marine IFF transponder was just on the other side of the heat pump.

The last thing Kinsey's compromised Marines would expect out here is for their transponders to be picked up by hostiles. For one thing, they were short range only, designed for fire-team coordination, not long-range detection. For another, the signal was meaningless unless you knew what it was and the colonials didn't know.

Paul wryly congratulated himself for ensuring his own transponder was off, but then, he was trying to be sneaky. He considered asking Oliver for help in cracking the suit's operating system, but, despite the Maegi's recent improvements to the two HMA suits used by Rodrigues and Armstead, he had no experience breaking into a deployed suit.

And he didn't have access to the kind of quantum computing power that resided in Paul's sinuses. The Nathaniel family's investment in him had paid for itself many times over and now it would help free the colonies from the grip of a Gray instigated civil war.

He found the Marine suit's login protocol and hacked the password by brute force. His core was able to throw billions of guesses at the login simultaneously. He found the life support routines and initiated an oxygen warning.

Damn it! The transponder was moving his way! He stepped back into the harsh shadow between the heat pump and some kind of large boxy thing and froze.

The Marine walked past, mag-plates in his soles allowing an ungainly but relatively rapid progress. The slap of the man's boots reverberated through the hull plating, sending faint echoes of sound up through the air in Paul's own suit.

This was why the instructors at the Twenty-Nine Moons station insisted that hull sentries never use their mag-plates and it was why Paul had worked his way out here, handhold by handhold.

He let out a breath he didn't know he'd been holding as the sentry disappeared among the jumble of modules, headed inside to have his atmo-cycler checked.

Space always brought out the absurdity of human reflexes. How could that Marine have heard Paul's breathing? He moved past where the man had been standing and continued on.

"Wait," Oliver suddenly commanded after Paul had gone another thirty meters. "Back-track about three meters. Signal index was growing fine but then started dropping. Looks like you just passed the best spot."

"How's that?"

"Good. Settle in while I find the best place to hide our codes."

Paul looked around, settling on an array of heat-sinks mounted a half meter above the hull plating. He wedged himself under them, figuring he'd look like more miscellaneous crap to any casual observer.

He treated himself to a small sigh. He had the most advanced processer in the entire sector lodged in his head and, here he was, acting as a mobile relay station. At least he'd get *some* of the fun.

He'd been in this operating system before, when they'd almost sent the kill signal that would wipe out all conditioned Humans. He quickly found the security module and cracked the password cascade in a heartbeat.

"We're in," he told Oliver. "It's all your show now."

"One of these days you'll have to tell me how you slip into hostile systems so easily," Oliver muttered.

"Not without a better argument than that," Paul retorted. "I thought you Maegi were supposed to be freakishly persuasive."

"Nah, we just put that in the recruiting posters," Oliver replied with a slight distance in his voice. He was probably already at work. "We do take our dental plan seriously, though..."

Paul forced himself to keep quiet. He didn't know if Oliver worked better or worse with distractions, so he figured he'd leave it up to the Maegi. He scanned around for signs of sentries, but the Grays in charge of this signal operation probably had their species' lack of understanding when it came to ground-pounders.

Their idea of security was a cordon of heavy cruisers. A clone species with no finite life span, the Grays showed no inclination to fight and die with a rifle in their hands. It offended their sense of group solidarity. If one of them were to die in combat, they'd prefer to die along with a ship full of crewmates, thank-you ever so blandly.

Did that indicate a belief in the afterlife?

"OK," Oliver cut into Paul's musing, "here's the plan. For a start, we leave all the existing code intact. We don't want conflicting commands triggering a suicide imperative before they get a chance to act on our own addition."

Silence for a moment, then a flurry of key strokes.

"We'll just add in an additional nested line..." barely audible humming, "... here. This line gets accessed a hell of a lot, I'd imagine. They actually regulate the subjects' eating habits. I suppose they don't want to go to all the trouble of brainwashing us only to have us keel over from heart disease a couple years down the road."

The Grays would rather have their subjects perpetuate the Human civil war and then eventually die in combat against other Humans. It helped reduce the nuisance represented by the colonies and it wouldn't force the Imperium to get involved.

More keystrokes.

"Alright. After each meal, they'll have a compelling urge to top it off with a tube of FMG. Hm..." A few more strokes. "We'll put it at the start of the suicide imperative as well. Kind of a *time to end it all, but I'll have a last puff before I snuff it.*"

Paul frowned at his heads up displays. "Oliver, wouldn't an important line like that be more likely to get checked out by their programmers?"

Oliver laughed. "You've never met a Gray programmer, have you? They do it right the first time. Why the hells would they ever feel the urge to waste valuable time looking at code they've already written?"

"Fine," Paul conceded. "This is your area of expertise."

He grunted as he slid out from under the heat exchangers. "Order me something in a quarter centi. I'll be right down."

He made his way back to the docking port on the aft side of the central block and climbed onto the dorsal surface of the long-range, export-model Hichef shuttle they'd arrived in. He cycled his way through the escape trunk and stepped out of his armor, leaving it to retract itself into a collection of neatly stored plates and fabrics.

He stopped at the front console to check the system before leaving through the airlock to enter the station.

The elevators to the habitat ring had a longer line than expected. He must have arrived during a shift change. Still, by the time he stepped out into the rotationally generated gravity of the ring, it was pretty close to the time estimate he'd given Oliver.

The station was even more impressive than the one orbiting Ganges. This one was the same diameter but twice as wide. Two rivers flowed around the ring, with inlets and small lakes offering connections between them. The habitable area curved up the sidewalls, giving way to forest and crops where it neared the seam with the roof.

It all curved away behind the roof in the hazy distance, rivers appearing to flow uphill as they followed the circumference of the massive ring and, yet, the large cargo ships floated placidly along on the water.

The Imperium had long since lost the sense of grandeur represented in the old ring-station designs. It wasn't simply the question of grav-plate cost. The ancient architects could have easily relied on maglev trains for the station's inter-zone shipping needs but they chose to create a river out of the station's water supply.

It was slightly less efficient, after comparing load size with travel times, but the end result was far more pleasing to the Human spirit.

Paul took a slidewalk in the direction of the riverfront café where Oliver waited. He gazed off into the distance, suddenly aware of why stations like this always managed to awe and depress him at the same time. They were stark reminders of how Imperial architecture was increasingly a statement on the death of the individual.

This station's design made concessions to how inhabitants would *feel*. Efficiencies were sacrificed when alternative choices might prove more pleasing to the eye. The cities out here were made of soaring *individual* towers, unlike the Imperial arcologies where millions lived and worked in a single massive structure.

Every day, Imperial citizens got ready for work in six square meter apartments where, if you could afford the extra rent, you might be able to rise up on your knees without hitting the ceiling. The rapid transit capsules carried them to work like blood cells in a massive organism.

It made Paul shudder with disgust just thinking about it, and yet, when he was growing up in the mines on Hardisty, he'd envied those people with a passion. Not having to live in a hole off the side of a mining shaft, being clean...

In the Imperium, there was always someone whose lifestyle wasn't quite so terrible as yours. It gave folks a twisted kind of hope for something better.

Out here, hope came more from imagination than from emulation. Minds were free here.

Living conditions were far better for the average citizen in the colonies. Even the meanest apartment on Roanoke had two-meter-high ceilings and windows. They even had separate rooms for sleeping, talking and eating.

They could actually prepare their own food out here. Paul's suite on Home World was lavish by Imperial standards but he didn't have a *kitchen* as the colonials called it. It simply had a prep space and refrigeration-cube for use by caterers. Not eating in licensed establishments was illegal. Only the very wealthy could afford to buy a temporary license and have caterers cook food in their homes.

Kitchens aside, he could easily find a much better place to live on Roanoke and at a fraction of the cost he'd paid back home. His sister actually lived in a *house*. A real house with walls and a roof. He knew some of the great families of the Imperium maintained such things. Julia had grown up in one, but then, her father was the Governor of an entire planet.

He edged his way toward the slower-moving regions of the slidewalk as he neared his rendezvous, stepping off entirely as he reached the right cross-street.

He had no intention of ever returning to his old life.

He smiled as he spotted Oliver at a street-corner patio. A server was just setting down a large mug filled with a latte. Fresh gods-damned coffee! Made from real beans and served in a ceramic mug instead of a polymer bag.

This was how Humans were supposed to live.

"You checked?" Oliver asked as Paul slid into the seat opposite him.

Paul was looking at the flow of pedestrians past the low wrought-iron fence marking the limits of the patio. They had such purpose in their stride – well, most of them. There were always going to be those who hated their jobs...

He turned back to the Maegi. "Yep. Buried in the personnel folder where nobody bothers to look, unless they're adding crew." He'd done a quick search of the shuttle's systems before coming down for his coffee.

Oliver leaned forward. "So, the audio system was active?"

Paul took a sip, concentrating for a moment on the flavor before setting the mug down and nodding. "Not so the panels would show, but yes. The sounds match the character associations found in the original conditioning. It's enough to put your message into any conditioned crewmember's mind, unless they're deaf."

"Well," Oliver shrugged, "you can't have everything..."

"And we'd already received thirty passes from the other ships at the station," Paul added. "By now, the update has probably run the circuit of every ship here."

That didn't mean much here, where the station itself was embedding Oliver's code in every visiting ship but, after they left, they'd be spreading it to every ship they came in contact with.

And those ships would spread it even further, every time their transponder code was read.

The price of FMG was about to skyrocket.

A.G. Claymore

STIRRING THE HORNETS

Cat Among the Pigeons

ow are they looking?" Pulver asked, just coming onto the bridge to start his shift.

Julia glanced back at him, careful to keep the boredom from her expression and voice. "Still stable for life-support," she said. "Propulsion is a complete mess, though. They've made very little progress on that front."

"If only they knew there were a few hundred Imperial engineers watching them from this nebula," he said quietly. "I doubt they'd find it amusing."

"No doubt," she agreed, "but we can't waste such a golden opportunity to introduce ourselves. The Grays will come, Captain." She turned away from the hologram to face him. "We'd already started cutting back on the *distress call* ambushes and the Grays have ramped up their abductions accordingly."

She looked back at the holo where a crippled passenger liner was sending its perfectly legitimate distress call. "They'll come."

Pulver made his rounds, checking in with each department and getting the latest tactical picture. He returned to the command holo and opened up an orders screen and perused the latest entries.

Julia took a deep but controlled breath. Patience. This called for patience. The passengers and crew on that liner might be worried about falling into the wrong hands while their ship was crippled, but worry wouldn't kill them.

158

Pulver turned to her. "I am ready to relieve you, ma'am."

"I am ready to be relieved."

"I relieve you, General."

She'd grown unaccustomed to the strict Imperial protocols while serving as a colonial officer. "I am relieved. Attention on the bridge. Captain Pulver has the deck."

She touched her palm over her heart in the standard response to a salute and headed for her quarters. The process had been ingrained in her but now it seemed a little stuffy.

Though she was in charge of the small fleet, the *Sucker Punch* was staffed by engineers and short on qualified deck officers. She'd volunteered to do double duty as a deck officer and it had surprised her how this ambush seemed to drag on.

Now there were large swathes of time where she was stuck on the bridge. She couldn't just wander the ship and meet the crew. She couldn't even retire to her quarters.

Now she could, though. A hot shower would take some of the tension away. She'd managed to get halfway out of her uniform when the contact alarm chimed from the panel by her door.

The desire for a shower had done the trick. If she'd been trying to force fate by *pretending* to want a shower, it wouldn't have worked. She strode briskly into the bridge, ignoring the startled glances from the crew. It wasn't like they'd seen any critical targets. They were just surprised at seeing an officer with a partially undone uniform.

Contact with the enemy didn't wait while you finished buttoning your tunic in privacy. It was said that Monty himself fought the Serpents at Gol Hartha while in his underwear and a ratty old undershirt.

159

"Four cruisers and four frigates. Diamond envelopment with the frigates in reserve." Pulver told her as she approached the holo.

Julia took a quick look at the slight twist on the standard Gray attack formation. The shuttle bays on the cruisers were already vomiting a haze of small craft to begin the abduction process. She unclenched her jaw.

What she wanted – really wanted – was to have them all destroyed but, if you kill them, they won't learn anything.

And she wanted them to learn caution.

Windemere's image appeared slightly to the left of the tactical display.

"Micro-jump your force as soon as you're ready, General," she ordered.

There was a slight shimmer and they were facing the Gray ships with the stricken Human vessel in their midst. "Hail them," Vance ordered.

The initial thinking had been to let the Grays hail the Humans but they'd realized it wasn't in the same character as the breezy, friendly persona Vance would be projecting to the enemy.

It also increased the possibility of the Grays firing on the Human ships.

A Gray officer appeared in the central holo. If he was surprised at finding an Imperial fleet, centered on an LHV-class attack carrier, he didn't show it, at least not so Vance could tell. The Grays took a lot of practice to read and

General Urbica had given him an overview of the topic, but he'd still need a lot of practice.

"Greetings!" he boomed. "General Vance deLaCouer Windemere of his Imperial Majesty's Engineers at your service." He sketched the rudiments of an elaborate court bow and found, to his surprise, that he was enjoying himself immensely.

The Gray tilted his head to the right, his skin registering as a few lumens lighter than standard. If Urbica was right, it meant slight confusion and a touch of fear.

Were there any Gray albinos? Strangers would be forever trying to reassure them...

"State your reason for being here," the Gray captain droned.

"Just a routine mission of mercy," Vance said. "A Human colony needs technical assistance so we'll drop in and see if we can help."

"Which colony are you..."

"I see you've found some of our people in distress," Vance cut him off. As there was no colony in distress, he had no intention of answering the Gray's questions. Better to set the tune and see if the little bastards knew how to dance.

"As you can see," he ploughed on, "we're in an excellent position to render assistance to them as well." He sketched another bow. "My thanks for your willingness to help our people, and our Emperor's thanks as well. No doubt a commendation will make its way to you through the appropriate diplomatic channels in a few decades.

"In the meantime," he said, adopting a more brisk tone, doubting such a subtlety would register with a Gray, "we'll take it from here. You can recall your shuttles."

With a wave, he closed the channel.

And allowed himself a deep breath.

Then he realized the tension was still there. He leaned closer to the holo and zoomed it in on the haze of Gray shuttles. They were still heading for the Human passenger liner. Should he repeat the request for the Grays to stand down?

He shook his head. It would weaken his position. No officer acting on Imperial authority would so such a thing. "Launch all aviation assets," he commanded. "I want a CAP around the fleet and the rest will escort the technical teams to the Human ship."

Vance had seen combat action, before taking over Nidaveller, but he'd never been up against the Grays. What he was doing right now would have triggered an all-out fight, if he were facing most other species.

He hoped Urbica was right about these guys.

"CAP established, sir," the Tactical officer announced. "Assets forming up before moving to render assistance."

"Very well." Vance looked back to the holo. He was putting his small force on a combat footing. Would the Grays back down or would they...

The Gray shuttles had stopped.

Glory be! It looked like Mrs. Windemere's little boy would live to see another day.

"Relief force ready to deploy, sir."

"Send 'em in."

She'd been right. With no overt provocation, the Grays were backing down. The numbers simply didn't add up to a fight and so they'd probably recall their shuttles. They could hardly carry on with their intentions. Abducting Humans under the nose of an Imperial force wasn't how they operated.

Vance zoomed his view back out. The green icons indicating his own shuttles as well as their escorts were reaching the halfway point between the two forces. As they passed the middle, the Gray shuttles began moving back toward their own ships.

"Hail the Human vessel."

A Human figure appeared in front of Windemere. He let out a whoop and reached out of the image to slap someone on the back. "Never would have thought I'd see Imperials with my own eyes," the man said. "but I'm sure as hells glad to meet you, Captain."

Vance knew better than to get huffy about a civilian captain from outside the Imperium not knowing military insignia. "General Windemere, Imperial Corps of Engineers," he introduced himself genially. "Can we render assistance?"

"Imperial Corps..." The man stared at Vance for a moment. "Are you having a laugh? Here we are, with a dead engine and four decks open to space and the Universe just decides to drop engineers in my lap? I'm certainly not complaining, but this does strain credulity a bit."

Vance knew it wasn't as much of a strain as the man thought. If the Universe *had* dropped him in their laps, it had done so quite a while ago and they'd been watching the stricken ship for days like a peeper in the bushes.

"We picked up your distress call," he hedged. It was true, it just wasn't *all* of the truth. "Stand by to receive damage control parties." He killed the channel and turned to his tactical officer.

"The Grays are hailing us, sir."

Vance raised his eyebrows at the tactical officer, a tight-lipped smile on his face. "Very well," he replied patiently. "Central holo."

He turned back to find the Gray captain, presumably the same one, but who the hells could tell the difference?

"You have the rescue well in hand," the Gray said. "We will leave you to your labours."

His head tilted slightly forward, or his forehead suddenly got larger, which wouldn't really surprise Vance in the least. From the simple primer with Urbica, that would seem to indicate curiosity.

"Odd, wouldn't you agree, that you're here in Gray territory?" the Gray said with so little inflection Vance couldn't really tell if it was meant rhetorically or if an answer was wanted.

Not that he gave a rat's testicles.

It was the perfect opening. If Windemere's force was going to bluff, now would be the time. He was going to bluff alright, but he'd do it by not bluffing. He had to appear as though he were steering the discussion away from the reason for his presence.

"Odd is a matter of perspective." He waved a dismissive hand. "Many would call my taste in wine odd, though more would call it abominable."

"I don't see how that applies."

"Well, isn't it obvious?" Windemere leaned his head back in what he'd first thought to be surprise, but belatedly realized meant disgust to a Gray. Oh well, he'd be shooting at the bastards in a week or so. No harm in pissing a few off now. "I find my taste in wine to be the very soul of normality."

He decided to play the disgust card to the hilt and get rid of an annoying conversation at the same time. "If you're going to be deliberately obtuse, I see no reason to continue this conversation."

With a gesture, he killed the channel.

A quick glance around the bridge told him he'd at least given them a good show. There were grins all around.

All in all, a good day's work. They were rescuing a few hundred civilians. Those Grays would probably jump for the nearest repeater node and wave their precious Quorum about an unexpected presence, starting a shit-storm...

Did the Grays defecate? Pellets maybe?

Anyway, the Gray leadership would be dropping pellets trying to figure out why Imperial ships were poking around colonies they'd always pretended didn't exist.

This sure beat sitting at Nidaveller, waiting for CentCom to have him killed off.

Phase 3

Ava nodded at the armorer's instructions and put her left heel into one of the two indents in the cube shaped stack behind her. She pressed down.

"Good," dragoon Warrant Officer Stiles said encouragingly, even though she hadn't really done much. He'd doubtless been through this process hundreds of times. "Now give the scanner a moment to map your body. We don't want anything getting broken." He gave her a grin.

"Do I have to do that every time?" Ava asked. "It seems like I wouldn't have time for this if we stumble onto an enemy force."

"First time in the suit, you always calibrate," Stiles said. "Every subsequent use, you just step in and it deploys. Faster than getting dressed." He looked down at the cube as it emitted a series of clicks and chirps.

"Calibration's done, Commodore. You ready to put on the best armor in the Universe?"

"Better than HMA?"

To his credit, Stiles just barely managed to stop himself from spitting on the deck plates. "That committee-designed, government-issued *gavno*? Sure it stops bullets better, but I'd rather be in a position to be the one *firing* the bullets than stopping them.

"Second heel," he ordered.

Ava lowered her right heel onto the second pressure plate. "Oh!" she exclaimed involuntarily as the stack of plates leapt into motion, knitting themselves together around her legs.

Her eyes grew wide and her breathing rapid as the suit enclosed her upper body and arms before snapping a helmet into place from somewhere behind her head.

A heads up holo-display, no more than a centimeter thick but seeming much deeper, came to life before her eyes. She could see Stiles and one of Pulver's engineers standing in front of her. Data callouts showed their mass and state of armament along with a stack of closed windows for items like health, supply and orders.

"Now retract the helmet," Stiles instructed.

Ava focused on the task. She sub-vocalized the command, minute muscle movements sending the actual command to the suit's sensors.

She jumped slightly as the helmet snapped out of the way.

"Good." Stiles gestured to her left. "Try a short walk around the hangar."

She took her first step to turn and stopped immediately to regain her balance. The suit seemed a little too eager to help. Her leg had come up much farther than she'd intended.

"Keep at it," Stiles urged. "Takes a little practice to get used to the power assist, for you and the suit both."

She took another step, aiming herself down the middle of the ornate arches spanning the *Rope a Dope's* main hangar. She stepped off, wobbling as the suit tried to propel her towards the ceiling with every step. The effect was quickly lessening as the suit learned her regular walking gait. By the time she reached the aft hangar doors, she'd pretty much managed a normal-looking walk.

"Excellent," Stiles shouted, barely audible amid the clanging tools and heavy duty air exchangers of the hangar deck. "Now jog back."

Ava glanced up at the ceiling. She subvocalized and the helmet snapped back into place, startling her again even though she knew what to expect this time. She didn't want her brains spread all over the panels above.

She set off at her regular jogging pace and found herself bounding along like a Thompson's Chromelle. She had to be lifting two meters from the deck with each stride. This part of the calibration was as much on her as it was the suit. She reduced her push-off, decreasing the altitude of each bound until she reached a suitable jogging pace.

She had to adjust her suited jogging gait if she wanted to preserve the impressive leaping ability of the suit; otherwise, it would simply be calibrated out. She reached the armorer and turned to head back down the hangar.

The pace was an easy one, but she was covering the distance as if she were almost running flat out. It might prove more useful in ground combat than on a ship, but she knew she'd be leading attacks on some pretty large Gray vessels. She returned to the two men and retracted her helmet.

"Alright," she said, barely breathing heavily after her run, "I'm sold on these things. I just wish we could get the project rolling immediately."

"We need to give Pulver's team a little time to put together the CAD-Holos first," Stiles replied, "and then we can start sourcing local suppliers. That will go a lot faster once we start knitting the colonies back together. I don't think we could source all the parts on a single colony."

"Nor should we," Ava flexed her right arm. "This should be something that helps tie our economies back together. The suits will almost certainly be used in conflicts between the colonies, but they'll be our own fights, not Gray puppetry."

Stiles held up a large pistol in a holster, nearly twice the size of a regular model. "Seven millimeter, linearly accelerated rounds," he said in the matter of fact voice one used in quoting stats. "The power cells draw their charge from induction plates on your palms and the holstering plates on your hips or chest. If you drop it and an enemy with no suit picks it up, they only get a couple of shots off before the cells die." He slapped the weapon onto a holstering plate on her right hip.

"How many rounds?"

"Four hundred per magazine and the standard mag clip holds three spare mags." Stiles held up a flat object with three magazines protruding from the front. He slapped it onto the left hip, mags facing ahead and slightly upward. "That gives you sixteen hundred rounds," he said with evident satisfaction. "And they'll punch out the seam on an HMA suit's fixatropic plate, if you get the right angle."

He tapped Ava's armored shoulder. "At sixty-eight percent of the armor protection of HMA and one-hundred-seventy-nine percent the mobility, this suit will get you in position to do just that."

It might just come to that. With renegade Marines still loose in the colonial territories and a war that would probably draw in the Imperium, nothing could be ruled out.

Ava flexed her fist, smiling at her enlarged hand. "Let's make the recording." She stepped over to a crate and pulled out a recording ball.

She walked over to one of the dragoon ship destroyers, stopping just to the side of the crest on the hull, and tossed the ball into the air in front of her.

A holo replay projected below the ball showed her what the recording would look like. She activated a control holo and slid the ball to her left, bringing the three stars and the letters '1GD' into full view over her right shoulder.

"Begin recording," she ordered.

"This is Commodore Ava Klum of Roanoke," she began. "We have been absent for some time now and it's because we've learned a terrible secret. The Grays are responsible for creating and fueling the civil war that's kept us divided for so long. They were behind the attack on Dresden and they've been very busy since then.

"We've been silent until now because they have captured thousands of our people over the years and have implanted conditioning that increases the desire to carry on the fight. Even now, some will see the attached data proving our assertions and still argue for a continuation of the war.

"These people are under the influence of a host of deeply imbedded behavioral imperatives and, if they're pushed, they'll attempt to kill themselves. Exercise extreme caution around them and, if they ask for FMG, let them have it. Tetrahydrocannabinol, the active ingredient in FMG, has been discovered to have great effect in eliminating this behavioral conditioning.

"I urge all who hear this to cease operations against their fellow Humans and to prepare for what is coming. The Grays have done this to keep us from posing a threat to them and, now that we have revealed their schemes, they will consider us to be extremely dangerous.

"We must unite and we must do so immediately." She gestured toward the ship destroyer behind her. "And we don't need to defend ourselves alone. There are those who aren't welcome in the Imperium anymore but who are willing to join us in our struggle. This is their home now and they're eager to fight for it."

She didn't need to explain what the symbol behind her meant. The holovids brought out on each *Fools' Hope* ship kept the colonies up to date on Imperial news and the 1st Gliessan Dragoons were widely admired.

"By the time you see this message, we'll be deep behind the Gray frontier, degrading their ability to support an attack on the colonies. Use that time to organize the defenses. Elect leaders, just as we always have. Don't allow Imperial-style squabbling over seniority to eat away at our ability to fight.

"We must unite," she re-iterated, raising an armored fist in front of herself, "and, though chaos awaits us, it is infinitely preferable to annihilation. People of the colonies, this is our moment. Either we seize it and become a force that even the Imperium would fear to provoke, or we allow our enemies to destroy us at their leisure."

She steeled herself for the next bit of showmanship, or was it showwomanship? She subvocalized a command and her helmet snapped into place with brutal speed. It was a bit melodramatic, but you needed that kind of thing when you were trying to convince your people to save themselves.

"End recording," she commanded.

She retracted the helmet.

She'd take the ball back to her quarters on her own cruiser and do a little editing. By the time Julia opened a wormhole, she should have it ready for the public.

Spreading the Word

"**W**e have the beacon, ma'am." The communications officer turned to look back at Julia. "Commodore Klum's ship is moving toward the outbound end."

"Very well." Julia looked over to Pulver. "I'll be in the hangar."

When she arrived, Ava's shuttle was just touching down on the deck. As the ramp touched the plating, the intercom approximated the sound of a bosun's pipe. "Commodore Klum, arriving." The ship's voice announced.

Ava stepped out and the smile on her face made Julia suddenly aware of how much she was missing Paul. Ava didn't bear a strong resemblance to her brother, but many of their facial expressions were the same.

"Good to see you." Julia returned the smile. "You've got the recording?"

Ava pulled out a data crystal. She nodded toward the drone bank, just to the starboard side of the main hangar door.

They walked over and loaded the recording in the drone bank's memory. All forty drones started blinking an amber light on their control panels.

"Continuous transmission?" a drone-tech asked them.

"Yes," Julia answered, "but the first launch will remain silent until it receives an activation code." She stepped forward as the tech stepped back and turned away, giving her the chance to enter a code without his seeing it.

She input the code she'd already agreed on with Paul, wishing she could add a personal message as well, but she didn't want to distract him during a crucial moment. It was enough for him to know she'd prepared this drone.

Ava reached up to her ear. "The last of my ships are through."

Julia looked up from the drone, stepping back so the technician could resume his work. "Let's launch the drones first. That'll let us go over the latest target data before you head out."

Going Viral

"**W**hat possesses a man to think short shorts are ok to begin with?" Oliver squawked through the speakers in Paul's helmet.

"C'mon, Ollie," Paul urged, "he's just expressing himself."

"It's putting me off my coffee," the Maegi groused. "I can't look left. The damned crack of doom is there, at the next table, waiting to scar my eyeballs."

"So, don't look left."

"Don't look left, he says. You're lucky you're not down here to see this."

Paul chuckled. Oliver was doing his best to entertain him. He'd been crammed under the same heat exchanger for the last two centi-days and his butt was starting to lose circulation.

An image suddenly flashed up on his HUD. "*Cai bu shi!*" he exclaimed. "I thought you were making it up." He closed the image but two more popped up. "C'mon, Ollie. Have pity on me."

"Alright, but you owe me the next coffee."

One image closed but then two more opened.

"*Wei*! You said you'd stop..."

"I said I'd have pity. I was gonna fill your screen with hundreds of close-ups..."

Paul suddenly grabbed a stanchion and pulled himself sideways slightly to get a better view through the fins of the exchanger. "Hang on! Knock it off, Ollie. I think I see the drone beacon."

The images cleared from his vision and Paul forced himself to not focus on any particular point in the star-field. After a moment, a series of faint flashes caught his attention.

"That's it alright. You ready down there?"

"All set, Paul. I just need the file."

Paul slid out from beneath the heat exchanger, took a quick look around the area for sentries and then braced his left arm against the side of the cooling fins, aiming in the general direction of the drone.

The reticle projected around the drone by his HUD turned green. "I have a secure link to the drone," Paul told Oliver. "I'm shutting down its beacon before it draws unwanted attention."

He'd download the message using a communications laser, built into the pad on the back of his forearm. Utilizing a variable-slit interferometer, the link was relatively secure from casual interception. The pattern of the data would simply collapse if an interloper used a method like beam-splitting.

The other drones, sent throughout the colony, would be transmitting in omnidirectional mode, spreading the word about what the Grays had done and how to cure it. This one drone would transmit to Paul only, allowing him to sneak the recorded message into the stations systems and from there, into every ship visiting the busy hub.

"That's all," Oliver announced. "We'll make use of the convenient back door the Grays left for us and just slip this in with the code we inserted earlier." The Maegi was silent for a few moments. "Ok, the nest is coded; we just need to upload the video file."

A progress bar showed up on Paul's HUD.

"Ollie, should we set a delay for the video?"

"A delay?"

"Well, yeah. Think about it. A real life virus that kills the host within a few milli-days tends to disappear pretty quickly because the host rarely lives long enough to pass it on. If this just pops up on ship-wide holo screens the moment it loads in, they'll drop everything they're doing and dig it out of their system."

"Huh."

Paul could almost see the man rest his chin against his right hand as he considered the problem. Meanwhile, he cracked the security protocols in the Traffic Control department and found the data he'd be needing.

"So..." Oliver must have paused for a sip. "... we'd need to know the average transit time of all ships departing Cerberus..."

"Three point nine days," Paul cut in.

"What? How the hells..." Another pause. This time it was probably for a bemused head shake. "Never mind. I'll set this to activate four days after installation."

"Better make that four days after *departure*, Ollie," Paul advised. "Remember, the average ship spends point eight days in the docking clamps and another point zero three waiting for a departure window."

"Again, not sure how you're getting your info, but I'm glad you caught that, Paul. Saved me from a major brain-fart, buddy. Damn near hot-boxed the whole deal."

"It's always the mundane details that unravel an otherwise ingenious plot," Paul told him. "I saw a treason plot come unraveled because the conspirators falsified maintenance records for a Marine unit but forgot about the third-party refurbishing companies."

"You followed the money trail, huh?" Oliver chuckled. "Cherchez les credits..."

"Speaking of credits, are you signing on with the armor project?" Paul would have kept quiet, but he'd learned Oliver did his best work while conversing.

"I might, but I'd only be able to help with the operating system, so I don't know how much of a contribution it would be. Sure, the system is bloated, but how bad can it be?"

"Ollie, I'd say that seventy percent of all fire-teams heading dirtside in a combat shuttle at any given moment will have at least one poor bastard wearing a *bag-n-burn* suit 'cause his HMA wouldn't boot up. The stuff the dragoons use is a little better but you still see them freeze up in combat. You need to be on that project. The colonies are going to need every edge we can get our hands on."

"I'll definitely give it some thought," Ollie told him. "We're gonna have to come up with a way to get it into the public eye as soon as possible so the demand is there when we start rolling suits off the droid rows."

"Sounds like you're in."

"And speaking of *in*," Ollie said, "it's time for you to drag your arse back down here. I'm all done with the video. Shall I order the usual?"

Smash and Grab

"**W**e have a fix on our position." The navigator updated the system and Ava's command holo changed from grey to orange, distant planets and asteroids appearing. "We're well within micro-jump range to Tel Khorgo."

"Very well," Captain Korolev acknowledged. "Lay in a course for the shipyards at Tel Khorgo and pass it through the fleet. If we have any navigational errors, I'd prefer we all make the same mistake together."

Ava approved. It was a standard Imperial practice that Ava had given little thought to in the past, but it certainly reduced the danger of having a ship drop out of distortion behind the rest of her fleet. One simple error could wipe out half her forces and, if it happened in front of the enemy, they could expect little in the way of mercy.

She watched as her ships slid into existence on the holo, appearing as though they were growing out of a flat plane in space. She shuddered. It was great having the captured wormhole generator at their disposal, but it was a two-edged sword. The Grays wouldn't have been stupid enough to keep the technical details on only one planet, would they?

The attack on Tel Ramh had set the Grays' program back severely, but how long would it take for them to start producing more ships with source-directed wormhole drives? This was going to be more than a messy border skirmish. The Grays had to be knocked on their bony little asses or Humans had to get their hands on the secrets of the drive on the *Sucker Punch*.

"Hail from the *Sucker Punch*. It's for the commodore."

"I'll take it here," Ava replied.

Julia appeared in front of her, life sized. "The last of your ships are through the wormhole, Commodore. Good hunting!"

"Thank you, General. We'll see you at the rendezvous." Ava cut the link and turned to Korolev. Formerly the chief engineer locked up by Captain Fall, he'd been elected to the captaincy of the *Burt Rutan*. As Ava had chosen the Gray cruiser formerly captained by Fall as her flagship, that made Korolev her flag captain.

"Captain, we'll jump in at your discretion."

Korolev nodded. "Aye, ma'am. We're just lining up the last ships now."

Nineteen ships would be jumping into the fight. Four were captured heavy cruisers like the *Burt*. Another seven were Gray frigates and the remaining eight were a mix of Human-built privateer ships of varying configuration. Most of them had been freighters before their conversion and they still had vast cargo spaces as well as quick load systems.

There would be no attempt at impersonating the Purists this time. The Quorum knew that group was no longer capable of an operation of this magnitude.

A chill ran down Ava's spine. Like all colonial citizens, she'd grown up in the shadow of the Gray Quorum. They were a technically advanced species that viewed Humans as little better than lab specimens. They'd have no qualms about wiping out every last Human if they deemed it to be in their interest and here she was, about to launch an overt attack on one of their major logistics centers.

There'd be no backing down from this; the ram was at the gates.

Perhaps in sympathy, the Universe shivered as well and her holo was repopulated with a view of Tel Khorgo. Several dozen stations ringed the planet in geosynchronous orbit, allowing each station to be replenished from the surface daily.

"Reading eight cruisers and seventeen frigates on the near side," the tactical officer announced, highlighting them on the tactical holo layer. "Only one cruiser and three frigates currently underway. Assess active ships as the planetary combat orbital patrol."

Ava checked her interface, confirming that all the ships could receive orders directly from her holo. She ordered an acceleration to attack speed, primary targets being the four active vessels. Their plan remained mostly intact for the moment. They'd focus fire on any ships that were currently underway and then continue on a high speed pass around the planet, destroying warships as they went.

She opened a separate window to the privateer ships.

Initial scans from the near side of the planet showed four very promising targets. The stations sprouted long lattices from every surface. They held cargo containers designed for quick loading into Gray freighters or easy docking with the warships they were intended to replenish.

She decided to detach one privateer to each station as they passed. They might not be as efficient with the alien containers, but the converted freighters would be able to use their load rails to fill their holds in short order. The captains already knew to prioritize the units with green ordnance glyphs as well as those with engineering red.

It was one thing to seize warships from the Grays, it was quite another to keep them supplied with parts and ammunition and they'd be going through a lot of both in the months to come.

"The COP is heading for us," Tactical announced. "Based on standard doctrine, I believe they'll try a micro-jump in the next milli-day. Come at us from the side."

"Very well," Ava acknowledged, reaching back into the display to change the selection of the first four privateers. "Changing the lineup for the first smash-and-grab," she advised. "We'll trade cargo capacity for guns by putting the *Walter Currie* in the group and taking the *Flower of Rotterdam* out. All four to begin their deceleration now and stand by to fire on the COP, if it appears on our flank."

She frowned at the display for a moment and then reached out to add one frigate to the smash-and-grab team – Robin Metzker's ship. They could use the extra firepower against the COP and it wouldn't hurt for them to have a little insurance while the rest of the fleet was travelling around the planet.

She hoped Metzker didn't just get elected captain because she'd been one of the two crewmen who'd rescued Paul and Julia from the Grays.

Her newest order icons went green as the five captains involved acknowledged.

"If they're going to jump us," Tactical warned, "their own template would suggest it'll happen any micro now."

"Understood," she replied. "We're going to speed up and turn for the secondary orbital insertion. Changing formation to arrowhead." She watched as the icons went green again. The main group was now pulling away from the first grab team but that would be very difficult for the enemy to see at this distance.

As would the course change.

"They've jumped!" Tactical declared. He updated his view to show the general area surrounding the two groups of

Human ships. "No sign of them. They're either running or they're doing a second jump to come at us from behind."

"Well, they're sure as hells not running from their assigned station," Korolev growled. "So they'll be up our backsides in less than a milli, or at least they'll be sitting where they *thought* our backsides would be..."

"There they are!" The tactical officer was gripping the sides of his console. "Just over a hundred klicks behind us – we're about twenty degrees outside of their firing envelope."

"But they're smack in the center of our five ship's envelope," Ava said, zooming in on the trace. The five Human ships fired on the cruiser first and the effect was devastating.

Hitting the Gray ship from behind, the rounds impacted on the engines and mechanical compartments. Power levels would be severely impacted throughout the ship and her weapons were all based on linear acceleration. Gray guns were devastating, but they were power hogs. After firing their current loadout, it was doubtful they'd be able to recharge even one capacitor bank for a main gun.

In fact, her chief engineer was likely trying to convince the captain to give that stored power back so they could use it to keep the systems running.

The frigate captain, assigned overall control of the small human group, must have come to the same conclusion because the second salvo now streaked toward one of the Gray frigates. She made a mental note to commend Metzker, if they both lived through this raid.

The second target took its medicine with even less grace. The smaller ship appeared to have completely lost her engines and one round even over-penetrated, coming out the bow without even vaporizing against any part of the ship.

The firing shifted to the next Gray frigate, but Ava suddenly realized that the firing rate, held in check by Metzker to gain the psychological effect of coordinated salvos, meant they wouldn't have time to hit the fourth frigate before it could open.

The enemy ships had begun turning quickly when they realized they'd missed their targets and that they now had hostiles aft of their position. It would certainly be too late for the first three ships, but that last Gray frigate was going to get a chance to shoot back.

Ava could hardly be angry with Metzker for something *she'd* only just noticed, but it was hard to watch nonetheless. It was far too late to send a warning. All she could do was hope for the best.

It wasn't as though the coordinated fire would only give psychological benefits – dubious against Grays – there was also the fact that it efficiently removed ships from the equation. Four damaged enemy ships could do more return damage than one undamaged ship.

The third Gray frigate withered under the focused fire and stopped turning to meet their threat.

That left one enemy ship and her bow was swinging to point directly at the primary threat, the Human frigate.

As Ava watched, the Gray frigate vomited a cloud of plasma as her mains fired. The rounds impacted almost immediately as the two forces were only a few kilometers apart. The front of Metzker's frigate was obscured by a cloud of debris and a large section of one of the engines was cartwheeling off into the void.

The privateers opened fire, scoring hits on the enemy's engines and imparting enough force to throw her off axis, her guns aiming off impotently into the blackness.

And that was where they parted ways. Ava sent the privateers a command to continue on to their assigned targets. They needed to complete their objectives quickly rather than hang around a debris field. She would have to organize a rescue attempt on their way out.

She released the remaining enemy stations and ships on the near side for gunnery and portioned them out to her ships to avoid wasting time on overlapping fire.

As soon as the icons began turning red, Korolev leaned forward slightly, eyes roving over the display like a kid in a candy store. "Tactical – weapons free. Mains on the cruisers and secondaries to concentrate on frigates."

They had two stations, three cruisers and six frigates to kill. The Grays would have been caught with their pants down, if they had any use for pants. As it was, the ships were all in various states of resupply. Several were even being worked on in open space docks and Ava was pleased to see the tactical team had put those vessels at the bottom of the priority list.

A soul-rending scream vibrated the decking as the two-hundred-kilo-slugs of depleted uranium went streaking down the gravity well of Tel Khorgo, trailing a brief flash of plasma. Two slugs were targeted to each of the first two cruisers.

"Time to impact?" Korolev kept his eyes glued to the holo display.

"Just over three milli-days, sir." The tactical officer looked back to the captain. "Next rounds will be up any moment now for the mains. Should we target the third cruiser?"

"Give her two and one each for the two stations."

Streaks of vapor slipped past the bridge windows. Even the Grays were unable to contain all of the cooling carbon dioxide in their weapons.

"Mains are pumped," Tactical declared. "Vacuum confirmed. Firing."

Again the shriek, and again Ava's bones rattled. She knew it was normal for these ships, but it still surprised her that the supposedly superior Gray engineering seemed so similar to its Human counterparts.

"Coming into the range for secondary guns," Tactical announced.

As if in agreement, the secondary batteries began to howl at each other like a graveyard filled with demented souls. Each fired as soon as its rails could be cooled, pumped and reloaded with the smaller ninety-kilo slugs. The sound was probably easily ignored by the Grays but it raised the hair on the back of Ava's neck.

"Three certain impacts on the first targets!" the sensor officer crowed. "Clean hits and multiple secondaries in the engineering sections. Looks like their magnetic fluid went up."

"Quiet on the bridge!" Korolev roared over the sound of cheering. "We've got a lot more shooting to do before we can call this a win. Our next targets might even be in the mood to shoot back, just to be friendly, so keep your minds on the job."

"Seeing hits on the frigates," the sensor officer declared, sounding more businesslike this time. "Two broken up entirely, and one looks to be venting atmo from several areas. The fourth hasn't..." He leaned in closer to his holo, squinting up at the image. "Correction on the fourth;

185

multiple hits now and the bow, as far back as the gunnery capacitor bank, has sheared clean off."

He opened his mouth to say something but stopped, making a distinct effort to master his reaction. "Impact from our mains on the third cruiser. One hit. Vaporized a ten meter hole, dorsal to ventral, just forward of the engineering spaces. I'd say she's probably a dead'un."

It was a quirk of Gray weapons design that the smaller rail systems could handle higher muzzle velocities. Once you closed to within range of the secondary batteries, the engagement was often over before another salvo from the mains could reach the target.

Ava reviewed the overall situation, silently chiding herself for focusing on Korolev's fight. Destruction of the remaining targets on this side of the planet seemed well in hand. She selected all of her ships and grouped them into seven teams of two each.

As the targets came into view over the horizon, they'd be assigned a group. She didn't want to miss a target because everyone had fired at a previous target and were too busy reloading their main guns.

It was easy enough to get colonial privateers to fire on an enemy, but getting them to stop firing and switch to something else could be an exercise in frustration. Far better to hold some in check, giving each their turn, but always having several ships ready to take on new targets.

She took another look at the icon for Metzker's frigate. It showed little information, but that didn't mean they were all dead. She'd have to figure out how to mount a rescue attempt on the way back, but it was going to be tricky, with the fleet moving in the opposite direction to the stricken warship.

Some might just cut the bullshit and call it impossible.

Grab and Run

"**N**o," Robin said calmly but firmly. There's no use having Damage Control working on the weapons if they can be used to help fix our drives. If we get them going, we're not staying around to fight; we're gonna show 'em our cute little asses and scamper."

"I don't have *any* teams working on the engines, Captain," Little, the chief engineer, told her. "That hit tore our port assembly clean off and smashed the entropy shunts. No way of getting underway short of a six-month stay in a good dockyard."

"So, there's nothing we can do except shoot at anything that happens to drift past our guns?"

"If we can even get them working," Little said dubiously. The forward ends of the mains are a mess. We'd have to cut..." He stopped talking as Metzker grabbed his arm and led him over to the main holo. He wasn't offended, just pragmatic enough to know when his boss was about to drop something batshit-crazy in his lap.

It was the kind of drinking story every engineer loved to tell but hated at the time.

"If we can't get our ship running," she said, pointing at the disabled Gray frigate, "how about that one?"

Little was shocked, but only for the briefest of moments. Then professional pride stepped in like a traffic cop and began marshalling his thoughts. "That last hit wasn't too severe," he allowed. "They should really be underway by now, but they aren't, which tells me they probably lost their coaxial stabilizers. If they had spares, they could fix that in a heartbeat."

He shook his head, lips drawn tight. "Dammit, Captain. They probably don't have the parts or, same thing again, they'd be turning their guns on us right now, assuming they're even aware we're still alive over here."

"Do *we*?"

"Ma'am?"

"Do *we* have the parts?"

Little shook his head.

"So our stabilizers were hit as well?"

"Captain," Little began, taking great care to avoid using the voice engineers often use when trying to explain technical matters to barely-educated combat officers, "they're intact but, if we pull them, we kill life support."

Sometimes you just had to point out the blatantly obvious.

Robin was having that same thought.

"Are you telling me that the enemy ship probably has no life support? That any living crew are bundled up in EVA suits, just waiting for us to come over and shoot them?"

"Well, I suppose..."

"Well then, that settles it." Robin gave him a satisfied nod. "Computer, ship-wide intercom."

She waited until the speakers overhead hissed into life. "All hands, this is Captain Metzker. Our ship is finished, so we're going to take the enemy frigate home instead. All personnel not needed by Chief Engineer Little to pull some equipment are to suit up and report to their assigned escape trunks. On my command, we will abandon ship and commence boarding operations."

She turned back to Little. "If we're not staying here, we don't need the stabilizers installed on this ship, right?"

His ears were slightly red as he chuckled. "Well, when you say it like that, it seems obvious!"

"Tactical," Robin shouted over the clamor of a bridge crew getting suited up for a pulse-raising adventure.

"Ma'am?"

"Put your best fighters on the command shuttle. I'll take them in through the ventral engineering trunk and secure the self-destruct. When I give you the all-clear, you take the rest of the crew over. Secure the bridge and then we'll come at the rest of the crew from both ends."

She was pleased to see that her orders had been taken seriously. When she arrived at the forward shuttle bay, her command shuttle was packed with troops. There was no room left to stand but she didn't really want to pull anyone off.

"Mosh pit!" one of them shouted and, before she could respond, they grabbed her and pulled her in above their heads. It may not have been the most dignified way for a captain to travel but, with your own ship dying and a fight to the death ahead of you, who had time to worry about prestige?

She nearly got wedged between shoulders when the shuttle exited the ship and banked hard to head for the target. With a little jostling, they managed to keep her aloft. The ten-kilometer trip went quickly and she thanked her luck that they'd been drifting closer together rather than farther apart. At the start the fight, she'd ordered a further deceleration for her small force so they'd have more time to fire on the enemy.

She frowned in the privacy of her helmet. That part had worked, but she wasn't certain she'd made the right decision in focusing fire on one target at a time. Intellectually, she knew there was no way to know if she'd been right or wrong, but she still had a hundred twenty three dead crewmen. Though the number may have been higher if she'd fired on all targets simultaneously, it offered little comfort.

She still had hundreds of people depending on her to make the right moves now. Even a half-assed or bad move, as Julia had once advised her, could mitigate a disaster. A commander who froze up and stopped making decisions was sure to get her people killed.

She looked up with relief as the overhead light, a few centimeters from her face, turned green – the Gray color of blood and warning. Time to go and she was fairly certain she was making the best decision out of a pretty limited set of otherwise terrible options.

The rear ramp opened, the frigate hull filling the entire view, and she was carefully handled out to float in front of her team. The ventral escape trunk was five meters away and she grabbed a rail at the top of the shuttle opening. With a light push she crossed the distance, catching one of the handrails around the trunk and flexing her arms to slow her body.

One foot hit the hull with a light thump but she doubted it could be heard inside an engineering space filled with machinery and frantic technicians. She waited as her advance boarding party crossed over. One of them held up a portable spot-welder and she gave him a thumbs-up while silently chastising herself for forgetting the need.

She waited till he moved next to her and then opened the outer hatch of the escape trunk. The hatch snapped out of the way, oddly silent given its violent speed.

The crew inside would probably have heard that. Time to abandon stealth in favor of speed.

Her crewman reached into the housing and put a temporary spot-weld on the door retaining clip. He pulled back immediately and Robin reached in to pull off the access plate inside the trunk. She yanked on the lever for the hydraulic bypass before pulling back out of the way.

She'd just caught a glimpse of the disappearing inner hatch and the rush of internal gasses or, rather, the dust kicked up by the gasses. She held onto a railing as the shimmering atmosphere vented past her and her team. Three Gray crewmen tumbled out the trunk in their EVA suits.

So Little must have been right. Life support was down, leaving only waste gasses inside. She fervently hoped that meant he'd be right about the repairs needed.

The force of the venting gas quickly abated and she yanked on the handle to pull her way inside, not wanting to let her men be the first to risk taking fire. She floated up into the chamber at an angle, seeing enemy crewmen – *crewclones?* – picking themselves up from the floor. She drew her sidearm but drifted into the grav effect of the deck plating and tumbled to the deck before she could pull her trigger.

The next man in rolled immediately to the side, having been drilled in this kind of work, and began firing on the enemy.

By the time the third security operator came in through the trunk, the chamber had been cleared.

Robin was already on her feet and raced to the center pedestal to pull the cable linking terminals throughout the ship to the self-destruct device. She fogged her visor with relief as she looked down at the thin red disconnected optical cable in her hand. If this had been installed on a

Human ship, the cable probably would have been replaced with a length of licorice a long time ago.

She was cold. There was no life support to heat this vented compartment and she'd been sweating profusely with the adrenaline rush of the initial boarding action. She ignored the discomfort, gladly accepting the cold over the searing heat that could have been unleashed.

"Tactical, this is the captain. All clear. I say again, all clear. Commence boarding operations."

She went to work on the self-destruct as her security team fanned out to clear the adjacent engineering spaces. She started with a calming breath. It was bad enough she was shivering from the cold. Being jumpy was the last thing she needed right now.

She jumped, nonetheless, as the amber circle around the cable housing suddenly started to blink in green. Someone on the bridge had just tried to blow the ship.

It had been pretty close, but to her adrenaline-fueled mind, it seemed like ages since she'd pulled that cable. She settled down to the task of deactivating the circular array of firing circuits, each one needing its power supply disconnected.

By the time she'd finished, the second wave of boarding teams were entering the ship. The security officer would be leading a large group to the bridge but there weren't enough shuttles for the whole crew. Several dozen escape pods would be docking with the pod portals on this ship.

Hundreds of armed crewmen would come swarming through the bottom hatches of the enemy escape pods and into the ship at multiple locations.

She stepped back from the nuke with a satisfied sigh. The ship was hers. The previous crew was now just a nuisance to be dealt with.

She saw motion and spun around, her pistol in her hand, though she didn't remember drawing it. Little's helmet protruded into the compartment from the escape trunk. "Permission to come aboard, Captain?" His voice sounded oddly distant through her helmet speakers, despite only being three meters away.

"Come on in," she waved him up. "You got the parts?"

"We'll know pretty soon," he replied carefully. He went over to a control panel on the port side of the compartment and hit a green button.

Robin resisted the impulse to jump back as the large floor hatch snapped open. It was all the more startling because the impact vibrated the deck plates and the soles of her boots, propagating the sound up through the air in her suit. She was growing accustomed to the silence of vacuum and the appearance of a sudden apparent drop through the hatch, accompanied by the startling noise, was a strain on her already heavily taxed nerves.

A hastily wrapped pallet of parts floated up through the opening, accompanied by the techs who'd remained behind with Little. The big square hatch was rammed shut again and they drifted gently to the floor, bouncing lightly before the grav-plates reached full output, holding them firmly down.

Another tech came in through the escape trunk, and it closed behind him. Robin distinctly heard a double impact through her suit and realized he'd cut the temporary weld on the safety clip.

"Well," Little's voice sounded in her helmet, "they needed the entropy shunt alright. We should be able to get her fixed in no time."

Robin turned to look for him, but he wasn't in sight. Knowing, from the fact that her proximity vox was picking up his musings, that he had to be within a limited range, she moved around the self-destruct pedestal and walked through the only open hatch in the compartment.

Her security chief reported that he'd secured the bridge. Confident that he had the fight well in hand, she decided to concentrate on finding out how soon they could get underway.

"*Bozhemoi!*" Little exclaimed. "You *Oblom* piece of *gavno!*"

Robin quickened her pace to find Little kicking angrily at a mounting pedestal in the middle of the compartment. It was covered in a slimy blue substance. Small fragments of clear glaz-casing slid down the sides of the structure, accelerated slightly with each kick.

"What's the problem?" Robin demanded.

The engineer turned to her as his technicians entered, carrying parts over to an alcove where a smashed glaz-case tube was sparking erratically from its now-exposed conduits. "This is a new problem," he told her grimly. "Long story short, this is, or was, an energy filter. Makes sure that power to the distortion drive is clean enough. Too many variables when you're trying to shift the Universe past your ship and BOOM!"

Robin was coming down off her adrenaline high by this point so she wasn't terribly startled by Little's outburst. "So, where does that leave us?"

"Well," Little glanced over at his techs just as a new sound began humming beneath the deck. "It leaves us in the middle of a junkyard. Might be we could find the right parts, seeing as the dead ships are all the same model as ours. And there's a spot of good news as well..."

He looked down at his wrist pad as a chime sounded in their helmets. A good news type of chime. He pulled off his helmet.

Robin started to look at her pad but turned the motion into a reach for her own helmet release. If Little wasn't grabbing his throat in panic, the chime obviously meant the oxygen levels had stabilized.

"Told you we'd get that repair done in no time," he reminded her cheerfully. "Now we've got life support as well as theoretical power for the mains; we just need to scrub the power if we want to use 'em."

"You said you have good news..."

"Oh yeah." Little grinned. "Bad news is we have to go search the wreckage for a new scrubber, but the good news is we only have two ships to search before we find out if we're still humped or not."

Robin took another calming breath. "You know, that just sounds like you're trying to stuff bad news into a mini-skirt."

"Did I mention we can use the pitch drives?"

"Really? Hells, why didn't you say so? Now we can limp back to the rendezvous in eighteen months or so. Maybe even pull the grav plating and make a big old-fashioned gravity sail like the first colonists used to have..."

Little's eyes lit up. "Now that'd be fun! We could just use the..." He stopped as Robin waved him off.

"Right, right," he conceded. "Work first, play later. If you can get somebody up in the bridge to move us closer to one of the frigates, I'll get a team together to do a little browsing."

Just Smash

"That's a big one," the sensor officer declared. "More than enough containers down there that we'd have to run this raid five or six times just to clean em out."

"Sending our last three freighters in." Ava acknowledged, updating the holo command lists. There was no sense in spreading the converted privateers if they could fill their holds at one station. It would also give them an added measure of security if enemy ships happened to show up.

They'd been lucky so far, but it was a luck of their own manufacture. This sector hadn't seen much fighting in the 'Purist' conflict. Most of the vessels were freighters, bringing containers to the stations where they were consolidated and re-loaded onto other freighters and taken to their ultimate destination.

Some warships were being replenished or refitted here, but Tel Khorgo was mainly a massive distribution center. It had been chosen as a target because it would be lightly defended and rich in valuable goods that, if denied to the enemy, would damage their ability to project force into Human-held territory.

With the last freighters assigned to shopping duty, the raid became a simple matter of shooting anything they laid eyes on. It took very little to destroy a station. The fleet was orbiting in the opposite direction of the stations and the rounds fired were imparting an incredible amount of kinetic energy.

Aside from the actual damage done by the impacts, the stations as well as the cargo and docked vessels were fatally slowed to a point where they were no longer balancing the force of the planet's gravity. The cargo containers mostly broke free of their moorings or entire lattices snapped free of the station, but they'd still been slowed enough in the process to fall into the grip of Tel Khorgo.

"Next station coming over the horizon," Sensor announced. "Sweet zombie Stalin, this facility has more than five times the cargo of that last one."

Ava fought a momentary sense that she'd missed an opportunity, shoving it aside as she remembered that the last station had more than enough cargo to fill her privateer ship's holds. "This raid just keeps getting better and better," she said, just loudly enough for the entire bridge to hear.

"I'll say," Korolev affirmed. "We're already leaving with full holds and we *still* get to destroy several more times that in Gray supplies."

Ava nodded, glad to see he'd caught her point. "The next best thing to stealing something from the enemy is ensuring he doesn't get to use it himself."

"Contact!" Tactical announced. "Three frigates coming up from the surface. Still at very low velocity."

Ava activated a group icon. "Captain Korolev, they're all yours."

Korolev shot her a nod of thanks. "Aye, ma'am. Helm, slave to fire control. Let's get our mains pointed down there before Higgins can swing that slovenly bucket of his around. I've got a bottle of Stoli that says we can take the first target."

Their ship continued along with the formation, but she and the second ship in her temporary grouping rotated to aim down into Tel Khorgo's atmosphere. Teams on both ships were working frantically to be first to fire.

"Loading black hats," Tactical advised. The carbon-matrix coating on the 'black hat' ammunition were needed if you wanted to fire on an intra-atmospheric target and have anything solid left for impact.

So far, the raid was going well, but Ava couldn't help but wonder about the frigate she'd had to leave on the way in. It would be another couple of centidays before they could swing back around and try to make contact.

In a damaged ship, two hundredths of a day could be an eternity.

Or an introduction to eternity...

A Break Can't Be Caught

"Thank the gods," Little heard one of his techs exclaim. "Their scrubbers are intact."

That was a bit of good news for a change, and on the first ship they'd checked. Little drifted into the central compartment to find three of his team working to detach the units. "Good," he said, turning back toward the hole they'd come in through. "I'll go out where I can get a clear shot – let the captain know the good news.

They were using laser comms, unsure of what surprises may be lurking in the wreckage. No sense letting them pick up radio transmissions and learning that revenge might be a possibility.

Before he reached the hole in the hull, a brilliant flash shone through it, casting harsh shadows inside the compartment. Then another, and another, and another.

"*Bozhemoi!*" Little glided toward the opening and peeked through a tear in its side. Four cruisers. They must have just arrived for supplies. The Grays would never dispatch four cruisers to fight a force like Commodore Klum had brought here. They'd be hopelessly outgunned.

Their own recently acquired ship, however, was in far more danger. If the new arrivals stopped to investigate the debris field they'd just dropped in next to, things would get very interesting.

"Come on," he whispered to the Gray ships. "Worry about the stations in orbit. They're your priority. Ain't nothing here but dead Grays."

The four human ships left to grab cargo on this side of Tel Khorgo had already moved off, having fired enough rounds to destroy the stations and knock them out of orbit.

A lot of those stations wouldn't have started burning up yet and rescuing the crews might just give the newly arrived enemy ships a sense of urgency.

The sight of the nearest cruiser filled his visor and he felt a shiver of fear, but she continued her silent progress toward Tel Khorgo. He glanced over at his own ship. Metzker knew her business. She'd be keeping the crew out of trouble until this was over.

He looked back. One cruiser was turning their way. Little turned and moved toward the aft passageway, seeing his team approaching with the scrubbers.

It was enough to make you cry. They had what they needed to pull off a heroic self-rescue and, yet, it was starting to look like they were going to get a 200-kg enema after all. He held up a warning hand, motioning for them to wait there, and, waving his hand palm down, aimed at his own mouth in the standard 'shut your pieholes' gesture. He moved back to the hole.

The cruiser was coming closer and Little was racking his brain, comparing his damage assessments for the frigate they'd seized as well as the one he was currently floating in. Limited propulsion in their new ship, two mains damaged but the other two still in good working order. Metzker would have those loaded right now but she'd have to swing the ship around to bring them to bear.

The ship they were salvaging parts from might have had one gun in working order, but it would take far too long to get his team down there and there weren't enough men to work the weapon and run the targeting solutions.

An absolutely useless waste of time and energy, and he was just turning around to issue orders to get his team started on it when his eyes fell on the self-destruct terminal.

"Karkada, MacAdam, get to work disconnecting that self-destruct. We might need it soon."

Little drifted over to the damage control locker and pulled out a pair of comm-links. He stared down at them, wondering if their range was enough. He grabbed a third and moved over to the pedestal.

He might be able to do something about the cruiser coming his way, but the other three would turn back and he had no clever plan for that. He shrugged. You rarely fix a big hairy problem all at once. Start with what you can deal with and go from there.

Fate

"The rest of our fleet should be coming around the edge of the planet, ma'am," Tactical advised. "Any milli now."

Robin was fighting back a wave of panic that threatened to completely swamp her and the interruption came at just the right moment. "Very well," she replied. "We'll have to hope we can have their help with some of our new guests." She almost didn't believe those calm words had come from her own mouth, but she knew there were problems she could do something about and others that were beyond her control for the moment.

They were currently alone. The other captains had been given very specific orders not to stop until the objectives had been achieved. Any rescue would have to wait until after the fleet returned from the far side of the planet and she wasn't content sit idle in the meantime – not when there were other options.

The cruiser was coming in very close to the debris field. Perhaps it was going to search for survivors. She knew they'd find the Humans on this frigate soon enough. "Helm, slave to Tactical."

"Helm slaving to Tactical, aye, ma'am."

"Tactical, we don't move till we have to. If they just run a scan and then move on, that's just fine by me. Our priority is to get our crew back to the RV." Robin waited until the tactical officer turned to look back at her. "Hold firing till I give the word, then we open with the secondary batteries. The shield generators on those bastards are always shifting the seams so I want them found before you use up the two rounds we have loaded in the main guns."

"Aye, ma'am," he replied, "fire on your order only, secondaries first to identify the seams."

She looked back to the tactical holo. That cruiser was damned close now. It just wasn't fair, but then combat never was. They'd managed to steal a chance by taking this ship and there was at least a fifty-percent chance that Little had his hands on some workable scrubbers by now. All they wanted to do was drag this busted-ass frigate back to the rendezvous point.

And then this fully functional cruiser had to stick its nose into their business.

Her eyebrows shot up. "*Wo de tian a!*" It was almost close enough for her to consider carrying the cruiser by boarding. Wouldn't that be a hell of a story? Just like General Urbica's taking of the *Sucker Punch* after taking and abandoning a Gray cruiser in Irricanan orbit.

Or how Urbica and Grimm had seized a Gray cruiser only hours after Robin had found them locked up on another Gray ship.

She looked around her bridge, wondering if it might be a good idea to trade up again. It would mean fighting only three cruisers instead of four.

And a cruiser did have bigger main armaments...

FUBAR

"Hold it ready," Little ordered. "One hand on the edge of the hole, the other on the nuke."

Karkada and MacAdam floated into position, the nuclear device held as far inside the compartment as they could. The reflection of the enemy hull filled their visors as the cruiser drifted past them.

They would still have three enemy ships to deal with, but nuking the closest one should help preserve the one tactical advantage his own ship still retained. The enemy had no idea that one of the damaged frigates was in Human hands. They might be able to get off a devastating surprise hit against one of those cruisers, but it would only be a surprise the first time.

After that, it would be one damaged frigate against three cruisers. He shrugged. That was Captain Metzker's problem. He'd give his captain the best situation he could engineer; the rest was up to her.

The ship appeared deceptively close. Little knew he had to resist the urge to 'eyeball' it. Like some cartoon character running out of momentum halfway through jumping a canyon, he didn't want the weapon to intersect the ship's path after the vessel had passed.

He wanted it to go off as close to the engineering spaces as possible. Given her low velocity, now that she was inside the debris field, the time to throw the nuke was...

"Now!" he ordered quietly but with unmistakable urgency.

Karkada and MacAdam heaved, almost in unison, and the self-destruct device went tumbling toward the enemy's shields.

Little pushed off with his left foot and drifted over to them. Karkada grabbed his suit to position him in the middle of the hole. With one hand clutching the comm-link that was holding the weapon's firing circuit open, Little wasn't keen on trying to grab anything. Reflex might kick in and ruin his clever scheme.

"Thanks, Vik." Little watched the nuke grow smaller. He had no way of knowing the range of the comm-links in open space, but he knew it wouldn't reach as far as the cruiser. This time, he *was* eyeballing it, and he'd better get it right. He pulled a second comm-link from a utility pouch at his waist and handed it to Karkada.

The two techs pulled him out the hole in the hull and stood on the outer hull using the mag-plates in their boots. It was indecorous and they were loving every minute of it. With a second heave, they sent their chief hurtling toward their new ship before pushing off behind him. Two other techs had already reached the ship and were working at installing the scrubbers.

"That should be close to halfway, Vik," Little advised. He watched on his HUD as the comm-link icon separated from Karkada, creating a link in the chain that would extend the reach of their emergency communicators. Little would rather have sent all of his men on ahead, just in case the links didn't have enough range, but he didn't trust himself to keep the trigger pressed on the dead-man's switch he'd rigged to the link while jumping off.

He passed through the shielding and concentrated on trying to grab on without forgetting the dead-man's switch. He'd considered a simple press-to-detonate scheme but preferred the absolute certainty of detonation afforded by the dead-man. He got his left hand onto a tie-off railing a heartbeat before the rest of his body slammed into the hull with all of the force imparted to him by his two techs.

The air was forced out of his lungs and, when the ducts finally cleared the fog from his visor he looked back at the enemy ship in alarm. "*Chto za huy?*" he yelled. "What are you fools doing? I go to all this trouble to buy us an advantage and it's for nothing?"

He watched, mind racing through the variables with furious speed as the slow-moving nuke passed the enemy shield and bounced slowly aft along its hull, grabbed here and there by the lateral bleed from the grav-plates in the ship's decking. He looked down at the link in his hand as the blue shield shimmer announced the safe arrival of Karkada and MacAdam.

"*Polnyi pizdets!*" he muttered. The best shot was probably to go for it and try to pre-empt what his crewmates were doing. He let go of the trigger.

The Cavalry

"The other three are still coming our way," Tactical advised. "Tango charlie one still investigating the debris field. Metzker's ship is swinging around to bear on them as slowly as they can without looking like it's on purpose."

Ava dismissed the urge to hail Metzker. An approaching enemy force made a good distraction for those four cruisers but, if that force suddenly started trying to make contact with someone in the debris field... "Very well," she replied. "Focus fire on tango charlie three."

They'd come here expecting combat losses. That was the nature of the game they were playing, but they'd gotten lucky. Most of the enemy warships had been caught in the middle of replenishing. It was an ironic weakness, the efficient nature of Gray logistics. Few ships were waiting their turn in orbit with alert crews.

She'd begun to hope that the single frigate would be her only loss and she'd still held out hope of rescuing some of the crew.

Now it looked like they'd take a few more lumps after all. She'd have simply ordered a jump out of the system, if not for her crippled frigate crew. If only there was a way to know for sure whether they were alive or dead.

"Targeting solution active and disseminated to the fleet," Tactical announced. "First target is tango charlie three. Fleet will switch focus to tango charlie two on our signal. Maximum effective envelope in one-six millis."

"Helm..." Ava began.

"Lords 'amighty!" Tactical exclaimed as an orange haze doubled the size of the icon representing tango charlie one. "Looks like a nuke went off inside their shield."

"Stay on target," Ava ordered. "We're still starting with tango charlie three."

Job Satisfaction

Little's visor darkened as the cruiser suddenly disappeared behind a brilliant, shield-contained glow. The glowing shape was roughly twice the volume of the ship and almost the same form. Sheets of violent energy escaped along some of the weaker seams where the shields met.

The engineer knew that tendrils of destruction were also worming their way into the ship, killing crewmen and shattering bulkheads. He flinched as one of those tendrils reached an aft shield generator and vaporized it. The force was released, propelling the quickly disintegrating forward half of the vessel, still shielded for the moment.

It raced past the frigate he clung to, smashing into the one they'd been forced to abandon. He reflected that it would have been nice if the damn thing could have crashed into one of its other companions, but you can't have everything.

At least it had missed *this* ship.

He started pulling his way over to the nearest escape trunk.

Fighting Chance

"**W**hat the hells?" The tactical officer, to his credit, began re-targeting the main guns before Robin could even voice the order, despite the sudden and dramatic destruction of his original prey. The ship had swung almost all the way around to face the incoming cruiser. Now it began swinging back toward the other three enemy ships.

"Fire on the next closest vessel," Robin ordered, just to be sure they were on the same page. "And we can thank our chief engineer for preserving our element of surprise for a precious few seconds." She sincerely hoped he'd made it back before the explosion because the wreck he'd been scrounging in had been torn apart by the blast.

At least two of his techs were back aboard, installing the scrubbers.

Still, it looked like they'd finish sometime after they lost this fight, so running wasn't going to be an option. She was about to give the order to open fire when the sensor officer interrupted.

"Fleet is coming back our way," the tactical officer announced. "The three enemy cruisers are turning to meet them."

"We hold fire," Robin ordered, frowning at her tactical officer. He was staring intently at the holo, his finger hovering above the fire control panel. "You hear me, Mister Merton? We hold fire till the moment is right."

Merton looked back to Robin, breathing rapidly, the understanding slowly working its way across his features. He jerked his hand away from the panel. "Understood, ma'am. Holding fire."

Robin didn't want to simply shoot at the enemy and do as much damage as she could before her ship was destroyed. She wanted to wait until the enemy were committed to another target, the Human fleet in this case, before adding her own contribution. It also might just give the engineering techs enough time to get the distortion drive running again.

She opened the damage control channel. "Comms are still offline?"

"Yes, ma'am," Little's voice replied, "but we'll have that fixed in a few micros. Distortion is almost ready to go as well. Another couple of millis and we'll be ready to jump, though we might still explode a little bit..."

Robin grinned. "Little, you magnificent bastard! The whole crew's gonna get you roaring drunk when we get back!"

She closed the channel. Ordinarily, she'd wait until they were out of danger before patting anybody on the back but she thought it might help morale for the bridge crew to hear that some things, at least, were going well.

"Our fleet is firing their first long-range shots," Tactical advised. "Looks like they're focusing on the ship nearest them."

"Good," Robin walked over to the tactical station, stopping where the operator and his officer could both see her.

"I want you to concentrate on the other two," she told them, reaching up into their holo display as she spoke. She activated the two icons. "Port secondaries open up on this one, starboard on this one."

She looked at both, waiting for the nods. "Find the shield seams and put one main round into each. They'll be drawing power from the aft shields to reinforce forward. With that many contacts coming at them, they'll barely have anything at the rear."

"We'll have to be very quick," the tactical officer advised. "If we take too long firing on the seams, the enemy'll have enough time to shift power back to the aft sections."

She nodded. "So fire as fast as you can. Do we have enough traverse in those two mains to hit both targets at once from here?"

Tactical shook his head. "At this distance, we'll have to rotate the ship and use the elevation and depression instead. The *yuben* Grays keep on putting shuttle bays right in the middle of the bow. Cuts eight degrees from traverse toward the centerline."

"Very well. Helm is still under your control. Put us in firing position and find those shield seams." She started back for her own station. "Crack em open, gentlemen. Let's beat 'em like rented mules." She had no idea what a 'mule' might be. It was just another archaic word from the mists of time, but it sounded good, for the crew's sake.

The ships showing in her holo began rotating as the frigate moved into a firing position that would let her shoot at both assigned targets simultaneously. Though the main guns were limited in their side-to-side traverse by the shuttle bay, they could elevate and depress more than enough to put the two targets in their firing envelope.

"Firing," Tactical stated calmly.

The mournful howl still made the small hairs on her neck stand up, but it felt good to be firing at the enemy. She enlarged the view of the two closest ships just as the deeper wail of the main guns vibrated her feet.

The wait was relatively short, given how close the targets were. At roughly fifteen kilometers, the rounds arrived on target in roughly the time it would take to say the word 'kilometer'.

The target to starboard had a relatively weak section of shield seam and the round penetrated easily, smashing its way into the heat exhaust from one of the pitch drives. The round, now converted into an ignited vapor, must have struck the magnetic shielding for the main distortion drive because it was channeled out the side of the vessel's hull, preventing any further damage.

The ship's thrust was thrown out of balance with the loss of the engine and she veered toward the other targeted cruiser, just regaining control in time to avoid a collision.

The round targeting the ship to port failed to penetrate the shields but, with weakened power to the aft shields, the grip that the energy fields had at their overlaps became weaker. Rather than dissipating the force of the impact over the entire shield, a jagged orange pattern showed where slippage occurred in the protective fields.

The slippage was too much and two of the aft shield generators were torn loose from their mountings, crashing through bulkheads, severing conduits and, of course, failing to emit their shields anymore.

The secondary batteries kept up their fire, now tearing into the cruiser's stern with ruthless brutality. The smaller rounds had less penetration and kinetic energy, but they chewed away at the ship like a swarm of carno-bats.

"Portside target, now the ventral target, has lost propulsion and shields," the tactical officer declared. "She's coasting but she can probably still fire her weapons. Starboard target, now the dorsal target, is underway but at reduced velocity. Venting atmo in the area of the starboard pitch drive compartment. Assess as still combat capable and the greater threat."

"Very well," Robin replied coolly. She realized she should've insisted on having Tactical give proper target designations at the start of the engagement. Even with three enemy targets, it was becoming unwieldy. "Focus on dorsal target first, then we'll..."

"She's coming around!" Tactical interrupted. "Firing on her flank. I think we'll find... Bingo! A big gap in her shields over that hole we made. Firing the mains..."

The shriek rattled her bones again and two heavy slugs sliced into the hole in the Gray cruiser at fifteen times the speed of sound. An orange flash showed on the far side and a small cloud of debris began appearing from behind the ship.

"Overmatched!" Tactical warned, his lips drawn back to show his teeth. "Both rounds went nearly all the way through before vaporizing. The real damage is coming from our secondaries."

"Understood." Robin could see from the holo that the secondary batteries were now making a scrapyard of both ships. Getting them from behind, while they focused on a Human force to their front, had been what she would describe as an incredible stroke of luck.

It didn't occur to her that she'd manufactured that luck by ordering Tactical to hold fire and wait for the right moment.

"As soon as we get the mains reloaded, let's save 'em for the third ship," she ordered.

"Aye, ma'am." The tactical officer nodded, his eyes alight with the thrill of not being dead.

"Distortion alert!" The tactical operator called out. "The last target is spooling up her jump drive!"

"Quiet on the bridge," Robin shouted. Maybe she was just caught in the adrenaline of combat, but she didn't want that ship getting away. It was just one more ship to fight later and they had her stern.

There was no better place to be. The enemy's mains were in her bows and the engines took up most of the aft sections. Critical target plus minimal defenses.

The other two cruisers – she really had to enforce proper target designation protocols – were drifting hulks, barely keeping their crews alive. "Bring us around. Target all gunnery on that last cruiser. I'd rather destroy her now, while we're behind her, than a month from now in a head-to-head engagement."

In That Case, Never Mind

"**L**ooks like tango charlie three is going to jump before our rounds impact." The tactical officer raised an eyebrow. "Captain Metzker is turning her ship to fire on them. At least, I'm assuming that's her and not a ship crewed by extremely confused Grays."

It had to be her. Ava had been worrying about how to rescue them on their way out of the system and here they were, plastering four cruisers with a damaged, captured frigate. From the rate of fire, it looked like two of their four main guns were out of service and, yet, they'd seen an opportunity and they'd jumped on it like a pack of wolves.

No need to worry about giving their position away by contacting them. The Grays certainly knew they had a hostile ship behind them. "Hail that frigate."

"Commodore," Metzker's voice crackled from the bridge speakers, "we thought you might need a hand with these cruisers." The moan of the captured ship's main guns increased the background static for a moment. "Crippling hit," Metzker said approvingly. "Good shooting, Tactical."

The casual cheek of her opening comment had brought a surprised laugh from Ava and her crew.

"They've disabled tango charlie three," Tactical confirmed. He glanced back at Ava, shaking his head in bemused admiration.

"It's good to see you've managed to find a working ship, Captain. How badly damaged are you?"

"Ma'am, we've scrounged enough parts from the other ships to get this one operational. We should have clean power for the jump any moment now." A static filled chuckle filled the pause. "If we're wrong about the power, we sure won't care about it for very long."

"Do you need assistance?" Ava turned to open an inventory screen. "We might have parts."

"No need, Commodore. We have the parts. It's more a question of what else might have taken damage that we can't diagnose in the time available. My chief engineer assures me that the probability of a successful jump is in the high nineties, which is a hell of an improvement over our original situation.

"The chances of you running into trouble if you stop to take us all off is much higher, so we'll take our chances on the *Brawler*."

Ava grinned, though Metzker couldn't see it. "An appropriate name for your new ship, Captain."

"Thank-you, ma'am. We'll just mop up here before jumping. Metzker out."

Loose Ends

"So we're the *Brawler* now?" the tactical officer asked with a chuckle. "It'll still have to pass a vote with the crew, but I don't see any problems there."

It was standard privateer procedure. The captain nominated senior officers as well as ship names. If the crew didn't like the choices, then she had to keep coming up with alternatives until one of them got approval.

"Captain, Little here." The engineer's voice sounded a little clearer. He must have a damage control team working on the comms system.

"Go ahead, Little."

"Scrubbers are installed. We're ready to jump."

"Thank you, Little. Standby, we have a few loose ends to tie up here first." Robin turned to Tactical. "Their shields are a mess, load HE and fire at will."

"Loading HE, aye, ma'am."

The three remaining enemy cruisers had large shield gaps and deep holes in their structures. At this point, even the secondary batteries would start to overmatch with kinetic rounds, passing straight through the ship with minimal vaporization. The high explosive rounds had been designed for just this purpose.

The first rounds started chewing into the cruisers. They penetrated a bulkhead or two before the outer shell deformed enough to activate the detonators. The ten-kilogram charges converted to gas with incredible energy in the enclosed spaces, turning bulkheads and stanchions into projectiles.

The spherical area of destruction was far more effective than the relatively linear path of damage created by the kinetic rounds, but they needed their kinetic cousins to 'open the door' for them.

"First two are scrap," the tactical officer judged. "Taking fire from the secondaries on that last one but not for long…"

The remaining enemy ship came into the firing envelope as the *Brawler* finished her turn. Two plumes of plasma accompanied the thrilling howl of the main guns, one shortly after the other. Robin was surprised at how quickly she'd grown to like that noise. This had been her first fight from the captain's station. Her other fights had been from the helm and she'd never liked the sound of the guns.

Now that they represented an extension of her own will…

"Good hits!' Tactical exclaimed.

The first hit impacted the already failing shield and tore one of its generators loose. Not having a firm, overlapping grip with the other shield segments, the generator's mounts took the full force of the detonation, rather than sharing it equally with the mounts of all the ship's shield generators.

The loose generator would have tumbled through the ships bulkheads, causing even further damage, but it wouldn't make much difference at this point because the second round detonated its one-hundred-fifty-kilo charge at a point near the vessels centerline. Large sections of hull were blown off, taking their shield emitter nodes with them. Critical connections throughout the ship were severed by the force and debris of the explosion, cutting all controls and isolating the engines from the cooling plants.

"Reading a heat buildup," Tactical announced. "Their engines are about to go critical."

"Helm," Robin called out, "line us up and jump when ready."

She should say something to the crew. She looked at her holo and realized she might not get a chance later. The *Brawler* was almost aligned for her jump and the jury was still out on the state of her propulsion systems. Small though the chance of catastrophic failure might be, she didn't want to die without congratulating the crew.

"Comm, open channel – ship-wide address."

"Ship-wide channel open and ready, ma'am."

"*Brawlers*, this is the Captain." She liked the name, so she might as well tie it to the victory they'd just won. It would make the eventual vote on the name more likely to swing in her favor. "Considering that this isn't the same ship we brought to the fight and that we managed to get the drop on four enemy cruisers, I'd say we all did a hell of a job today.

"Chief Engineer Little and his away-team managed to destroy one of those cruisers with nothing but some ingenuity, a few wrenches and an insignificant little nuke!" She paused to let the inevitable laughter run its course.

"Their quick thinking gave us the opportunity to lay low for a few crucial moments and strike the enemy once they were committed to another fight. If you see one of them planetside, buy them a drink."

Cheers rang through the hull.

She felt a shimmer run through the Universe, something most people never sensed but a small minority were able to feel. The tension began draining from her shoulders. "And now that we've jumped, I can safely say that we're going home! Well done, *Brawlers*!"

She worked her way around the bridge, shaking hands, punching shoulders and slapping backs. There was another hour till they dropped out at the rendezvous point, then a thirty hour hop to their next attack.

She wanted nothing more than to return to her quarters, take a shower and crash. She frowned, stifling a curse.

Her quarters, her clothes, the modular shower unit they'd been installing in captured frigates – they were all on the frigate they'd left behind. She looked down at the coveralls she was wearing. Her only clothing.

This would take them out of the fight. The usual retrofits that made the Gray ships usable were more than just comforts. The shower modules, the laundry facilities, food service – they were necessary for the health of the crew.

She looked over to an officer leaning over the damage control panel, racking her brain for the name. He was senior enough and he was here. "Leong, go to the captain's cabin for now and rack out. I'll send for you to come take the conn once we've jumped from the RV point."

She didn't want to be half asleep while explaining the situation to the commodore. She could hang on long enough to talk to Klum and then get the ship underway for Roanoke. A huge yawn escaped.

She was pretty sure she could stay awake.

Fighting Chance

"**We**'ll be there in a centi," Daffyd assured Paul. "Get your shuttle moving as soon as you can."

Paul closed the channel and stood from where he'd been crouched in the shadow of a transmission array. As long as you stayed on the right side of the thing, you wouldn't get fried. He started back toward the berth where his shuttle was still docked. Oliver was already aboard. No need to go back in the station, just get permission to break umbilicals and get moving.

He was thinking about his pending departure from Cerberus as he rounded the corner of something large and grey only to find himself face-to-face with a Marine sentry in HMA.

This was bad. Paul might be fast, but the Marine had been carrying his weapon in his hands like any self-respecting Marine on hull sentry duty. That weapon was now aimed at Paul's center of mass.

"Oliver, I've got a problem out here," he warned. "A sentry has the drop on me."

"Just walk away – you're wearing that fancy dragoon armor."

"Not your best advice ever, Ollie. He's a Marine. His weapon stands a good chance of firing through my armor. Better than good, actually."

Nonetheless, it was a good thing the dragoons had outfitted their favorite cop with a suit. A chime sounded in Paul's helmet. The sentry was pinging him with a comms request. He accepted the link.

"You're not from around here, are you?" The Marine's tone made it more statement than question.

"I'm from the Eye."

"You're from the... *cai bu shi*? The Eye?" His weapon didn't falter. "How do I know you're not using that dragoon armor to play me for a fool?"

Paul had caught a note of hope in the man's skepticism. He might just be looking for a way out of his current situation. He activated his transponder. "Read me," he said simply.

There was a pause as the Marine picked up Paul's signal.

"*Wo de ma!*" the sentry exclaimed. "It's you!"

Paul was used to being recognized as the man who'd executed Seneca on the podium of the Grand Chamber but this was something else.

"You could probably fake a transponder," the man hedged, "but if you are who you claim to be, then you'll know why I'd let you live. You met my brother-in-law a while back – Harry Clark."

Paul's CPU kept track of that sort of stuff for him, but he didn't need it to remember Harry Clark, Lance Corporal, 538 MEF. He nodded, the gesture visible through the visor. "Yeah, I met Harry. He helped us out by not detonating the nuke meant to destroy the factory ship on Santa Clara."

The Marine lowered his weapon a fraction. "There was a compelling reason behind Harry babysitting that nuke."

"His daughter," Paul confirmed. "Kinsey was holding the girl somewhere to ensure Harry didn't lose his nerve at the last moment."

"That's right," the Marine said, "and you got her out. Never even promised Harry you'd do that, but you found her and got her back to my sister. After they made an example of Harry, I told Eve I'd try to take up a collection, keep her and little Emma from going into indentured servitude. Y'know what she told me?"

Paul shrugged, though he knew what was coming.

"She said some fancy-ass knight had come to her place. Told her how her man had given his life to save the Imperium and that a hero's widow shouldn't have to live in poverty." He paused for a moment, his weapon returned to cradle in his left arm.

"She's set up with a nice apartment with six-foot ceilings, her own little shop down on the main floor and little Emma's getting a proper education. D'you know what I think, Inspector?"

"What?"

"I think I'm looking at that same knight. Your senator friend got you made an equestrian, and they say you're rich as Roland himself..."

Paul laughed. "I *was* rich," he corrected, "but that was in the Imperium and I don't plan to go back. I might be rich again someday, though. We've got a few ideas that might take hold out this way."

He nodded over his shoulder. "Why not come with us?"

"Hah! Like you'd be keen on somebody from the 538 tagging along. You'd be nuts to trust us."

"We've already got a few of your boys that've seen the light," Paul told him. "Armstead and Rodrigues joined us on Roanoke and they were holding my niece hostage. If I could trust them, I'd sure as hells have more reason to trust you, wouldn't I?"

The heavily armored shoulders shrugged. "Well, I sure as hells have good reason to want to throw my lot in with you, after what you did for my sister."

"Well, we've got a rendezvous to make," Paul turned and started walking. "Let's go."

He could feel the heavy feet hitting the decking behind him and he added the man's link to the channel with Oliver. "We're all good out here, Ollie. A new recruit's joining us from the Imperial Marines."

He used the IFF code to bring up the man's data from the records he'd used to stop Seneca's plot. "Private Sean Orlowski, meet Oliver – no last name, apparently – a Maegi who's been helping us clear up a lot of trouble with the Grays."

"A Maegi?" Orlowski exclaimed. "I thought they were just a fairy tale folks on the Rim told their kids."

"Welcome to the land of legends," Oliver quipped. "I've got clearance, Paul, so as soon as you boys are aboard we can cast off."

"Suits me just fine," Orlwoski said cheerfully. "The sooner I get away from that *goucaode hundan* Kinsey the better."

Paul turned and waited for Orlowski to stop. "Are you saying he's actually *here*?"

"Better part of a year. Why?"

Paul could think of a dozen questions he'd like to ask, all at once, but he'd rather do it without helmets and commlinks getting in the way. He turned and resumed his progress toward the dock where Oliver waited.

They climbed in through the escape trunk and shut their suits down, stepping out of them as they folded away. Orlowski's HMA took roughly twice the space that Paul's dragoon armor required in storage.

Oliver came through the passageway linking the crew compartment from the cargo area. He held out a hand. "Welcome to the team, Orlowski."

Orlowski waved his hand over Ollie's, his face showing mild surprise, perhaps at his easy acceptance. He turned back to Paul. "So why did you stop out there when I mentioned Kinsey?"

"He's responsible for a lot of dead people," Paul told him. "In the Imperium and out here in the colonies."

"We need to find him," Oliver insisted. "Let's get in there and punch his ticket."

"It's not as easy as just walking up to him and shooting him," Orlowski warned. "He's been here for close to a year now, with a sizeable contingent of Marines. They've taken over a major crime syndicate to cover his expenses while he waits for his Gray masters to show up." Orlowski spat on the deck.

"So he's hard to get to?" Paul asked.

"I haven't seen the guy in six months." Orlowski sat on one of the benches that ran the length of the cargo space on both sides. He stretched his legs. "Even in HMA, sentry duty can be a real pain in the legs."

A barely perceptible shake of the head. "He'd been getting increasingly paranoid the last few months. Kept insisting that folks wanted him dead..."

"He wasn't paranoid," Paul interjected. "He's right."

The Marine shrugged. "Anyway, it got so you'd have to have a pretty damned good reason to talk to the guy. Used to be he'd make the rounds, keep in touch with the boys from the 538. We were his power-base, after all. If he lost us, he'd have a hard time keeping his new criminal pals in line.

"Then he stopped dealing with us directly. Gunny Laval would bring us our orders, even though the silly bastard had to climb out of his bottle to do it. He's been sober a lot more lately, now that he's been forced to do some work."

"But we can find him," Paul insisted. "We don't need a lot of his time, just long enough to..."

"You won't get it," Orlowski said harshly. "If Kinsey thinks you or General Urbica is closing in on him, he'll go to ground. He'll rabbit and you'll be back to square one."

"Well, we have to try," Oliver said. He turned for the cockpit with a sigh. "I'll cancel our departure clearance."

"Sure," Paul nodded absently, staring at the decking. He frowned, looking up at the Maegi's departing back. "No, wait! Ollie, we're going. We'll keep our rendezvous with the *Rope a Dope*."

"Paul," Oliver protested, "Kinsey's right here. You saw the holos from Uruk. That *hundan* had his men assisting with the wholesale slaughter of anyone who couldn't be brainwashed."

"And if we go after him, he'll run." Paul reached out to put a hand on the Maegi's shoulder. "So we'll make *him* come after *us*."

Oliver's eyes narrowed. "And you have a clever plan to make that happen, do you?"

"So clever," Paul assured him, "you could put a tail on it and call it a weasel." He laughed. "Actually, it's pretty simple, which is the hallmark of a good plan. What's the one thing a crime lord can't abide?"

Ollie's eyes showed understanding, but it was Orlowski who answered first.

"A rival."

"Man like you," Paul said, nodding at the Marine, "should have had his majesty's commission a long time ago. Out here, you can make something of yourself, but first..." He looked over at Ollie. "...We need to get going. We've got a turf war to wage and we need some muscle of our own."

Incite

"**T**hey have dozens of collectors," Orlowski said quietly, even though the thug was too far away to hear them. "Once a shop owner resigns himself to paying protection, they don't bother sending a larger group. He knows what'll happen to him if he gets feisty."

Paul watched the man walk into a pastry shop. "And this is the end of a route?"

"It is. He'll be on his way back to his aggregator now with the week's take."

"Good." Paul left the mag-train station with two of the fifty dragoons he'd brought back to Cerberus station. Orlowski, even with a fresh haircut, was too recognizable and stayed on the platform. He'd take the train to their temporary command center and wait for them there.

They were roughly twenty meters away when the thug left the shop and headed toward Paul and his two comrades.

Paul had rehearsed this with all of the dragoon volunteers before choosing who to bring. The thug saw nothing alarming in the three approaching men. They all seemed wrapped up in their own problems, like any ordinary citizens.

The distance closed steadily.

Paul had dealt with hundreds of guys like this as a military policeman on a dozen Rim worlds. Low-level muscle, used to milk hard-working people of their ability to pay the Emperor's taxes. An Imperial citizen's entire reason for existing was to pay taxes.

The law was understandably aggressive in such cases. A cop only had to document their activities. Trials represented an even greater strain on the Imperial Exchequer and so law enforcement had very clear protocols regarding guys like this one.

Paul had no qualms as he reached the correct distance. He wanted powder burns. He brought his pistol out of his pocket and shoved it up against the startled man's forehead. The small-caliber weapon made a pneumatic popping noise as the man's head pitched backward. The round was too small for any sort of dramatic exit wound. It fragmented as it tumbled through the man's brain, not even reaching the skull on the far side.

He kept watch as his two compatriots went through the dead man's pockets.

Mason held up a currency chip.

Paul nodded and they turned down a side alley, jumping an alumifoam-panel fence and strolling nonchalantly onto the street in the next block.

The attack would be interpreted as the act of a rival syndicate. The station was a big place; the point where it curved out of sight was nearly lost in the haze of distance. There would be several groups vying for control at any given time and the local police, if they were allowing Kinsey's group to operate, would almost certainly brief him on the death of his collector before he'd be missed by his own aggregator.

One attack might be interpreted as the result of a rash decision. A junior member of a rival group might try such a thing to prove his abilities, although it would almost certainly earn him a new hole in the back of his head. Management couldn't afford to have subordinates starting wars on their own initiative. Such things had to be planned out.

And the result of a planned war would be multiple attacks coordinated by a central individual.

Advance

"**S**low down," Daffyd urged. "It's too crowded on this street but he's coming up on the same alley he started from. We'll incapacitate him once he's out of the public eye."

The protection money collector veered to the right, ducking into the same alleyway that Daffyd had been counting on.

"Civvies have no gods-damned sense," Eddie mused, waving his hand across the vehicle's control board, taking them into the alley. "Using the same route for ingress and egress?" He shoved his hand forward across the board and the vehicle surged, thumping with a muffled sound before halting.

"Monty's hairy nuts!" Daffyd exclaimed. "What the hells are you playing at?"

"What?" Eddie looked back to Daffyd, gesturing out the windscreen. "You said incapacitate him."

Daffyd held up a stun launcher that Orlowski had secured for them. "*I* was going to incapacitate him."

"Uh uh," the squadron commander contradicted. "You said *we'll* incapacitate him." He jabbed a finger at his chest. "Any attempt involving us as an aggregate would tend to indicate the use of our conveyance. It seemed the most efficient way for us both to incapacitate our target."

"Tell me again why you're here and not running your squadron?"

Eddie waved a hand. "Wanted to see the place," he said. "and I've got good subordinates to mind the shop while I'm here..." He suddenly spun his head back around to the front.

"Looks like you'll get the chance to use your launcher after all." He nodded out the window. Their target was pulling himself down the alleyway by holding onto one of the conduits that ran along one the walls, hopping along on one foot.

"*Tamade!*" Daffyd pushed a slide switch forward and cracked his weapon open. He pulled out one of the tiny balls and waved a hand to open the side door. With a quick look up and down the alley, he stepped out and walked briskly up to the man. "Why the hurry?" he asked as he jabbed the ball against the small of the man's back.

Tiny darts deployed as the pressure simulated a normal impact. They were enough to penetrate his clothes and embed in skin. Four thousand volts sent the man into spasms.

When the device was drained, Daffyd slipped it back into his pocket. Paul had been adamant that they leave no evidence behind. If Kinsey's people found the ball at the abduction site, they'd realize they weren't dealing with a rival syndicate. Imperial weapons indicated someone with a little more clout.

Eddie pulled up and helped secure the man before loading him in the back. "That was pretty easy," he said, "but there are so many ways it could have gone horribly wrong..."

Daffyd climbed into the back seat and sat with his feet on their prisoner's head. "Let's just get back to HQ before a cop comes along. This crime-lord thing is risky as all hells."

"Pfft," Eddie responded, climbing behind the controls of their small mag vehicle. "Paul's the crime-lord. You and me, we're just his lowly foot-soldiers, putting in the time, hoping for a chance to move up the chain."

"Whatever." Daffyd leaned back and closed his eyes. "Let's just get back to the ship."

The Next Objective

Paul was on the bridge wing, looking out across the river at a stretch of the shoreline where several derelict buildings had been torn down. A crew was bringing in construction equipment to put up something new.

Daffyd leaned on the worn, but otherwise solid, wooden cap of the railing. Without weather, the station's fixtures tended to last a lot longer and this freighter, though rusty along her waterline, was in very good shape otherwise.

It had been Daffyd who'd found her in a nearby derelict yard and got her propulsion back online. For the most part, freighters on Cerberus just had to load up and let the river take them where they needed to go. The engines were just there to maneuver in and out of docks, but they were good at keeping station offshore.

"You look like *gavno*," Daffyd observed.

No answer.

Daffyd sighed. "You give a fella a compliment and all you get is the cold shoulder."

Paul snorted. "I just wish we could see an end to all the fighting is all…"

"That happens for everybody," Daffyd said quietly, "eventually. If you want peace, you need a bullet in your head cause strife is the gods-damned Human condition."

He turned to lean on his left arm, looking over at Paul. "This is about you and the General, isn't it? You'd like to settle down but you figure it's too risky."

Paul nodded, still looking out over the water.

"Well you better not get any silly ideas like running off to some remote world together," Daffyd insisted. "If you do, you'll still end up fighting the same battles, just on a different scale." He chuckled. "Somebody like a local crime lord..."

"Speaking of which," Paul mused, "we need to move this along so we can get back to the fleet."

"We've got a prisoner," he told Paul.

"Figured you would," Paul said, still watching the shore. "You and Eddie are the only ones to bring anyone in so far."

"At least it'll let us move up the food chain."

Paul nodded. "Still like to get a few more. Come at em from more than one direction. A couple of gunners from Dmitriy's squadron are working an angle on a drug pusher up by the university. I think their chances are pretty good."

"Are we pushing too hard too fast?" Daffyd voiced the concern that had been nagging at him since his arrival. "Won't we spook Kinsey?"

Paul shook his head. "A group trying to muscle in wouldn't just tickle him, they'd be going for maximum impact. They'd want to disrupt Kinsey's cash flow and undermine his subordinates' confidence in him.

"Have you ever seen something like that?" Paul nodded toward the riverbank.

"Like what?"

"Those guys are getting ready to fabricate buildings. *Individual* buildings."

"We have stations like this back in the Imperium."

"Sure, but less than a fraction of a percent of all Humans have ever seen them." He looked at the engineer. "Have you?"

"No."

"Making a standalone building with its own little purpose," Paul mused. "Seems crazy, but it feels so much more natural."

"It's delightfully inefficient," Daffyd said. "These colonies seem to exalt the individual, rather than making us all into cogs in some drab machine."

"That's exactly what I've been trying to put into words," Paul turned from the view to grin at him. "The engineer philosopher!"

"*Feihua!*" Daffyd stepped away from the railing. "If you're done torturing *me*, let's get below and you can start in on our guest." He headed for the stairs.

Their *guest* was conscious now. Trussed up from an overhead pipe, his head was hanging back, staring up at the cable runs and pipes above. His head jerked forward at the sound of approaching footsteps.

"Welcome aboard the *Jolly Badger*," Paul said mildly with a nod toward Daffyd. "Don't get me started. It was *his* idea."

"I got her running so I get to pick the name."

"And what the hells is a badger?"

"Beats me, just some old origin-world fairy tale creature." Daffyd pulled a chair over to the wall where he could lean back. "Y'know, like the Toe Fairy."

Paul looked over to the prisoner as he slipped a knife from his sleeve holster. "Can you imagine having to work with this guy? The nonsense he comes up with." He waved the knife carelessly, the prisoner's eyes focussing on it. "Just yesterday, he was telling us about a date with this woman..."

He darted a glance at Daffyd. "This time you're *sure* it was a woman, right?"

"Oh, for the love of the gods!" Daffyd raised his voice, jumping into the improvisation with ease. "That was just the once. How the hells was I to know what that district was all about? I'd never been to that world before."

Paul turned a longsuffering gaze back to the prisoner. "You really can't tell this guy anything," he complained, bringing the knife back up in front of the man's face, waving it to emphasize his points. "Rim worlds are safe enough, if you go to the local MP outpost and get a briefing. They really don't mind if it saves them the trouble of pulling some *dumbass* out of a hermaphroditic brothel."

"I believe you said *don't mention it,* at the time," Daffyd groused, "and here I am, listening to you mention it."

For a completely made up event, the story was in serious danger of taking on a life of its own.

"I never said *I* wouldn't mention it." Paul grinned at the prisoner. "But we're being rude to our guest." He slid the tip of the knife into the man's right nostril. "I have simple questions," he said softly, "and they have simple answers. I should warn you, before you consider playing this the hard way, that I can stand a considerable amount of pain."

"You mean when you're inflicting it, right?" Daffyd asked.

Paul shrugged. "Well, yeah. I figured that went without saying." He pressed the tip of the blade against the inner side of the nostril. "So how's it going to be? Do you feel like answering a few simple questions?"

There was very little apparent danger in agreeing with such a simple question. There was no actual information being given up yet, so the man made the most likely response.

"OK."

Once you start talking, a good interrogator can milk you dry. If you start talking with an affirmative like *yes* or *ok*, it just speeds things up even more.

"What's your name?"

239

"Frank."

"Did you grow up on the station?"

"Yes."

"Who do you work for?"

"What?" The man's eyes grew wide. "Are you kidding me? We never see him; he probably doesn't even exist. You're wasting... Aghhh!" He jerked his head away turning the cut Paul had made to the inside of the nose into a clean slice all the way through.

"Ah," Paul remonstrated, "now that's mostly on you. I was just putting a little cut on the inside to warn you. No external damage to scare off the ladies, but you had to jerk your head..."

"You said if I answered your questions, it would go easier for me." The prisoner was breathing rapidly.

"Not if you're going to piss in my pocket." Paul leaned in, his face now six inches away from his prisoner's. "I asked you a simple question and you tried to muddy the waters with talk about the leader of your syndicate."

He slid the knife into the other nostril. "Who gives you your marching orders? After you're done robbing your victims of their credits, where do you take the chip?"

Frank's eyes darted to the side.

Paul was reasonably sure another attempt at misdirection was in the offing. "You want us to turn that pretty nose into a pig snout?"

"What the hells is a pig?" Daffyd asked from his perch behind Paul.

"It's the animal that pork comes from," Paul said over his shoulder.

"Really?" The front chair legs hit the deck. "There's an actual animal? I always thought it was just engineered from Human tissue."

"That's disgusting!" Paul removed the knife and turned to face Daffyd. "You thought you were eating Human tissue?"

"No," Daffyd corrected, "I never ate the stuff because I thought it would make me a cannibal."

"Oh sure," Paul nodded. "Hard to make friends if you're always trying to take a bite out of them."

"Would have been useful right now, though. Hey?" Daffyd chuckled. "I could've started at the feet and worked my way up till he talked."

"You guys are messed up," Frank complained, "and you're in way over your head. We've got Marines calling the shots. Some real grade-A hard cases and you wanna muscle in on them? I'll tell you whatever you want, but I'd forget the whole thing, if I were you."

Paul hid his relief. The station was a big place. With more than six-hundred square kilometers of useable space, there was room for more than one crime syndicate. They were pretty sure they'd set up in the middle of Kinsey's territory, but confirmation never hurt.

"Marines!" Paul acted impressed. "Saying, for a moment, that we *believe* you," he added sarcastically, "there should be no danger to your bosses in telling me where to find them, right? It's not like we're going to get the upper hand against *real Marines*!" He looked over and shared a laugh with Daffyd.

"How much you wanna bet the Toe Fairy works for them too?" Daffyd asked.

"Don't say I didn't tell you," Frank warned.

"Y'know, I'm starting to like this guy," Paul said. He turned to the prisoner. "C'mon, Frank. Answer time. Help me fight my deep-seated urge to use blades on folks."

"Alright," Frank blurted, eyes back on the blade. "The daily collections for this sector go to Seamus – I swear I don't know his last name – at his pub on the corner of Liberty and Coleson."

"Its name?"

"Place is called *Your Name Here*."

"Inventive," Paul remarked. "What kind of muscle at the bar?"

"Usually three Marines," he said. "One out front, acting like your average barfly, two in the back, where the credit chips are held."

"All in plainclothes?"

A nod.

"And when do they take it to the next guy in the chain?"

A pause. "First day of the week."

"You realize that if you steer us wrong, here, and we don't come back, somebody's gonna make slippers out of your ass cheeks?" Daffyd added.

A nod.

He didn't look particularly alarmed at the prospect, so Paul figured he'd been telling the truth. "Nothing you'd like to recant or adjust at all?" He spread his hands out. "No penalties at this point, if you've been bullshitting me and decide to come clean."

"No need to lie," Frank said simply. "Just make sure you carry a holo eye, or something, so your people know I didn't lie. Those Marines are gonna hammer your bones flat."

"We've faced Marines before," Paul said mildly. "Isn't that so?"

"Technically," Daffyd corrected, "Frank, here, is facing one right now."

"What do you mea... Hey!" Frank twisted his head in a vain attempt to avoid Paul's right hand. Strong fingers grasped his jaw.

"Hold still," he ordered, tossing the knife on the floor and reaching out to Daffyd for a small dispensing nozzle.

"What is that?"

"*Prison yard sutures*. Don't worry," Paul soothed. "This glue is industrial strength."

Frank seemed on the edge of screaming as Paul ran a thin bead of the adhesive along the outer edge of the cut in his nose. "Yeah, it stings," Paul admitted, "but warning you really wouldn't have helped. You'd just be more likely to twitch."

He guided the edges of the cut together, holding them so the glue could bond. "You ever see this done when you were locked up on Mictlan?" he asked Daffyd.

A headshake.

Frank seemed to forget all about the pain in his nose. "You did time in Mictlan?" His voice had taken on a nasal quality that he hoped wasn't permanent, but his sense of alarm quickly overrode his concern. He'd been assuming he was being held by a bunch of misguided fools. The kind of people who'd never last two micros in a fight with Marines. If one of them was a Marine himself and the other had managed to survive in the Imperium's most notorious super-max prison... well... that changed a few equations.

"What's the story with his leg?" Paul asked.

"Bad sprain, but it'll mend," Daffyd told him. He sighed at the look on Paul's face. "Eddie hit him with the car before I could use the stunner."

"Hmmm..."

"What?"

"Not a bad call, really. If you'd fired the stunner, there'd be tiny scorch marks on the walls and pavement from the balls that missed."

"*Bozhemoi*! Not you too?"

"That should have occurred to me earlier," Paul admitted. "Stunners should be last resort and, even then, single ball if possible. Too much evidence, otherwise."

"That's what I did," Daffyd told him, "eventually. He started hauling himself down the alley, so I gave him a jolt."

"You're a tough bastard, aren't you?" Paul grinned at the prisoner. "C'mon. Let's get him onto a cot. He'll have to stay here till we're done. Then you need to hit the stores. I've got a schematic for you to work on."

Let's Be Hasty

"**T**here they are," the sensor tech said with quiet urgency. Though there was no need to speak loudly in the cramped confines of their *Hasty Ferret* he did so out of reflex. The enemy was only a few thousand kilometers away from their lone scout ship. "Two cruisers, five frigates."

"So they're finally adapting their tactics to compensate for General Urbica's ambushes," the pilot/commander mused. "Trying to make themselves a harder target."

The sensor tech cursed softly. "Ain't right, 'Vampire', leaving those poor bastards to the Grays..." A holo display in the center of their windowless craft showed a horde of Gray shuttles moving between their ships and a Human freighter.

Vampire chuckled. "Send what we've got, 'Fungus', and don't you worry about leaving anyone," he insisted. "The old man might look at the numbers and call it all off, but the General knows what we can do. Hells, our three heavy gunboats alone could run 'em off. They might only have two thirds the displacement of a Gray cruiser but they've got twice the mass. Gunboat armor can shrug off the biggest nukes the Grays deploy."

Though both Windemere and Urbica were of the same rank, everybody in the fleet knew who *the General* was.

"There's also our antimatter rounds. One good AM hit on a Gray cruiser can rip her open, once you get past the shields."

The sensor tech sent the signal back to the open wormhole, well beyond a Gray cruiser's maximum detection range.

He looked down at a pulsing icon in the holo display. "Looks like we're lit up," he reported calmly. "No sign of any change in activity yet, though."

"So..." Vampire pulled a couple of coffee bags out of an overhead bin and handed one to his tech. "... What will our Gray commander decide to do, knowing he has an Imperial Navy scout watching him?"

"Smart money'd be on scampering."

"Smart money rarely follows the Grays," Vampire advised, "because their thought processes are too different from ours. They say learning the language helps to understand their mindset."

"Tried that at the sensor school," the tech admitted. "Wanted to go into intercept analysis but the language just sounds like constant moaning. Damn classroom sounded like a brothel."

"Sounds like fun."

"Not for eight hours a day, it wasn't. Anyway, I didn't have the ear for it so now I'm stuck working for your sorry ass..., sir."

"Well, the job does have its perks." Vampire waved a hand at the holo. "Front row seats to the fight."

"You really think we'll commit?"

"I'd put a year's pay on it, if we were still working for the Navy and not running our own little sideshow. The General's had our data long enough to make a decision. You know she doesn't waste any time making up her mind." He nodded at the comm-log window in the holo.

"No new messages recalling us, which means the fleet is gonna be coming through the wormhole any time now."

As if to prove that Vampire had access to inside information, six icons sprang into life, just on their side of the wormhole.

"*Wei*! You were right, oh Wise One! They're jumping in!"

The icons disappeared as the six ships slid the Universe past their positions, reappearing to the side of the Gray ships but far enough off axis to prevent destroying them with the drop-wash.

Now the game would escalate another notch.

Unconventional

Julia stood outside the pick-up range for the ship-to-ship holo system, face-to-face with Windemere but at three meters' distance. Letting Windemere do a bit of play-acting was one thing, but this was going to be a much hairier engagement and she wasn't about to take any chances on a relatively untried officer. Windemere's combat experience was entirely as a junior officer.

He was still useful as the face of the operation and so she kept him in the middle of the pick-up circle. It wouldn't do for the Grays to learn of her involvement, at this time. They considered her to be a renegade from CentCom. Her presence would blow the impression they were working so hard to create.

She checked the deployment. As already planned, the carrier approached from behind the three heavy gunboats and the two frigates. "Tactical, sitrep," she demanded.

"Aye, ma'am," the tactical officer replied, still looking at his reports. "Showing no capacitor buildup consistent with prepping their main guns. The shuttle activity has come to a full stop. There's bound to be Humans on the return legs but we can't see inside the hulls. One comms burst, but it's on the new encryption key, so we can't crack it."

"How much you want to bet it said 'everybody stop what you're doing while we sort this out'?" Windemere ventured.

"Remind me never to play cards against you." Julia nodded his way. "Rattle their cage, Vance. This time, we're taking the initiative and we'll shove it right up their pellet-holes."

A Gray shimmered into holographic view in front of Windemere.

"We've picked up a distress call," Windemere spoke over the Gray's beginning remarks. "We're here to render assistance to Humans in distress."

"We will gladly deliver them to your vessels," the Gray droned, "but it will take some time to complete the transfer. Our shuttles are insufficient to move large numbers with any real haste."

Julia's lips drew back at the corners. There was a very good reason that the phrase 'let's go to that Gray improv theater' had never been uttered anywhere in the Universe. This one was playing for time because he'd been caught with gods know how many Humans already in stasis – something he'd be hard-pressed to explain.

The Grays were certainly able to move large numbers with haste. They'd been doing just that when the Human force had surprised them.

She gave Windemere a nod.

"No need for the wait," Windemere told the Gray. "As you can see, we've brought our own aviation assets. Stand by to receive our shuttles."

Julia used her menu to cut the channel. She selected a fleet-wide channel, nodding at Windemere again. "All vessels, this is General Windemere. Execute Romeo Seven Two."

Twelve heavy combat shuttles left the main hangar door in three waves. They split up, one each heading for a frigate while two angled toward each of the cruisers. The remaining three moved toward the vessel the Humans had been stranded on.

The Iron Hands came next. The brutally ugly Navy fighters bristled with weapons and three squadrons of them began moving around the Gray ships. The threat was implicitly obvious, for the most part, but there was an element to their menace that the Grays were unlikely to notice in time.

The INV *Dark Star* was a Navy carrier, so she didn't carry a heavy ground attack force like her Marine counterparts, but she did have a sizeable Marine contingent aboard to handle shipboard security as well as assisting in boarding operations. At just over one hundred twenty enlisted men and six officers, the Marine complement was more than sufficient for their current mission.

As the shuttles reached the halfway point to the enemy ships, the pattern flown by the Iron Hands gradually coalesced. Each Gray vessel had an IH fighter pass beneath their ventral Engineering trunk at roughly the same moment, slowing for a brief moment.

A fire-team of Marines detached from among the clutter of sensors and antimatter auto-cannons of each IH and drifted toward the escape trunks on the Gray ships. They used thrusters to align themselves and to slow their final approaches, landing softly on the enemy hulls so as not to alarm the crews inside.

At a coordinating signal from the *Dark Star,* the fire-teams, arranged around the Engineering escape trunks, initiated the boarding process, opening the hatches and forcing their way in past the rush of escaping air. Ignoring the dying Gray engineers, the Marines moved to secure and deactivate the self-destruct devices on every ship.

By the time the combat shuttles had reached their assigned Gray ships, the Marines of the first phase had removed the nukes from their cradles and had secured the Engineering spaces.

It was more than likely, once the Grays shook off the surprise of being caught in the act, that they would give serious consideration to blowing their ships. Once the first combat shuttles landed in their bays, that likelihood would only have increased. Deactivating the self-destructs would open up tactical options and taking them away afterward would only deepen the enemy's sense of humiliation.

"Tactical, any sign of a change in their combat stance?" Julia's face was aimed toward the Captain's holo, but from the other side, seeing as Vance was standing in the command circle. Her own internal CPU was linked to the ship and three small holo-projectors near her left eye gave her a HUD that moved with her.

It was still difficult to monitor everything, though.

"No change, ma'am."

"Keep a sharp eye," she ordered. "If they're going to think about fighting, it will be in the next few micros."

The first combat shuttles thumped down onto the Gray deck plating, causing some sections to buckle slightly under the heavy Human-built craft. The back ramps were already half way down and smaller doors snapped open on each side, disgorging armored Marines.

They fanned out from the shuttles, weapons at the ready, pushing the Grays back. One of the Humans, a Marine captain, stepped away from the perimeter, approaching a long row of capsules floating on suspensor fields. He retracted his helmet and leaned over to gaze through the inspection window of a capsule.

His face grim, he opened an unsecured channel, one that the Grays, as well as the Humans, would hear. "Command, this is Foxtrot Two Six Six. The Grays have our people in stasis pods. This is an abduction. I say again, this is an abduction. Request command concurrence that the conditions of the Rim Armistice have been breached, over."

The Rim Armistice, which had ended hostilities between the Gray Quorum and the Imperium more than five centuries earlier, spelled out clear consequences in the event of any attack by one party on the other.

It had been ignored by CentCom after the failed Gray attack on Irricana, but that didn't mean it had no teeth.

"Foxtrot Two Six Six, this is Command," Windemere's voice responded. "Video feed from your call sign viewed and verified. Command concurs. Armistice breached. All call signs foxtrot, seize all Gray vessels and conduct inspections. Command out."

"Forward!" The Marine captain shouted. "Alpha, link up with the team in Engineering and then clear the lower decks. Bravo, take the middle. Charlie and delta, with me.

The gloves were coming off.

Any Gray foolish enough to stand in their way was hammered aside with a rifle butt or a simple swat of an armored hand. The captain led his team to the forward riser and two of his men leaned in the shaft, aiming their weapons up to cover the route. He hopped into the zero-gravity column, his momentum carrying him up toward the bridge deck. The rest of his team followed as he reached back to push off the rear wall, falling out into the transverse hallway behind the bridge with a heavy clang of armored feet.

He moved immediately toward the bridge, his men hammering onto the decking behind him. Just as he reached the bridge hatch, the Gray captain must have come to his senses because it slammed shut, leaving one enemy crewman outside.

The Marine captain grabbed the Gray by the arm and tossed him away from the hatch. One of his two fire team leaders stepped up to the door, pulling a half-kilo charge of C32 from a small heated chamber on his torso. He pulled at the elastic mix, creating a long ribbon of explosives that he used to frame a rough door to the right of the sealed hatch. He stepped back a few paces and looked to his officer.

The Marine captain sealed his helmet. "Blow it."

The blast, though heard, was barely felt inside the heavy armor. The two fire teams rushed into the bridge, shouting and pulling crewmen away from terminals. The officer entered and approached the Gray captain, who appeared slightly disoriented from the blast.

The alien didn't seem to miss a beat, despite the shock of the breaching charge. "You have no right to board our vessels. We are in the territory of the Gray Quorum."

The Marine officer retracted his helmet. "You were found to be in possession of Human prisoners, taken from a Human vessel broadcasting an Interplanetary Standard distress call."

"Prisoners?" the Gray droned. "You are mistaken, we..."

"They were in stasis," the Marine cut in, looking down at the Gray, "and those who weren't yet incapacitated on your other ships are reporting that they were removed from their ship against their will. It seems they were given to believe that their vessel would be destroyed and them along with it, if they failed to surrender."

"They were intruders in Gray space..."

"The Rim Convention only mentions attacks. It lists no provisions regarding the location of those attacks," the Marine interrupted again and with more force in his voice. "Your ships are in violation and we intend to adhere to the letter of the law. Any ships found to be involved in attacks on Humans will be seized in reparation."

The Gray's skin grew very light. "*Himchellan, quoranta est*," he declared.

The Marine officer stared at him calmly. He was no linguist, but he knew the Gray command for self-destruct and he knew the inclusion of *quoranta* was intended to activate the self-destruct on his entire flotilla. "You just about done?"

The alien's skin regained some of its color now that it was obvious that the ship wasn't going to blow. "There will be repercussions for this act of piracy."

The Marine leaned in. "So, you claim to being engaged in an act of piracy? I'm not sure I buy that. I think you're just trying to shield the Quorum from the fallout." There were distinct advantages in forcing an adversary to use your language.

"That was not my intended meaning..."

"Your final disposition will be determined by our commanding officer." The Marine turned to his men. "Corporal Ward, take your team and help get the Human prisoners rounded up and identified. Check 'em off the manifest we got from their ship. Sooner we get 'em all accounted for, the sooner we can get off this bucket and finish our dinner."

He put a hand to his ear. "Roger that, if he's only been in stasis a few minutes... Exactly. Bring him up here so we can involve him in the process."

He turned to the Gray captain and shoved him into one of the holo-pickup circles. "Wait there."

Windemere looked at the three individuals shimmering before him. Urbica stood behind the image of the Marine officer, a large holo display projected from the left side of her face.

He turned to the middle holographic image. "Captain Chase," he nodded politely, "we're very glad to have been of assistance, but I'm afraid we don't have the necessary parts to repair your vessel. Were you carrying much in the way of valuable cargo when you were attacked?"

The civilian captain shook his head. "Just wheat, but the consignee had insurance. We were dead-heading back to the Masran system with a few hundred religious pilgrims to help pay for the repairs that, obviously, I'd put off for a little too long..."

"What's your capacity?"

"Ten thousand cubic meters," the captain replied. "I know it isn't much, but she's our livelihood. We've got every cent sunk into her."

"Sorry, Captain, but she's a dead stick," Windemere insisted. "Under the provisions of the Rim Accords, a plaintiff is entitled to lay claim on seized goods in replacement of lost property. I'm thinking one of those frigates would suffice."

"Wait," Chase looked to the side, spoke to someone and then looked back. "General, are you suggesting that I take one of the frigates that attacked us?"

"They displace eighty thousand cube and already have about six thousand storage," Windemere said. "If you pull a couple of those main guns, you'd double your existing capacity easily."

"The remaining guns would give you the ability to protect your passengers and cargo as well," the holographic Marine captain added.

"Pardon my mistrust, gentlemen, but my better nature has already taken quite a beating today," Chase said, looking from the Marine to Windemere. "What's the catch?"

"The catch," Windemere said, looking back at the holographic list Julia was projecting, "is that I can't leave you on a dead ship and I just don't have room to take you all aboard my own fleet. Space is always at a premium on a warship.

"The Accord gives us a perfectly reasonable solution," he continued, "and those Gray guns are modular. My boys could have those out for you in a few centis. We can float them over to the *Dark Star* and grav 'm down in a corner of the flight deck. I'm sure we can find a use for them."

Chase frowned down at the floor, perhaps trying to figure the value of the guns against the cost of having a dockyard remove them. In the end, having the ability to take on more cargo on his next stop must have won out. "That sounds acceptable, General, and thank-you!"

"You can't give one of our ships away," the Gray insisted.

Julia's holographic teleprompter simply said; *You've got this. Have fun with him.*

Windemere smiled at the Gray in front of him. "Oh, certainly not, but your ships are now *mine*. Now, don't be a sore loser, Captain. You've been caught with your head up your pellet-hole and it's time to pay the price for that."

"And how do you propose I get our crews home?"

"I'm not in the business of offering travel options," Windemere corrected. "I'm far too busy serving His Imperial Majesty to be running a gods-damned rickshaw service for disgraced pirates."

"You accuse us of piracy and yet you plan to murder my crews?"

Windemere rolled his eyes. "Gods! It's a wonder you have no entertainment industry, what with all the drama every time I run into your kind." He affected a thoughtful expression for a moment.

"Here's what we can do," he said suddenly. "We'll leave you one ship so you won't die waiting for rescue."

Having expected death from exposure to space, the Gray seemed willing enough. "Very well. As we have no choice, we'll remain aboard my flagship."

Windemere chuckled. "You'll do nothing of the sort, *Sonny-Jim*! I'll issue orders for you to be transferred to the freighter you were caught raiding." He turned to the Marine captain. "As you remove Humans from the stasis pods, start putting the Gray crewmen into them."

He looked back at the now dark-gray captain. "Propulsion is out and life-support's on its last legs," he explained. "Wouldn't want you to die before your people find you, now, would we?"

The Marine officer grabbed the Gray captain as soon as the holographic projection of Windemere disappeared. "Let's get you down to the hangar bay. O'Neil, bring the rest of the bridge crew down with you. I want them asleep first. Who knows what mischief a bridge officer can cook up if left too near their stations?"

Though the rest of the bridge crew were being herded along on foot, the Marine officer chose to throw the captain over his shoulder like a sack of coffee, just to grind in the humiliation a little more.

He slid down the riser and bounded heavily out onto the hangar deck, the Gray on his shoulder smacking his head on the armor with every step. He stepped over to one of the pods and dropped the captain in next to one of his crewmen. "These should be big enough to take two Grays each," he declared over the battle net.

"You can't put me in here with an ordnance technician, third grade," the captain protested blandly.

"Well, we couldn't find an ordnance technician, second grade," the Marine told him cheerfully. "Look at the bright side: when they find out how you lost your ships, the disparity in rank will get a lot smaller."

With that, he slammed the cover shut and activated the stasis field.

Feint

"**S**ensors are back up," the tactical officer confirmed. "Target is directly ahead; distance is forty-five thousand klicks."

"Beat to quarters," Ava ordered.

The rest of the fleet has come through the jump successfully and their reported positions are well within tolerances," the sensor officer added. "We...

"Contact!" Tactical interrupted. "One times frigate turning to meet us. Designating as Tango Foxtrot One."

Ava considered it to be a good sign. The Grays were guarding their production facilities after all. That hadn't been true a few weeks ago, when a scouting ship had passed this way. The raids were starting to have an impact on the Quorum. They were spreading their forces out in an attempt to cover as many installations as possible.

How thinly would their high-value targets be protected if they were wasting ships out here?

"Focus fire on Foxtrot One first," Ava ordered. "We'll hit the mine once we clear their defense."

A single frigate was no defense at all – not when the Humans were attacking in force. Being on the offensive conferred a major advantage. Ava was keeping her forces concentrated, allowing her to completely overwhelm any defenses found at her targets. The Grays, on the other hand, had thousands of stations and installations in need of protection and no idea which one might be hit next.

"We could fire a few rounds at the mine from here," the tactical officer suggested. "The frigate's an impossible target at this distance but the asteroid can't move out of the way.

There's a chance the frigate might try to block the shot, seeing as it's their duty to protect the mine."

"Tempting, but no," Ava replied. "If he doesn't block the shot and we take out the mine, then there's no reason for him to stick around, or us, for that matter. He'd just jump out and report the loss. We need that frigate dead and we need the miners screaming... well... mumbling for help."

The tactical officer shook his head. "You're right, of course. I didn't think that through enough before I mentioned it."

"Nothing wrong with that," she reassured him. "I'd rather hear ideas that miss the mark than have you hold back. We could miss a good idea that way."

"This still gives us an advantage," he said. "The frigate captain will expect us to fire on the mine instead of at him. We should fire the mains at twenty thousand and aim for the mine. If we load the sub-munition rounds, we can adjust them onto the frigate at the last second. He'll never expect it."

Ava nodded thoughtfully. "Should catch him off guard." She grinned at him. "See why I don't mind half-baked ideas? Work up the firing solution and fire when ready."

The tactical officer turned back to his station where his rating was already working out the timings and angles. They were almost within firing range now.

"Starting to resolve the locations of their communications gear," the sensor officer advised. "Marking the long-range array for the final shots."

"Stand by for firing of the main guns," Tactical announced.

"Standing by," the helmsman replied. "Steady as she goes."

261

At maximum distance, there was little need to slave the helm to fire-control. The traverse of the main guns was more than sufficient to bear on target.

"Firing."

The demonic moan of the mains shook the deck, rattling Ava's bones, and the four rounds streaked away.

"We're picking up signal activity from their long-range array," Sensor advised, "*lots* of activity."

"Good," Ava acknowledged. "As long as they think there's still a mine to save, the Grays will send help." She darted a glance at the chronometer where a countdown was running.

"Rounds are changing trajectory." The tactical officer leaned in closer to the holo display.

Sub-munitions were ejecting from one side of the main rounds, imparting a slight amount of force each time and nudging them toward a path that would impact the Gray warship. At five kilometers, they released the remainder of the sub-munitions, hitting the ship with a cloud of rounds at fifteen times the speed of sound.

If the Gray captain had realized what was coming, there was no way he could have reacted in time. The last-micro change of target had worked perfectly and his ship was now drifting with a buckled hull and ruptured conduits and it was venting atmosphere.

Ava opened a fleet-wide channel. "All call-signs will focus fire on Foxtrot One. Weapons free for targets on the trace in order of prioritization."

At the moment, the mining complex and the long-range communications array weren't on the trace and Ava had left her captains in no doubt as to their fate if they fired on those targets without authorization. She needed the mine to keep calling for help.

A hail of fire was unleashed on the damaged frigate. The already weakened shields were no match for the heavy rounds from the cruisers and one shield generator was torn loose from its mounts and forced out through the far side of the hull, a cylindrical segment of shielding fading around it as the built-in backup power was depleted.

Some of the ships were still firing at the frigate but most were already moving on to other targets on the list. Satellites, support structures and storage facilities began wilting under the barrage.

"Tactical, Foxtrot One is out of the fight," Ava ordered, opening the fleet-wide channel. "All call-signs, turn to orbital insertion path."

The icon for the frigate went gray to stop her captains wasting ammunition on it.

"Another burst from the long-range array." The sensor officer turned to Ava. "It's a match for the first transmission but with more added to the end."

A second call for help and, probably, a warning that the Humans were moving into orbit rather than destroying the mining complex right away. It represented a chance to catch the attackers flatfooted.

"Target the long-range array," she ordered.

It was out of the traverse arc of the mains but it would have been overkill anyway. The secondary batteries screamed a salvo and, though her Gray-built cruiser was light on secondaries, it was more than enough for the task.

"Long-range array destroyed," the tactical officer announced, looking to Ava.

She nodded. "All call-signs, focus on the mine as we pass. Stand by to jump when the countdown hits zero."

Trying to coordinate a jump using regular communications was too imprecise so they were all running the same countdown clock. When it hit zero, they'd jump out.

Ava spent the next ten minutes searching the sector holo for signs of inbound enemy ships while keeping an eye on the damage they were doing to the surface. The time to jump crept up on her faster than she would have expected.

"Eject the shuttle," she ordered.

An older shuttle, one that they'd been cannibalizing for parts, was pushed out through the shielding of the port landing bay. It went tumbling down into the atmosphere, quickly acquiring a shock-layer of ionized, high-temperature air. There were too many openings in the small craft and, as it tumbled, the heated gasses found their way inside, tearing the vehicle to flaming shreds that rained down near the wreckage of the mining complex.

"Jumping," the helmsman called out, "in three, two, one..."

The planet shimmered and slipped away as the fleet moved the Universe past their position.

"Fifty centis to the target," the nav officer said. He craned his neck from side to side, working out the tension of the previous engagement.

"Very well," Ava replied. "Secure from general quarters. XO, make sure everybody gets food and rest before we arrive. You have the conn."

"I have the conn," he confirmed.

She headed for the mess hall. Half a day to the *real* target, which meant, hopefully, a half day in transit for the target's protective force as they tried to respond to the emergency call from the mine. Considering the delay required to organize and launch a relief force, she should have slightly more than half a day to deal with whatever they found at the Gray shipyards.

And the debris from the sacrificed shuttle might convince the enemy that the Humans were genuinely interested in the mine for some reason. It was a long shot, but it increased the probability that the Grays would stick around to scan the site just a little longer.

She usually preferred to attack replenishment sites but the shipyards reportedly had more than eighteen cruisers in the final stages of construction and they'd be far easier to destroy in space dock than they would with a full crew and ammunition load. The yards would also be of use in repairing battle-damaged Gray ships, so the target still satisfied her primary criteria.

Stalk

"**H**e's coming out," a young dragoon said over the secure earpieces Paul's team was wearing. "Just one man but he looks like a *teufelhund,* alright. Gods, you actually have to *order* these guys to stop getting haircuts, don't you?"

"Tim, you're up." Paul shifted his gaze to the man leaving the bar behind the Marine. "Just a splash is all we need." He resisted the urge to start his vehicle right away and move closer.

They'd given thought to kicking in the front door and interrogating the Marines inside, but Paul had talked them out of it. Talking about capturing and interrogating an Imperial Marine was one thing; actually doing it was quite another.

And there were better ways to find out who the Marines at *Your Name Here* were reporting to.

"*Goushi!*" Tim feigned a stumble as he reached the bottom step and splashed his beer on the bag in the Marine's hand. He was looking back accusingly at whatever had *tripped* him when the Marine stopped.

Tim turned to leave, wobbling slightly, when he seemed to notice the angry Marine glaring at him. "Shorry, bud. Did... did I get shome on you?" He wavered apologetically, taking a quick emergency step to the side to regain his balance.

The Marine shook his head, turning to resume his course and Tim stumbled off in the opposite direction. There were cameras everywhere so he'd have to stay in character till he could get off the street.

"Starting to get a read." Daffyd was frowning down at a holographic interface projected from a small ball-shaped module he'd set on the floor between his feet. It was nearly the same size and shape as the sensor pickup that was reading the signal from the nanites.

He glanced over at Paul. "The nanites need to dry before they activate. We're building signal but it's slow."

"You're the one who insisted we use beer..."

"Well, we could hardly just toss a miscellaneous powder on the bag, now, could we?" the engineer shot back. "I built a nanite farm, designed the bots and grew them all in less than a day. Sue me if they don't have an anaerobic cycle. Better ideas were taking priority at the time."

"I would but you don't have anything I want..."

"Signal strength is getting better," Daffyd interrupted. "Let's keep him within five hundred meters, just to be safe.

Paul started up the vehicle and slid out into traffic. They pulled off every time a parking spot opened up and gave their quarry a chance to rebuild his lead on them. They came to an intersection and the barriers came up, stopping their lanes but no traffic was flowing in the other direction.

The Marine ignored the flashing red signs and walked across the empty lanes.

"*Gavno!*" Daffyd leaned forward. "We're going to lose him! He's already near the limit for this pickup."

"We're boxed in." Paul shut down the engine and the vehicle settled to the pavement.

"What the hells?" Daffyd demanded. "He's getting away and you're just gonna park in the middle of the lane?"

"Just grab your balls and come on." Paul slid the doors open and hopped out, giving an apologetic wave to the honking vehicles behind them. "Sorry," he shouted. "A recall just came through the link and shut her down. Something about exploding fuel cells with unusually high noise sensitivity."

The honking ceased before he made it around to Daffyd's door. "C'mon! We're not going to catch up sitting here like a couple of idiots."

Daffyd shoved the pickup ball in his pocket and stepped out with the holo unit in his left hand. "About as inconspicuous as a Bishop on Narbonne. I can't read the interface and run at the same time..."

"Move!" Paul turned him in the right direction and started jogging toward the slidewalk. He stepped on and scanned the stretch on the other side of the intersection. By the time Daffyd stumbled onto the walk, Paul had already been carried along by at least ten meters.

He hurried to catch up. "I've lost the signal," he panted. "We could try again next week."

"You think he might start getting suspicious when somebody spills beer on him once a week till we get this right?" Paul shook his head. "No. We managed to get your bots on the bag. I intend to find him. Sooner or later, they'd check the public feed and see Tim hanging around and..."

His eyes narrowed. "*Tiancai!*" He started across the empty intersection, the red warning light turning green halfway across. "Put the projector in your pocket."

The public network gave full coverage of the entire station and, here they were, fiddling around with a half-kilometer-range pickup. He'd already cracked the station's security protocols. It was child's play to access the sensor net.

He started with a query, tracing Daffyd's projector ball back to the pickup, finding the signature of the nanites they'd sloshed on the Marine's bag. He quickly found the same signature using the station network and overlaid it on his own view of the station rather than projecting a retinal image that he'd then have to read as a map and translate into the surrounding terrain.

A bright orange shape was bobbing along to his right, one block over and heading back the way they'd come. "He's doubled back," Paul told Daffyd.

"Are you sure?"

He nodded. "I tapped into the station's sensor feed. He's still moving at a regular pace. I don't think we spooked him; he's just engaging in a few countermeasures out of professional pride. Must be one of the special operators from the 538."

"Come on." He led Daffyd back the way they'd come, his CPU mapping out the edges of the buildings and showing him where alleys and tunnels would allow them to shift over to the street where their quarry was now walking. "Let's follow him from this side of the block for now."

"He's almost halfway back to the bar at this point," Daffyd muttered. "Probably gonna turn soon or he's on one hells of a detour."

"Which is why we're staying on this street," Paul explained. "If we move over to him and he turns right, then it looks odd for us to turn back again."

Sure enough, their target took a right turn and Paul put out a hand. "Let's slow the pace a bit," he said quietly. "We don't want to get ahead of him."

The Marine crossed the street forty meters in front of them and continued on toward the river.

"Hope he's not heading for a boat," Daffyd said quietly.

"That *could* prove problematic," Paul replied mildly. Though he suddenly had a feeling as he looked down the gently curving canyon of buildings to where an island was visible in the middle of the river.

A series of turbines on the upstream side appeared to have been the power source for an abandoned industrial facility on the island. Whatever they made there must have used a lot of water or it certainly would have been more efficient to put the site on the station's mainland.

Whatever they'd made there, they weren't making it anymore. The place was obviously deserted and had been for years. He knew Kinsey would have seen the advantages of such a location. They had a clear field of view in all directions and it would be a difficult place for a rival gang to assault.

A man convinced he was being hunted by Imperial agents might find some measure of security on a small island like that.

It became more likely as they followed their quarry. Having made his one perfunctory attempt at throwing off pursuit, the Marine now headed steadily toward the riverbank, sped along at twice the normal walking speed as he strode along the constantly moving slidewalks.

He crossed the riverside street and took a stone stairway to the riverbank.

Paul and Daffyd jogged a couple of steps as they walked off the end of the last slidewalk and reached the low stone wall just as a small boat hummed away from the jetty below.

"Just as well we left the van behind," Daffyd said, "or you'd be asking me if I could turn it into a boat right about now."

"We *are* going to have to get someone inside that facility," Paul insisted. "Kinsey may be in there or he may be somewhere else entirely. We need to know before we try to raid the place."

"Well..." Daffyd pulled out his holo projector and nodded down the stairs. "... I did mention having higher priorities than making the bots active in water, right?"

They moved down the stairs, away from the crowded street, and sat on a bench under a small stand of apple trees.

Daffyd held up the ball. "Link me up."

Paul fed the nanite data to his projector and a menu sprang up in front of them. Daffyd set the ball on the bench, the projector keeping the menu in place based on the position of his face.

He scrolled through a few menus and opened a command line. "When I activate this," he warned, "we'll have limited visual capability for a short time before it kills the power cells."

"Firstly," Paul said, "*Cai bu shi*! And secondly, how long will it work?"

"Yes way! And I'm not really sure but it should be at least a half centi."

Paul looked across the water to where their target was walking from the dock to the abandoned building. If they started too soon, they might only get a glimpse of a few hallways. The man disappeared inside and Paul closed his eyes.

"I'm watching his movements on an overlay of the building," he explained. "Let's hope the plans on file are accurate.

"He's moving down the hall to the main office. Hang on, he's waiting outside the office that belonged to the plant director. The bag is on the ground; I think he's waiting on a chair or a couch."

"Just tell me when," Daffyd urged.

"Ok, the bag is moving again. Start the video feed." Paul opened his eyes and, once he started seeing the slightly hazy image from inside the building, he routed the data to Daffyd's projector.

A hallway sprang up around them. A guard opened a heavy gray door and stepped aside. A man with short-cropped hair stood just inside with a 10mm pistol in his hand. As soon as the bag reached the doorway, the image stuttered and then faded entirely.

"*Cao wo!*" Paul exclaimed "What happened? Did the power fail?"

Daffyd shook his head. "That stutter – it wasn't the power cells; it was countermeasures. I'm sure of it." He picked up the ball, checking to ensure that it had at least stored what they *did* manage to see. "Whoever that was, it wasn't Kinsey."

"He's a lieutenant from the 538." Paul sighed. "For all we know, Kinsey is in that room right now, but that officer blocked our view."

"So what do we do now," Daffyd asked, "hit the place or watch it?"

Paul looked out across the river, chewing on the inside of his cheek. "If we set up observation posts, the only way we confirm Kinsey's presence is if he *leaves* the place and then we're back to square one again. That means the assault option."

"And if he isn't in there?"

"Then we grab whatever intel we can and move on it immediately." Paul stood up, waiting for Daffyd to collect his projector and turn it off. He led the way up the stairs.

"The clever chess game is over. Now for the mad scramble."

Approach

"**S**ignal coming back from the scout," the communications officer announced.

"I'll take it here." Ava activated the holo feed from the incoming signal and studied the trace sent back by one of the Hasty Ferrets they'd borrowed from the *Dark Star*.

Nurazhal was a major shipbuilding node for the Gray Quorum. Located at the center of a concentration of mineral-rich planets, Nurazhal itself possessed little in the way of minerals, but it had a stable climate and the crops raised there helped feed the massive shipyard that ringed the planet.

Its position placed it in the middle of a resource-rich sector. No doubt the Grays had run endless simulations and linear transport optimizations before deciding the planet represented the most efficient place to bring the riches of the surrounding worlds and convert them into ships.

The Hasty Ferret, sitting far enough away from Nurazhal to be almost undetectable, was now beaming a treasure-trove of tactical data back to Ava's flagship, which was well beyond the known detection range of Gray long-range sensing.

The HF's hull consisted of a network of flat facets, each one coated with a matte black material that excelled at converting electromagnetic energy into heat. Cooling systems carried that heat away to the entropy shunts, capturing and imprisoning any light or radar that might otherwise return to the Grays and give away her position.

The Ferret crews were a pragmatic bunch and kept mostly to their own kind. One pilot and one operator were assigned to each of the small craft and they made their living sitting under the enemy's nose. A combat shuttle sitting at the same range would be detected immediately and destroyed.

Their sensor suite was second to none and the data flooding back to the fleet presented Ava with a tough decision. "Tactical." She looked over to find him watching her, along with most of the bridge crew. She chuckled, expanding the view to full size, filling the open space in the center of the bridge. "Looks like half their forces are still here."

The tactical officer approached the other side of the projection. He nodded, lips drawn tight. "Twice our forces, at the least. Frankly, we suspected as much. We never really expected them to send everything they had for a single mining outpost."

He moved slowly around the projection, coming to stop next to her. "Not sure I'm keen on fighting against these odds."

"Nor am I," Ava mused, and then a grin spread across her face. "But what if only half of us fight them?"

GLOVES OFF

Fate

eems a shame," Daffyd said wistfully. "I hate to damage a good ship." He ran a hand along the smooth wood of the bridge railing. "Never even saw a ship made to float on water before. There's something about it that just feels right. Less claustrophobic than a spaceship."

"You get claustrophobic?" Paul arched an eyebrow at him. "An engineer? You've got all those enclosed spaces to crawl through and you're claustrophobic?"

"That's different. When I'm in a conduit run or climbing in behind a module, I'm there because my ship needs me. It's... symbiotic. I keep her alive and she returns the favor. When I'm off duty, the walls start closing in."

"Mictlan couldn't have been much fun for you."

Daffyd chuckled. "As opposed to all the other inmates who enjoy living in a supermax prison so much."

"Well, once things settle down, you could come back here and find another ship. Maybe make a living carrying cargo around the station?"

"Nah." Daffyd waved off the notion. "I'd go nuts staring up at this ceiling every day." He nodded up at the curved roof. "I'll just have to put up with cramped spaceships." He took a deep breath. "Sure will miss the fresh air, though."

Paul laughed. "That's just the smell of bird shit and algae."

"The air's filtered by the trees here," Daffyd insisted. "Up to sixty percent, which takes a huge load off the atmo cyclers."

"Can't you just pretend the station's just a really big spaceship?"

Daffyd shrugged. "Maybe. Anyway, what do you think are our chances of finding Kinsey on that island?"

Paul looked ahead. The island was coming up fast, now only three hundred meters away. "I'd say more than seventy percent. It feels right. Can you think of a place he's more likely to be?"

"Seeing as I've only been here for a few days, no," Daffyd said. "How often do you rely on feelings and hunches as a cop?"

"You'd be surprised. A hunch is usually based on data I've seen but haven't consciously put into perspective yet. It's my subconscious' way of saying *hey, dumbass, look at this!*"

Daffyd grabbed Paul and shoved him toward a stairway leading down to the main deck. They descended and ran toward their crewmen who huddled near the bow.

"I hope dumbass was paying attention, 'cause it's time to brace for impact." Daffyd found a suitable corner formed by a ship's rib and the outer hull. "Hang on!" he shouted at the men around him, all crewmen from the *Rope a Dope*. "Here it comes!"

They all closed the helmets of their light dragoon armor.

The ship screeched as she tore through the hydroelectric array that sat upstream of the island. Large modules tore loose and rolled beneath the freighter's bow waves. The light metal catwalk used to maintain the array shattered like matchsticks as the bow ran up through it, heaving up onto the shore with a sigh of mud sliding against steel.

"Go," Paul roared as they leapt over the bow, their armor making light of the ten-meter drop. He raced ahead, jumping the low retaining walls that terraced their way up to the main structure.

He came across a single guard, walking a sentry beat around the island in plain clothes. Before either could raise their weapon to fire, a shot from a dragoon behind Paul finished the man off.

He wished, momentarily, that he had thought to use suppressed weapons so the sound wouldn't give their approach away but he realized it would have conferred little advantage, if any. The ruckus of smashing their old freighter ashore would certainly have alerted their quarry.

It was still preferable to the slow, laborious maneuvering required to bring the ship into the receiving or shipping docks on the sides of the island.

He reached the upstream door of the main wing and slammed his way through to find three armed men in the hallway. He fired a burst, cutting two of the unarmored guards down while another dragoon downed the third.

He could hear heavy footfalls and knew what was coming. "Cover!" he shouted into the helmet's pickups. "Take cover. Heavy Marine Armor ahead."

Paul ducked into a side door, stumbling over an overturned prototype printer and sprawling onto his face. He rolled to get up and saw, through the door, that a dragoon was standing in the middle of the hallway, firing his assault rifle down the hall. Before Paul could repeat his warning, a three-round 20mm burst punched through the man's armored torso, hurling him back down the hall and out of Paul's sight.

"*Zhentama!*" Paul came to his feet and raced for the downstream wall. "Get out of the *goucaode* hallway! Just fire around the corner at him and keep him busy for a moment."

He hit the thin office wall, smashing through the weak barrier with ease in his light armor. The suit doubled his mass but also added to his speed and agility and he powered his bulk through the intervening walls to reach the Marine's flank. He turned hard, tearing up the flooring fabric as he launched himself into a dive, smashing through the wall and back into the hallway at his enemy's feet.

Before the armored man could react to the new threat at his feet, Paul shoved his weapon up into the crevice beneath the HMA breastplate and squeezed the trigger. The rounds broke the seam holding the flexible, fixatropic abdominal armor to the breastplate. The segment of flexible armor affected by the round's impact went temporarily hard but it also pushed back into the Marine's abdomen driving his breath from his lungs and leaving a gap for Paul's second burst to slice up into his chest cavity.

He came to his feet as the HMA suit slumped into the rest position. The dragoons came out of the side offices and moved toward him but suddenly stopped and brought their weapons up as Paul heard the faint whine of micro-servos and mech-muscle tissue.

Paul turned as the HMA suit returned to a full standing position. "Platoon flow," he warned. "That means there's at least one more active suit within fifty meters and I'm betting it's in the main office. Let's go. The longer it takes to get there, the longer Kinsey has to run off."

He raced off down the hallway toward the office. "Daffyd, take your team in from the neighboring office on the upstream side," he ordered. "I'll bring the rest in through the hallway wall and we'll have 'em in a crossfire. He reached the doorway and ran a couple of strides past it before turning and smashing his way through the wall, just ahead of the rest of his team.

An armored man was in the center of the room, aiming at the door. He turned in surprise, running to his left as he brought his weapon to bear. Paul dove, relying on the aid of his implant to put a burst of full automatic fire into the man's abdominal plates. The rounds sprayed the fixatropic sheeting, the fluid inside temporarily hardening in response to the impact of the small caliber rounds and preventing them from penetrating.

Because he'd hit the abdomen while the Marine had been running, the plates froze at an awkward angle and, when the man tried to angle toward his target, his upper body couldn't flex to maintain balance and he thundered into the carpeting, face first.

Daffyd's team burst through the side wall and, seeing their target on the floor, the engineer stepped over the prone form and slid his muzzle under the back of the cuirass, squeezing the trigger several times to break the seam and finish his enemy.

It was only then, after the armored target was neutralized, that Paul's suit registered the sound of heartbeats and heavy breathing coming from a door at the back of the office.

He stepped over to the door, grabbed the handle and tore the door from its hinges, tossing it aside with ease.

Rufus Kinsey stepped back, holding his hands out in a warding motion as he stumbled and fell backwards to sit on a mouldy toilet.

"Make a good obituary," Daffyd suggested as he came to stand next to Paul. "Rufus Kinsey, former Marine Colonel, dishonorably dismissed for high treason, killed hiding in the crapper."

Kinsey's hands came down and he scowled at the two men in front of him. "You won't be killing me today, gentlemen."

"Oh no?" Daffyd hefted his assault rifle. "These boys are from 1GD, you *hundan*. More than half of them have lost someone to your shenanigans. If Paul or I don't kill you, one of them sure as hells will."

"And how will you get back home?" Kinsey sneered. "With my capture, you'd be heroes again. CentCom would have to welcome you instead of arrest you. Then my patrons can make a deal to get me released." He laughed in their faces. "You need me alive!"

"This is the problem with selfish people," Daffyd told Paul, his tone conversational. "They all think they're the lead character in their own little story so they assume the Universe will just arrange itself to their liking."

He looked back to Kinsey. "We like it here, *ni tamade*." He shoved his rifle up against Kinsey's chest, waited a heartbeat to see the fear, and pulled the trigger.

Three rounds hammered into his chest cavity, tearing a hole through his heart and destroying one of his lungs.

Paul turned from the dying man, ignoring his last moments. "Who'd we lose on the way in?"

"Fredrickson, from Eddie's squadron, and Kalashnikov took a bad hit to the shoulder. Might lose an arm."

"Hospital?"

"We can't afford to pay," Daffyd spat the words out.

"I've earned some funds since coming out here," Paul told him. "I should have enough but, first..." He scanned around the room, walked over to an ornate carved wooden box on the desk that sat next to a credit chip terminal. He smashed the delicate lock on its front. A neat stack of credit chips were inside.

"I'd say we can afford to have Kalashnikov looked after." He handed Daffyd the box. "I'll call in an air ambulance."

The look on the dragoons' faces was worth more than all the money in that box.

Intrusion

Primary Javelin Mthellan knew his skin was several shades darker than normal. His head inclined forward and to the right by just a fraction before he mastered his rage and brought his unseemly histrionics under control. He'd been a ship's javelin when the upstart Humans were still patting themselves on the back over their new pointy sticks.

He knew better than to let his anger make a fool of himself and yet his self-control had failed him in front of his own bridge crew.

The nerve of those Humans! Using an artificial singularity generator to disrupt a busy transit lane wasn't terribly new. Raids had been carried out by their privateers from time to time.

But this was different. This time, a naval force from their precocious Imperium was tripping Gray ships out of distortion and *boarding* them, claiming they were looking for abducted Humans.

That they were certain to find some had no bearing on the matter. What damaged Mthellan's calm was the fact that they were here, in Quorum space, projecting their will on sovereign Gray vessels. They were forcing their way aboard each ship and searching it as if they actually had the right to do so.

He had half a lobe to fight them, but his was the only warship among the six stopped vessels and he had little doubt as to the outcome, should he attempt to bring his mains to bear on the Humans.

It only added to his rage and humiliation that his cruiser had been assigned to protect this shipping lane. Here he sat, meekly awaiting a shuttle filled with the cursed Humans' Naval-Infantry.

He blinked. Marines. The Humans called them Marines for some bizarre reason. Though Mthellan's kind disdained infantry combat as an anachronistic throwback, he couldn't deny the effectiveness of the concept as applied by the Humans.

They liked to get in close with their ships, which carried far more in the way of secondary batteries than their Gray counterparts. It made targeting harder as the cone of a main guns firing envelope grew smaller as you got closer to the muzzle.

It also opened opportunities for their Marines to get aboard Gray ships and seize them. Mthellan managed to stop himself from a haughty tilt of his head. Still, he wouldn't fail in his duty to scuttle his ship in such a situation, as so many other javelins had. He was not so enamored of his long existence that he'd forget his duty.

"A shuttle approaches," his vizier, tertiary grade advised, his absolutely neutral tone a possible rebuke over Mthellan's earlier outburst of physical anger.

He opened a holo image of the forward landing bay and watched as the shuttle settled on the deck. He fought the anger as he noticed the gouges and dents made by the armored craft.

Like the ship that had launched it, the shuttle bristled with weapons. And the medium-bore rail gun protruding above the cockpit could easily destroy his ship if they were to fire it while inside the landing bay.

Heavily armored Marines came from the rear ramp as it hit the decking and they moved off in pairs to start their search of the ship. One of their number, their officer by the markings on his armor, went with the team heading for the cargo bay.

Mthellan once again fought the urge to open fire on the Human ships. How dare they board his ship and not even report to its captain?

"Gray vessels, this is General Windemere," a harsh voice grated on the bridge sound system. "Any unauthorised movement will be met with severe penalties. Gray freighter seven-two-chimela-six-six, you are ordered to heave to or we will open fire without further warning."

Mthellan looked back at his holo. The freighter was turning out of the line, ignoring the impertinent Human's demands.

The javelin watched in fascination, silently encouraging the freighter captain's defiance until the icons representing the Humans' Iron Hand fighters began converging on the ship.

He knew they carried 30mm guns, mounted beneath the crew compartment and protruding out the front of the small craft.

They weren't converging on the freighter at all. Mthellan realised they were arraying themselves in two groups, one aimed at his starboard flank, and the other at his ventral surface. They were meant to keep him in place.

He realized that the combat shuttles were being diverted to deal with the lightly shielded freighter. They fired only enhanced-conventional rounds, easily penetrating the shields and crippling the engines.

Of course it made sense, when Mthellan reminded himself that the Humans suspected the vessel might be carrying some of their people. Using their Iron Hands to stop the freighter may well have worked, but there would have been little left for them to search.

Two shuttles made their way into the freighter's forward bay. The infantry must have found what they were looking for because a swarm of shuttles suddenly issued from the carrier.

Mthellan realized the freighter captain may have been trying to destroy his vessel by running. His civilian ship had no self-destruct and so he may have been counting on the Humans to do the job for him and erase the evidence.

He decided to recommend the captain for a note of commendation, though it was uncertain what weight his words would carry. Sitting meekly while a far younger species gave insult to the honor of the Quorum was hardly the way to burnish one's reputation.

It had taken thousands of years and more clone bodies than Mthellan cared to count for him to reach his rank and now he'd probably get his first negative note-to-file. He couldn't even remember his original body anymore but he could recall the revulsion he'd initially felt upon seeing his first clone host.

He silently cursed the shapers for putting his kind in a prison that he couldn't bear to escape. It was a mystery why they worked among the Humans.

"The soldiers are re-boarding their shuttles," the vizier, tertiary grade announced.

Mthellan watched as the small craft left the ship. Of course, there was nothing illicit for the Humans to find on his vessel but it wasn't the point. Even if they'd known, he was certain they'd have boarded and searched the ship anyway.

The Humans were sending a message – a very provocative message.

Coming so close to the sudden attacks by the colonial privateers, he had to wonder if they were connected. He was certain any attacks against the colonies would be noticed by the Imperium. It was almost as if they were trying to build a justification for war.

Curious. He'd watched the Imperial Humans for centuries and he'd been sure they had lost their appetite for expansion. They seemed content to slide into chaos as their expansion-based economy turned inward, feeding upon itself.

Yet now they were here, acting as though they owned this sector, and the implications were troubling.

"Gray cruiser, this is fleet traffic control." A bold voice announced. "You are now clear to depart. Remain on your assigned heading until you clear the jump threshold or you *will* be fired upon. Control out."

Dismissed by a member of an inferior species. Mthellan's head tilted back a degree. He knew he was embarrassing himself and his entire staff with this fresh outburst but he didn't care.

An Inspired Defeat

Grand Ballista NGark stood with his feet three centimeters farther apart than was normal. His shoulders were drawn back slightly and his chin a degree or so higher than one would expect.

His blatant preening might have been out of place for a civilian post but he was responsible for the defenses of the Quorum's largest shipyard and he'd just completed a full inspection tour, visiting each and every one of the warships guarding Nurazhal. He'd shown the same attitude during his tour, hoping to buoy the confidence of his forces. A military governor had to show confidence.

The yards at Nurazhal were one massive structure, ringing the planet above the equator and capable of producing more than thirty warships simultaneously. With the recent colonial raids and the more troubling activity of Imperial warships, production at Nurazhal had been ramped up to full capacity.

The Quorum had sensibly decided to prepare for war. They had taken far too long, in NGark's not-so-humble opinion, but at least they'd come to their senses.

A flurry of logistics craft shuttled back and forth between the storage wings and the material conveyors, ensuring a steady flow of goods for the automated fabrication systems inside the ring. Even more logistics craft unloaded freighters at dozens of locations around the planet-girdling ring.

Thirty vessels, a mix of frigates and heavy cruisers, moved along the assembly-line rails of each individual construction dock. Three frigates were almost ready, approaching the small bulge of administrative habitats that marked the line between each dock in the ring. Each of the three had taken their crews aboard and the final loadout teams had come aboard with cargo shuttles, each carrying the food, supplies and ammunition needed to turn the massive constructions into living, breathing killers.

Unlike most of his kind, NGark had been career military *before* the transition that had granted his kind immortality. Most of his fellow officers had eventually grown bored of the life and moved on to science or politics but NGark had stayed on, advancing over the millennia to reach flag rank.

He knew his current, overblown stance harkened back to the reproductive displays of a past long forgotten by most of his kind but he was relatively unique in his refusal to show disgust at such ideas. He'd be considered a degenerate if he chose to voice his opinions, but he dimly remembered the act of sexual reproduction as something rather enjoyable.

If he recalled correctly, from deep in the mists of time, he'd been something of an enthusiast.

He was also one of the few original officers left from his species' final generation and his people feared his displeasure at least as much as they did the enemy.

That didn't mean he was immune from political meddling. He'd been certain the mining outpost on N'Zhil was a write-off, but he knew he had to send a strong response to the colonial raid. To simply ignore it would have energized competing factions at the high chamber and his dismissal would have used as a convenient stepping stone for an ambitious *apparatchik*.

He'd sent half his forces and he begrudged even that much. He was well aware that the raid might have been a feint to draw his forces away from Nurazhal, leaving the yards open to destruction at a time when the Quorum needed every ship it could get its hands on, but he also knew he'd be accused of timidity if he sent too few ships, especially after the miners had sent a message claiming the Human raiders were moving to enter orbit.

It would still be a half-day before the first scout jumpers could return with word from N'Zhil and NGark was silently cursing his lack of information. He doubted very much that any Humans would still be there. They'd know how long it would take for a reaction force to arrive.

He looked at his large-scale tactical holo. If the Humans had any sense, they'd be coming here to take advantage of his decisions.

As if in confirmation, a vizier, first grade, interrupted his thoughts. "Multiple distortion alerts on the N'Zhil approach vector, thirty five thousand cubits out."

NGark assessed the variables. Either his force had been tumbled from distortion before reaching the mining outpost and then had to flee back to Nurazhal or the new inbound contacts were the enemy. Either way...

"Recall all forces from the far side of the planet," he ordered. "We concentrate here to block their orbital insertion window." Even if the incoming ships were his, it probably meant a pursuing enemy arriving behind them, soon enough...

"Vessels are of our design," the technician advised. "No response to hails as of yet, and..."

"A second wave of distortion alerts," the technician, second class, who sat next to him declared abruptly. "Human ships and we're seeing mass separation. It appears the second group is firing at the first."

Well, that, at least, gave NGark a clear target to fight. Why the Gray ships had failed to respond to hails was a concern, given the near-instantaneous performance of radio or light-based signals at such close distance. Still, his captains were mostly untried in combat, having held their posts for little more than a century or two, and they may have been overwhelmed by the urgencies of the fight.

He leaned forward, his head inclined slightly to the left, and the entire bridge crew was suddenly acutely aware of his wrath. "Signal our inbound ships," he ordered. "Get them out of the way so we can fire on the Humans."

He straightened slightly, inner eyelids becoming straight lines across the middle of his dark eyes.

Misdirection.

The cursed apes had told him a story and he'd believed it. The perfectly plausible arrival of Gray-built warships followed by a clearly hostile force of Humans. The supposed firefight might well be a show to lull him. The Humans would have to be firing their main weapons if the sensors were resolving mass separations at this distance.

And if they were...

"Vizier, what damage to either of the two groups of inbound vessels?"

"Difficult to resolve at this range, sir, but it appears to be minimal at this stage. Our own ships have managed to evade the heavier rounds from the Humans, so far."

NGark felt the chill of lightening skin. "What of those enemy rounds," he demanded. "Plot their trajectories."

The holo began to populate with green lines showing the path of the enemy ordnance. The lines all intersected the shipyards. NGark's flesh chilled. To be gulled so easily by those apes. They'd only recently come down from their trees and yet they'd played him like a *zithra*.

"Full combat footing. Fire at both incoming groups. Launch all shuttles and attack craft," he said with the slightest emphasis on the first syllable, a warning to any who might be slow in passing his orders. "Position one on each inbound track or the dockyards are lost."

"But, sir..." the senior dagger at the tactical station turned to face him as the first howl rumbled the decking... "such an order means certain death for the pilots and I am compelled to refuse the order and log a complaint..."

He fell in a heap, reddish brown blood turning green as it pooled around his form.

NGark kept his sidearm in his hand. He hadn't fired it often because it had been designed for his original form and clone bodies lacked the physical strength needed to effectively handle the recoil.

He looked pointedly at his secondary tactical officer. "Do you also wish to refuse a lawful command in a time of war?" he asked calmly.

The officer turned to his station and passed on the orders.

That would block some of the enemy rounds, but it was no long term solution. He looked at holo, the fragile station still going about its business. The shuttles scurried back and forth.

The shuttles.

"Tactical, have the computer commandeer all the cargo shuttles. I want them to each collect one container and move out to intercept the enemy fire. Three quarters of the shuttles will continue to ferry containers while the rest will remain out here with us to position them as obstructions.

"And get those freighters out here immediately."

"Sir, I must protest..."

"No, you short-telomere degenerate," NGark rounded on the tactical officer. "I want the containers they have in their *holds.* We have a tenth of a standard day before those enemy rounds get here but the enemy will carry on firing during that entire time. The only questions are: do they know about the mines we've sowed and will we run out of containers before they find them?"

Never Reinforce Failure

"**W**e have inbound traces" Tactical warned. "They appear to be targeting both of our forces. Just over a deciday till the rounds get here."

"Very well," Ava acknowledged. "Fire everything we have at the station. Let's get the secondary batteries going. Ignore the defensive fleet for now. Set all call-signs to independent evasive action."

She could hardly complain. They'd gotten off several volleys before the enemy commander came to his senses, even if he'd figured out their ruse more quickly than expected.

Given the size of the Grays' military, it was inevitable they'd run into a decent commander sooner or later. She just wished it hadn't happened today. Still, it shouldn't matter. The rounds were on the way and it wasn't as if the Grays could move their station.

"Ma'am," the sensor officer turned and walked briskly over to her station. "I've been watching the target zone and I'm starting to see a pattern forming in the light reflections." He gestured to her holo with a questioning expression and she waved her assent.

He opened his own overlay. "We think these are the heavy cargo shuttles," he said, pointing at the cloud of dots, each too small to have an icon of its own. "It looks like they're hauling the raw material containers into positions where they can intercept our rounds. Kind of like ablative armor."

He pointed at the larger dots, this time with icons. "Still too far out to be certain, but these look like container ships."

"*Jian gui!*" Ava sighed, looking up to catch the tactical officer's eye. "Run a simulation," she ordered. "Work with Sensor's data and find out what percentage of shots they might block, and get it done quickly. Time always runs out faster when you're shooting."

"*Tamade!*" the XO groused. "Who's been fiddling with our forward shielding? It's been pulled in to within half a meter of the hull!" He opened a view from the forward shuttle bay and grunted in surprise. "I suppose we did declare weapons free but this is taking things to useless extremes."

Julia looked over at his holo and a startled laugh escaped her.

A small group of crewmen stood at the forward edge of the hangar deck, just inside the shield and they had armed themselves, pushing the muzzles of their linearly accelerated assault rifles out through the blue haze. They were firing in the general direction of the station but, with nearly twenty thousand kilometers still separating them from their target, the chances of hitting it were slim.

The XO looked over when she laughed and he shrugged. "Their action station is to repel boarders in the forward bay, so no real harm done. If I went after everybody who ever acted like an idiot, we'd run out of officers inside of a week."

"Speaking of idiots," the tactical officer cut in, "I might just qualify. The computer gave a ninety-eight percent intercept prediction and then went on to suggest we fire around the poles of the planet instead of just at the narrow band of station we see from this side."

Ava nodded. "We all should've thought of that. Either the enemy fails to realize what we're doing and we get some hits in or he catches it and has to block those shots as well."

"Which dramatically increases the area he has to block," the XO added.

"Already on it," Tactical assured them. "It drops their intercept ratio to ninety-six percent."

"Ninety-six?"

"Aye, ma'am, but it's better than ninety-eight."

They raced down toward Nurazhal, putting as much ordnance into the equation as possible, until they reached their predetermined disengage line.

"Standby to jump," Ava said as calmly as she could. They'd seen a lot of explosions but they'd all been too far out from the station.

Whoever commanded the defenses knew what he was doing. His scheme of using the cargo containers to block incoming shots was a clever improvisation that she'd never have expected from a Gray. All of their rounds were used up in vaporizing the containers and the materials within. With so much kinetic energy converted to heat, the rounds had no chance of reaching their intended target.

The slower secondary rounds might have a chance, but it seemed the tactical computer's simulation had erred on the side of optimism.

Regardless, the time to leave was upon them. She'd come here to damage the shipyards, not to get into a pitched battle with a strong force, especially not a unit as well led as the one guarding Nurazhal.

Her upper body jerked back in alarm as one of her ships was suddenly wiped out. No incoming trace had been detected. "Mines!" she shouted, activating the fleet-wide channel. "Minefield – all call-signs brace for emergency jump!" She reached up to the blinking red icon and touched it, sending every one of her ships a signal that activated their distortion drives.

It was a standard operating procedure since Julia had implemented it, months ago, and Ava was glad to have it. Julia had wanted to be sure her more hot-headed captains would withdraw when ordered and so the sub-routines had been added to slave all the fleet's distortion drives to the flagship. One icon would launch them all to a pre-specified rendezvous point, regardless of what the individual captains might feel about running from the Grays.

As the stars shimmered out of focus, she saw one more icon disappear and she fought the urge to vent her frustration. She'd known losses were possible, even likely, but she'd been certain they could do enough damage to put a major enemy asset out of commission. Now, it seemed she'd lost good people for no gain at all.

From the Jaws of Victory...

"The Humans are gone," a vizier, first grade, announced.

"Keep those containers coming," NGark ordered. "The Humans may be gone, but some of their ordnance is still inbound." He returned to his earlier stance. No graduate of the academy would have thought outside the manual and used cargo to save the station.

They would have charged into battle, destroyed many of the inbound ships and then died without saving the station. NGark had seen it before. The newer officers relied too heavily on the battle drills learned at officer school. Battle drills wouldn't save the Quorum's ability to build warships.

His leg and shoulder muscles twitched slightly, a faint vestige of an ancient fight-or-flight reflex. "Vizier, what was that series of impacts on our shield?"

"It appears to have been small-arms fire from the Human ships."

NGark tilted his head, raising an eyelid in amusement. Those apes should have known they could never harm a warship. Even the nav-shielding would...

He straightened slightly, his neck seeming to grow longer. The station didn't travel. It needed no shielding in the pristine orbitals of Nurazhal. "Is any of that small arms fire heading for the station?"

"Impossible to tell, sir. The rounds are too small for our sensors to resolve."

Those apes!

Though the chances of impact had been slim, the crewmen on Ava's ship weren't the only ones with the idea of firing from a forward bay. Dozens of crew had fired thousands of rounds and - with almost all of them aimed at the station, the chances of impact had grown accordingly.

The Grays had concentrated their defensive efforts on stopping rounds from the main and secondary batteries, and they'd succeeded, but the smaller rounds streaked past, mostly unnoticed. Almost all of them passed harmlessly by the massive ring to burn up in the atmosphere below.

A single, three-round burst of 10mm depleted uranium penetrated the outer hull in a strategic storage zone, red streaks slicing through the air as they tumbled through the deck plating to disappear into the machinery beneath. They caused an inconvenient amount of damage but they'd narrowly missed the conveyor line of nuclear armatures destined to become self-destruct devices.

They also missed the mildly startled Gray technician servicing one of the robotic arms that installed the firing circuits. Before the clone could look up at the hissing holes behind him, the holes combined.

The metal parts of the station had survived centuries of flex as it dealt with the pull of Nurazhal's two moons. Over the years, the cyclic gravitational forces had led to the nucleation of millions of microscopic fatigue cracks throughout the station. As the abuse continued – the moons were still there, after all – the cracks grew and united, gradually weakening the structure of the entire station.

The impact of the three rounds had hit a particularly weak junction where the presence of stabilizing walls were few and far between. Only the final components, such as self-destructs, were stored and installed in this section and the structural frame-lattice had less support.

The section of hull around the three holes was snatched away into the darkness and the sudden increase in escaping air grabbed the technician and slammed him against the fatally weakened panel, tearing the entire section of hull plate loose.

The wall panels on the interior side of the chamber were not secured tightly enough to deal with such a sudden pressure differential and the air on the inboard side pushed it violently toward the growing hole in the hull. They struck the robotic arms on their way out and one arm, having just completed the insertion of a firing trigger, was grazed by a power conduit that trailed behind the panel.

The conduit was still live and it grounded against the robot arm for just long enough to send a flow of electricity to the firing trigger.

There were dozens of self-destruct devices on the conveyor line but only one of them detonated. It was more than enough to cause severe damage.

Originally developed to prevent advanced Gray technology falling into hostile hands, the devices had sufficient yield to make any attempts at salvage a waste of time.

Many of their ships had been captured by Humans and turned against the Grays, but that only served to give the devices a new purpose. If a Gray captain was faced with the boarding and capture of his ship, then his responsibility, indeed the responsibility of every Gray aboard, was to destroy the vessel and deny its use to the enemy.

The blast tore a massive hole in the geometric lattice-work of the station's frame and the few segments that still held the gigantic ring intact had suffered under the same cyclical stresses as the hull panels had.

The moons were both on the other side of Nurazhal and their combined pull, already translating all the way around the shipyards, made short work of the few remaining frame segments, severing the circle, leaving a circular shaped line segment and one end of that line had been given momentum toward the planet.

In eerie, awe-inspiring silence, one broken end of the station, easily twenty kilometers in width, began drifting lower than the other, girders, conduits and conveyors tearing apart as the two ends moved past each other, trailing debris.

The dropping end accelerated, now several kilometers below its twin as it led the way toward the killing atmosphere below.

NGark stood with his feet a little closer together.

It had to be the small-arms fire, because whatever had caused the damage hadn't shown up on their sensors.

Though the Humans didn't know it, their foolish gesture of firing from their bows with small arms had managed to doom a marvel of engineering. A station that had taken Gray engineers three and a half centuries to build was now spiraling to its death because of 10mm rounds from an assault rifle.

And a healthy dose of unfavorable probability.

Though it would take a few days for the station to completely deorbit, there was no saving it and that meant that the massive industrial investment in the surrounding planets had been nullified as well. The Grays could certainly ship the minerals to other locations but they had been optimized to service the yards at Nurazhal. The containers that served the shipyard conveyors wouldn't work at most other facilities and so changes would have to be made.

This represented a massive loss to military capacity.

And NGark would now have to explain why his clever defense had all been for nothing. He doubted his anachronistic mind would save him this time, not when probability had decided to have repeated and unpleasant congress with him.

Cause for War

Julia stood in the pickup circle for the command holo of the INV *Dark Star*. The time for playacting was over and now the Grays would see who was really calling the shots.

She'd returned to wearing the underarmor suit and the Marines aboard had managed to find her a suit of HMA that she could calibrate to her body. It sat ready in the flag officer accommodations.

Windemere had done an excellent job, giving the Gray Quorum the impression that the Imperium was now taking an interest in this sector of space, a sector the Quorum claimed as their own despite the massive Human population. Now it was time to make them think that interest went farther back than they had originally estimated. Her presence among the recently arrived Imperial force would have them worried that she may have been scouting for more than just prisoners.

It would look as though CentCom were searching for a pretext to justify an invasion. Considering their recent meddling in Human space, it wasn't hard to imagine, unless you knew how sluggish and disinterested the Human command structure really was.

The generals of CentCom were too involved in the political maneuvers of the senatorial families to care much about a Gray incursion at Irricana and Santa Clara. Even considering the threat posed to circuit production and, by extension, the Imperium itself, they'd simply dispatched a security force and left it at that.

The Grays didn't know that, however, and the slugs at CentCom would forget it soon enough when Gray ships once more crossed the Rim in force.

"Report coming in from Vampire's call-sign, ma'am." The comms officer routed it to her station.

There were two Gray frigates at Uruk, watching over a small fleet of their freighters. A flurry of cargo shuttles were moving back and forth between the freighters and the ground station below where Windemere and his engineers had rescued the *Pony Express*.

"Hiding the evidence," Windemere muttered from his new spot to her left.

Julia nodded. "Seems you've done your job well. They're worried what we might do if we discover how many of our people they've killed down there."

"It certainly makes a good *casus belli*."

She laughed but it was a dark, chilling sound. "As if they didn't leave other causes for war strewn about the colonies. Their causing a civil war among Humans springs to mind..." She dragged a copy of her fleet icons to Uruk and set them up in a formation that could box the enemy vessels in against the planet's gravity well.

"But this," Windemere insisted with some force, nodding at the holo, "is far more clear-cut. We don't need to sell rumors of war when we have footage of wholesale, industrialized slaughter. The media will devour every pixel and beg us for more."

Julia made sure the system was recording the holo feed. A shot of the Grays scrambling to hide their atrocities would make a good lead-in. She shivered. "Those poor people down there died simply because they couldn't be conditioned," she said. "Their legacy will be the downfall of those who killed them."

She gave Windemere a nod then unmuted her channel to the rest of the fleet. "All call-signs, this is General Urbica. Stand by to initiate the engagement."

She double checked to ensure that each ship had the coordinates she'd assigned them and pressed the hovering icon to initiate the fleet wide micro-jump.

The stars shimmered out of focus, barely blurring into the bluish gray of full distortion before winking back into view. She pressed another icon and every ship in her fleet launched their aviation assets, even the gunboats who only had a few small shuttles with point defense armament.

The squadrons of the INV *Dark Star* began to swarm out from three launch portals and the Iron Hand fighters were the first to turn toward the Gray ships.

The fleet had arrived flank-on to the two defensive ships and they had the gravity gauge on them. The Humans could approach the Grays with the assistance of Uruk's pull but the Grays had the planet at their backs and could only try to claw their way up out of the planet's gravity well.

"Hailing channel," she ordered.

A Gray shimmered into view in front of her. "This is Brigadier General Julia Urbica of his Imperial Majesty's Marines," she announced. "We have credible evidence of illegal confinement being carried out at this site. You are ordered to cease all activity and stand by for inspection teams. Any failure to comply will be construed as a hostile act."

She cut the channel.

"By now," the tactical officer said, "they know what we do with the ships we catch carrying victims. It only stands to reason that they'd... *Tamade!* They did it. The frigates both destroyed themselves rather than fall into our hands."

Sour-faced, Windemere handed Julia a credit chip.

"Secure those freighters. I'll be on the surface with the evidence team." She turned to leave.

"And our Marines," Windemere added forcefully.

She waved a hand noncommittally as she left the bridge.

"It's right through here," Pulver told her, leading the way out onto an open walkway where the rain pounded down on them. "Stay clear of that gate at the end. It kills whoever comes in contact with the field it generates."

Steeling herself, Julia stepped to the railing on her left and looked over. She recoiled, raising a hand to her mouth. The mound of skeletons and decaying bodies staggered the imagination.

She'd seen death before, even caused quite a lot of it herself, but the sheer unthinking magnitude of what the Grays had been doing here tied her stomach in knots. One small skeleton still grasped the rotted remains of a stuffed toy and she fought to keep from imagining what the victims must have felt as they were marched toward the gate.

The camera orbs had been following her since the micro-jump that had brought them here, but there was no need to tailor her actions to them now. Her true reaction to the spectacle spoke volumes that words could never match.

Finally, after mastering her rebellious stomach, she stepped back to the railing and a sensor tech on the *Dark Star* nudged the cameras forward to show what she was looking at.

Julia's grip on the railing was turning her knuckles white, though it wasn't visible to the cameras, not in the driving downpour. A camera lowered to capture her in a close profile shot, catching the rage in her eyes.

She'd heard of this place from Windemere and his men. Daffyd had also described the place in horrific detail and she'd known it would be useful when they were ready to push the Quorum into a full war with the Imperium. Remembering how she'd planned to use this atrocity now threatened to bring her to tears.

These people had suffered horribly, watching their loved ones die and knowing their moment was coming as well. They didn't care about borders, policies or inter-species politics; they just wanted to raise their children in peace. Now she would use their pain for her own convenience? To advance her own idea of what the Imperium should have already done after the attacks on Irricana and Santa Clara?

The rage boiled inside, directed in equal measures against the Grays, CentCom and herself. "No more," she whispered.

"No more!" she shouted up into the oppressive rain. "They've gotten away with too much already. This stops now." She looked over to Pulver who was wiping his chin with the back of his hand.

"Back to the ships," she ordered. "Get everyone back to the ships, including the Grays we seized down here."

The ride back to orbit was a turmoil of noise as the heavy rain lashed at the hull of their combat shuttle. Fifteen Humans they'd found in a holding pen were in the back with her, babbling with excited relief but Julia sat staring at the deck, astonished by the strength of her anger. She struggled to channel it, to forge it into a tool.

307

The pounding of the rain abated and the rescued Humans looked out into the blackness, jeering and cursing at the sight of Gray freighters.

When they landed inside the *Dark Star*'s hangar deck, she let the others exit the craft first. She walked out past the group who were already beset by a team of medics and headed straight for the forward riser.

Windemere understood the look on her face when she returned to the bridge. He'd been down there himself. He gestured to a holo interface at an auxiliary helm terminal. "Freighter crews are secured in their own holds and the controls are ready at this station. Our boarding parties are all off the Gray ships."

She took a deep breath, letting it rattle out slowly over her anger. She was still furious, but she had it under control. She'd stick to the plan for its own sake, not simply to slake her rage. "Auxiliary Freighter Control, line them up."

She selected the waiting icon for the *Sucker Punch*. "*Sucker Punch*, this is Urbica."

"*Sucker Punch* standing by," Pulver's voice answered.

"Open the wormhole, Captain."

A circular area in front of the lead freighter shimmered before suddenly stretching to give a view of a stark world. There wasn't a single place where green things grew and even the seas, if there had ever been any, were gone. It was a massive sprawl of buildings and transportation corridors.

This world, if you believed the intelligence reports, was the home-world of the Grays and the seat of the Quorum.

She opened a general channel. "This is General Julia Urbica of His Imperial Majesty's Armed Forces. My forces are currently in orbit around a planet listed in the convention annexes as Uruk and we are deeply disturbed by what we have found here."

She touched a blinking green icon. "We are sending you a copy of the report we have made for our Emperor. In it, you will see the monstrous scale of the crimes committed against our people.

"You have been seizing Humans and conditioning their minds to keep the colonial civil war going – a war you created for your own convenience. Those who proved resistant to the process were either used as research subjects or killed outright.

"We have seized four freighters that were engaged in an attempt to remove the bodies and equipment at your facility. Under our standing orders, we are entitled to seize such ships and deal with the crews as we see fit; however, the vessels are tainted by what was done here. They are of no worth to us and so we send them back to you."

The officer at the auxiliary control, upon hearing her declaration to return the ships, activated their engines, sending the four Gray freighters through the wormhole, directly into the atmosphere of the Gray home-world. He'd already maxed out the nav-shields, not caring if the doomed crews had life-support and the four ships accelerated toward the Gray capital at roughly sixty meters per microday, every microday.

The inhabitants below would be hearing the faint sonic booms as the ships exceeded the speed of sound while still high in the atmosphere.

Huge shock-layers of superheated air built up around the bows but the shields protected three of the freighters as they roared toward their final port of call. The fourth, the ship in the lead of the doomed formation, had a poorly aligned emitter and the nav shielding was far weaker than what the Grays mounted on warships.

As the shock-layer pounded at the bow, a stream of the superheated gasses managed to force its way through, shearing away hull plating and sensor arrays until reaching the forward emitters on the starboard side.

The shielding collapsed entirely on that side of the freighter and the incredible energy of the shockwave was unleashed on the interior of the vessel, shattering everything in its path. Within a matter of heartbeats, there wasn't enough left to even pose a navigational hazard for the following ships, just a cloud of fire and smaller debris that nav-shielding could easily deal with.

The remaining three freighters punched through the fireball and continued along on their path. Where they would strike was a matter of pure chance. Rather than attempt to locate any strategic target, Julia had simply ordered the *Sucker Punch* to open a direct wormhole. She'd been tempted to crash them into the Quorum chambers but she wanted them left alive or the war needed by both the colonies and the Imperium would fizzle out before it even began.

"Spreading them out," the helm officer advised. "No sense crashing into the same spot three times."

The three ships moved apart, but at their current distance and speed, the impacts would still be close enough for their areas of effect to overlap. Travelling at fourteen hundred meters per microday, more than four times the speed of sound, the three freighters thundered into the structures on the planet too fast for the naked eye to process the devastation.

From their position on the other side of the wormhole, essentially the same as being just outside low orbit, the impacts were visible but small. To anyone on the surface, the effects would be devastating.

Three ships of a million tons each, impacting at four times the speed of sound, made for a statement that couldn't be ignored.

"We are leaving Uruk as we found it," she told the Gray home-world. "And I am declaring it off limits to Gray ships."

She cut the channel to the Gray world. "*Sucker Punch*, restore normal geometry and secure the reactor."

Impulse Shopping

Paul shrugged. "They aren't here, Dmitry. All I can tell you is that they *were* here in the last couple of days."

"Figured that out all by yourself, did you?" the squadron leader grinned, nodding at the low resolution image of the deorbiting station around Nurazhal. "I suppose you learn that kind of super-sleuthing when you work at the *Eye*?"

The enormous space station, a ring circling the entire planet, had been severed and one end was continuously feeding itself into the atmosphere, drawing the rest down after it like a long ingot into an arc furnace.

The *Rope a Dope* was trying to catch up with either of the two friendly forces after their slight delay at Cerberus. They had only gone there to insert a message into the station's system but finding Kinsey had elongated their stay. He was capable of too much damage for Paul to leave him alive.

They had spent the better part of a day drifting toward Nurazhal and now they were prepping for their next jump. Paul had no idea how far along the program Ava and Julia might be, and he decided to forgo further attempts to join the fighting of the current phase.

They'd jump directly to the Uruk system and, if nobody had arrived yet, hide in the orbiting debris field.

"*Ohooiet!*" Dmitry raised a hand to shield his eyes. "*Chyort voz'mi!*"

The flash was above them and several hundred kilometers away, but it was still bright enough to outstrip the aging ship's window shading system.

Dmitry, currently the officer of the deck, shot an angry look at the sensor coordinator. "*Ey, parshivy!* Just because we're focused on the planet doesn't mean we don't keep our eyes open. What just showed up in my sky?"

"Planet killer, sir," the red faced man replied. "Two frigates as escort. They're sliding in very slowly and hailing the planet."

"*Oh zhe zhen shi ge kuàilè de goucheng!*" Paul exclaimed. "We might want to consider jumping right about now."

"Now, hang on," Dmitry cautioned. He activated the vector traces, comparing the relative velocities. "You'd be surprised just how often we get ignored because we look like a floating pile of *gavno!*"

"They could ignore us just as easily if we weren't here," Paul pointed out helpfully.

"Yes, but with a little adjustment from our docking thrusters, we could be ignored from a much closer distance." Dmitry had that glint in his eye. He had some serious mischief on his mind.

"Right," Paul acknowledged, the insane idea infecting him quickly. "They'll have a self-destruct. We're going to need Daffyd to come along."

A sigh. "No doubt that pastry-eating *tolstak* will claim all the glory." His smile took the edge from his insult. "Let's get him up here, we don't have much time."

The holo of the interior was incomplete, to say the least. Paul, Dmitry, Daffyd and three dragoon lieutenants specialized in shipboard combat were looking at the less-than-perfect projection.

"I was only conscious for this section." Paul pointed to the crisper area of the internal map, showing where his rescuers had led him to freedom. "But my eyelid twitch must have kicked in while they were taking me aboard and putting me in storage over here." He indicated the storage room where Dem and Robin had first found him, next to Julia.

"My old Military Police CPU stored what it could and began building a Marine-standard map from the visual record." He saw no need to let them know about the advanced CPU that really resided in his sinuses. A military standard model was more than sufficient to map the interior of an enemy ship.

"They had to take a turn to the starboard side right here," Daffyd mused, indicating a jog in the corridor. "Going off a rough estimate of what a gun like that would need for power, I'd say there's a fairly large reactor right there and it would probably have to tie back to the main reactor in the engineering spaces. That would explain why there's no cross halls in the area, just those access hatches."

"So where do you think the nuke will be?" Dmitry raised an eyebrow.

Daffyd used his fingers to align a cube and he stretched it out over the engineering sections. "Somewhere in there but probably close to the main control stations. They always like to put the self-destruct in a spot that's constantly manned."

"And where are the panels?" one of the boarding officers asked.

Daffyd waved at the holo. "Somewhere in this cube," he declared with mild annoyance. "It's not like they took Paul on a tour of the ship so we have to do a bit of searching."

"This means we don't do the usual fast-and-dirty insertion," Paul insisted. "It works when we know where to go but, if we pop the airlock hatches, somebody on the bridge is going to figure out why a decompression alarm is going off before we can find the device and disconnect the remote link. I'll go in first. I'll cycle in through the air lock and clear the first compartment, then we bring everybody else in."

"Yes," Daffyd agreed. "Everybody goes in through the same airlock and joins the search for the self-destruct. We only take people who know how to deactivate it."

"Makes sense," Dmitry conceded. "Make sure she doesn't go boom first, then spread out and kill the crew."

"We've got a plan!" Daffyd rubbed his hands together. "Any more detail at this point would just bog us down. How long do we have to suit up?"

Paul was still two hundred meters away from the planet killer, but he now had to crane his head around to see anything other than the huge ship. He had to give Daffyd credit for a good idea. He'd improvised a launcher using large-diameter ventilation ducting and carbon dioxide from the weapon-rail cooling system. The boarders were being fired out the open launch bay of the old passenger liner cum combat carrier and it had put Paul on target for the cluster of ventral engineering hatches.

Doing a shuttle catapult would certainly have been noticed and would have marked the *Rope a Dope* as a potential hostile, rather than as drifting garbage.

Paul reached out and caught one of the hundreds of antennae that protruded from the planet killer's underside. It flexed, slowing his approach until it snapped off in his hands, letting him tumble to the hull where he just barely managed to grasp the base of a sensor dish.

He was less concerned about the noise he'd made than he was about the error message the broken antenna might have triggered. A number of warnings and messages would be cropping up on various stations around the massive ship and someone might put them together before the Humans could find the self-destruct.

He worked his way over to one of the escape trunks and opened the hatch. A quick look over his shoulder told him the rest of the boarding party was either already on the hull or just about to land and so he slid into the trunk and activated the entry cycle.

The inner hatch snapped open and he clambered out, grateful for the increased agility of his dragoon armor. HMA was overkill when trying to clear a Gray ship, especially now that they had no Marines on board. Kinsey had withdrawn entirely from his association with the Grays, concentrating what few Marines he'd had left on Cerberus to build his little criminal empire.

He brought up his Nuttall Special and fired into the head of the crewman who'd come to investigate the opening hatch. The silencer Daffyd had made for it eliminated the sound of the shot, leaving only the clacking sound of the slide as it inserted the next caseless round.

He looked down into the trunk, seeing a helmeted Human outside, and he gave a thumbs-up. The inner hatch snapped shut and the outer opened to let him into the trunk.

Similar thunking noises sounded around him as other hatches began to open. Boarders began climbing in.

He moved past a bank of small EVA suits to check the hallway, then shut the door. Judging from the equipment in the room, it must have been designed to facilitate exterior damage control by large teams.

They'd selected this section as their entry point precisely because of the concentration of escape trunks. Very considerate of the Grays to design a way to get large groups into their ship.

"I'd expect more suits for an emergency DC chamber in a ship this size," Daffyd said behind him, "but the Grays always did build for small crews. Lots of automation."

"What direction do you think we should go?" Paul indicated the closed hatch as well as the one on the other side that had already been closed when he'd come aboard.

Daffyd pulled out his own pistol. "My finely honed senses tell me we should try the aft door." He nodded at the one that had already been shut.

"Probably just leads to the latrine," a crewman said morosely.

Daffyd waved a negligent hand. "If it's their pellet hole, you can stand guard over it, Edrich." He started toward the door but Paul stepped in the way to stop him.

"You're a ship's engineer," he explained. "I'm a cop. Right now, we need engineers more than cops. I'll clear the way; you keep the ship from blowing up."

"We're fighting Grays hand-to-hand, right?" Daffyd asked. "With dragoon armor, you can just give 'em a good kick. Their small-caliber weapons can't penetrate our suits."

"Fair enough," Paul conceded, "but their small-caliber fingers can blow the ship if they see you stumbling around a corner and they can get their hands on a terminal."

He turned and stepped to the hatch, waving Daffyd and the other boarders back to where they wouldn't be visible once the portal was opened. He pressed the button and brought his weapon up almost by the time the heavy door had snapped out of sight.

Two Gray crewmen were standing at a control pedestal and he fired off two rounds at each, hitting them in the center of mass. No messing around with tricky headshots now. That first crewman had been less than a meter away but these two were more than fifteen meters from the open hatch and he had to prevent them from any further use of the controls they stood at.

He moved into the large chamber, seeing and downing two more crewmen before they could think to run. There were three other exits from this room and one of the boarding officers led his team toward the first exit on the right. Paul looked back to see the other two officers gesturing at their men, getting them moving into the large chamber.

He twisted the silencer off his pistol. It had helped, but his accuracy was suffering and the time for silence was now at an end.

Stealth had gained them their foothold, but it would be foolish to expect their incursion to go undetected for very long. Now came the time for speed and focused aggression. The first team lined up by their door, each man tapping the helmet of the man in front to signal readiness.

When the line was ready, they opened the hatch, tossed in a stun grenade and streamed inside the next chamber, the first two men moving to the left and right corners while the next pair took up positions inside the room to either side of the door. The lack of weapons-fire indicated an empty room and the team moved farther in to reach the next door.

Stun grenades were even more effective against the finely tuned eyes and ears of the Gray clones. The flash and sound tended to incapacitate them for almost twice as long as they did Humans.

The second team entered the second room after deploying a stun grenade and the firing began immediately. The man on the right shot a Gray at point-blank range, as the alien was blocking his path to the corner domination point. The other Grays were working at a large circular array of control panels and they stood in poses of shock as the soldiers cut them down with short, aimed bursts.

Having cleared the room, they moved on down a hallway at the far side. Ten meters down, another hall led away to the right and the first two men took up positions on either corner, covering as the team moved past.

"This looks like the kind of place we might find a self-destruct," Daffyd declared, strolling into the chamber. He looked around at the large circle of panels. "Don't see one, though."

"Maybe the monkey should push the green button?" Edrich groused, nodding at a large green touch pad on a column in the middle of the room.

"Maybe the other monkey should shut the hells up and start looking the room over," Daffyd snapped. "I'll go see what our boys are finding aft."

Paul and Daffyd followed the team's path, coming into a medium-sized room with banks of equipment and a few terminals. The sound of small-arms fire crackled up the hall, punctuated by the heavy thump of a flash grenade.

"This is just Entropy Control," Daffyd shook his head. "That last room would have to be Central Engineering. It's how they lay out their ships."

"We have to find that nuke quickly," Paul warned. "The assault is too loud to go unnoticed. Won't be long before they realize they're under attack."

"I know!" Daffyd was holding fistfuls of his own hair. "The last thing they'll want is to have one of their precious new planet killers fall into the hands of a pack of hairless apes that..."

He let go of his hair, turning wild eyes on Paul. "*Bozhemoi!*" He turned and ran back into the chamber they'd come from, shoving Edrich away from the central column. "*Davai*, Ed. The monkey needs to find a nuke." He put his palm on the touchpad, causing it to blink in green.

The column began to rise like a meter-wide periscope. A half-meter hole through the column revealed a self-destruct device. Daffyd pulled a glowing blue conduit from the top housing and the line's color faded.

"Help me with the triggers," he shouted at Edrich.

Edrich began to remove the three triggers on his side of the column. "Hard on the back, this," he complained. "Should have built in a setting for Humans."

"Maybe you can suggest it to the Quorum." Daffyd removed the final trigger and stepped back, blowing out a deep breath as the column began to lower.

"I realized nobody'd ever seen one of these beasts until after they'd been losing ships." He grinned. "Takes them a while to react to new situations, but they should at least have tried to make their self-destruct a little harder to find.

Maybe hide it in the floor..." He waved a hand at the descending column.

"All so simple," he explained, "for a genius-level fella like myself." He frowned. The column was still descending into the floor. The touchpad descended out of sight and a meter-wide hole slid down into view from above. A blue line led to a second device and a slight whine was coming from the conduit housing.

"Oh, you dirty little *shluha vokzal naja*". He looked at Paul. "Let's hope there are only two of the damned things."

An Ironic Reprieve

NGark was seething but managed to present an air of professional calm. He didn't have to wait for the transponder codes to know who'd come to relieve him of his command. PShelt always had his eye on what was best for *PShelt* and he'd been quick to demand the Quorum's second planet killer as his personal flagship.

He would have volunteered to carry any bad news to his old commander and he had the connections needed to get such an assignment. NGark wished he'd given the short-telomere degenerate a strong enough punishment to break his military career but it was too late to go back and change it now.

It had been nearly two thousand years since he'd demoted PShelt but the youngster had climbed his way back up the ladder quickly, thanks largely to his backers.

And now he was approaching the minefield with a message and that message was almost certainly a recall order. NGark was finished.

He tilted his head slightly. The ships should have stopped by now to request passage through the minefield but they continued, albeit slowly. It would be just like PShelt to force his former mentor into deactivating the field on his own, just to show who was calling the shots. Too proud to make the proper request of a disgraced ballista.

Or perhaps he'd forgotten about the minefield?

NGark gave it a moment of reflection. He wouldn't mind at all if the fool killed himself, but his ship had taken nearly two years to build and the crew didn't deserve death simply because of who they worked for.

Just before he could command a hailing channel to warn the incoming ships, his vizier, first-grade, announced the incoming hail. "Central holo," he ordered.

Let the humiliation begin.

PShelt's image appeared before him. "Grand Ballista." He oozed with politeness to the point of sarcasm. "You have suffered grave misfortune."

"The station was destroyed," NGark replied simply. He wasn't one for excuses.

"And yet your ships have taken no damage," PShelt said, his intonation betraying the unseemly pleasure he was taking from this conversation.

It was pointless to explain how they had saved the station only to lose it to random small arms fire. "If you have come here to deliver a message, then do so. If you have come for resupply, you will have to move on as we are obviously experiencing technical difficulties, at the moment."

PShelt's chin tilted down and inward at the odd statement, but he recovered his composure. "I have been sent to relieve you of your command. All your ships will transfer to *my* flag where they might see more effective use than they have here."

"No doubt orbiting home-world will give them the experience they'll need to fight the Humans," NGark droned politely. "It will be a lesson in patience, if nothing else."

"Their duties are no longer your concern," PShelt replied, eyes wide and skin slightly darker. "If you had been properly vigilant and your forces more competently led..." He stopped in mid tirade to look to the side. A voice in the background was too low for NGark to make out.

"Boarders?" PShelt sounded incredulous. "How can there be Humans on this ship?"

NGark nearly chuckled. He'd come close over the last few millennia but never so close as this. He'd almost been startled into it by the absurdity of PShelt's sudden predicament. In the midst of lecturing him about vigilance and preparedness, the fool had let the enemy sneak aboard one of the Quorum's two greatest vessels?

"Perhaps you could finish your discourse on the value of vigilance after you resolve your current problems?" NGark suggested. "Though I fear duty allows only one outcome when a ship is being over-run."

PShelt had always been quick to blame other leaders for allowing their ships to fall into enemy hands. He turned back to face NGark. "I will show you what preparedness means, Grand Ballista. I am *fully* prepared to do my duty." He turned his gaze slightly to look at one of his tactical officers. "Initiate the self-destruct."

There was the briefest of pauses which then grew into an uncomfortable moment before finally achieving its full potential as an outright disaster. PShelt cast his gaze about his own bridge, his complexion growing very light.

"Not as prepared as you might have thought," NGark offered helpfully. "My only regret is that your shame will have to be posthumous."

PShelt didn't appear to have heard him and he seemed as though he'd lost the ability to make decisions. He simply stood there, the nictitating membranes flicking sideways across his eyes in denial until his head suddenly lurched toward NGark.

The Grand Ballista nearly reacted to the sudden motion before reminding himself that he was only watching a hologram. His nemesis tumbled out of sight and a Human stepped into view, looking down at PShelt for a moment before facing NGark.

NGark gave the man a polite nod. "I should thank you," he said politely. "You've taken one of our capital ships, but you've also removed an imbecile from our ranks. Given the damage he could have caused, I believe the Quorum has the better of the deal."

Flashpoint

"**D**istortion alert!" The sensor coordinator grabbed the sides of his station, leaning back from the display in alarm. "Only two traces but one is gonna be big. They're bringing a planet killer!"

"Beat to quarters!" Julia broke off her discussion with the quartermaster, stepping into the pickup circle for the central holo system. She shot an angry look to the left. "Tactical, my display shows no indicators."

The tactical officer's head lowered as if he thought he could hide it between his shoulders. "Sorry, ma'am. Linking through now."

She'd had to train her privateer bridge crews and thought she'd catch a break, now that she had commissioned Imperial officers to work with, but these were all engineers. The sooner she got her dragoons back aboard the *Sucker Punch*, the better.

"If this is an attack run," she mused to nobody in particular, "they're awfully far out, and why such a small escort for a capital ship?" She activated the fleet-wide channel. "Nobody fires, unless the inbounds fire first."

"*Wei*!" The sensor coordinator leaned in to squint at the image. "*Tianxiaode* what's going on, but that's the same hunk of *goushi* that made fools of us at Nidaveller!"

Julia couldn't help but laugh. Right in the middle of her wishing for her beloved dragoons, they showed up.

And they brought their general a present!

"**H**and to the gods!" Paul insisted, grinning at the senior officers assembled in Julia's quarters. She kept a few couches arranged around a low table in one corner of the large room. It made for a good think tank. A place where officers could think more freely than they could in a formalized setting. "We think he was the guy in charge of defense at Nurazhal and he told me we'd removed an imbecile from their chain of command."

"He actually thanked you?" Windemere grinned. "Didn't think the Grays had a sense of humor."

"Technically, he said he *should* thank us," Daffyd corrected. "But he considered the ship to be an adequate trade."

"More than adequate." Paul leaned forward to snag a mug and the carafe of coffee. "He said the Quorum had come out ahead in the deal."

Julia snorted. "Did you kill him?"

Paul set the carafe down and enjoyed a sip. "Ahh! That's good! We ran out a week ago." He cradled the hot mug in his hands. "We would have killed the little bastard but, if he's as bad as that commander seems to think, and he's connected enough to get a planet killer..."

"...then he's of more use to us alive and serving the Quorum than he is dead?" Julia flashed him a grin.

"How do we know the commander at Nurazhal didn't just have an axe to grind?" Pulver asked.

"Oh, he probably has more than a few axes to grind," Eddie assured him. The dragoon squadron commander nodded at the coffee tray and Daffyd pushed it across the table.

"For one thing," Eddie continued as he poured, "we translated the intercepts after the fact and it sounded like our prisoner was coming to relieve the commander of the Nurazhal defenses."

"For what?" Ava leaned forward slightly to see the dragoon officer. "He pulled off a clever and highly unorthodox defense. We never got a single shot on target and we lost people for nothing."

"Might want to re-evaluate that," Eddie replied mildly.

"When we got there," Paul told her, "half the station was already down in the atmosphere and the rest was trailing in behind it. Something must have made it through."

"*Wo de ma!*" Ava was on the edge of her seat. "I have no idea how that happened, but it's a win and we'll take it!"

"A *big* win," Julia emphasized. "If we could find a way to match it at Govi Darkhan, we could seize the place instead of destroying it." It was a major logistics center for the Grays, serving most of the sectors on the Rim border, and it allowed their reach into the colonies as well, but they'd also learned from Brother N'Zim that a major research project had been set up there.

"Not with the kind of ground troops we have," Ava cut her off. "You know they're suited for lightning raids, not stand-up fights against heavy armor."

"I know," Julia conceded, "but you can't blame a Marine for wanting a stand-up fight against the only Gray ground forces we've found, so far." She waved it off. "Fine. We let them launch one raid across the Rim and then we'll try out our new planet killer on Govi Darkhan, even if it *is* in the perfect spot to support our own push against the Grays. Just destroying that planet would scare the Grays. Actually *taking* it..."

She shook her head. "I know, I keep coming back to it. Let's just get the crew transfer handled and we can get ourselves back across the Rim before the Grays come."

Windemere looked as if he'd swallowed a live rat. "Why don't we just take shuttles? The wormhole will put us next to Roanoke; why bother taking that piece of...?"

Julia held up a hand. "Remember, Vance; that ship has a special place in my heart as well as the hearts of the dragoons who made her and served in her. Park the *Rope a Dope* in a stable orbit and keep an anchor watch aboard. The accommodations are actually quite nice, if you can ignore the musty smell."

"It's just the anchor watch that'll be staying on the ship," Ava added. "For you, it's a short hop through the wormhole and a shuttle down to the surface." She handed Windemere a chip. "Go to my house and give this to Edward. He'll arrange lodging for your team as well as office and lab space."

"We're all staking you, General." Paul paused. "Perhaps we should start calling you 'Chairman'? Anyway, we're anxious to see a return on our investments, so the sooner you get set up on Roanoke and cranking out armor, the better."

Julia looked around the room. "Any other concerns before we get back to work?"

"Dmitry could use a few privateers to back up our skeleton crew on the *Mictlan*," Eddie replied.

"You named her after a prison?"

Eddie shrugged. "We named her after the same ancient underworld that the prison got its name from. And it makes

ApRhys feel at home, seeing as he spent so much time in lockup..."

"How many do you need to run that thing?"

He activated a holo in the middle of the table. "Planet killers have even more automation, ton for ton, than their cruisers but she still needs another twenty-five crew." He waved at the list hovering over the carafe. "The specialties are all broken out by division."

"We'll put out a call to the fleet." Julia grinned. "But I don't think there'll be any shortage of volunteers to work with 1GD."

Julia stood. "Eddie, let me know the instant our boys are aboard. We'll send our new engineering firm to their new home first and then it's back to the Imperium for us."

They had a war to spark.

The officers filed out as Paul set his coffee down and moved over to his pile of gear. He was moving to the *Sucker Punch* with the dragoons, while Julia would remain in the flag quarters aboard the INV *Dark Star*.

For the moment, though, they were in the same room and there was nobody else with them. When the door whispered shut behind Windemere, Paul dropped the bag he'd been looking through and turned, eyes widening in surprise as Julia pounced.

They fell onto the bed but she wrinkled her nose, sitting up astride him. "You smell like a mouldy old dragoon ship. I move we start with a shower." She deactivated the seams on her underarmor suit, smiling at the obvious hunger in his eyes. "Unless there are any objections?"

The motion carried.

Reinforcements

Julia walked onto the bridge, gripping her mug of coffee as a talisman against the monotony. Nearly two weeks of waiting for the Grays to show up at Santa Clara had left them wondering if they'd missed something. A quick glance at the status display showed that the Hasty Ferrets of 3rd squadron were currently out screening the fleet and keeping an eye on the Imperial world from an undetectable distance.

Though she missed Paul, it felt good to be living on a Human-designed ship. No matter how much time she spent on the Gray warships, they always felt alien. The ceilings were too low, even though they were designed around the same standard bulkhead panels and components used in the export market, and she didn't want to even mention the engineering needed to make Gray bathroom facilities accommodate Human digestive systems.

Captain Liu gave her a nod as she walked past him to the chair reserved for admirals, generals and other such nuisances.

"Anything new tonight, Captain?"

A nod. "A *carrier* group jumped in, right about the middle of the last dog watch. Looks like Marines and they came in ready for trouble. Had a combat air patrol outside the ship during distortion, tucked up next to the nacelles, and they spread out the instant the envelope collapsed."

She looked over at Liu. Like most Navy officers, he would only grudgingly admit that the Marines might have a sound reason for acquiring carriers of their own and he doubtless felt such an asset was wasted on them. Still, despite the way he'd pronounced the word 'carrier', she thought she'd detected a hint of admiration at the way they'd arrived in system.

More importantly, the presence of properly led Marines was unusual. She looked back at the display. They'd sent drones back to the Imperium from Uruk, detailing the atrocities committed by the Grays. The public would be in an uproar and His Majesty's government couldn't just ignore it without damaging the illusion of a democratic constitutional monarchy.

A force would have to be sent to investigate, even if just along the Rim, and a senator would have to put on his uniform and lead the effort as a praetor. Julia could think of very few senators who could be trusted to carry out the task and only one that would please the angry mob.

Time to stop hiding.

"Captain, please be so good as to hail the Marine carrier group."

Liu turned his head her way a tiny bit before mastering his surprise. "Aye, ma'am. Comms, open the channel."

Julia waited for the green icon in her holo. "IMC *Xipe Totec*, this is General Julia Urbica aboard the INV *Dark Star*, over."

There was a pause, long enough that she began to wonder if the transmission had been picked up, but the answer finally came.

"*Dark Star*, this is *Totec* Actual. I have to say, I expected to find you, just not right here, over."

Julia grinned. It was good to hear Tony's voice. "Tony, we've got enough Ferrets out to act as repeaters. Switch over to holo."

Tony shimmered into view in front of her. The newest leader of the powerful Nathaniel senatorial dynasty gave her a happy smile. "Good to see you, Julia. You've been busy, haven't you?"

"Well, CentCom sent me out there, so they can't complain about what I found, now, can they?"

"They sure tried," Tony said happily. "Blew up in their faces, though, so here I am." His face took on an expression of mock solemnity. "They've determined, in all their wisdom, that the Grays might decide we're pissed at them and that they might just attempt a pre-emptive attack on a few of our weak points."

"Lords almighty," Julia exclaimed. "Who are those people and what have they done with the real CentCom?" She rarely used sarcasm in front of her people, but she had no real intention of returning to the Imperium and neither did the crew of the *Dark Star*. The few who had loved ones in the Imperium would be arranging to have them brought out to the colonies.

Tony laughed. "So when do you expect the Grays?"

"Any day now. They're probably just busy discussing the mundane details at the moment. We've got Santa Clara covered but Paul could use your help at Irricana."

"Paul!" Tony nodded, clearly pleased to hear his friend and mentor was still alive. "The Navy has a couple squadrons of heavy gunboats and a pair of frigates there. What does Paul have?"

"He has 1GD, a couple of privateer cruisers and a frigate to help protect the Sucker Punch and a Gray planet-killer."

"Planet killer?"

"Yeah, but it's not like it's a one-shot weapon. It fires a series of huge masses in relatively rapid succession. Destroys a world's ecosystem, kicks up enough dust and debris to freeze the inhabitants." She shrugged. "They still have at least one more of the damned things."

Tony frowned. "Combine that with their source-directed wormhole engine and you've got a deadly combination."

"Which is why we need to hit them hard," Julia insisted. "If they're working to revive the wormhole program, they could open a hole over the Imperial palace and dictate terms to us. We need to push them into a corner where they can't get up to any more mischief."

"What sort of forces can the colonies bring to the fight?"

"The colonies?" Urbica leaned in. "They're just a myth, aren't they?"

Tony laughed. "One of my ancestors advised against abandoning them but he was overruled. We don't forget about stuff like that."

"They mostly have converted freighters," Julia replied. "The Grays have been steering them at each other's throats for a few decades but it's backfiring on them now. The colonials have a fair bit of experience at fighting and they've been seizing Gray ships and turning them against their former owners." She suddenly raised a hand, eyes wide.

"I almost forgot. Paul's sister is one of their foremost privateer leaders."

"Sister?" Tony stared at her for a moment. "I've known Paul for fifteen years and I never even knew he *had* a sister. You're with him for a year and a half..." He laughed. "No contest, I suppose. You're way prettier than I am..."

Julia shook her head in mock exasperation. "Get your ass to Irricana, General."

The holographic Tony bowed. "I defer to the senior officer."

Julia smiled as he shimmered out of sight. Tony could easily over-rule her by falling back on the title of praetor that the senate had almost certainly bestowed upon him before he came out here, but that wasn't the Nathaniel style.

If he felt she was wrong, he wouldn't hesitate to use his title to enforce his decisions, but he agreed with her and so he'd go where she said he was needed. The power of the Nathaniel family didn't come from their titles but, rather, from their actions.

If the Imperium had more like them, then this war wouldn't have been necessary.

ASCENDANCY

Carrier Warfare

The arrival of Tony's carrier group had changed the nature of Irricana's defense. Rather than waiting in orbit for a desperate defensive action, they'd been able to move the engagement zone farther out toward Gray territory.

They knew where the enemy force would be resupplying, seeing as Ava and her fleet had left only one option open to the enemy, and so they could predict their attack route with a large degree of confidence. That would let them dictate the location, if not the time, of the battle.

"Daffyd knows a place in Vermillion that makes *Arty Sings*," Paul told his holographic friend. "They're sending out a shuttle-load right now, free of charge, so we'll be stocked up again in no time."

Tony chuckled. "I'm *almost* surprised to hear someone's making classified gear out here but," he spread his hands in resigned acceptance, "it's the Rim."

The *Arty Sings,* or artificial singularity generators, were used by the military to force a passing vessel or fleet out of distortion where they could be engaged. The military version was roughly half the size of an adult male.

The units lifting off from the surface of Irricana right now were a little over half the size of the military version and Tony would probably turn his attention to military procurement if, he made it home alive.

Both the dragoons and the Marines were ferrying the AS units to their assigned locations, creating a screen that the enemy couldn't help but hit. Of course, if their limited power cells failed before the enemy arrived...

"Let's just turn them all on," Paul urged. "We've got a steady supply close at hand."

It was good to see Tony, but it was mildly awkward. In the past, Tony had been the younger of Senator Nathaniel's two sons and he'd always deferred to Paul.

Now Tony *was* Senator Nathaniel, and Paul was being careful to phrase things as suggestions, as efforts to build consensus.

As it turned out, the Grays arrived before the first AS net needed to be replaced. Five days into the seven-day power cells, a large group of Gray ships tumbled into space, right in the middle of the trap. Though the flash of their arrival had been seen from the fleet's position, they were sitting far beyond sensor range. A screen of Hasty Ferrets, thrown out into the space between the fleet and the AS net, reported their composition and activity.

This was the sort of engagement that carriers had been built for, at least in the opinion of the Nathaniel family, and it was an opinion that Paul shared. Many pundits claimed the concept was a redundancy.

Carriers, they claimed, gave up too much of their volume to their aviation complement and supporting equipment, cutting down on the number of guns they could mount. Those people were almost invariably tied to the sectors where more traditional vessels were built.

The ship destroyer squadrons aboard the *Sucker Punch* and the *Xipe Totec* mounted the standard 30mm launch rails, and the warheads packed a yield equivalent to a thousand tons of TNT. The SD didn't quite carry the equivalent firepower of a frigate's main gun but it was deadly, nonetheless, and far more maneuverable.

Ship destroyers were too small to have distortion engines but a carrier could put several squadrons into any fight and a single lucky shot could never eliminate all that firepower like it could with a cruiser.

And they opened up new threat vectors for the enemy to deal with.

"Right here looks good," Paul suggested to Eddie, pointing at a location above and slightly behind the enemy force.

His position aboard the *Sucker Punch* was an advisory one. Thanks to Julia's ruthless house-cleaning of the former SDF units, the officers of 1GD were proper professionals, rather than patronage appointees. That meant Eddie was able to turn his own squadron over to his immediate subordinate and take over temporary command of the entire regiment.

Paul served as the link between the privateer captains and the newly arrived dragoons. Tony and his Marines had worked with the dragoons before, but it was Paul that they knew and so he had become the de facto coordinator of the three forces, welding them together to stop the attack on Irricana.

Eddie nodded. "Should prevent them firing back through the wormhole at us." He touched the icon to authorise the coordinates. "Engineering, establish a wormhole on my coordinate marker."

The enemy ships, to their credit, had organized themselves and set a course toward their estimate of the enemy position but it would be a long trip before the two fleets came within sensor range. They'd brought three carriers with them but, if they'd launched fighters, the Ferrets were still too far away to resolve the smaller hulls.

They'd know soon enough.

The *Iron Hand* fighter squadrons slipped through the wormhole, followed by the dragoon fighters in their modified Gray hulls. The ship destroyers from both Human carriers followed as the first data began streaming back through the opening.

"*Wo de tian a!*" the sensor officer exclaimed. "The battlespace is packed with Gray fighters. Reading just over a hundred fifty Hichef-class fast fighters. No other variants appear to have launched, at this time. Three carriers, six cruisers and twelve frigates."

Paul nodded to himself. Their sixty Iron Hand fighters as well as the lightly armed, but more maneuverable, twelve ships of the Stiletto squadron were supplemented by the thirty-two Hichef-based fighters of the dragoons. IFF transponders were the only thing preventing the fight from degenerating into an orgy of accidental friendly fire.

"Transports are passing through," the tactical officer announced. The Khlen-based shuttles used by the dragoons carried a gun in the nose for softening up ground targets and the Marine shuttles, which also carried a 20mm rail gun along the dorsal spine, bristled with an array of smaller weapons as well. They'd been designed for insertion or extraction from hot zones and the Corps had always felt the best defense was a good solid kick in the enemy's gonads.

Regardless of their original design purpose, the shuttles could kill the enemy fighters and so they spilled out behind the Gray fleet and joined the fight.

"Damn it, Fedorov," Eddie hissed quietly at the holo, hands clasped tightly behind his back. "Don't get in so damned close. You don't have the fire-power that those Iron Hands have."

It was hard watching another man take your squadron into battle.

Paul realized that Eddie's concern illustrated a bigger problem. He opened an all call-signs channel. "Dragoons, don't close in with the enemy. Transponders won't keep the Marines from shooting you if they don't know which is which. Stick to the plan; stay on their flanks and support."

Eddie's lips drew tight across his teeth, showing his anger at himself. He'd focused too closely on his own squadron and forgot his role in the current fight. "What's the tally?" he demanded.

"We've lost four so far and the enemy have lost eighteen," Tactical replied. "That gap will widen more quickly as we continue to achieve battlespace superiority."

"Just be glad they haven't realized they could be using the guns on their Khlens as well," Eddie muttered, "or they might be enough to tip the scales back in their favor."

Paul shook his head as he watched an enemy Hichef slot in behind an Iron Hand, hoping for an easy kill. "As far as they're concerned, they built the Khlens for ground assault." One of the secondary armaments, mounted in the tail of the Iron Hand, fired a sustained burst and the Hichef disintegrated.

Paul looked over at Eddie. "It's not the proper tool for the job."

The Marines ploughed their way into the enemy fighters, weapons firing almost continuously. The Grays were quick to respond, turning to fire on the Human formation but the dragoons and the Marine Stilettos were providing a withering cover fire and the enemy Hichefs were being steadily pushed back from the rear of the Gray fleet.

Tony's holographic form stepped into view in front of Eddie and Paul. "The Grays are on their heels," he said. "I'm going to commit my heavy gunships."

The heavy gunships, originally designed for gravity-well operations such as covering a troop-landing from within an atmosphere, carried three 250mm guns in their bows as well as seven 150mm guns in turrets around the hull. They were surprisingly effective against frigates and larger ships but they did still suffer against concerted attack by fighters.

The three gunships of 488 Marine Expeditionary Force passed through the wormhole and they each turned on one of the three enemy carriers. If there was one thing a gunship captain hated above all else, it was an enemy carrier.

If the fight went any length, those carriers would be recovering their fighters and re-arming them to go back out and kill the gunships. They had a short window to prevent the scattered enemy fighters from responding.

Each gunship fired a salvo of three antimatter rounds from the main guns, hitting the carriers in the stern. They didn't penetrate the shields but the reaction between the antimatter and the rounds' casings unleashed the equivalent of thirty-two million tons of TNT.

Most of the blast dissipated quickly, as there was no air to propagate it, but the portion trapped against the shielding was more than enough to rip the shield generators loose from their mounts, buckling the protective fields at the aft ends.

Ever efficient, the Grays built the forward shielding mounts to handle greater stress. They estimated the majority of incoming rounds to be from the front and so they saved weight by using lighter mounts in the rear projectors. The increased acceleration, they reasoned, would give them an even greater chance to keep their bows facing the threat.

The generators became projectiles in their own right. The heavy units easily smashed through bulkheads, conduits and crewmen as they tumbled forward into the engineering spaces.

Two of the carriers went dead as their main generators were crushed. The third had taken heavy damage but it was now turning to face the fight at its rear and the second salvo from the gunship behind merely glanced off the half-buckled shield without achieving detonation.

The entire Gray fleet was turning, having found no enemies to their front, and their guns would be able to make short work of the three heavy gunships.

"I think it's time," a holographic Tony announced.

The artificial singularity generators were built into hardened cases but they weren't completely invulnerable and more than half of them had been knocked out by the gamma radiation from the antimatter detonations.

The enemy commander would soon realize he had the option to run and so the Human forces had to be held in check so as to give him the impression that he might still have a chance. If they committed everything at the start, they'd simply scare the Grays off.

"*Sucker Punch* to *Brawler*..." Paul waited for Robin to appear in front of him. "Get in there, *Brawler*. Good hunting!"

"Helm, take us in," Robin ordered. "All batteries, weapons free." She raised her voice. "And let's try to leave in the same ship we arrived in, this time!"

The chuckles helped to ease the tension.

Though most of the privateers were with Ava raiding Gray logistics centers, Robin had opted to join with Paul. She'd been the one to find and rescue him from the Grays when he'd first come to the colonies and she wasn't about to let them get him back.

Or fall into the hands of the Imperials. She didn't quite trust them, despite Paul's long-standing friendship with General Nathaniel.

Then there was the matter of Paul's ship.

She'd managed to draw escort duty for the *Sucker Punch* after returning from the refit. The ship's ability to put forces anywhere, on a moment's notice, meant independence for the colonies and she knew the most important mission the *Brawler* could draw was protecting that capability.

Her brother was on Roanaoke, taking care of her little girl, and the two were all she had in the Universe. Robin hadn't been the most involved parent, having been away fighting for the last five years, but she was doing it for little

Sarah and guarding the *Sucker Punch* was the best way for her to give her daughter a future.

"Enemy contacts coming back through the hole," Tactical warned. "Six Hichefs. Engaging..."

The moaning cacophony of the secondary batteries vibrated her bones as the enemy fighters streaked past.

"Splashed three," the tactical officer announced.

"The combat fleet patrol can handle the rest," Robin declared. "Keep moving forward. I want us turning toward Tango-Charlie-Five the instant we clear the hole. Tactical, fire as your guns bear."

The full tactical holo had been transmitting from the moment the first Human fighters had appeared behind the Gray formation. The cruiser Robin had selected was the closest to firing on a heavy gunboat. Imperial Marines had a near-legendary status in the colonies, where professional forces didn't exist.

Saving a Marine ship would link her own crew to that legend. She just hoped she wouldn't end up fighting them to keep the colonies independent.

The gunship was moving to evade, desperately trying to stay out of the way of the cruiser's main guns. The Marine ship was just too small to take any kind of pounding from a cruiser's mains. She *had* been designed to support ground operations, after all. The heavy guns in her bows had been added as an afterthought.

The Gray guns were creeping up on her, however, and it was only a matter of time...

"Firing," Tactical warned.

A mournful howl rattled loose fixtures on the bridge and the four rounds were on their way.

At almost the same instant, the enemy cruiser fired and she tore the front third clear off the Marine gunship. A cloud of debris, gas, and bodies expanded away from the front of the stricken gunship as the *Brawler's* rounds impacted the cruiser's shielding.

"Angle our approach," Robin ordered, fighting back the urge to curse.

She had no need to explain her order, not to this crew. As the ship altered course to approach at an angle, the ghostly moans of the secondary batteries increased. As the ship presented more of her side to the enemy, more of her secondary weapons could get a clear shot.

"Coolant failure on six-charlie-starboard," Tactical advised. "Damage control team is responding."

Robin was continually amazed at how the Grays would simply declare a design as sufficient and never revisit it again. The carbon dioxide system used to cool the gun rails was less than perfect, in her opinion, and another gun on deck six had gone down.

It was the second part of the reason for her approach vectoring.

"Mains up in five."

"Very well." She gave the tactical officer a curt nod. "Helm, bring us around on our next tack."

Tactical would fire the mains as they bore on target and then the portside batteries would get a turn to fire. Hopefully, Damage

Control would be able to get the coolant running to six-charlie-starboard by the time they swung back in the other direction.

The data transmitted back through the wormhole in the moments before the Hichefs had been smashed by the Human fighters patrolling their fleet had been enough to make up NGark's mind for him.

His fighters had already been losing the struggle before the arrival of the enemy gunships and now he'd caught a glimpse of what lay beyond the wormhole. He'd been considering a push through the hole, but he knew the enemy could simply move the opening at will.

His ships would never get near the entrance.

And on the other side of that entrance sat a long line of ships. Navy gunships, Marine cruisers, two carriers and the same Makers-be-damned planet killer that PShelt had lost to such amusing effect at Nurazhal.

A lesser commander would have ignored the odds and pushed ahead, but he knew there was no way for him to achieve his objective. He wouldn't be able to even approach Irricana, let alone conduct an orbital bombardment of the erbium mines in the capital city of Vermillion.

"Sound the recall," he ordered, "and all ships will standby to jump."

It was the one good result coming from the loss of two carriers. It had at least destroyed enough of the singularity devices that he could extricate his force without further loss. A commander needed to be lucky in combat but most officers failed to realize that luck was often little more than the ability to look past failures and see the opportunities that still remained.

PShelt's foolishness at Nurazhal, for example, had allowed NGark the opportunity to retain his rank. Of course, it had also led to his current predicament...

"But, sir," a sub-javelin, third grade, objected, "we've destroyed one of the gunships and, if we can..." He trailed off, blanching as he noticed NGark's hand was resting on the grip of his holstered sidearm.

It was an antique but it was intimidatingly large.

"The enemy has a horde of ships waiting on the other side," he explained, "and the only reason they don't all pour through is because they don't want to scare us off. They're so confident of the outcome that they want us to fully commit. That's when you'll see the rest of their forces come through."

"All ships report their readiness for the jump," the communications specialist, second grade, stated.

"Send the signal to jump," NGark ordered. "We'll fall back on Govi Darkhan." He was certain he knew where the Humans would strike next, and, when they did, he'd make them dance to *his* tune.

"But the recall..." Tactical protested.

"The loss of our remaining fighters will be mentioned at your trial," NGark assured him as the ship slipped into distortion. "If you had sent the recall when ordered to do so, we might have saved some of them." He looked for his master-at-arms and saw he was already leading a pair of security operators to arrest the tactical officer.

Not for the first time, he cursed the Makers for imprisoning his generation in clone bodies. His master-at-arms had served with him since before the sentence imposed on his race and he was one of the few that NGark could truly trust to do his job well. Everyone else aboard was a former doctor, lawyer, writer...

All had followed another path until the boredom had forced them to move on to another job that they still couldn't take seriously.

The longer NGark lived, the more his punishment made sense. It had seemed an odd choice, at the time – the opposite of punishment, in the eyes of many – but the Makers had punished genocide with immortality.

But not quite immortality, for the slowly degenerating telomeres of their clone chromosomes served as an effective death sentence – one that would take millennia, though it was no less inevitable for that delay. The species had thousands of years to reflect on their sins as they drifted down into oblivion.

He watched the next most senior tactical officer step up to the console and he wondered, suddenly, whether the Makers had decided to use the Humans to accelerate the end of the Grays.

Why else would they be working aboard their ships?

"That's the last of the enemy fighters," the tactical officer said with a sigh. "Nobody here but us Humans."

"Very well," Robin acknowledged. "Launch shuttles to search for survivors."

She stared intently at the playback on the holo. Shortly after the three fighters got through the wormhole, the Gray fleet had jumped. If only she'd managed to stop them, the enemy might not have escaped.

She knew she'd have to fight those same ships again, sooner or later.

The Road Ahead

Tony looked down at his mug in surprise. "What is this?"

"Real coffee," Julia said. "It grows on trees out here." Of course, *here* didn't refer to Masra, the dry world was simply the most convenient point to meet up with Ava's fleet.

The privateer commodore had just returned from cutting a swath of destruction through Gray territory bordering the colonies. Every planet that could support military operations had been bombarded, every station smashed.

Tony stared at Julia for a moment, then looked around at the group gathered in her quarters aboard the *Dark Star*. "Are you telling me they took a product that's manufactured in a chemical production line and found a way to make a tree produce it?"

The colonials in the room chuckled.

"The colony ships were sent out a long time ago," Paul explained. "Back then, we still remembered where our food came from. They were sent with seeds for coffee plants, pear trees, even ovum for cattle, pigs, chickens..."

Tony frowned down at his drink, clearly not understanding what the animals were or how they related to the beef, or pork he got from vats, but the coffee had been the original focus. "So, this stuff started out coming from plants?"

Paul nodded. "Then Imperial industry stepped in and developed a way to cut the labor out of the equation and you get the coffee bags we're used to."

"How about that," Tony mused to himself. "It's definitely better." He looked up, casting a nervous glance at Brother N'Zim before looking at Julia. He might be enlightened, by

Human standards, but Imperials mostly had a dislike for all aliens. "So, Govi Darkhan?"

"Govi Darkhan," she affirmed. "Brother N'Zim here has heard rumors about their research program." She leaned forward to activate the holo above her coffee table. An image of the targeted planet shimmered into view between them.

"The complex in orbit has the shipyards and resupply nodes." She enlarged the image to show the station, roughly five kilometers in diameter with long arms stretching out in all directions. She slid the view down to the base of the space elevator filament, on the surface of Govi Darkhan.

"This structure was enlarged five months ago and several shiploads of research personnel have moved in." She waved at the insectoid alien monk. "Brother N'Zim believes he knows what their purpose is."

"One of the ships captured at the Goats Head Nebula was involved in the transport of scientists to Govi Darkhan," the monk croaked. "The officers knew nothing but the crewmen, of course, had spent time with the scientists, getting them settled aboard the ship and showing them the emergency procedures."

He laughed, a dry rattling croak that made Tony's shoulders draw together in alarm. "It doesn't matter what species; it's always the crewmen who know what's going on. The scientists were very upset about the attack on Tel Ramh and they felt it was their duty to make the Imperium pay for it.

"Tel Ramh?" Julia leaned forward. "They're working to resurrect their wormhole program?"

N'Zim slashed his clawed hand from left to right, indicating how strongly he felt about the subject. "They must not be allowed to build such ships," he insisted. "If they do, they can dominate other species and they won't hesitate to eliminate any species that stands in their way."

A chill went up Julia's spine. This was the first time the enigmatic monk had volunteered information so quickly. His kind were always trying to get others to talk, only doling out enough information to keep the conversation going. N'Zim was clearly worried about what mischief the Grays might be cooking up and, if *he* was worried...

"We need to go to Govi Darkhan," she said. "We need to destroy it, if we must, but I think we should seize it, if we can."

N'Zim looked at her in apparent surprise but, before he could speak, Tony cut in. "Absolutely. They've already resurrected the program once. We need to ensure we have the same capability because, sooner or later, they'll manage to produce more than a single prototype and they'll come after us. If we can do the same to them, it'll make em think twice."

"Still," Paul cut in, "it could cause the war to fizzle out before it even gets going. Govi Darkhan is already their last major logistics node on this side of their territory. If they lose their research program along with it..."

"Then they might just get desperate enough to sue for peace," Ava finished for her brother. She held up a finger. "Our primary objective was to protect the colonies from the Grays and I think an armistice will achieve that. We've become too strong for them to risk an attack now."

She extended a second finger. "The secondary objective of keeping vulnerable but strategically important Rim worlds safe from attack will have been dealt with after we hit Govi Darkhan." She cast a wary eye at Tony as she extended a third finger.

"Lastly, we wish to avoid the spread of Imperial influence among the colonies. Our quality of life is superior. We don't have a bloated aristocracy or administration to support out here and we'd like to keep it that way. A full war was considered the lesser of many evils, when we set out, but now it seems unnecessary.

"If the Imperial military is sent here, the senate will expect to see a financial return on the investment and that return will come at the cost of our independence."

"Is it so onerous," Tony asked quietly, "to be an Imperial citizen?"

Ava snorted in amusement. "For a senator like you? I'm sure it's a lovely existence but, for the poor?" She looked up at him. "I've *been* a citizen. Paul and I lived in a hole in the rock on Hardisty until our father sacrificed himself to save us from being sold into indentured servitude. In the Imperium, hard work is simply *expected* of folks like us. Here, in the colonies, hard work can lead to advancement.

"My brother managed to advance through the Marine Corps and through the patronage of your family but that's a billion to one shot." She looked at Paul. "No offense, little bro. I know you earned your success but there are millions of citizens just like you that died in the streets without a credit to their names."

"No offense taken," Paul replied with a grin. "I know there was a lot of luck involved." He waved his mug at her. "She's right, Tony. The colonies are a better place for the average citizen and it would be a shame to ruin the place with a horde of Imperial tax collectors. Let's just grab Govi Darkhan and see what happens."

Tony took another sip from his mug and sat there for a moment, staring down at the steaming liquid as though searching for an omen. In the end, the quality of the beverage convinced him they were telling the truth about life in the colonies. He looked back up at Paul. "What the hell," he said. "We've got an *Ixtab* class assault-craft I've been itching to try out..."

The Ixtab, named for an ancient suicide deity, was a disposable docking platform for planetary assaults. It carried troop shuttles during high speed atmospheric insertions. The shuttles were launched just before the Ixtab herself thundered into the ground.

It was time to roll the final die.

And the goddess of suicide would be unleashed on the Grays.

Govi Darkhan

NGark opened a separate holo to examine the feed coming from his vizier. After four days of guarding Govi Darkhan, he was starting to wonder if he'd read his enemies wrong. They were supposed to be an impetuous species and, yet, where were they?

"As I said," the vizier repeated respectfully, "nothing more than a faint reflection and only for the briefest of moments. Hardly evidence of an assault fleet."

"But at the very edge of our detection range," NGark replied, still studying the seemingly insignificant sensor return. "Exactly where we would expect the Humans to employ their Hasty Ferrets."

He turned a fierce look toward his vizier. "Do you know what nature abhors?"

"A vacuum?"

"A coincidence. What we are seeing here is just one of a squadron of enemy scout ships and the fleet will be twice as far out, studying the data from their scouts and preparing to micro-jump down our throats."

And NGark would be fighting with the gravity well at his back.

He'd never won a fight by doing what the enemy expected of him and he wasn't about to try it now. "Tactical, signal the fleet to stand by for a micro jump. Fifth Squadron will remain here to guard the station."

He reached out to a point that was roughly twice as far away as the sensor ghost of what he fervently hoped was a Hasty Ferret. He closed his thumb and forefinger to create a location marker. "All other ships will jump to this point as soon as they confirm the coordinates."

"***T***amade!" Vampire cursed quietly. "The general was right about the enemy commander, alright."

His Hasty Ferret was all alone, unless you counted the enemy fleet that had just dropped out of distortion all around them, but Vampire didn't count them. Aside from his sensor operator, he felt *very* alone. "Looks like they all dropped out with us astern. They probably won't think to look for us."

"Well, that's the first phase of the battle going according to plan," Fungus, his sensor tech admitted grudgingly. "But that just means we're storing up the bad joss and, when this goes sideways, we'll be right in the gods-damned center of the shit storm."

Vampire's Hasty Ferret squadron had been stretched out in front of the enemy world but Vampire's own scout ship had been stationed where the fleet would usually be sitting. The fleet was twice as far out this time and Vampire's job was to relay data from the rest of his squadron as well as locate the enemy when they dropped out of their micro-jump.

General Urbica had seemed pretty sure they were going up against a commander who'd recognize the scout screen and that he'd attempt to take the initiative away from the Human attackers.

Vampire saved the current holo trace and appended it to the data queue. "Send the contact report, Fungus."

"As soon as I can," Fungus hedged. "We've got a *goucaode* heavy cruiser in the way but she's moving along with the rest of the bastards." He shook his head. "You rarely see the Marines dusting off their Ferrets."

"Marines?" Vampire snorted with the derision that usually came up when Navy men discussed Marines, or vice versa. "Like putting ballet slippers on a rhino."

"And most of the hangar space on their carriers is filled with Iron Hands and Hedgehog Shuttles?" Fungus suggested helpfully.

"And logistics shuttles to support ground ops," Vampire allowed.

"Cruiser's out of the way," Fungus announced. "Sending now."

"Send them a continuous feed as long as the beam won't be intercepted," Vampire ordered.

The report shot past the stern of the cruiser, the laser beam undetectable by the enemy.

"Now we just wait for the fight to start," he said quietly.

NGark missed cursing. It had been centuries since his blood had run hot enough for it and he'd quite forgotten what phrases he'd used. "They've set a trap," he declared, the tilt of his head betraying his rage. "They've set a trap and I've blundered straight into it, all the while thinking I'd been so clever."

"Shall we jump?" The tactical officer hovered his hand over an emergency override that would give him helm control.

"No," NGark gazed pointedly at the officer's hand until he withdrew it. "Move the fleet into a globe defense. If we're going to fight, we can at least fight without a planet at our backs. The only reason to jump from here is to escape the fight. Deploy mines in the center, but only the inner half of the radius."

"Wormhole opening," the vizier warned.

"Launch everything that flies." NGark had never considered using Khlen shuttles for space combat, but he'd been forced to leave most of his fighters behind at Irricana. "Concentrate them in the *center* of our globe, but make sure they know to stay clear of the mines in the very center."

There were far too few aviation assets left to him. He'd never be able to form an effective screen around his defensive formation and he was reasonably certain the enemy fighters would head for the center. None of the Gray main guns would be able to fire on the center, as they'd be facing outward, and the few secondary batteries that could bear on the inside of the formation would run the risk of hitting friendly ships on the far side.

He knew he was limiting his firepower but the enemy would put capital ships behind him if he assumed a line or planar formation; they *did* have a wormhole generator after all.

"Fornication," he muttered quietly. It didn't sound quite right. He knew it had been something of that nature, but cruder, somehow. Anyway, he'd just have to adjust his forces once the enemy was committed to one side of his globe.

The fighters came swarming through, streaming past two squadrons of heavy gunships and heading for the center as NGark had predicted. They were spitting out a hail of projectiles as they spread to flow through the gaps in the defensive formation.

And the lead fighters flew straight into the minefield.

In a matter of heartbeats, the lead Human squadron was wiped out but the following attackers mimicked the Gray fighters and stayed in the outer region of the center, dogfighting near the engines of the capital ships.

The Gray fighters were hammering the Humans in the enclosed confines of the chosen battlespace where the enemy couldn't bring their superior numbers to bear and the odds were beginning to swing in their favor.

But that was on the inside.

"They are deploying their artificial singularity devices," the vizier warned. "Jumping will not be an option."

More Human ships continued to pour through the wormhole, both Imperial and privateer, and NGark was stunned at the numbers. It was the largest force he'd seen yet and he knew they were more than triple the size of his own forces.

The battle was lost.

His mind drifted to the self-destruct devices aboard his ships but he dismissed the thought angrily. The Quorum would not be saved by the suicide of its crews. Far better to go down fighting.

"Bring us into a planar formation facing the wormhole," he commanded. He tilted his head back, ever so slightly, as he looked at the open wormhole. It led to a region of space where the artificial singularities wouldn't affect jump drives.

Perhaps what the Quorum really needed was to be saved from *itself*.

"Cone formation," he demanded. "Same orientation. Fighters to the flanks."

"Looks like they're trying to leave the party," the tactical officer advised Robin. "They're forming a swine-head and it looks like they're going to force their way through the wormhole."

Robin enlarged the view of the wormhole. "They're still in the center of our forces. They'll take a hell of a beating before they get clear."

"Should just move this end of the wormhole to the local star," a helmsman muttered. "I like a nice fried Gray…"

"Too late for that," Robin told him, grinning as the startled man turned to look at her. "They already have fighters in the hole so we can't change the geometry. We'll just have to kill whatever comes out this end."

She sincerely hoped the forces on the other side could thin them out a bit first.

"Two more frigates lost," the tactical officer warned just as a round penetrated the forward shields.

NGark's arm nearly moved to shield his face as the round gouged an opening in the outer hull near the security terminal. His clone body was so far removed from the original instinct-laden body of his species that his almost-reflex was more of a distant memory.

The metal gel beneath the outer skin of the hull, catalysed by exposure to vacuum, quickly expanded to seal the tear and save the bridge crew, or most of it.

NGark turned away from the security operator whose hindquarters protruded from the foam sealant. "We hold our formation," he admonished, dragging a ship's icon from the interior of the formation to replace a lost frigate on the flanks. "If they carve out an opening, they'll pour in like carrion crawlers and consume us from the inside out."

They were already feeding on the carcass from the outside. Another five ships lost acceleration and one of them was hit from behind by an undamaged ship whose crew had been too slow to react. The wreckage drifted back through the still accelerating fleet as ships dodged both the damaged vessels and the undamaged ones that blocked their evasive maneuvers.

It was a shambles, but that was the very nature of a retreat. He was leaving a squadron of ships at the planet – there wasn't time to bring them along. Likewise the ground troops guarding the research station on the surface.

They, at least, should make the enemy think twice about trying to seize the place. His nictitating eyelids stopped halfway across his eyes.

What if the Humans were planning to land their Marines?

"Emergency message to Fifth Squadron," he ordered abruptly. "They're to destroy the orbital station and ground facility and then jump for Home World."

By now, his crew knew not to question his orders and the transmission was sent just before the damaged carrier entered the mouth of the wormhole.

"**S**even hostiles identified," the tactical officer stated calmly as the holo replaced the image of the battle with a new scene showing the *Xipe Totec* and her escorts in orbit around Govi Darkhan. "Engaging."

Tony knew he didn't need to interfere. Harrison was his fleet tactical officer and he knew how to prioritize targets.

"They hit the station first," the sensor coordinator advised. "Just as they'd been ordered to."

That meant they still had a target worth seizing. "Initiate the Ixtab."

"**I**xtab 42, *you are cleared for separation.*" The clearance was picked up by every Marine in every shuttle docked to the planetary assault ship. It was a mantra of the Nathaniel family that a well-informed Marine was a more effective Marine and so the men and women of the 488 were usually tuned into the command net before being committed to action.

"About gods-damned time!" Skeat growled. He walked down the middle aisle of their assault shuttle, checking on his troops, grabbing each restraint and giving it a good tug.

"The restraints are the one thing that never fails, Sarge," Frizzel called out, raising his voice as the rumble of the cheap pulse engines of the main column kicked in. "Every time you check 'em, but it's the suits that'll kill us."

"Maybe I just like to give you the impression that I actually care about your booze-soaked hide," Skeat roared back, swaying slightly as the pilot maneuvered the assault penetrator away from the *Xipe Totec*. "Half of you squints are orphans; you gotta will your shit to somebody…"

"You can have some of mine right now, Sarge," Coleman shouted back. "After all this time waiting to deploy…"

Skeat laughed as he staggered to his own seat, near the back ramp, and dropped heavily into it. "Just keep it between your ears with the rest of it. Now, shut your festering fist-holsters so we can hear what's going on out there." The restraint-arms rotated into place, magnetically attaching to his armor, locking him in place as he looked right to see Obaid, the leader of Second Squad giving him a thumbs up.

Franklin skidded into view as the vessel gave another lurch. She managed to turn it into a graceful turn, dropping her backside neatly into the seat reserved for Third Squad's leader.

He sub-vocalized a command, reporting his squad ready for the assault and First Lieutenant Valeriya Nevsky's acknowledgement icon appeared next to it almost immediately. Skeat and the other two squad leaders in the platoon heartily approved of their new officer. She looked after her Marines when they needed her influence and she didn't play little games.

Their last platoon leader would have waited to acknowledge any input, trying to give the impression that he was busy with something more important. In Skeat's opinion, it was a bad habit that carried over into combat where delays were often fatal, as in the case of their illustrious leader, who managed to get himself trampled by an angry mob of secessionists on TC34553.

At least, that's how the report had been worded.

The order of battle report showed one enemy frigate remaining and it was turning to line up a desperate attempt at a jump out of the system.

"Come on," Skeat hissed. "Tell the pilot we can go. We don't need to wait on..."

"Cutpurse, this is orbital control. You are clear to start your insertion run. Be advised, the enemy defense grid is damaged but still active, over."

The column pilot's response was drowned out by the ironic cheers and the grinding thrum of the engines as they built up their first pulse. They all lurched back inside their armor as the engines dumped the first pulse of gravity ahead of the ungainly ship.

Ixtab class craft were long columns that usually rode docked to the underside of the Marine carriers. It was long enough to dock every assault shuttle and Iron Hand aboard the *Xipe Totec*. The pilot sat in an Iron Hand at the very front of the column, its forward shielding enhanced to deal with the superheated shock-layer of atmosphere as they plunged down toward their target.

In planetary assaults, speed was life but the aviation assets of the *Xipe Totec* couldn't handle shock-layers. They either had to ride down slowly and risk defensive fire or lock themselves to an Ixtab column and ride the thundering freight-train down to the planet.

"Shock-layer building," the column pilot advised, though the buffeting was more than enough clue.

"The mess was serving shepherd's pie tonight," somebody groused.

A twangy noise, like somebody hitting a high-tension steel cable with a bat, announced they were now taking enemy fire, but it was unlikely to penetrate the shock-layer and the shielding.

"Taking enemy fire," a mocking voice announced from somewhere to Skeat's right.

"Taking enemy fire," the column pilot announced.

Another ironic cheer.

"**C**ontact forward," the vizier warned. "Enemy frigate entering the far end of the wormhole."

"Lead cruiser is engaging," the tactical officer added. "The Human shielding is notoriously strong, at least for the Imperial vessels. I estimate a collision will occur inside the wormhole."

NGark knew what would need to be done. "Order the second cruiser in the line to fire immediately after the collision. Load enhanced nuclear warheads."

The tactical officer showed the slightest of pauses before passing the order.

As predicted, the first cruiser failed to destroy the frigate and simply ploughed into the enemy ship, both taking heavy damage, but the frigate, at a third the tonnage of the cruiser, was pushed back and both ships lost their shield generators as well as many of their secondary systems.

Not that it mattered, because the second cruiser in the line fired two rounds from her main guns into the stern of her sister ship. The rounds burrowed deep into the vessel before sensors in the warheads decided the center of mass had been reached and they detonated.

A nuclear warhead detonated in the vacuum of space yielded little more than radiation. That same warhead going off in the center of an enemy warship had far more matter to push around and the two weapons shattered the cruiser, taking the front third of the Human frigate along with her.

The walls of the wormhole rippled alarmingly and a hail of debris, confined by the narrow conduit of space, raced past the Gray ships, shattering almost all of the escorting fighters.

Two more rounds now streaked toward the frigate and easily burrowed in through her shattered bow. The explosions sent more debris toward the escaping Gray ships and some of the heavier, Human-built fragments were penetrating shields and causing damage.

"All ships remain operational," Tactical assured.

"The wormhole appears to be destabilizing," the vizier said in an oddly calm voice, as though he was simply interested in the phenomenon.

NGark could sympathize. He was also curious about the effects of explosions inside a wormhole, especially because the results would determine whether he survived the next few moments. Still, they had to concentrate on escape.

"The exit approaches," the vizier added.

The roaring vibration caused by the shock-layer had faded now and Skeat knew it was time to say goodbye to

Ixtab 42. "If you've got gods," he shouted down the aisle at his twelve Marines, "now's the time to bend their ears!"

"Want me to put in a good word for you, Sarge?" Waters shouted back. "I doubt the *Bull Slayer* wants you offering him green blood."

The other Marines heaped a torrent of good-natured abuse at Waters. The cult of Mithras had been the primary faith of the Corps for centuries and they could afford to take insults in good humor.

"Mithras likes variety just as much as the next man... or deity," Skeat shot back, "though I can always find him a cup of red, if you're willing..." He raised an eyebrow at Waters, who chuckled at the threat.

"He can have plenty from those colonials that are assaulting in their light shuttles but, if you want the personal touch..."

"Stand by for separation."

"Only if I can skip some of the degrees..." Waters stopped talking abruptly as their combat shuttle ejected from the central core of the Ixtab. The grav plating in the deck couldn't quite hope to counter the sudden acceleration but it could, at least, keep the Marines from blacking out.

The sudden roar of Govi Darkhan's battering atmosphere was a welcome sound because it meant they hadn't been smashed during separation, which happened three percent of the time. The sound eased as their own shuttle pilot brought the craft under control and vectored toward their landing zone.

The central column, true to her name, would be left to smash into the surface. An Ixtab never returned from deployment.

"If I'm gonna be on such an intimate footing with Mithras," Waters resumed his theme, "I should at least be made a *Heliodromus.*"

Before Skeat could think of a suitably witty retort, the green lights above them went to red. "Weapons!" he shouted.

They all reached up to the mag plates on the stanchions that held their seats. When their armored hands touched the hand-grips, the plates went to half power, allowing the weapons to be pulled down.

They checked their weapons without having to be told. They knew all too well that their lives depended on finding the problems before the problems found *them.*

The red lights began to blink and the rear ramp cracked open. Everyone lurched to the side as they banked.

"Tip for the driver," some wag called out, just before the sudden deceleration of the final landing cycle. Forty weapon muzzles rattled against the decking as their effective weight was suddenly boosted.

A quick series of thumps as the landing points hit dirt and then the restraints released, a chime sounding in everyone's helmet on the off chance they couldn't figure out they'd hit the ground.

Skeat followed his squad down the ramp, through the hazy air under the heat-sinks in the tail, and out to the sector assigned to his three fire-teams. They were twenty meters out from the shuttle and watching their third of the perimeter as the shuttle lifted off to link up with the rest of its squadron.

Until the time came for his Marines to leave, the assault shuttles would serve an air support role, firing on hard targets and keeping any enemy craft at bay.

"Skeat," Nevsky's voice crackled in his helmet, "your boys will provide the overhead for the approach."

"Rhodes, Ramsey, Klein," Skeat said over the prox net, "birds up."

The three Marines held still while a cluster of small drones detached from their back armor to ascend into the evening sky.

"*Crom Dubh!*" Ryan whispered. "Would you look at that..."

Skeat turned. The massive station, shot up by the Grays so it wouldn't fall into enemy hands, was now visible in the atmosphere. Its underside was wreathed in flames as it fell, hazy in the distance but an impressive sight nonetheless.

"Get your heads out of your asses," Skeat snarled, "or I'm gonna kick your teeth in and that'll involve a helluvalot of tearing. We came here to do a job, not to go sightseeing. Eyes on your arcs!"

The tactical map holo was filling in with all the detail from the platoon's drones and Skeat could see waypoints appearing as Lieutenant Nevksy began planning their approach. He grunted in approval. She'd only been with them for five months, and straight from the Twenty-Nine Moons, at that. He'd never known a new officer to be so sensible when it came to advice from her senior NCO's.

He grunted again as he watched the waypoints populate his map holo. She had a damned good eye for terrain, too.

"**W**e are clear of the wormhole," the vizier announced. "We can now form a stable distortion field."

"Standing by to jump," the helmsman advised. "Initiating the precursor..."

"Belay!" NGark set a targeting reticle on one of the three Human carriers they'd found among the ships on this side of the wormhole. It was crewed by Humans but it had been built at Tel Ramh.

"The rest may jump as they come out, but I want us swung around to bear on this target."

"The wormhole is collapsing." The vizier brought up a list. "We lost two thirds of our ships in there. What remains is mostly on the other side with the bulk of the Human fleet."

NGark suspected there was a note of censure in the vizier's voice, but that was now the least of his concerns. He'd lost Govi Darkhan, along with quite a few ships, but he could still give his people a victory if he could deprive the enemy of their greatest tactical advantage.

"Initiate the jump sequence," he ordered. There would only be time for a single salvo. After that, they could either run or die and he had plans for a shakeup of the Quorum.

The last two Gray contra-gravity tanks turned right as small-arms fire began to bounce off their turrets. The turrets swung around, aiming at a point triangulated by impact sensors in the armor, and they fired nearly simultaneously.

"Come on," Skeat urged. "You know you wanna run the monkeys over, instead of wasting HE rounds. Just hit the damned throttle already!" He wasn't terribly worried about casualties. Standard Gray tanking doctrine insisted on high explosive when engaging infantry. The problem with doctrine is that it fails to consider HMA.

The Grays must have been listening because they lurched forward, their low pitched whine rattling his bones and causing interference in his heads-up holo. The effect was short-lived, however, as three loud chirps announced the firing of Ice-Pick anti-armor weapons.

Propelled by the hydrogen launch-charge, the weapons used a thermodynamic precursor warhead to reduce the temperature of the targeted area, making the armor incredibly brittle. The secondary warheads penetrated easily and, suddenly, there were no more enemy tanks between the Marines and their final waypoint.

At least no operational ones.

"**T**hey're turning toward the *Sucker Punch*," Tactical warned. "A full salvo from a cruiser's mains might be enough to knock her out of commission."

Robin had seen the Humans in the stasis pods. She'd seen the bodies at Uruk. "Put us in front of her," she ordered. "Load shake-and-bake." The colonies were on the verge of gaining the upper hand and she wasn't going to let the Grays destroy Humanity's greatest military asset.

"Half kinetic, half nuke, aye, ma'am."

She closed her eyes, but the same old image of her daughter's face among the dead of Uruk came back to her and so she opened them. Those bastards wouldn't get her.

"Failure in the portside ventral conveyor," Tactical advised. "Ready for the other three mains. Enemy in the envelope."

"Fire."

The howl sounded like a fleeing soul and the decking rattled.

"They're firing."

"Weapons free, intercept mode."

The batteries of their frigate screamed in response but they were in a captured Gray warship and her secondary and tertiary batteries were fewer than those of her Human counterparts. The hail of ordnance was unlikely to stop all of the incoming rounds.

"The target has jumped."

"Intercepted one projectile..."

"Brace!" Robin shouted, forgetting to follow her own advice as the three enemy rounds hammered into their forward shield. She was thrown forward fetching up against the side of the helmsman's terminal, the hard edge breaking the ribs on her right side.

The impact should have killed her and she knew that meant the shield generator had torn loose, rather than having translated all the force of the impact into the ship. All of this registered in her mind in a heartbeat and she looked up just in time to see the remnants of one of the enemy rounds tumble through the upper part of the compartment's hull plating and pass on down the length of the ship.

The edges of the ragged hole bloomed with expanding metal gel but it was too wide and the seal never closed. She'd always assumed her last thoughts would be of her little Sarah, but her mind spent the last few moments fixated on the cold.

That hideous cold...

"**I**'d recommend against it, ma'am," Skeat urged. He was watching the enemy bunker while arguing over the unit prox. "We've already burnt three drones trying to crack that bastard. The missiles can't get through the shielding and the drones just die the instant they try to slow-dance their way past."

It was frustrating. They'd made it to the facility with light resistance but they and every other platoon down here had been balked at the entrances. Bunkers guarded every way into the underground facility and they had heavy shielding, at least on a par with what a capital warship would use.

The Grays inside those bunkers may not be proper infantry, but they could shoot out and the Humans couldn't shoot in. "Too close for shuttle fire too," he added.

"Agreed," she sighed. "They'd destroy the whole damned place."

"Well," Skeat mused, "what if we..."

A blur streaked toward the shielded bunker from somewhere to his left. A small explosion sounded just before it impacted and, somehow, the missile slipped right through the shield to smash the defensive structure.

"Shit!" he exclaimed.

"I know, right?" Nevksy chuckled. "And we thought those pirates were just cannon fodder. I'll get on the net – let the others know we've got a way in over here."

Skeat looked to his left and saw an enthusiastic but unarmored group of colonial privateers advancing on the wrecked bunker in pairs, one covering while the other moved up. Several of them had very strong upper bodies and carried the heavy recoilless rifles he'd heard about.

But how did they get through the shield?

"Forward!" he got up and led his squad to the bunker where the privateers were trying to lever a large piece of carbon-crete away from the tunnel opening. "Hubbard, Cook, Larsen!" He chopped a hand toward the debris.

The colonials stepped back as the three Marines stepped up in their HMA. The three of them were just able to shove the large piece out of the way and the privateer troops poured in past them.

Skeat retracted his helmet and nodded to one of the colonials with the heavy rifle. "What kind of round was it that got through the shield?"

The man grinned, leaning the weapon against a heavily muscled shoulder. "Ringworm," he explained. "Fires a metal ring at the shield, just before impact, and it slips into the energy field, making a hole for the warhead to get through."

Skeat turned to enter the tunnel, his three fire-teams already working their way down the long hallway. "We don't have anything like that." He stepped on what looked like a Gray torso, the ribs cracking from the weight.

"Neither did we," the heavy rifleman admitted. "It's pretty new."

"Huh," Skeat grunted. New wasn't a word you heard much in the Imperial military.

A familiar pattern of three thumps sounded from outside the tunnel mouth and he smiled. The assault shuttles were already picking up platoons who'd been balked at other bunkers and they were feeding them into the facility at this point.

His smile froze. A bunker cracked by unarmored colonials rather than by his Marines. "Oh well," he said, mostly to himself.

At least they'd be back aboard in time for shepherd's pie.

But first, they had a facility to pacify and, more importantly, the facility's scientific staff to capture. "Remember," he warned over the prox net, "we don't want to hurt the little darlings. Command wants the staff seized intact."

"What if they're shooting at us, Sarge?"

"Frizzel, if they're being kind enough to shoot at us, you can go ahead and return the favor. Otherwise, you secure 'em and move on. We gotta move fast. The enemy is likely to pull back from the other bunkers to help defend the interior, and I want the labs secured before they do."

"Well, they're only shooting a little and it's just 8mm rounds on low charge," Frizzel admitted, the sound of small-arms fire crackling from Skeat's helmet speakers. "I'll just go knock 'em down."

"Sounds like you've got yourself a well-led fire-team, Sergeant." The new voice drew Skeat's gaze around to the left. Someone in light dragoon armor had caught up with him.

The man retracted his helmet, extending a hand. "Ap Rhys, 1st Gliessan Dragoons."

"Skeat," he grunted in reply, "488." He squinted at Daffyd. "You the fella that invented that wormhole generator?"

"Sure, why not?" Daffyd replied negligently.

A chuckle. "So it's like that, huh?"

"Yep. A thin veneer of tauran shit spread over something even more unpalatable." Ap Rhys closed up his helmet as they neared the end of the corridor. The sounds of firing came from just around the corner but it stopped abruptly.

They rounded the corner to find a Marine in HMA kneeling to restrain three Grays. A fourth enemy had a badly broken arm.

"There's a lab!" ap Rhys exclaimed, running past the kneeling Marine before Skeat could stop him. A hail of rounds bounced off Daffyd's armor as he entered the room and he picked up a small chair. "Knock it off," he shouted, hurling the seat at the offending Gray.

Skeat had made it halfway to the door before the firing had ceased. He stepped into the lab to find the unconscious enemy laying on the floor, his rifle a few meters away. Holo screens projected along three of the four walls while the fourth wall was a sheet of dark glazing. A hallway led to more labs on the left side.

Another armored dragoon, four privateers and one of those creepy, insectoid monks flooded into the room. One of the privateers pulled off a backpack and opened it to remove a data module.

"Over there," ap Rhys pointed. "Those nodules can pull information from the entire complex. Get a copy made and get it back to the ship before some trigger-happy captain tries to give us orbital fire-support or something."

Several groups, each consisting of fifteen or twenty more men, passed through the room, a mix of Marines, dragoons and privateers.

The monk moved to a holo panel and activated the controls. A few quick gestures and the large dark window cleared, showing a chamber containing three huge, circular rings.

"*Tamade!*" Daffyd turned from his friend with the data module. He stepped over to stand next to the monk looking through the glass. "Let's hope this is a recent development."

Beyond the rings was a tunnel, exactly the same diameter as the middle ring, and its inner surface gleamed as though the rock had been polished to a perfect gloss.

"They cut that hole with the generator," Daffyd said, looking back to Skeat. "Opened up a short wormhole and slid the far end out to slice away at the rock. When they collapse the hole, the rock goes *tianxiaode* where, but it goes."

"They have managed to replicate their research," the Monk croaked. "We'll need to talk to the staff of this facility, one at a time. We need to find out how much is known only to the teams working here and how much the Quorum knows."

Ap Rhys nodded. "We can't let them have this technology again. Give the Grays an advantage and they'll beat you to death with it." He subvocalized a command to his suit. "All call-signs, this is 'Welshman'. Initiate 'Paper Clip' immediately. I say again – initiate 'Paper Clip'."

Skeat could hear small-arms fire coming from the corridor on his left. The enemy manning the other bunkers were starting to run into resistance from the Humans. His HUD showed him a three-dimensional map built by the scanners carried on the Marine armor, and the defenders coming back from the outer defenses were being stopped well away from the labs.

He could tell the fight was all but won by the Humans and something about ap Rhys' odd statement had him concerned. "What's 'Paper Clip'?"

Dragoons and privateers began coming back now, each carrying a Gray prisoner. They passed through the large lab and headed out toward the exit.

Ap Rhys waved a hand at the rings. "We'll get around to exploiting their research soon enough," he explained, "but first we need to get all of the staff separated and locked down. We need to find out just how far this knowledge has spread from here. We hammered their last research site flat but, here they are, building these *goucaode* engines again.

"We'll take 'em up to our ships and have the Brotherhood work them over. They have a way with the Grays."

Before Skeat could say anything in return, a red icon began to blink in his HUD. "We're being recalled," he said in mild surprise.

It wasn't as though he didn't think the local Human troops could finish mopping up. Hells, it had even been the privateers who got them all inside the complex in the first place. Still, it felt wrong, leaving the fight when there were still shots being fired.

He collected his team, pulling Rhodes away from the Gray corpse he was searching for souvenirs. They assembled in a flat area outside the smashed bunker and waited for the other two fire-teams to arrive.

Four shuttles approached. Three of them were Gray export models and they went into a holding pattern while the Marine assault shuttle began its descent. He cast another glance up at the other three shuttles and it struck him that it wasn't just his reluctance to walk away from an unfinished fight that troubled him.

This facility represented a strategic advantage. Why were the Marines being pulled out while the local forces were still pouring in? He checked his withdrawal order and saw that General Urbica had her name on it.

He hoped she knew what she was doing.

Anyway – shepherd's pie...

The Attack is the Message

"**H**ow many ships?" Julia demanded.

"At least a hundred, but we're just picking up reflections at this distance," the tactical officer of the *Sucker Punch* replied, turning to look back at her holographic projection. "They're probably just now hearing about the defeat at Govi Darkhan, so they wouldn't have had time to pull in forces to defend their home world."

Julia looked around at the circle of holographic captains, her eyes coming to rest on Paul, the only non-holographic presence in the circle. With Dmitry captaining the *Mictlan*, Eddie had insisted on returning to the fighter squadrons, leaving Paul to command the *Sucker Punch*.

Paul was far from comfortable in the role as he was no deck officer. He'd been stuck with the job because the dragoons had tended to follow his lead in the past and he had an eye on the big picture.

"Let their sense of duty kill them," Paul offered.

She nodded. "The *Mictlan*. Those captains defending their home world know what happens if they try to dodge the rounds from the *Mictlan*."

"They're sworn to protect the Quorum," Tony added. "As long as the Quorum is down there, they'll have no choice but to sit in the path of the incoming rounds and try to destroy them with defensive fire."

"Are we sure of that?" Dmitry asked from the bridge of the *Mictlan*. "They'll know a single round from us isn't going to wipe them out. It must take at least a couple hundred rounds before we make the place uninhabitable."

"If they do start evading the rounds," Ava warned, "then we lose the element of surprise."

"To an extent," Julia conceded, "but we can still open a wormhole at close range and wipe them out, one at a time. Let's try this first; test their resolve..."

N'Zim, standing next to Julia aboard the *Dark Star*, turned to her. "And how far will you take this assault? Once you have them at your mercy, what will you do?"

"As I said..." Julia turned to meet his gaze, "... we'll test their resolve."

"Our gunnery officer has her solutions resolved for all hostile targets," Dmitry advised. "We can have the first sixty rounds away in less than a centiday, but we'll need another half-centi to get the next magazine into position and cool the launch rails. Just move this end of the hole and give us the word."

Less than two hundredths of a day to wipe out a defensive fleet.

Or to wipe out a world.

It was frightening to think the Grays had gone to the effort of building these ships, but it was even more chilling to be in command of them. "*Sucker Punch*, have the wormhole adjusted for the *Mictlan*." She turned to Dmitry. "*Mictlan*, you are clear to open fire on the *defensive fleet* as soon as you have a clear shot."

NGark and his Master-At-Arms led a picked security team of thirty clones down the long corridor to the Quorum's main chamber. It was at least a hundred cubits beneath ground level and he had a sneaking suspicion its placement had been more a precaution against rebellion than alien assault.

Still, it had proved to be a sensible choice. He could hear the occasional distant thunder of a heavy round striking the surface, the shock wave sometimes taking a very long time to shake the subterranean corridor. Some of his brother captains were shirking their duty in the interest of prolonging their own monotonous existence.

He reached the blast door and stepped up to breathe on the sensor plate in the center. The massive circle rolled out of the way and he led his team down a short hallway and through a smaller, automated blast door to enter the main chamber of the Quorum.

He strode out into the large circular space in the center. On tiered benches, rising away from the center, forty faces looked down in surprise. One of the ruling members stood and gave NGark a condescending tilt of his head. "You were supposed to be relieved of your command..."

"Point of order," NGark cut him off. "As a Grand Ballista, I have the right to rise to a point of order." He looked to the chairman who, slightly dark with annoyance, gave a curt nod of approval.

"I am still a Grand Ballista," NGark continued, "because the fool you sent to relieve me lost his planet killer to the Humans, who are currently using it to bombard our home world." He pointed at the councillor who'd first spoken and forty heads tilted back in shock at the rude gesture.

"He has no business meddling in defense matters, not even to comment on them while in chambers." He turned and waved a hand at all of the councillors, an extravagant gesture and they shifted backwards in their seats in alarm.

"Your incompetent scheming has brought this war upon us and I move that we make changes in order to preserve what remains of our way of life." He let them mutter among themselves for a brief moment.

"All approved?" he called out.

Shots rang out from his security forces and the councillors of the Quorum were cut down in a matter of heartbeats. There were no guards, for they had not been needed in centuries.

NGark walked through the chlorine stench of the assault rifles to stand beside the slumped body of the chairman whose coppery blood was slowly turning a green, oxidizing as it spilled out onto his chest and ran down onto the floor.

"All those opposed?" he asked, looking around at the dead assembly. He put a hand on the chairman's neck and tipped the corpse into the stairs where he slid down to the central space.

"Motion carried." He sat on the chairman's couch.

"**M**ove the other end in closer," Julia ordered. "Just outside the atmosphere."

Paul, nodded to the engineering station where Edrich shrugged and turned to his controls.

"Gray Home World," She began. "This is Brigadier General Julia Urbica of the Imperial Marines."

A Gray shimmered into view. He was in a seated positon but he stood and gave them what passed for a polite nod.

The Humans shared glances. Nobody had ever seen a Gray nod before.

"I am Chancellor NGark," the Gray announced. "On behalf of the Quorum, which is currently indisposed at the moment, I welcome you."

"We are here," Julia replied, "because your crimes against the Imperium, the Free Colonies and their people have left us with no choice but to respond in force."

"It would seem I've been hasty," NGark admitted. He reached up to activate a menu and the view enlarged to show him, much smaller, standing in the middle of a large round chamber strewn with Gray corpses. "As you can see, I've already called them to answer for their inept leadership."

He returned the projection to the standard setting, showing him at full scale. "If you would like, I can have their patterns re-animated in new bodies. They should have transmitted into storage when I had them shot. You can punish them as you wish. Otherwise, I'd planned on emptying the buffer.

"As to their crimes, I apologize for the incursions into your space. They were unwarranted and poorly executed. It was an insult to you, assuming that such shoddy work would be sufficient to cripple your societies." He tilted his head back slightly.

"Regarding the treatment of your citizens, can you honestly say your own Imperium hasn't subjected them to far worse?"

"Stand by." Julia cut the link. Such words were inflammatory. If a copy of this conversation ever made it back to the Imperium, it could spark any number of revolts among the lower classes.

Humans could toil their entire lives in squalor and submission, but it only took one person to call it misery and a world would go into chaos. Chancellor NGark might even have known that when he said it.

"We should destroy the bastards," Tony urged. "They've come at us too many times. They've been on the brink of *destroying* us too many times. Will we let them keep trying?"

Julia shook her head. "Do you really think they can try again, Tony? Every asset they built for the effort has fallen into our hands. They'll be too afraid of our response to risk attacking you again. I won't be cursed through history as the person who destroyed an entire species."

N'Zim let out a creaky laugh of relief.

Tony frowned at the monk, then turned to Julia. "When you say *our response,* you don't mean the Imperium, do you? You mean the colonies."

"*Sucker Punch,*" she said, turning to Paul, who reluctantly nodded.

The wormhole to the Gray home world closed.

A new one opened to the Imperial home world.

"Is that all we have to say to the Gray chancellor?" Tony asked, though his tone indicated that his true concern lay elsewhere.

"The cat doesn't waste time telling the mouse that she's too full to chase it," Julia told him. "I'm sure the Senate is anxiously waiting for a report from their Praetor. It's time for you to go home."

"And what about Govi Darkhan?" he asked. "My Marines helped seize that research station."

"It's ours," she told him flatly. "If we allow the Imperium a toehold in our territory, there'll be no end of trouble. You wouldn't stop until you'd annexed every single colony."

She smiled sadly. "For centuries, the Grays let the colonies live because they feared Imperial retribution, even though the administration preferred to pretend no Humans lived out here."

"Not worth the time and effort," Ava put in.

"And the great irony," Julia continued, "is that, now, when we've proven how valuable we'd be to the Imperium, we no longer need its help."

"But the Imperium needs us," Ava added, gesturing to the tactical holo that hung between the projected captains. It showed a wormhole opened above the Imperial palace on Home World. The *Mictlan* held station near the opening, her potential threat obvious.

"Now *we* are the counterbalance to Gray aggression but, if the Imperium tries to annex us..." Ava let the threat hang unspoken.

"Sorry, Tony." Paul gave his old friend a sad smile. "But the way of life they've built out here is worth fighting for. If you'd had a chance to see for yourself, you'd understand."

A sigh. "It think I do understand."

"Then make sure the Senate does as well," Julia said forcefully, "because, if you don't, it'll mean war and it's a war you're not equipped to win."

Tony looked away, his expression troubled. Finally, he looked back at his friends. "I think you may be right."

Without another word, his image disappeared from the group projected in front of Paul.

"*Xipe Totec* and her escorts are moving to the wormhole," the tactical officer said.

Paul watched as the Marine ships passed through the opening and disappeared. He knew how hard it would be to convince CentCom and the Senate that the mighty

Imperium was no longer the big kid on the block, but there was nothing he could do about that. His old friend was on his own.

"Restore normal geometry and secure the reactor," he ordered.

It was time to get to work. They had seized a lot of Gray territory and it was time to consolidate their gains. He felt his heart lift a little as he saw Daffyd come onto the bridge, no doubt eager to get back to Govi Darkhan and pry into the secrets of the Gray wormhole program.

Out here, the future was what you made of it and they had a hells of a lot to work with.

A.G. Claymore

NEW RELEASE LIST

free stories

When you sign up for my new-release mail list!

Click this link to get started:
http://eepurl.com/ZCP-z

FROM THE AUTHOR

A few years ago, Chris Nuttall was kind enough to let me write in the *Empire of Ashes* (*Imperium Cicernus*) shared universe. I wrote *Rebels and Patriots* and, after incorporating some very helpful insights from Mr. Nuttall, it went live in August of 2014.

I have since written sequels to *Rebels and Patriots* and I've decided to list them as sequels of the *R&P* series, rather than keeping them under the *Imperium Cicernus* umbrella. This is partly to leave room for new writers in the *IC* universe and partly because it can get confusing trying to explain that my series was #'s 3, 8, 11 etc.... of the *IC* numbering system.

By branching off into a new series, we get:

Rebels and Patriots – Imperium Cicernus #3 / Rebels and Patriots #1

Beyond the Rim – Rebels and Patriots #2

The Gray Matter – Rebels and Patriots #3

Etc....

If you'd like to get an automatic email when my next title comes out, you can sign up here: http://eepurl.com/ZCP-z. Your email address will not be shared with anyone and I only send a message when a new story goes live or if I'm offering a free short story or novella. You can unsubscribe at any time.

I'm giving away several novellas (roughly a quarter of a novel each) to all subscribers. They tie into the various main series and *Spacers* is a free novella that provides greater depth into the events of this novel.

Drop by the link above and check it out.

A.G. Claymore

If your download link isn't in the welcome email from MailChimp, you can contact me at the email address below and I'll send you a copy. This story won't be sold anywhere, but it will always be free to subscribers. Feel free to pass it on to anyone you think may enjoy it. I'll be giving out a few more shorts to subscribers this year, time permitting.

If you have any comments, questions or just want to chat, you can always reach me at AGClaymore@gmail.com.

As always, thanks for reading this story and, if you enjoyed it, please consider leaving a review. Word of mouth makes a huge difference and even a line or two in a review helps to get a story discovered by new readers.

Made in United States
Troutdale, OR
05/17/2024

19953235R00239